W9-CLY-441

DATE DUE			

TO MY DAD, WHOSE HUMOR AND CAMPING SKILLS INSPIRED THIS BOOK.
". . . ARE . . ."   —S.M.

FOR NICOLE AND THE KLEINS: DAVE, CAMBRIA, AND AUDREY.
                                        —R.H.L.

Dial Books for Young Readers
Penguin Young Readers Group
An imprint of Penguin Random House LLC
375 Hudson Street | New York, New York 10014

Text copyright © 2016 by Scott McCormick | Pictures copyright © 2016 by R. H. Lazzell
Penguin supports copyright. Copyright fuels creativity, encourages diverse voices, promotes free speech, and creates a vibrant culture. Thank you for buying an authorized edition of this book and for complying with copyright laws by not reproducing, scanning, or distributing any part of it in any form without permission. You are supporting writers and allowing Penguin to continue to publish books for every reader.

Library of Congress Cataloging-in-Publication Data
Names: McCormick, Scott, date, author. | Lazzell, R. H., illustrator.
Title: Mr. Pants : camping catastrophe! / words by Scott McCormick ; pictures by R. H. Lazzell
Other titles: Mister Pants, camping catastrophe! | Camping catastrophe!
Description: New York, NY : Dial Books for Young Readers, 2016. |
Summary: "Feline siblings Mr. Pants and Foot Foot want to join the Rugged Rangers, but first they have to prove they can survive an overnight camping trip with their uncle and cousins" — Provided by publisher.
Identifiers: LCCN 2015022352 | ISBN 9780525428121 (hardback)
Subjects: | CYAC: Cats—Fiction. | Camping—Fiction. | Scouting (Youth activity)—Fiction. |
Brothers and sisters—Fiction. | Humorous stories. |
BISAC: JUVENILE FICTION / Comics & Graphic Novels / General. | JUVENILE
FICTION / Readers / Chapter Books. | JUVENILE FICTION / Humorous Stories.
Classification: LCC PZ7.M47841437 Mn 2016 | DDC [Fic]—dc23
LC record available at http://lccn.loc.gov/2015022352

Manufactured in China on acid-free paper

1   3   5   7   9   10   8   6   4   2

Design by Jennifer Kelly | Text set in Archer

**The artwork for this book was created digitally and
under the influence of chocolate chip cookies.**

CONTENTS

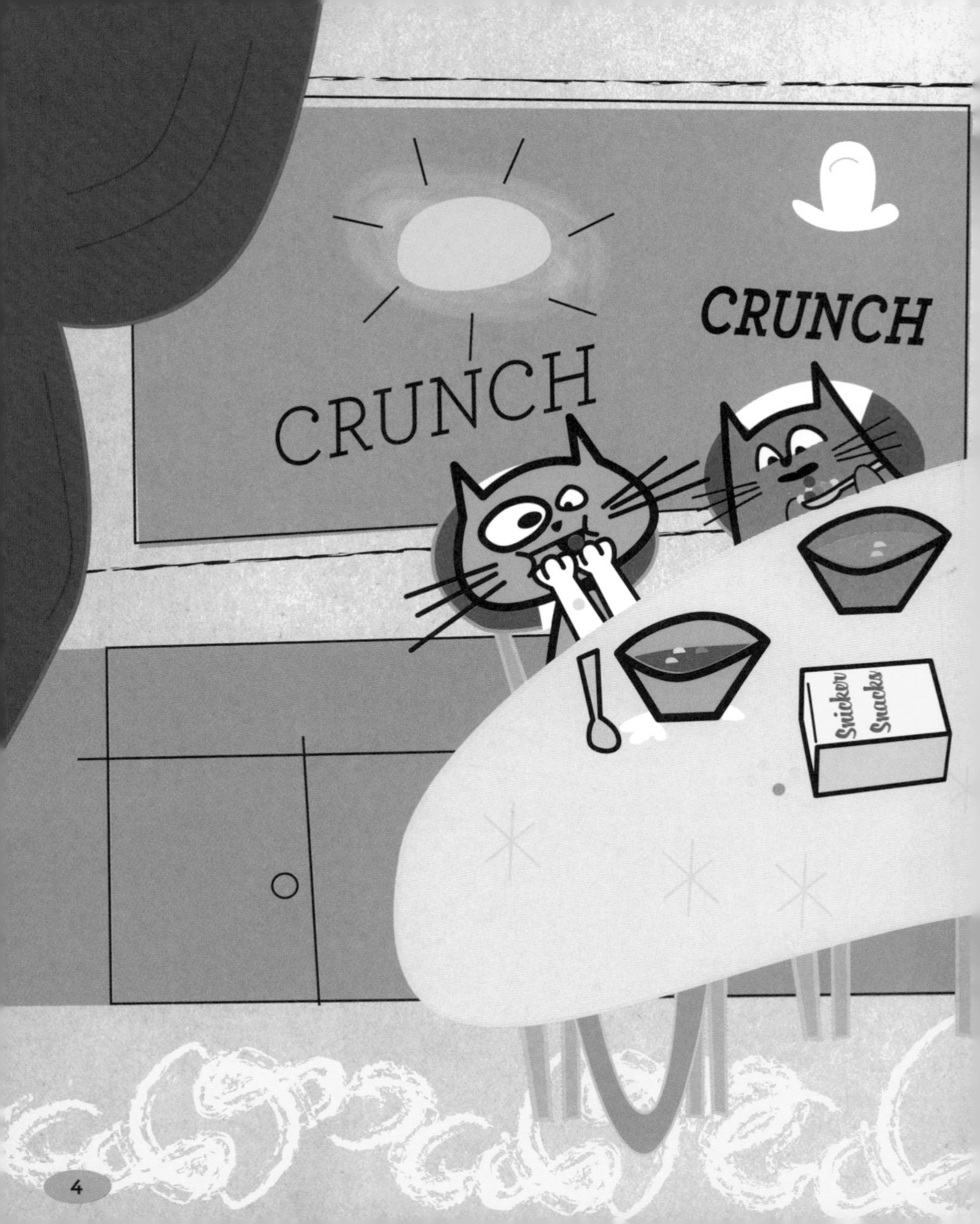
CRUNCH
CRUNCH
Snicker Snacks

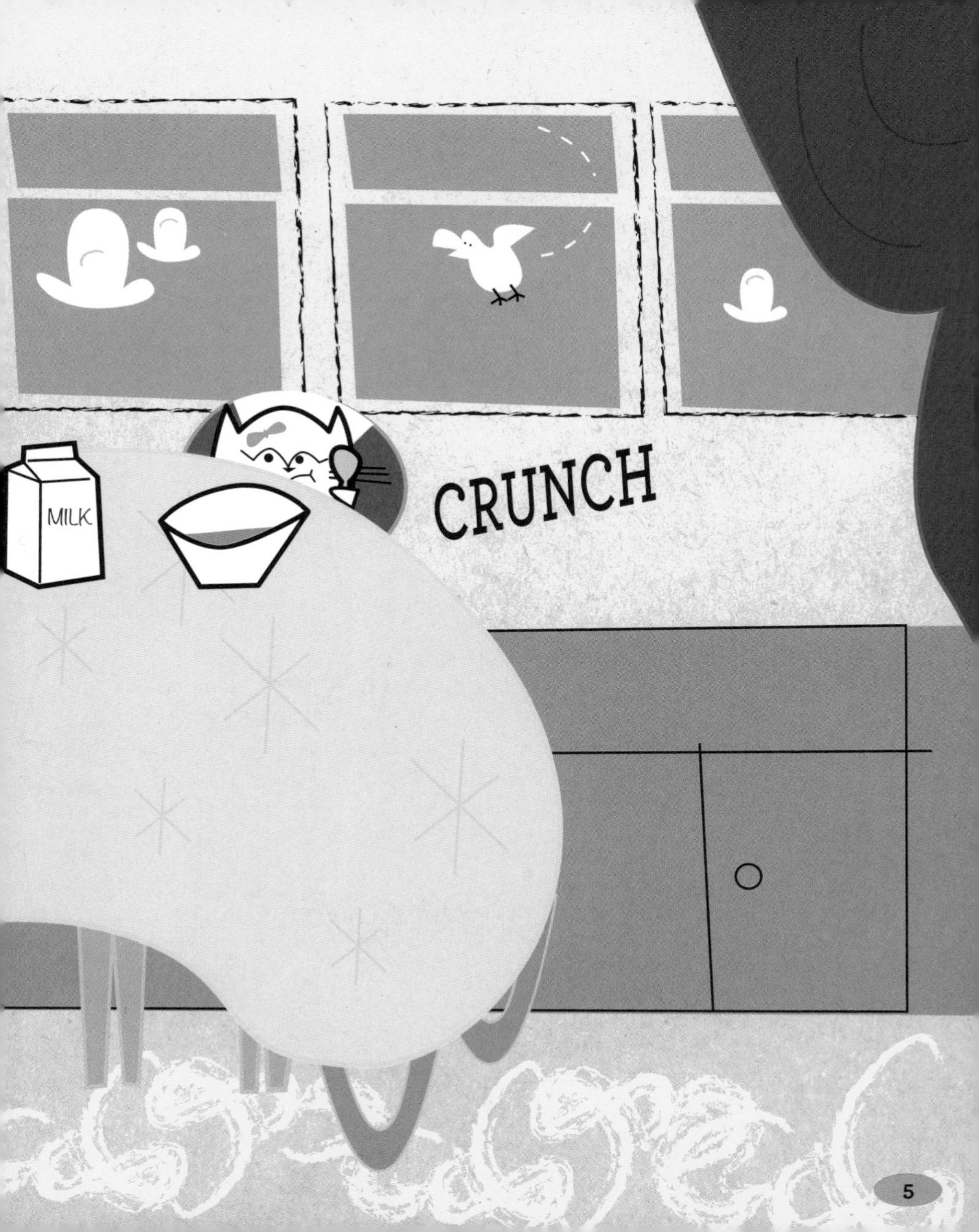
MILK
CRUNCH

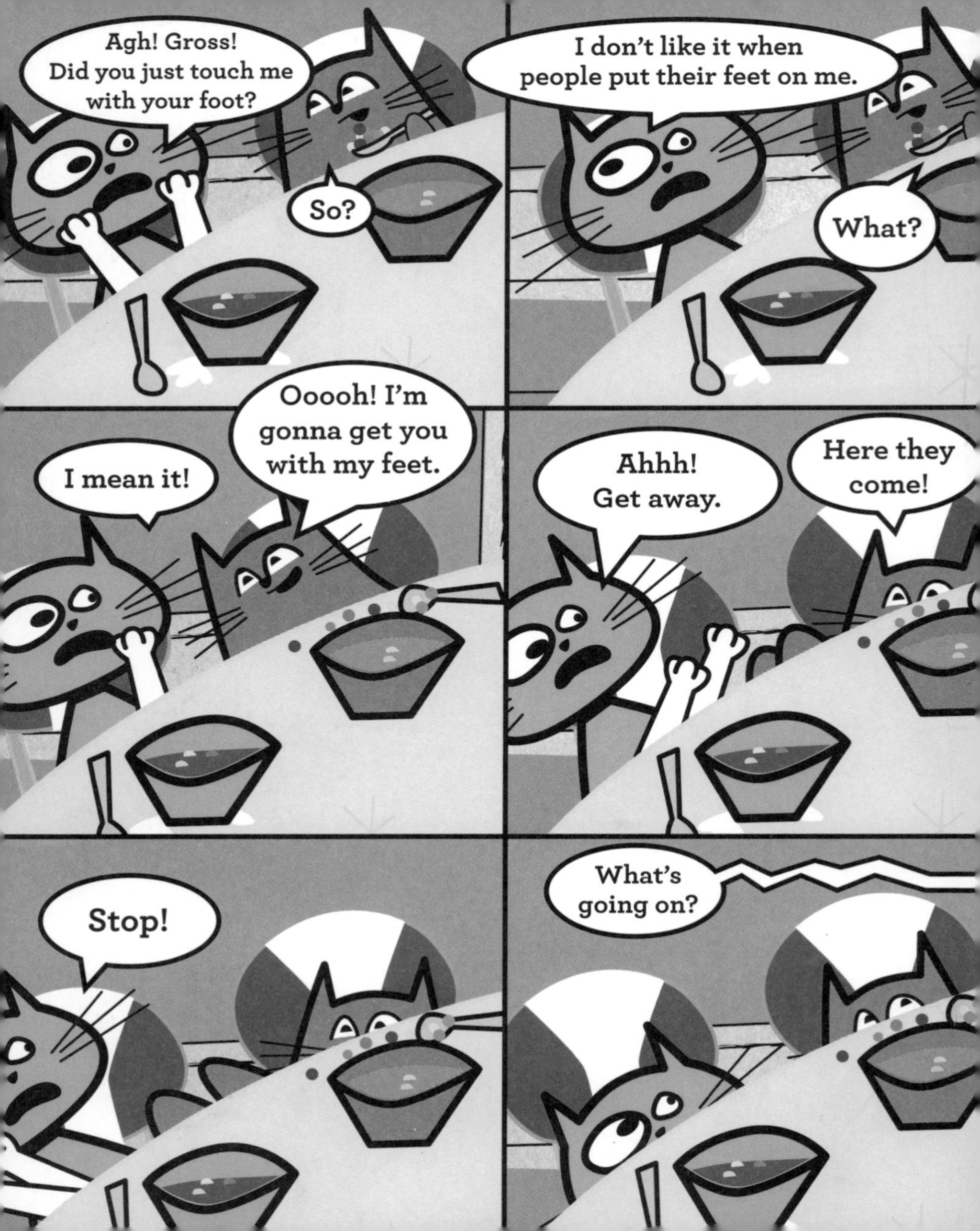
Agh! Gross! Did you just touch me with your foot?
So?
I don't like it when people put their feet on me.
What?
I mean it!
Ooooh! I'm gonna get you with my feet.
Ahhh! Get away.
Here they come!
Stop!
What's going on?

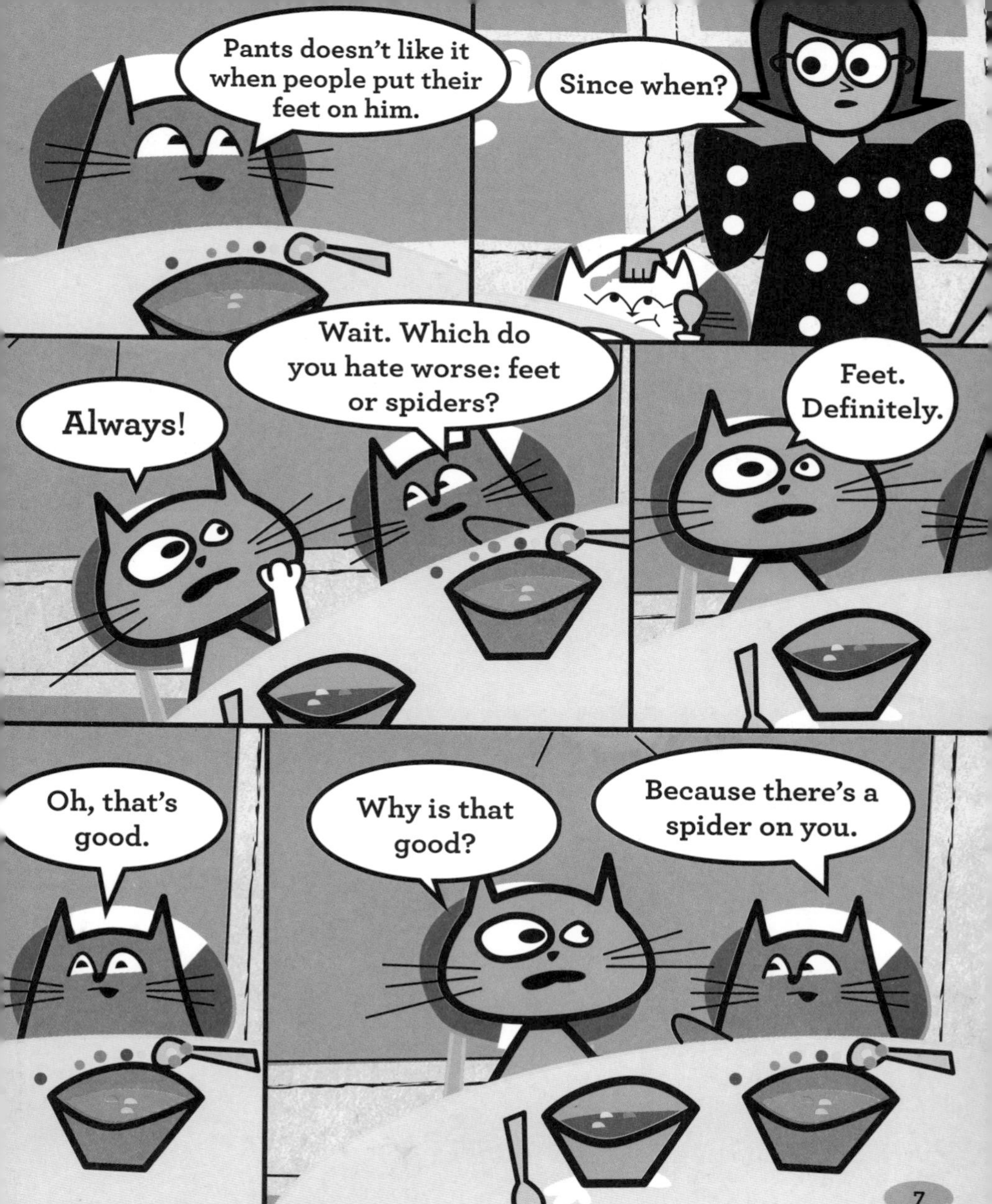
Pants doesn't like it when people put their feet on him.
Since when?
Wait. Which do you hate worse: feet or spiders?
Always!
Feet. Definitely.
Oh, that's good.
Why is that good?
Because there's a spider on you.

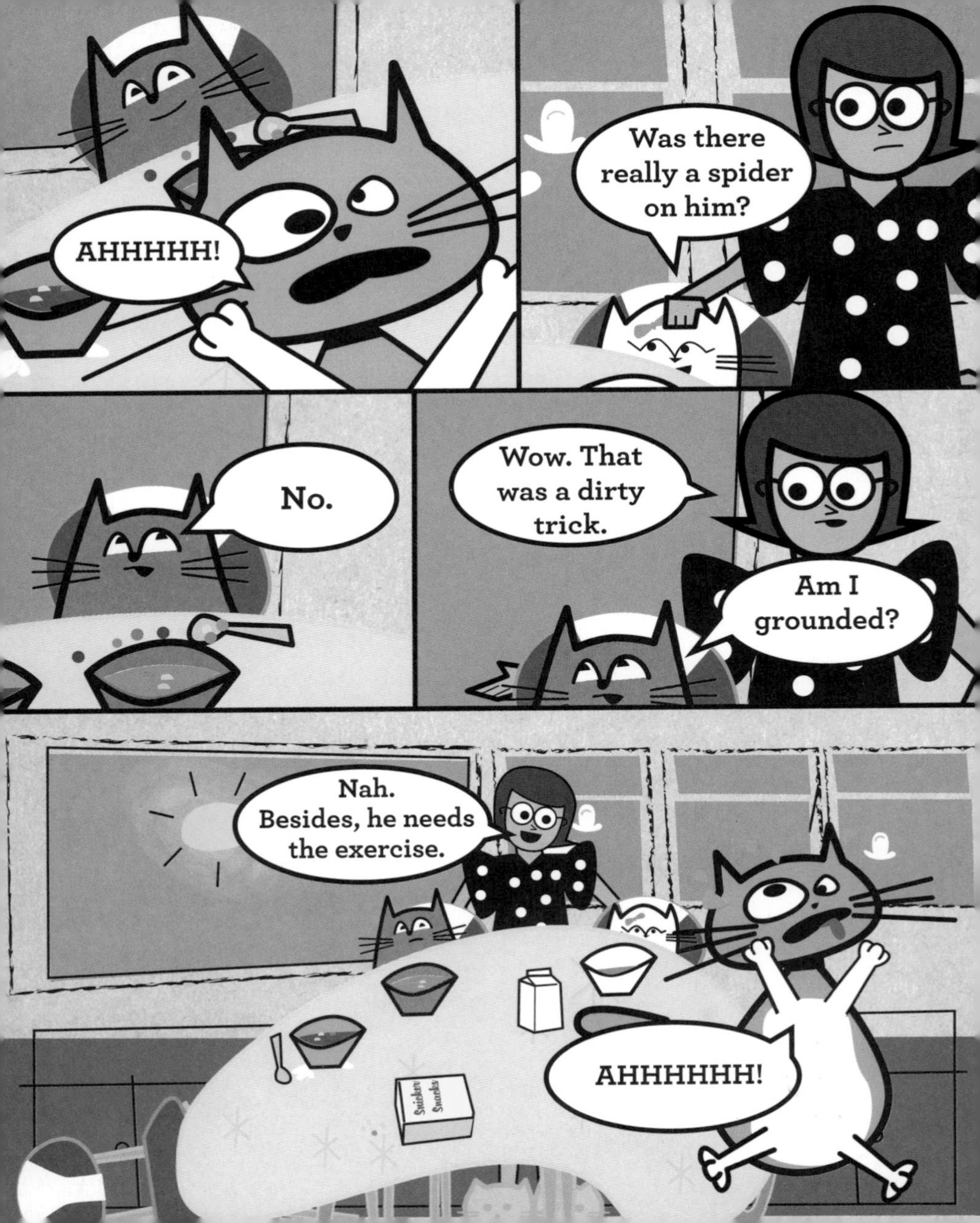
AHHHHH!
Was there really a spider on him?
No.
Wow. That was a dirty trick.
Am I grounded?
Nah. Besides, he needs the exercise.
AHHHHHH!
Snicker Snacks

Chapter One:
IT'S RANGER TIME!

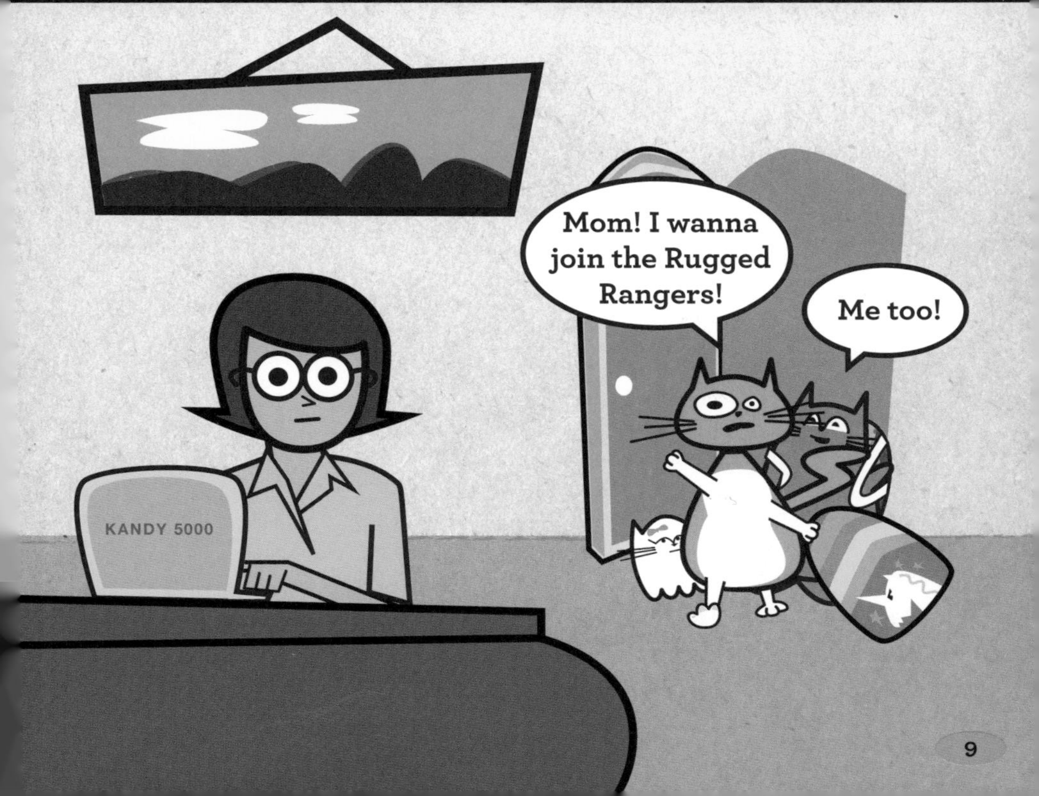
Mom! I wanna join the Rugged Rangers!
Me too!
KANDY 5000

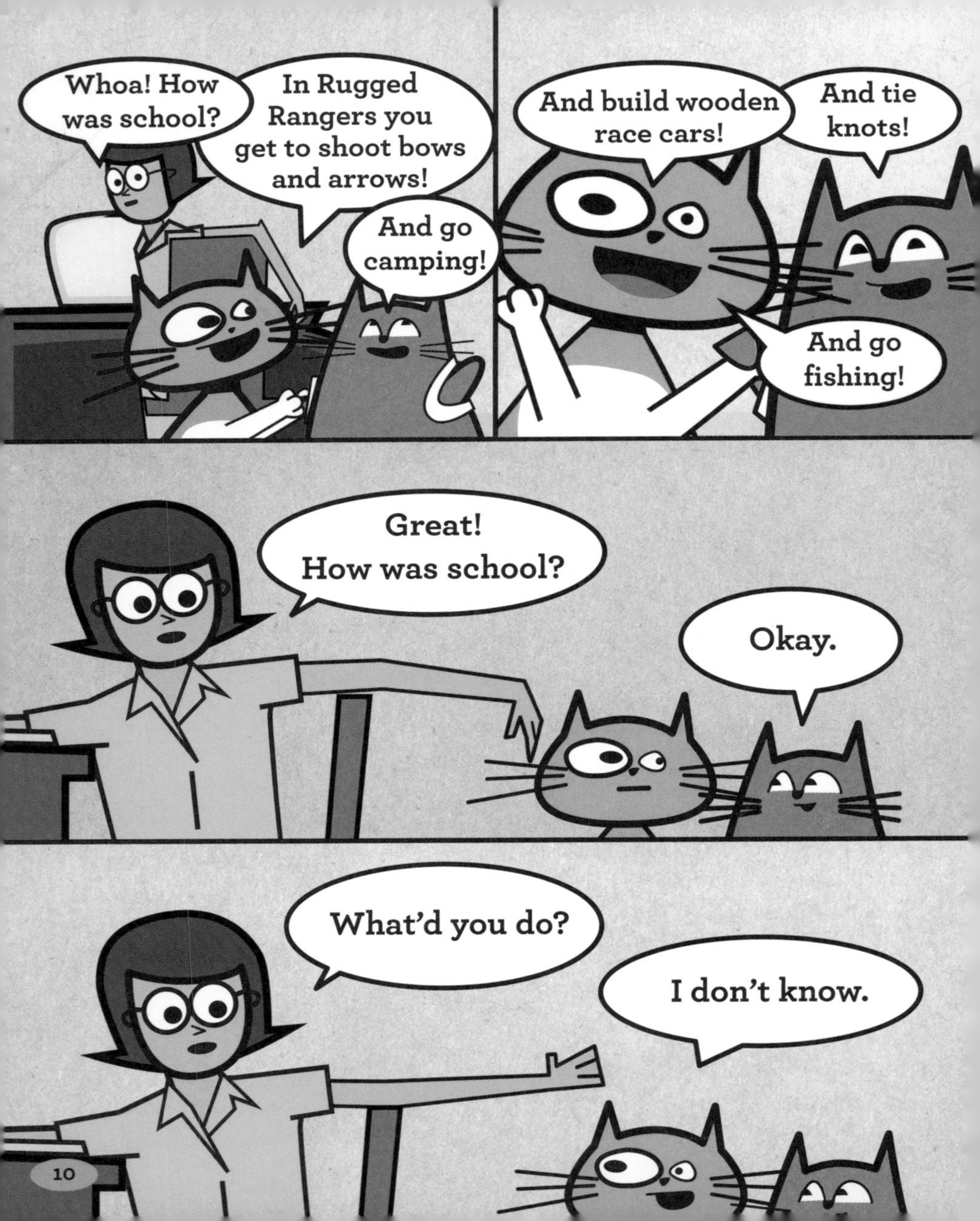
Whoa! How was school?
In Rugged Rangers you get to shoot bows and arrows!
And go camping!
And build wooden race cars!
And tie knots!
And go fishing!
Great! How was school?
Okay.
What'd you do?
I don't know.

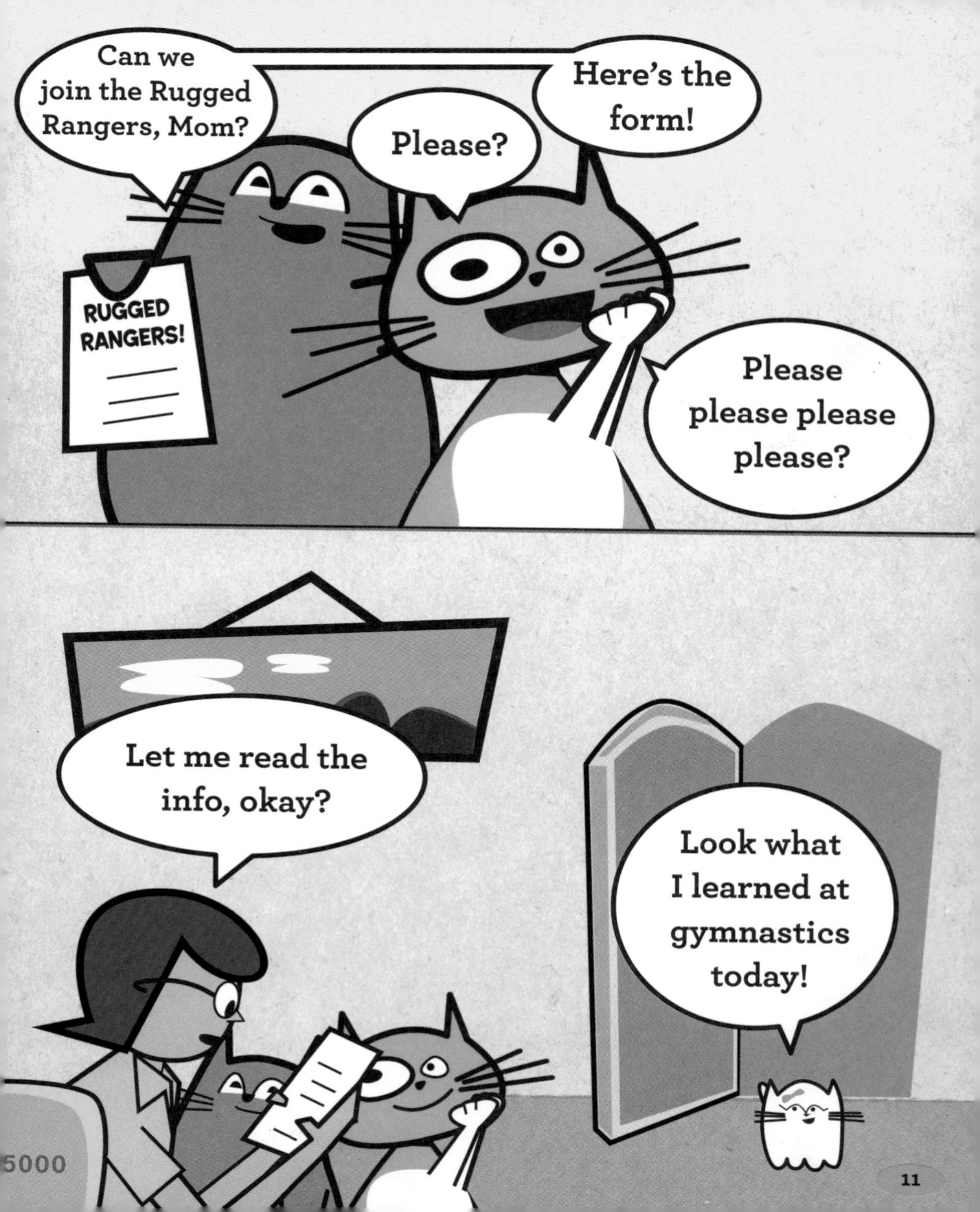
Can we join the Rugged Rangers, Mom?
Here's the form!
Please?
RUGGED RANGERS!
Please please please please?
Let me read the info, okay?
Look what I learned at gymnastics today!

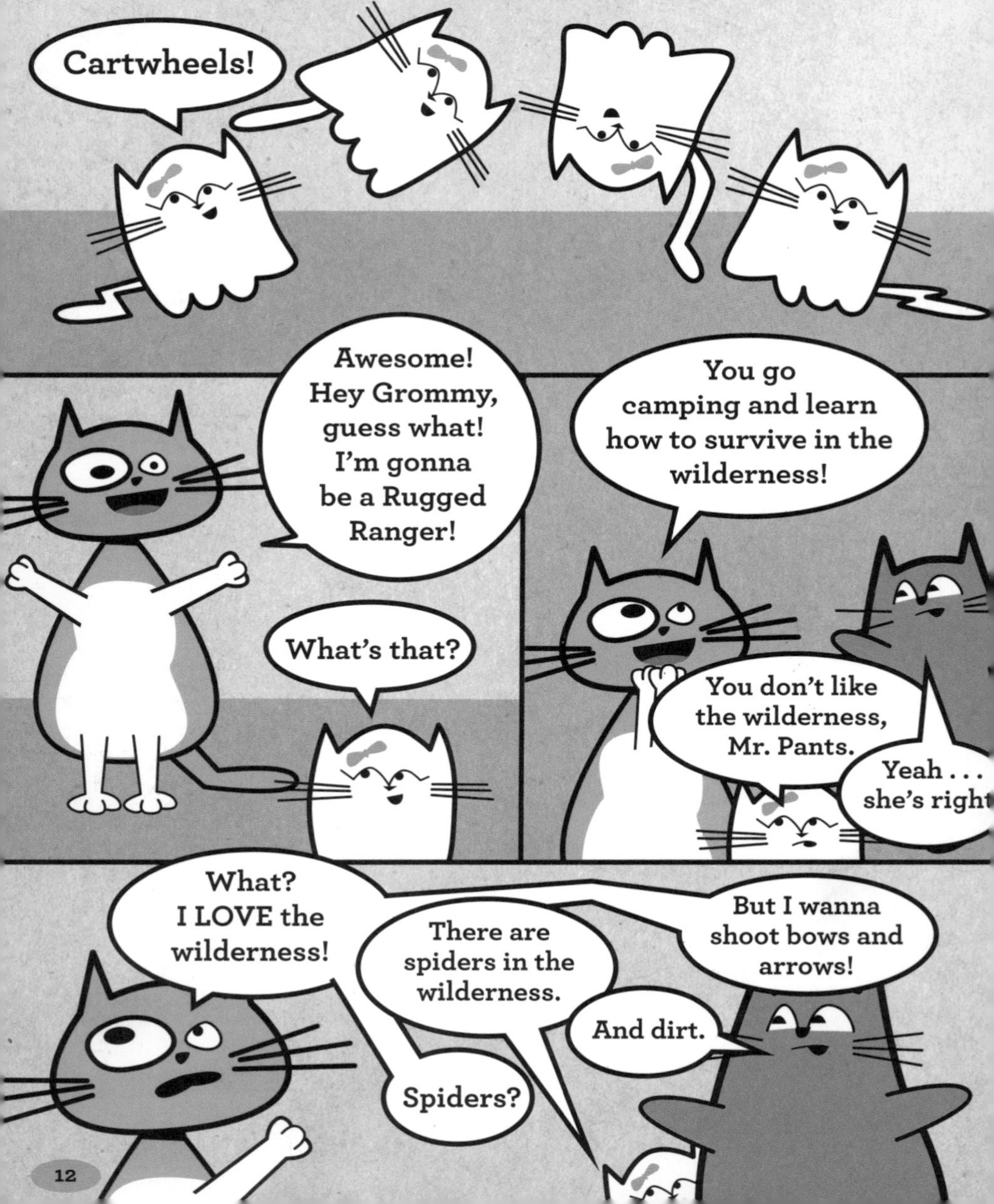
Cartwheels!
Awesome! Hey Grommy, guess what! I'm gonna be a Rugged Ranger!
What's that?
You go camping and learn how to survive in the wilderness!
You don't like the wilderness, Mr. Pants.
Yeah . . . she's righ
What? I LOVE the wilderness!
There are spiders in the wilderness.
But I wanna shoot bows and arrows!
And dirt.
Spiders?

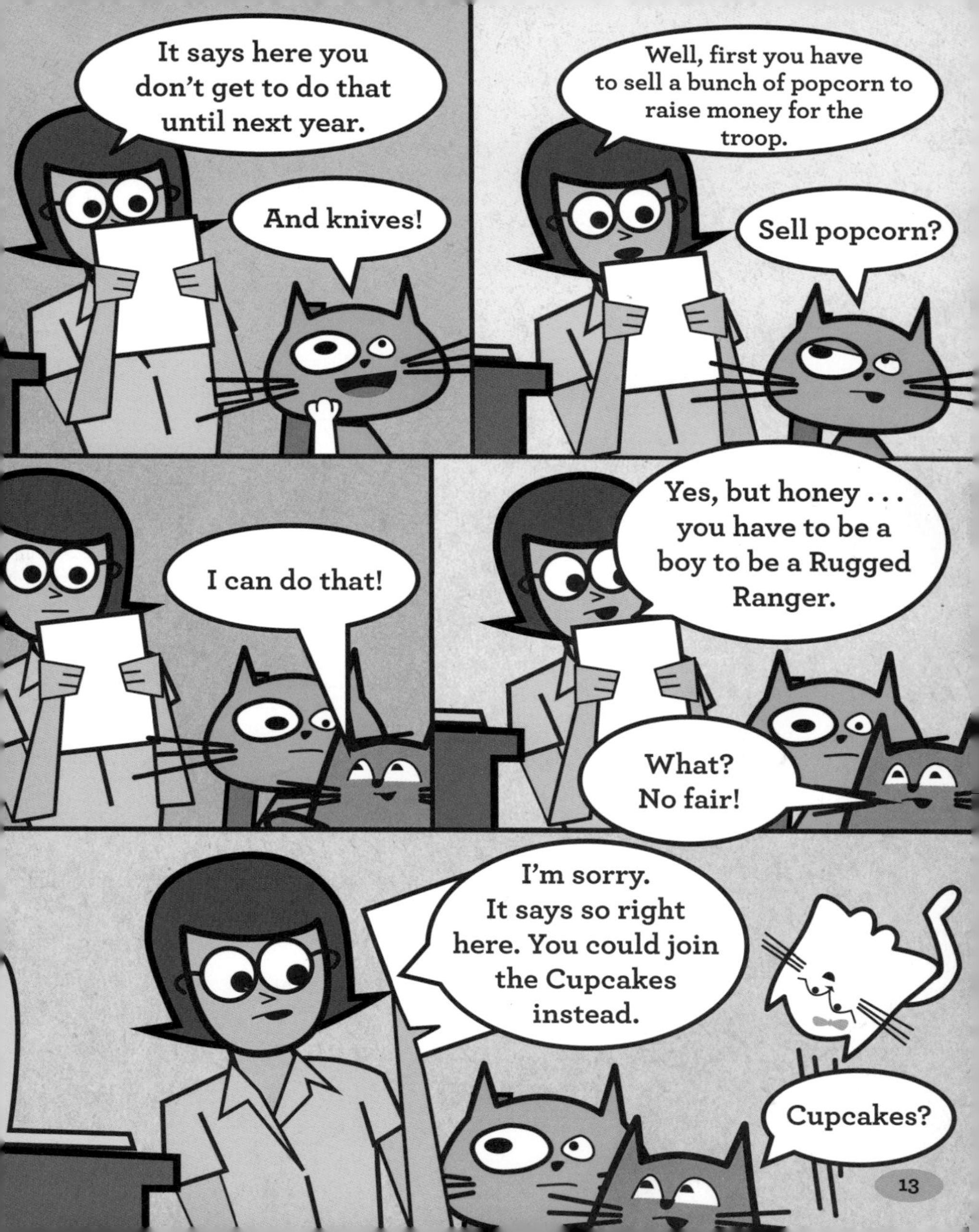

It says here you don't get to do that until next year.
And knives!
Well, first you have to sell a bunch of popcorn to raise money for the troop.
Sell popcorn?
I can do that!
Yes, but honey . . . you have to be a boy to be a Rugged Ranger.
What? No fair!
I'm sorry. It says so right here. You could join the Cupcakes instead.
Cupcakes?

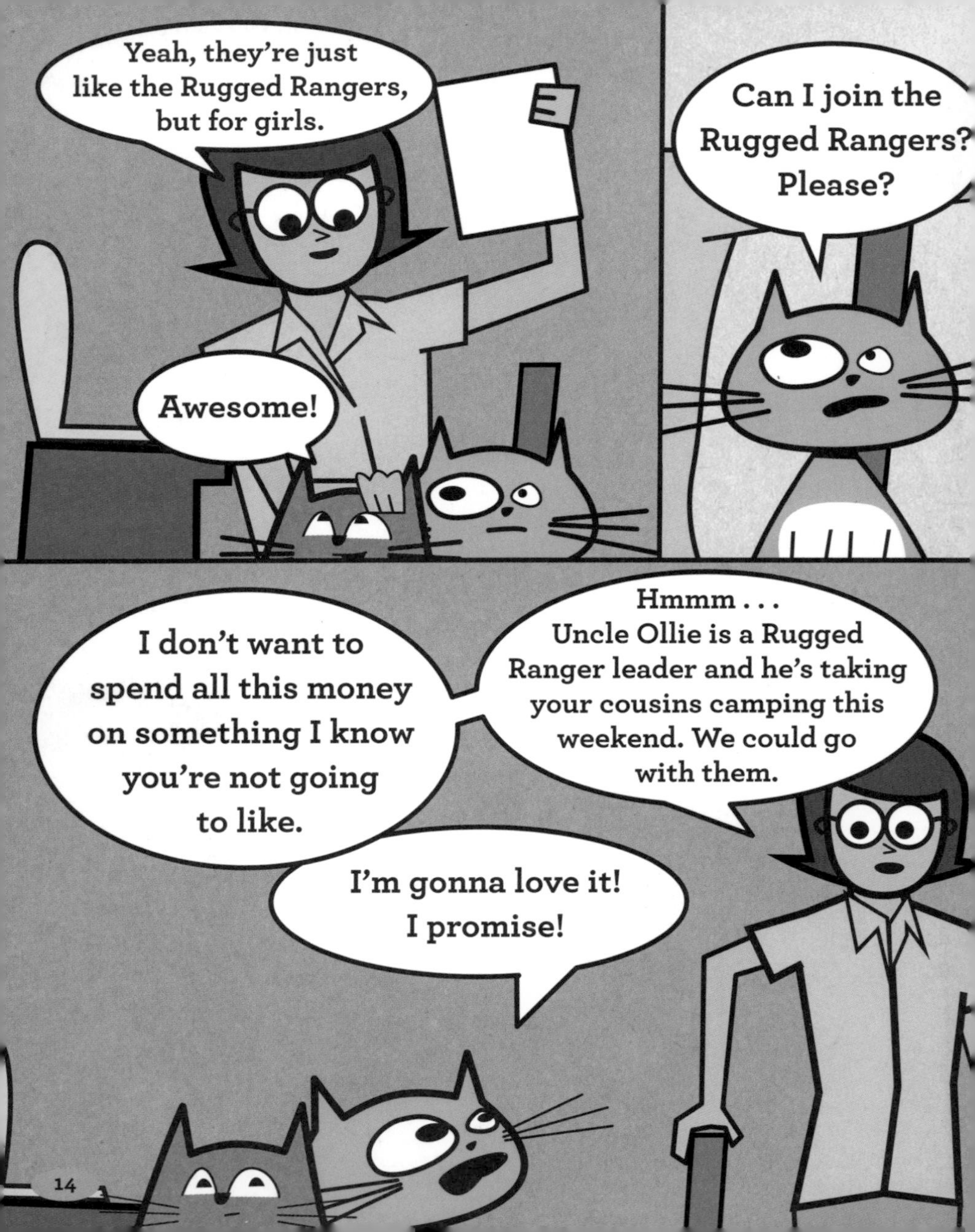
Yeah, they're just like the Rugged Rangers, but for girls.
Awesome!
Can I join the Rugged Rangers? Please?
Hmmm . . . Uncle Ollie is a Rugged Ranger leader and he's taking your cousins camping this weekend. We could go with them.
I don't want to spend all this money on something I know you're not going to like.
I'm gonna love it! I promise!

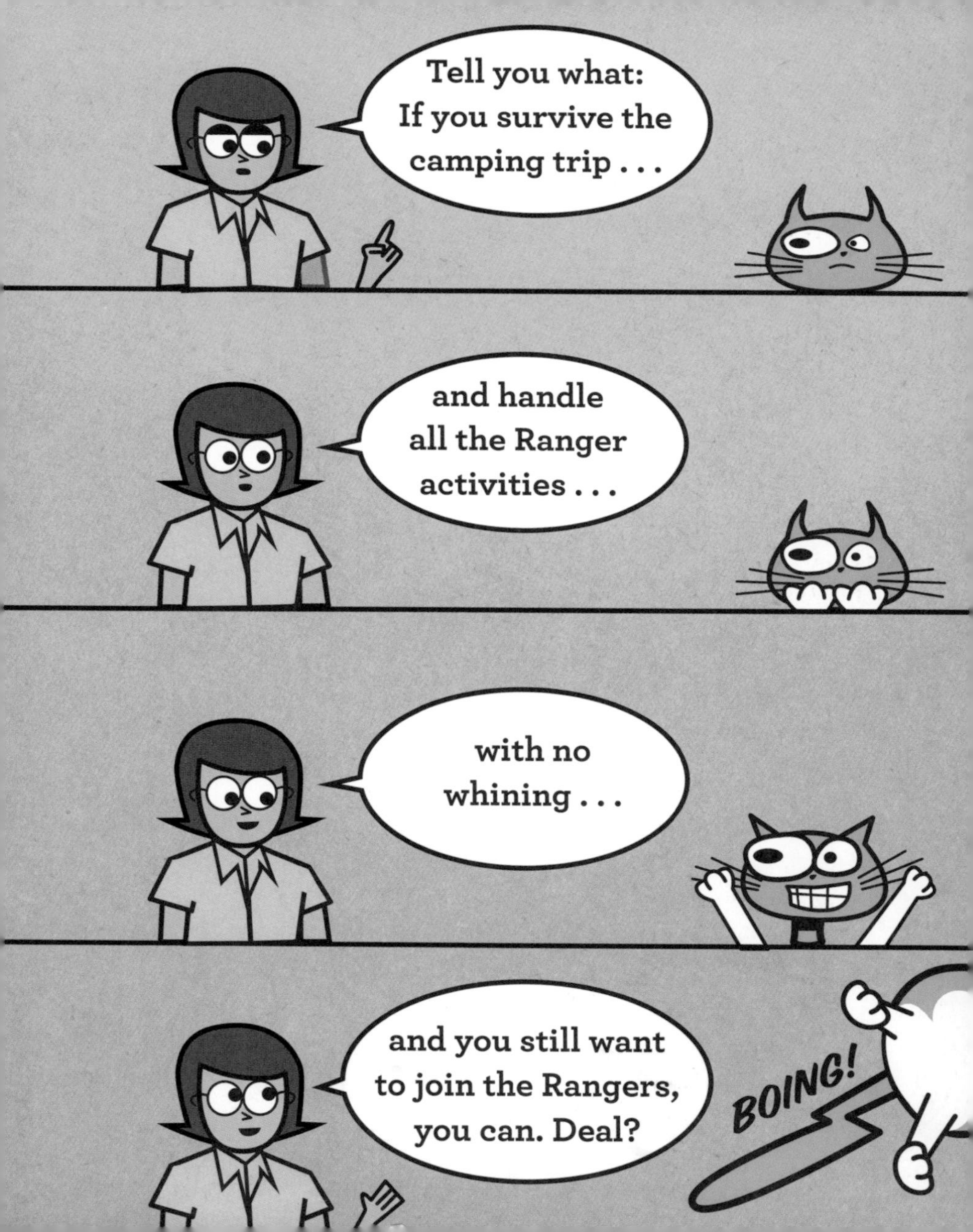
Tell you what: If you survive the camping trip . . .
and handle all the Ranger activities . . .
with no whining . . .
and you still want to join the Rangers, you can. Deal?
BOING!

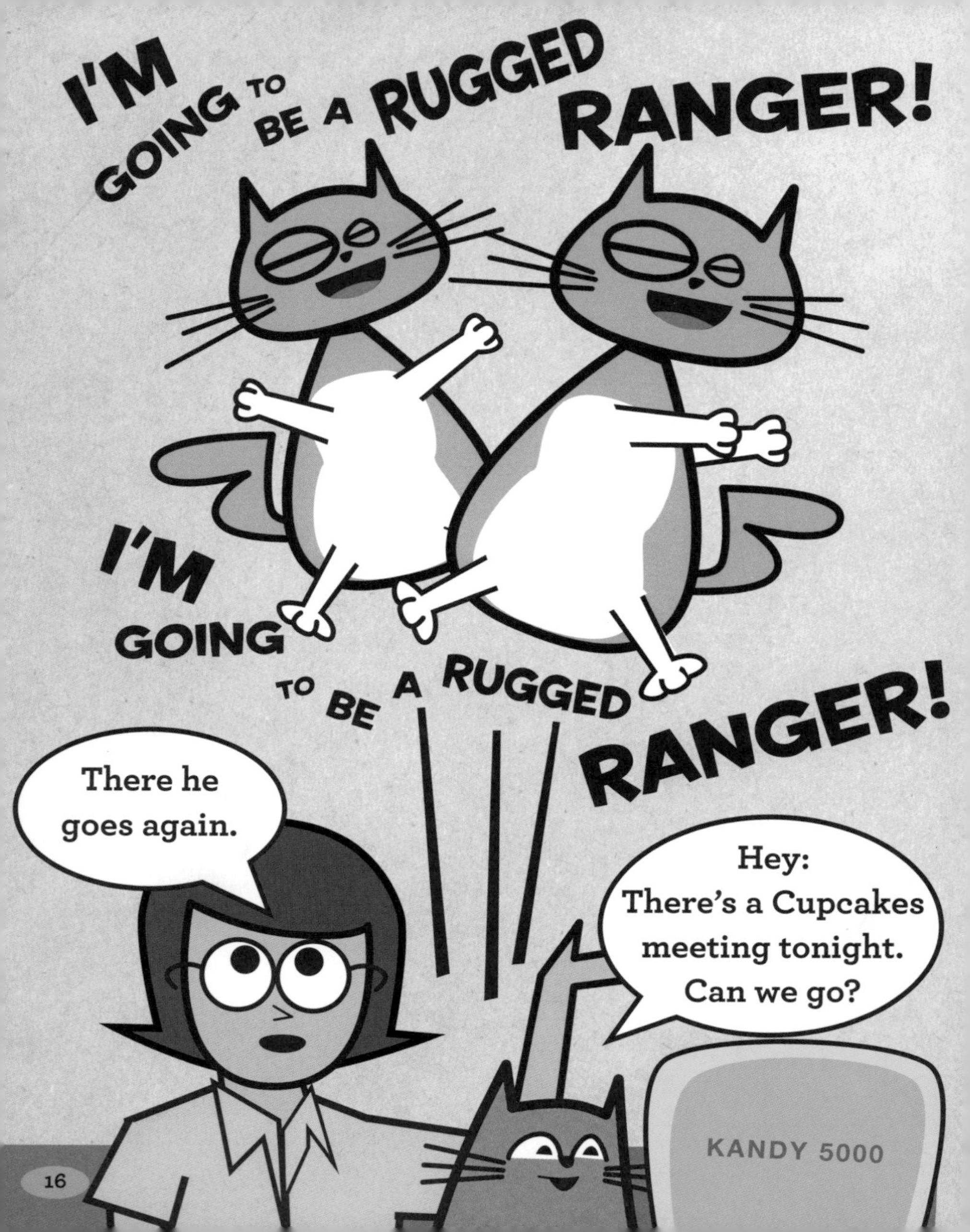
I'M GOING TO BE A RUGGED RANGER!
I'M GOING TO BE A RUGGED RANGER!
There he goes again.
Hey: There's a Cupcakes meeting tonight. Can we go?
KANDY 5000

Chapter Two: CUPCAKES

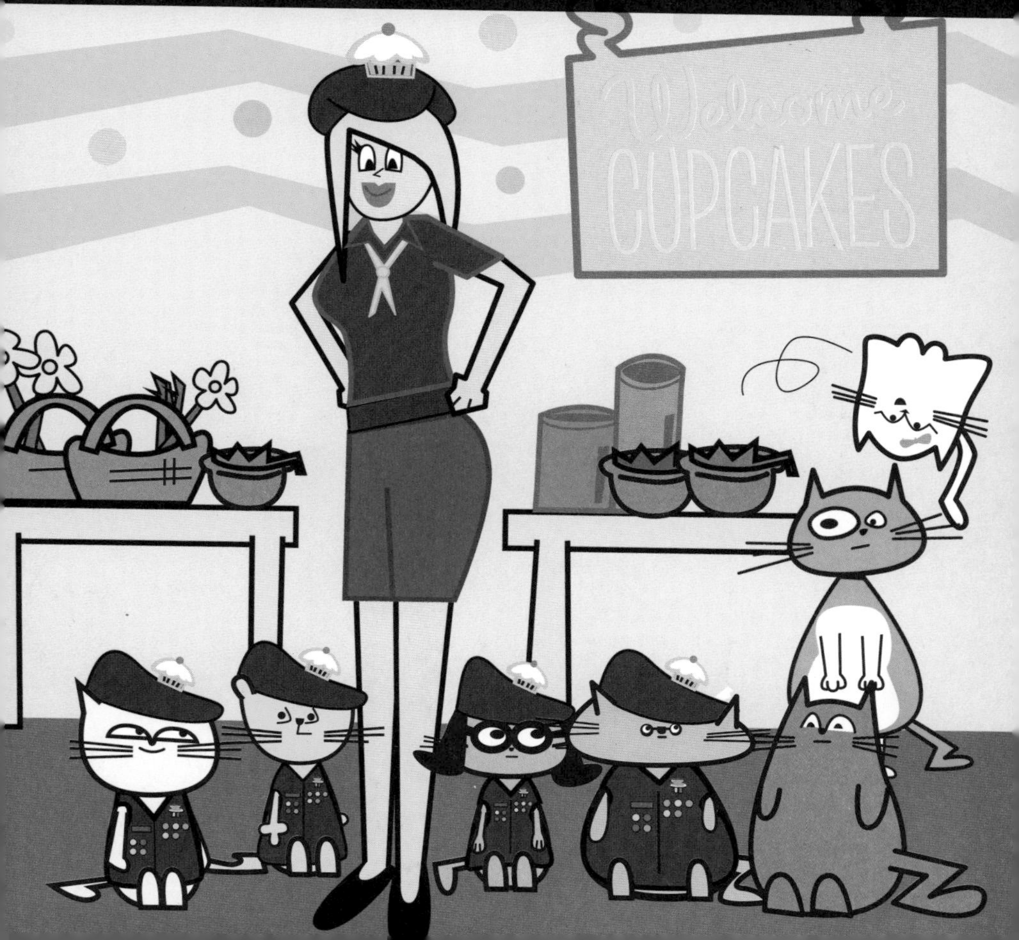
Welcome
CUPCAKES

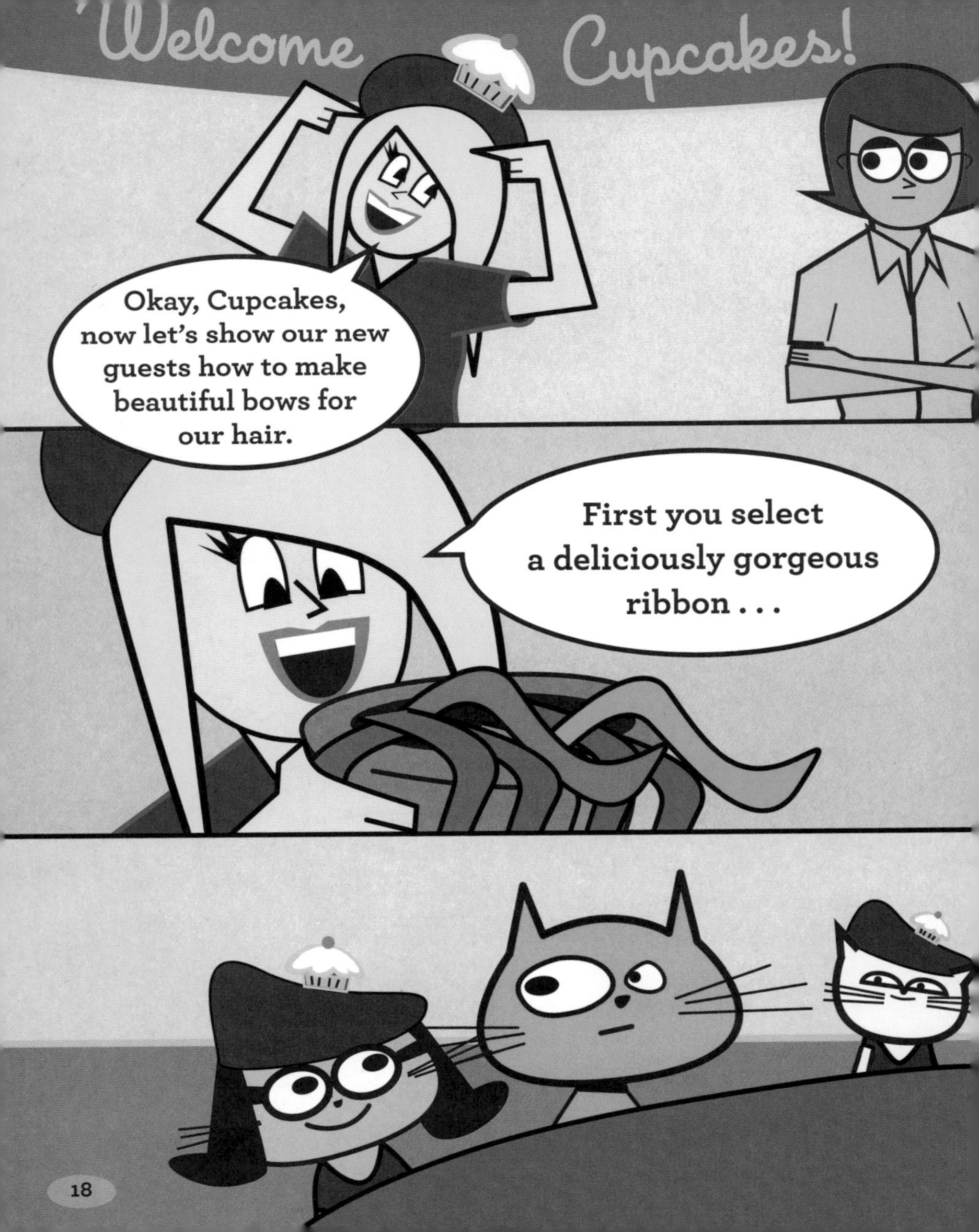
Welcome Cupcakes!
Okay, Cupcakes, now let's show our new guests how to make beautiful bows for our hair.
First you select a deliciously gorgeous ribbon . . .

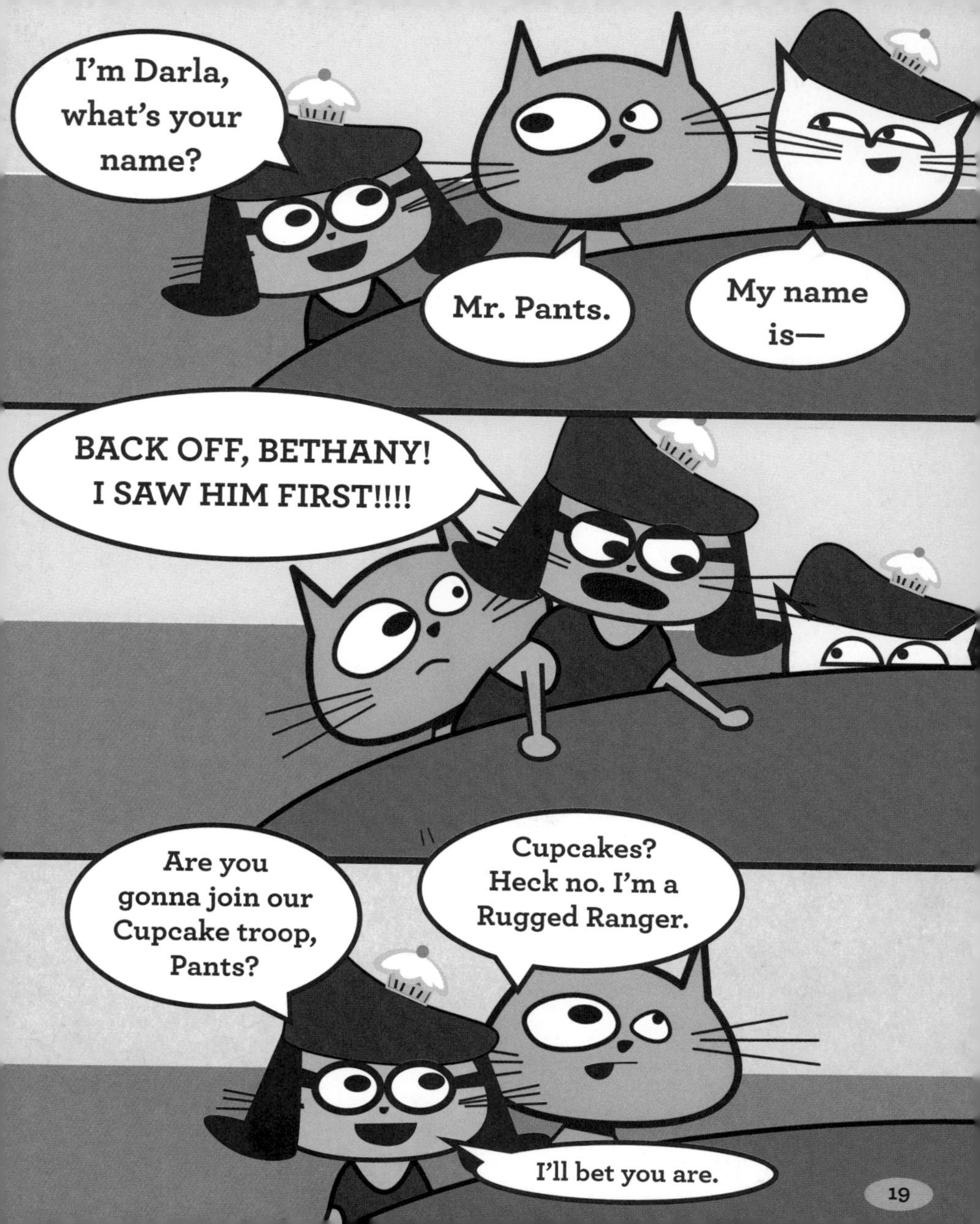
I'm Darla, what's your name?
Mr. Pants.
My name is—
BACK OFF, BETHANY! I SAW HIM FIRST!!!!
Are you gonna join our Cupcake troop, Pants?
Cupcakes? Heck no. I'm a Rugged Ranger.
I'll bet you are.

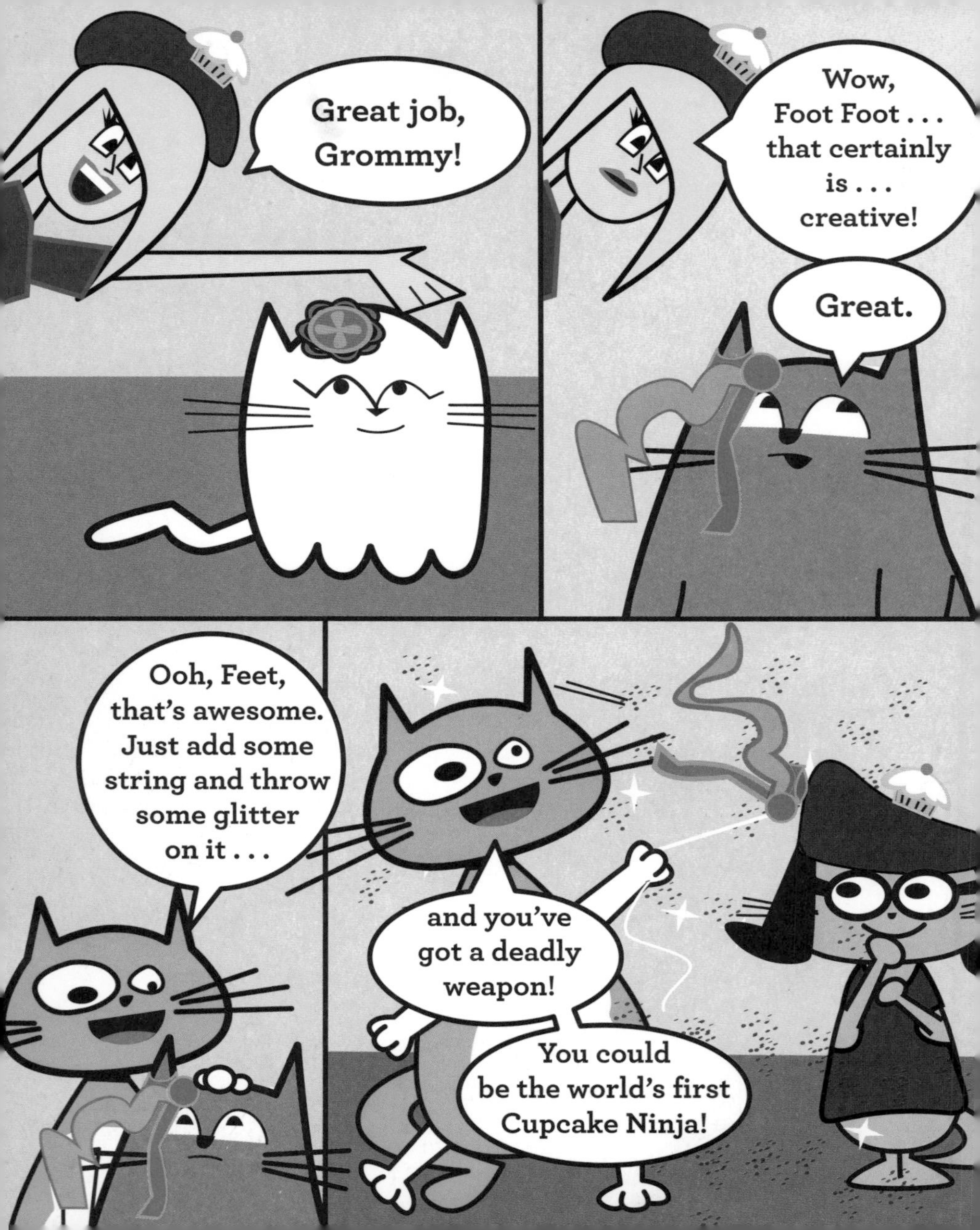

Great job, Grommy!
Wow, Foot Foot . . . that certainly is . . . creative!
Great.
Ooh, Feet, that's awesome. Just add some string and throw some glitter on it . . .
and you've got a deadly weapon!
You could be the world's first Cupcake Ninja!

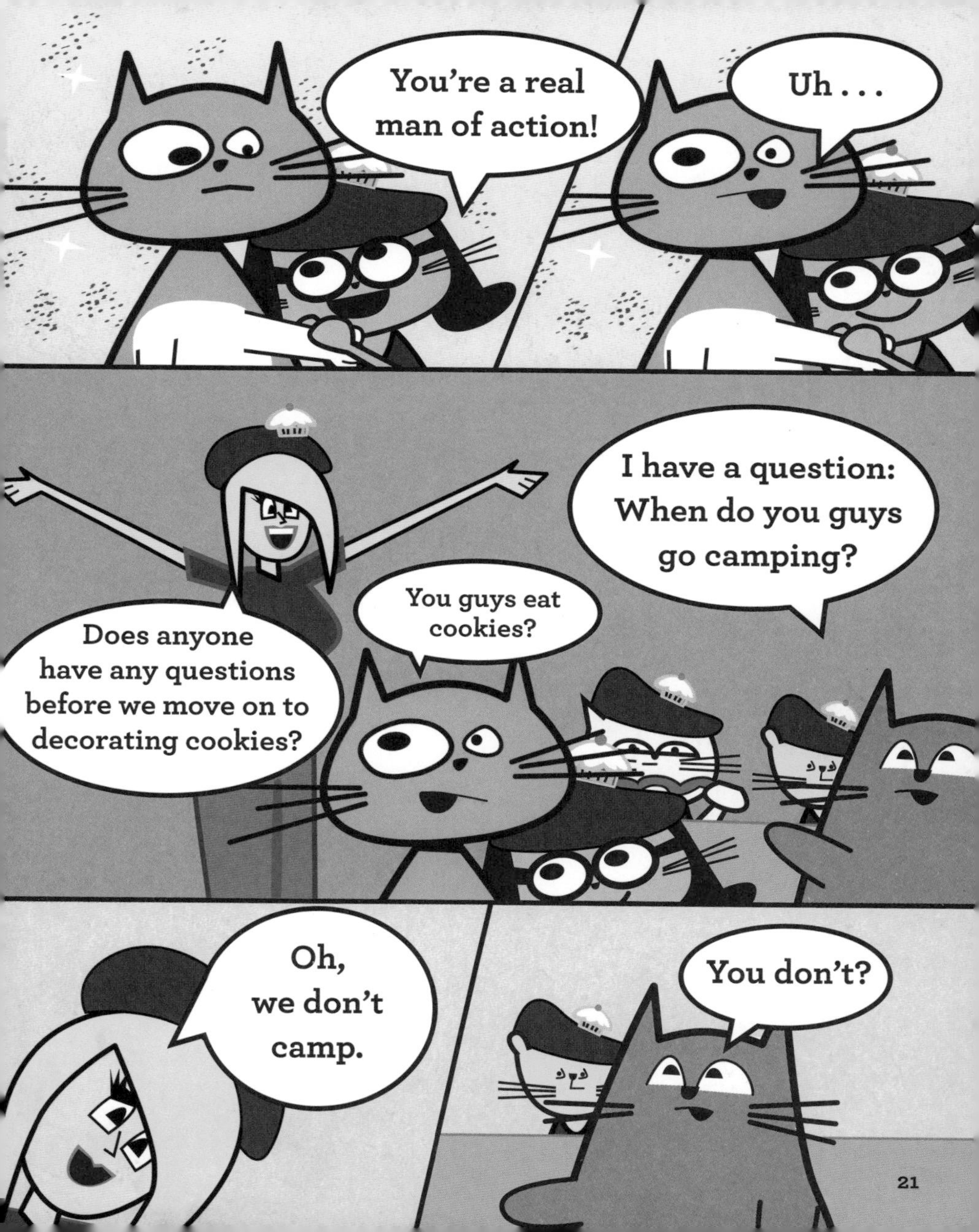
You're a real man of action!
Uh . . .
Does anyone have any questions before we move on to decorating cookies?
You guys eat cookies?
I have a question: When do you guys go camping?
Oh, we don't camp.
You don't?

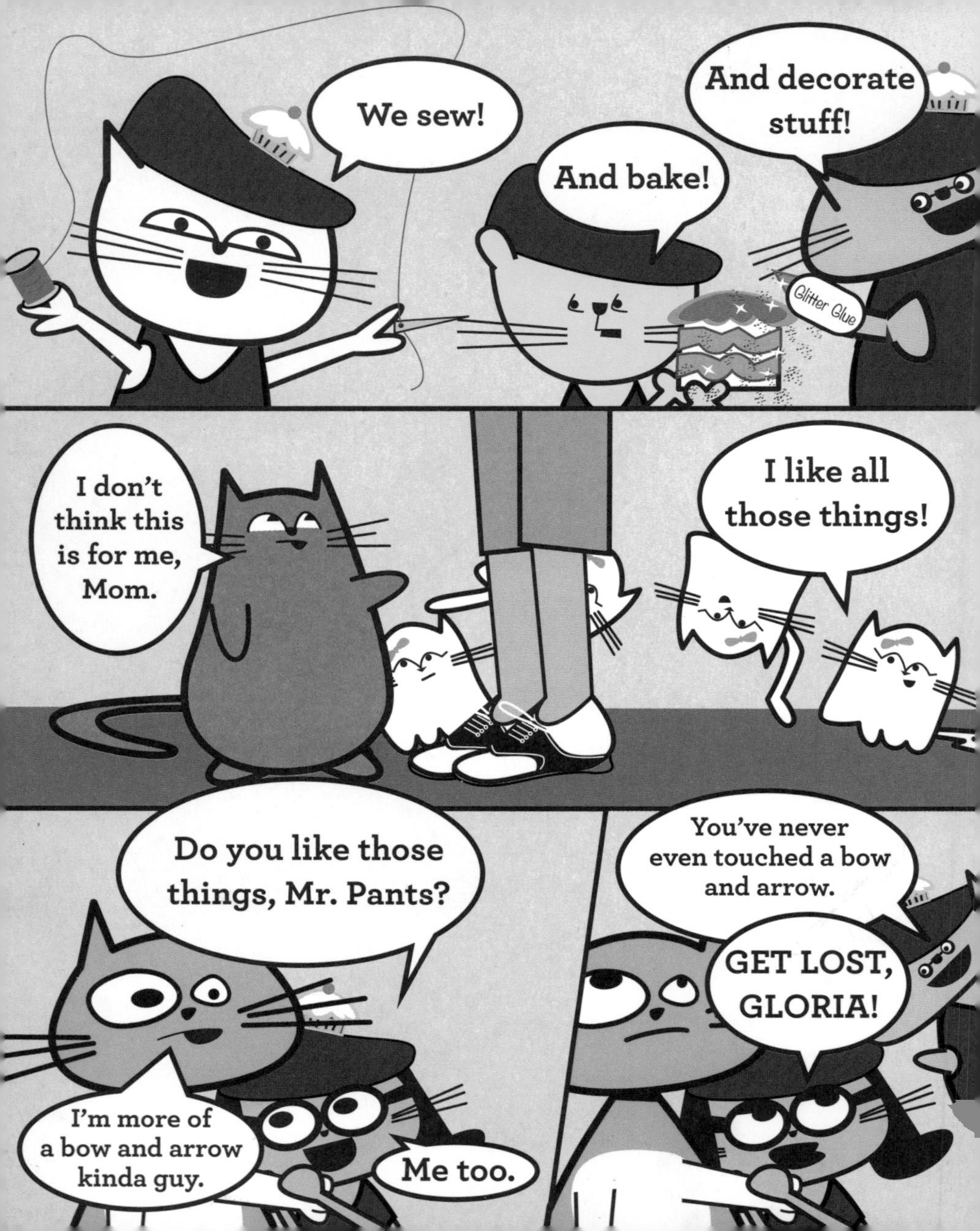
We sew!
And bake!
And decorate stuff!
Glitter Glue
I don't think this is for me, Mom.
I like all those things!
Do you like those things, Mr. Pants?
I'm more of a bow and arrow kinda guy.
Me too.
You've never even touched a bow and arrow.
GET LOST, GLORIA!

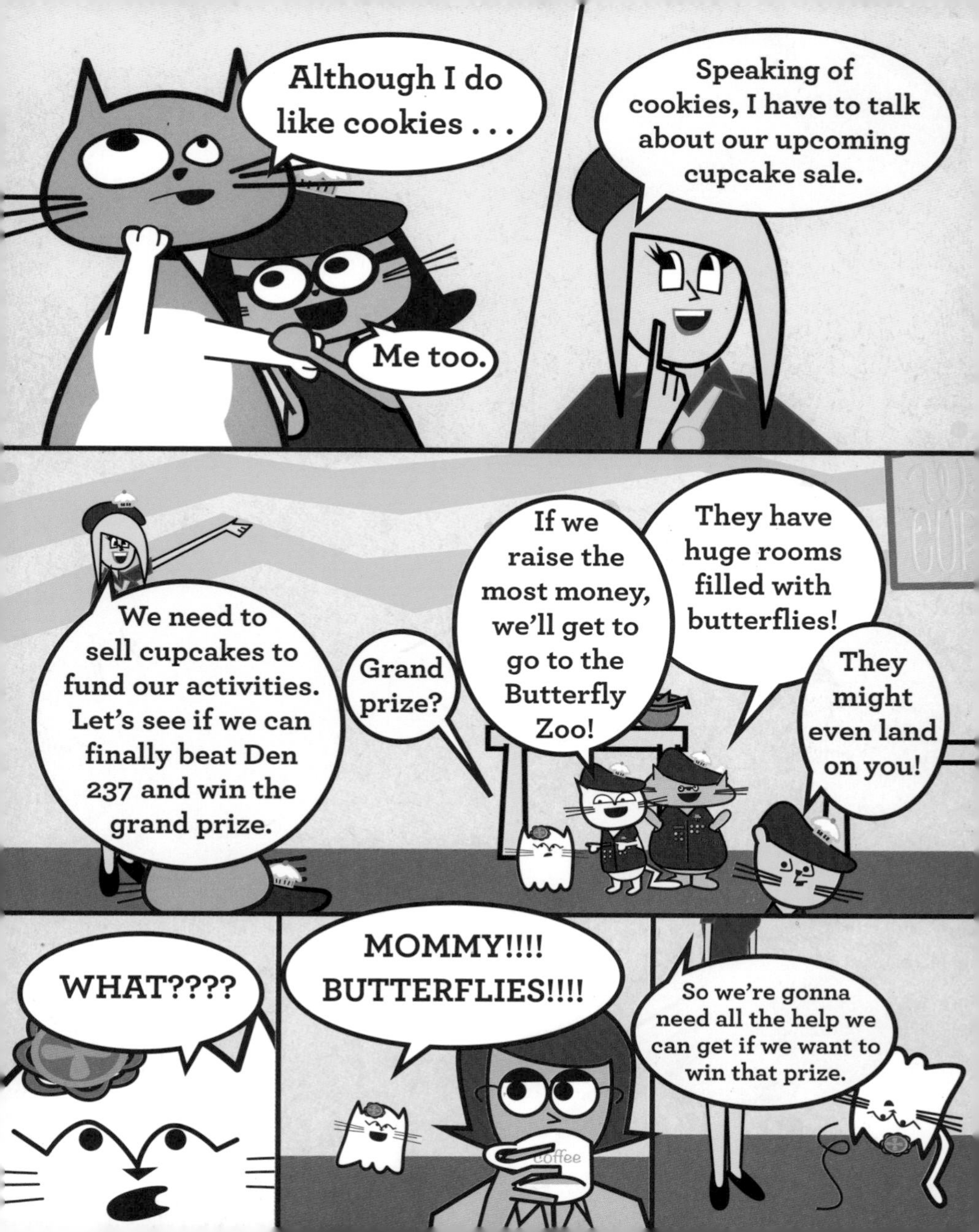
Although I do like cookies . . .
Me too.
Speaking of cookies, I have to talk about our upcoming cupcake sale.
We need to sell cupcakes to fund our activities. Let's see if we can finally beat Den 237 and win the grand prize.
Grand prize?
If we raise the most money, we'll get to go to the Butterfly Zoo!
They have huge rooms filled with butterflies!
They might even land on you!
WHAT????
MOMMY!!!! BUTTERFLIES!!!!
So we're gonna need all the help we can get if we want to win that prize.
Coffee

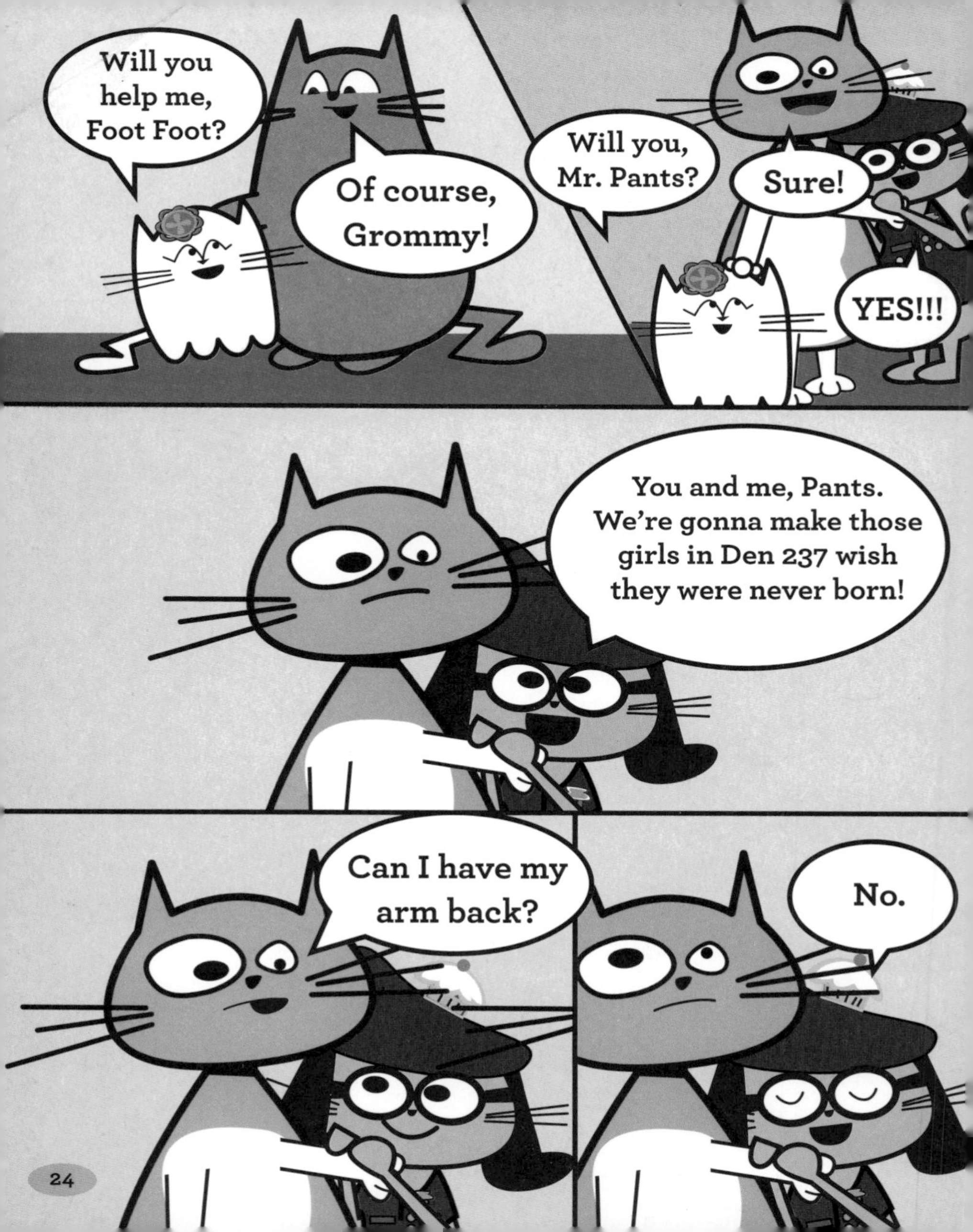
Will you help me, Foot Foot?
Of course, Grommy!
Will you, Mr. Pants?
Sure!
YES!!!
You and me, Pants. We're gonna make those girls in Den 237 wish they were never born!
Can I have my arm back?
No.

Chapter Three: SARDINES

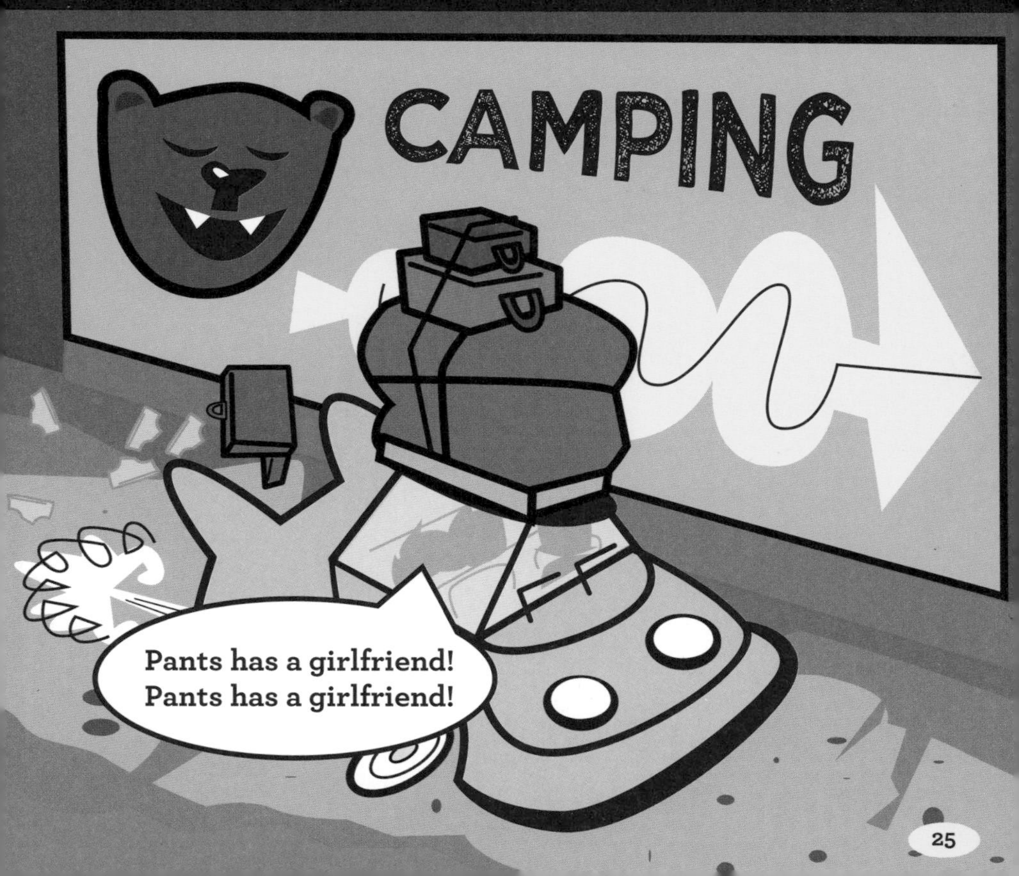
CAMPING
Pants has a girlfriend! Pants has a girlfriend!

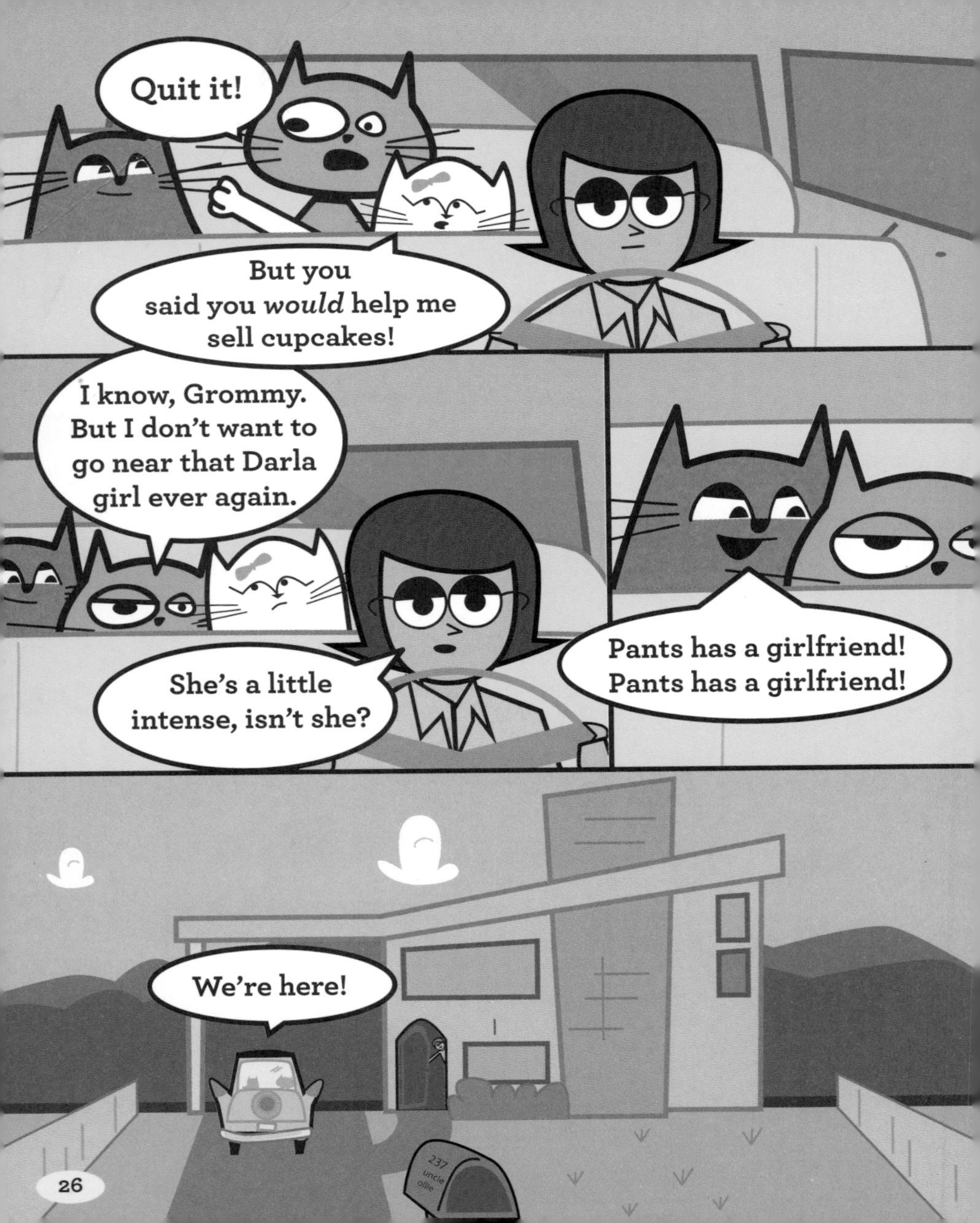
Quit it!
But you said you *would* help me sell cupcakes!
I know, Grommy. But I don't want to go near that Darla girl ever again.
She's a little intense, isn't she?
Pants has a girlfriend! Pants has a girlfriend!
We're here!
237 uncle ollie

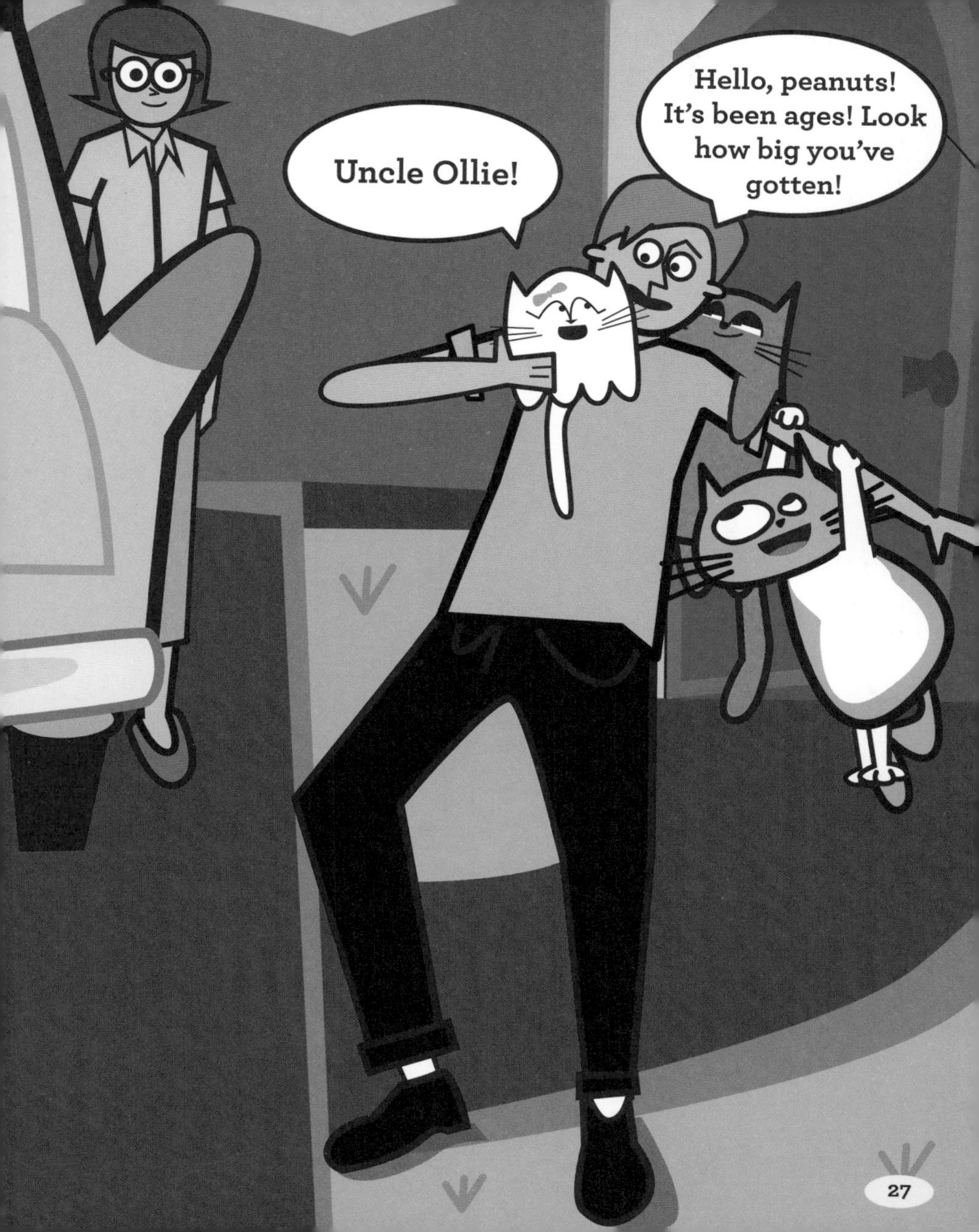
Uncle Ollie!
Hello, peanuts! It's been ages! Look how big you've gotten!

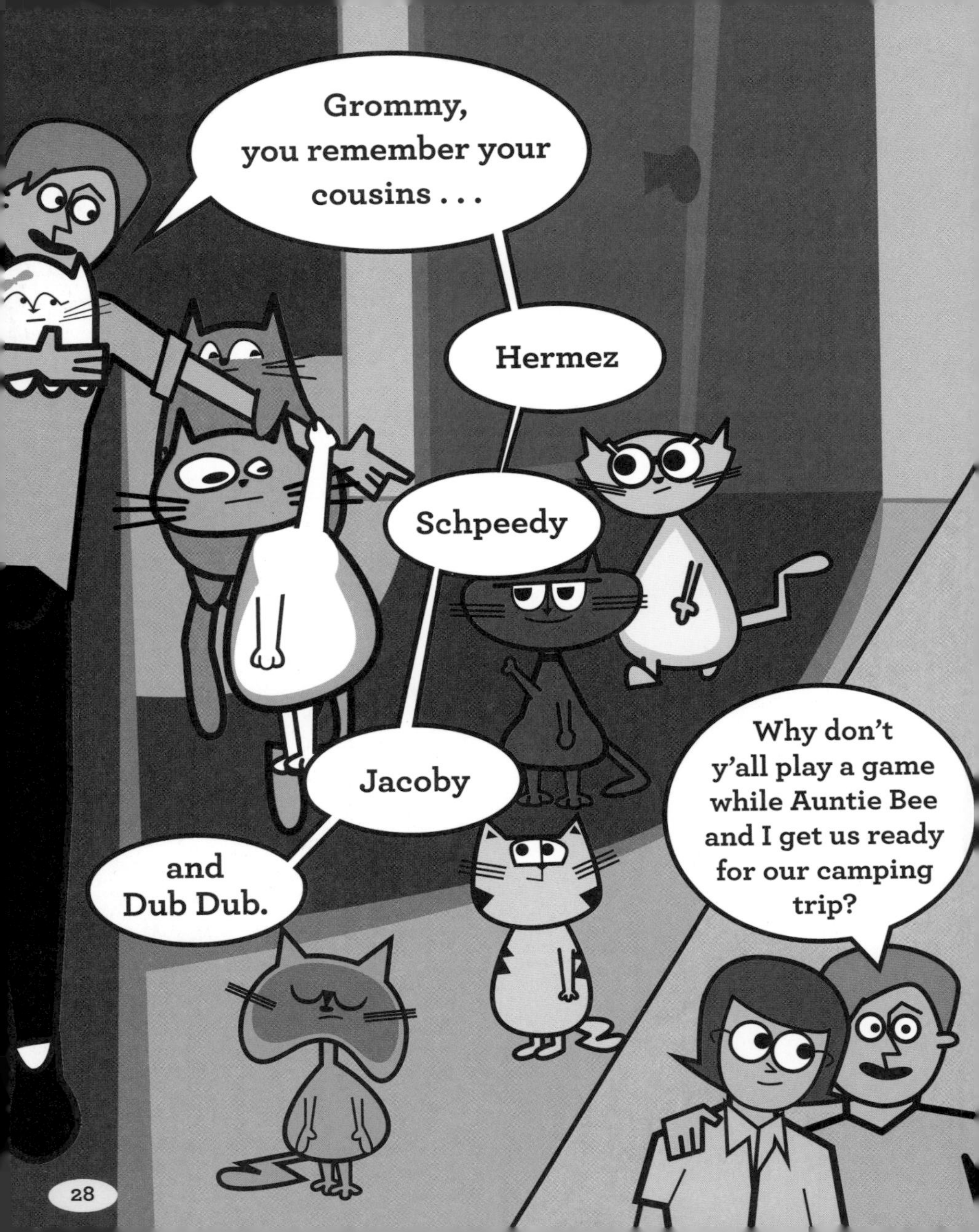
Grommy, you remember your cousins . . .
Hermez
Schpeedy
Jacoby
and Dub Dub.
Why don't y'all play a game while Auntie Bee and I get us ready for our camping trip?

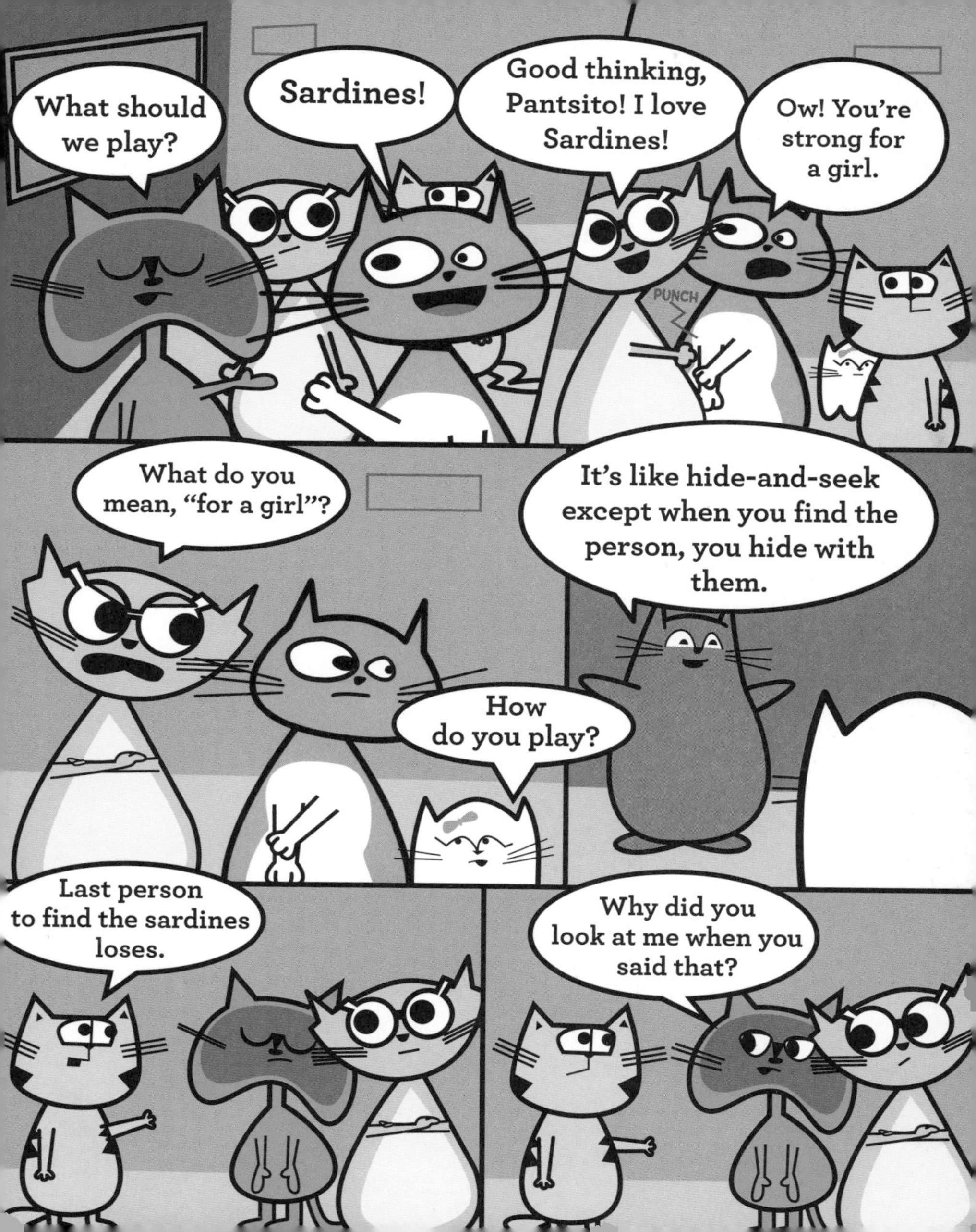

What should we play?
Sardines!
Good thinking, Pantsito! I love Sardines!
PUNCH
Ow! You're strong for a girl.
What do you mean, "for a girl"?
How do you play?
It's like hide-and-seek except when you find the person, you hide with them.
Last person to find the sardines loses.
Why did you look at me when you said that?

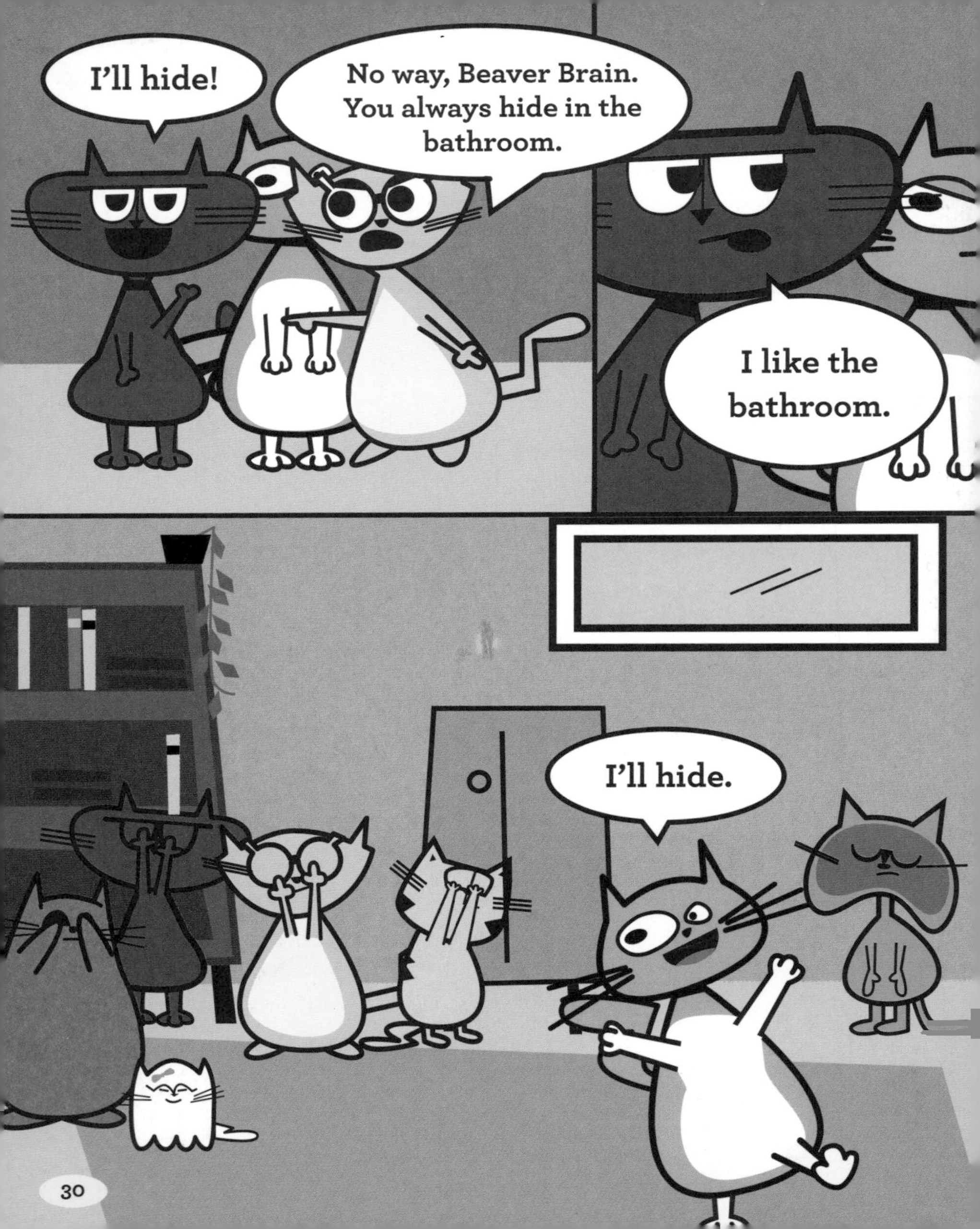
I'll hide!
No way, Beaver Brain. You always hide in the bathroom.
I like the bathroom.
I'll hide.

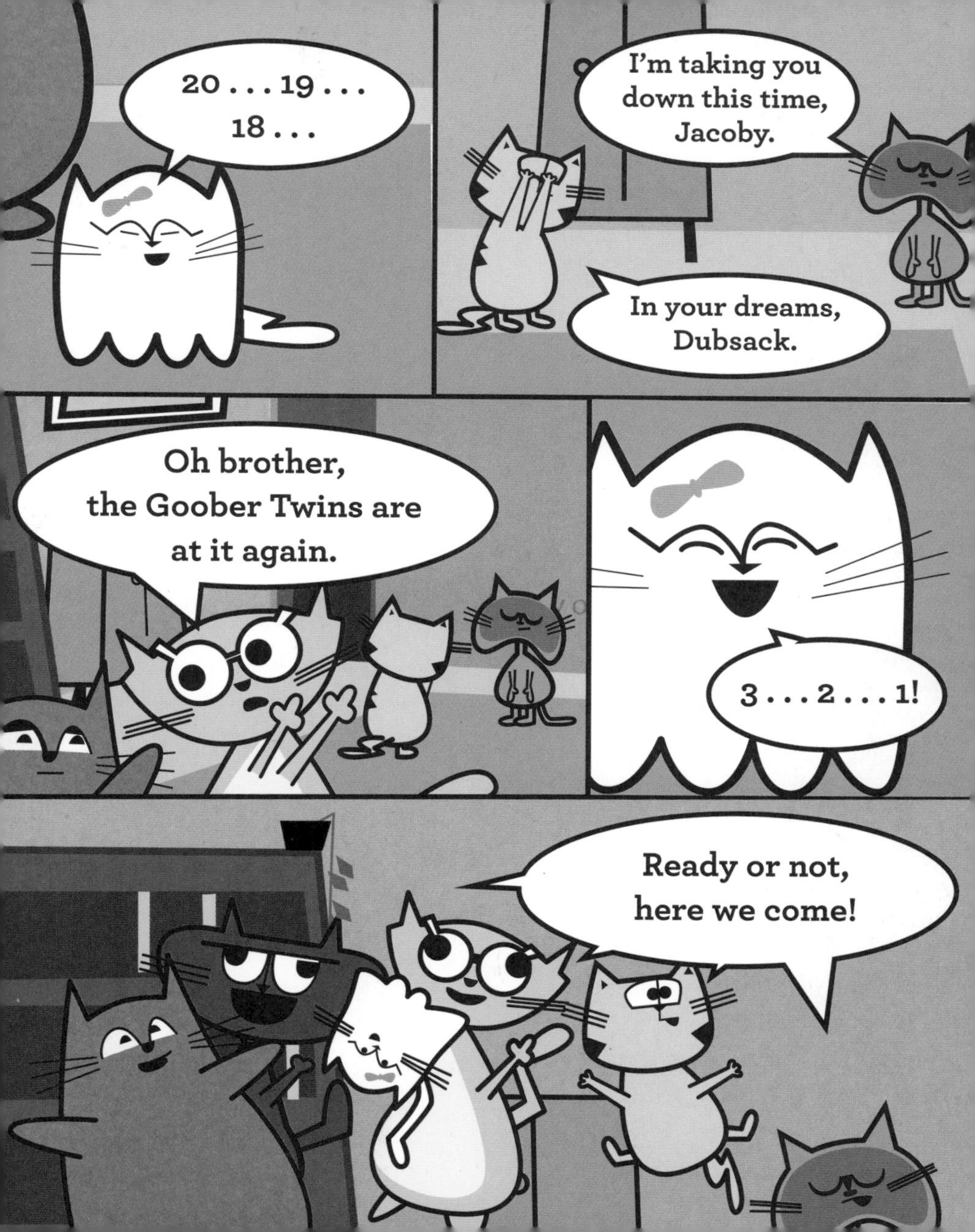
20 . . . 19 . . .
18 . . .
I'm taking you down this time, Jacoby.
In your dreams, Dubsack.
Oh brother, the Goober Twins are at it again.
3 . . . 2 . . . 1!
Ready or not, here we come!

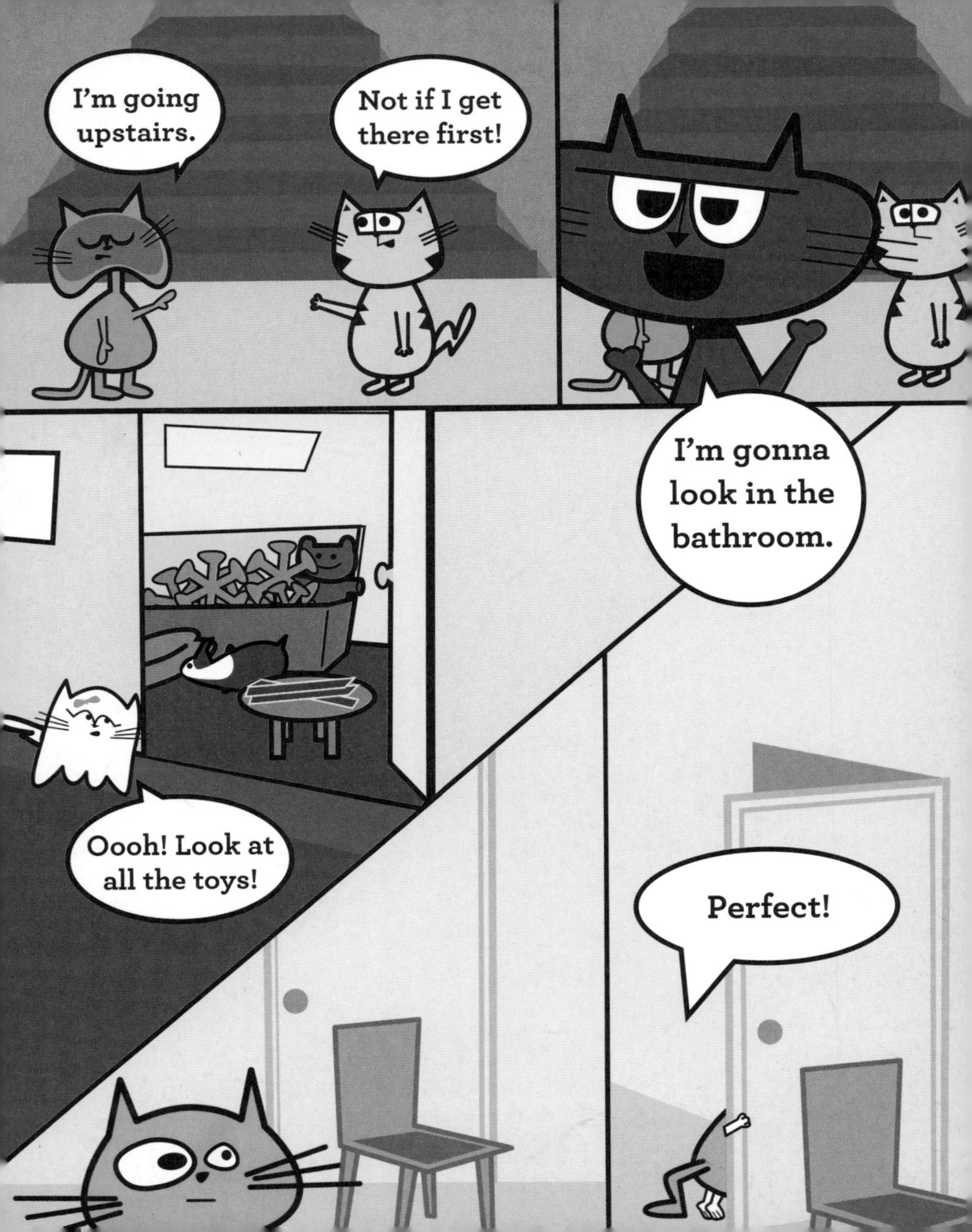
I'm going upstairs.
Not if I get there first!
I'm gonna look in the bathroom.
Oooh! Look at all the toys!
Perfect!

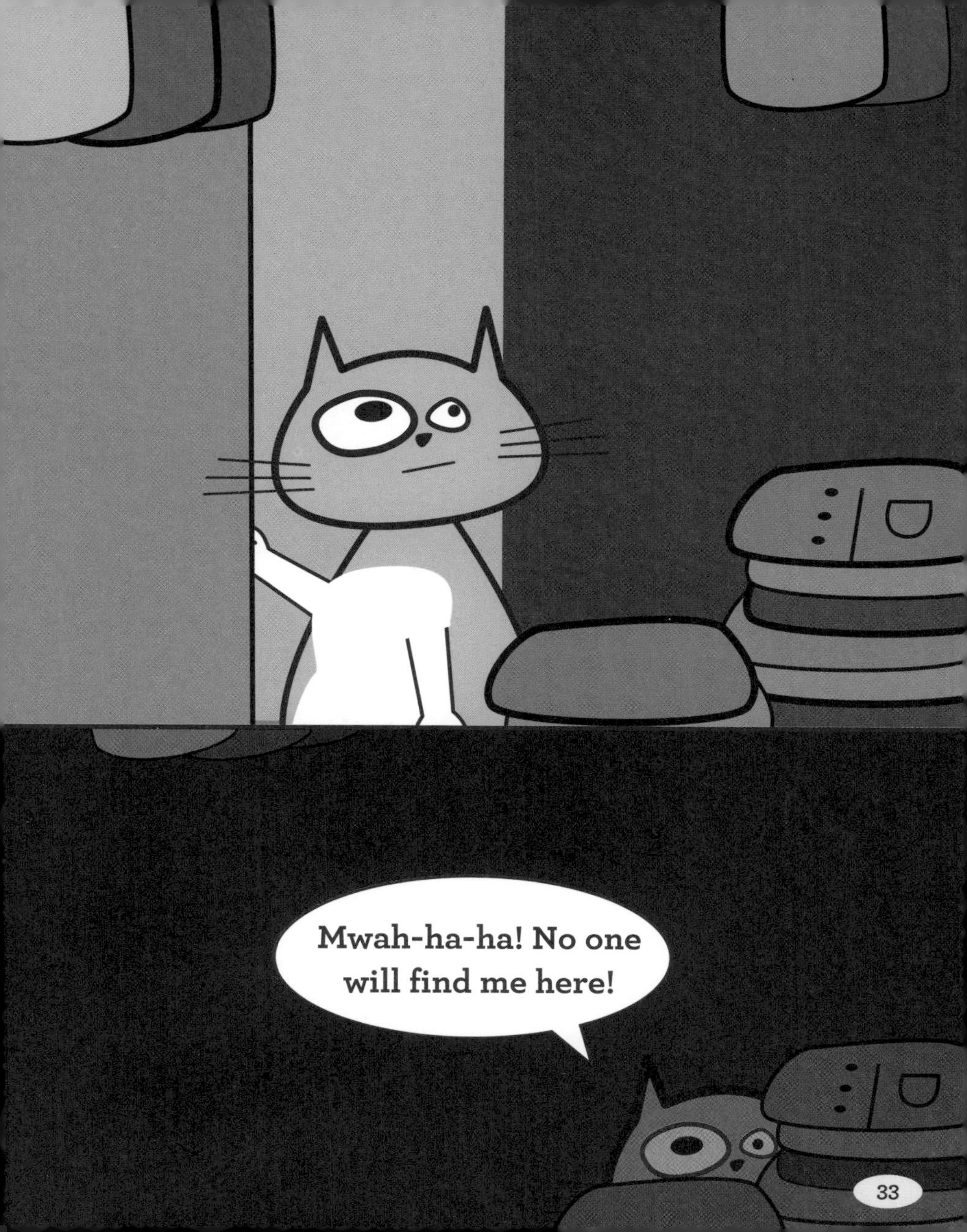
Mwah-ha-ha! No one will find me here!

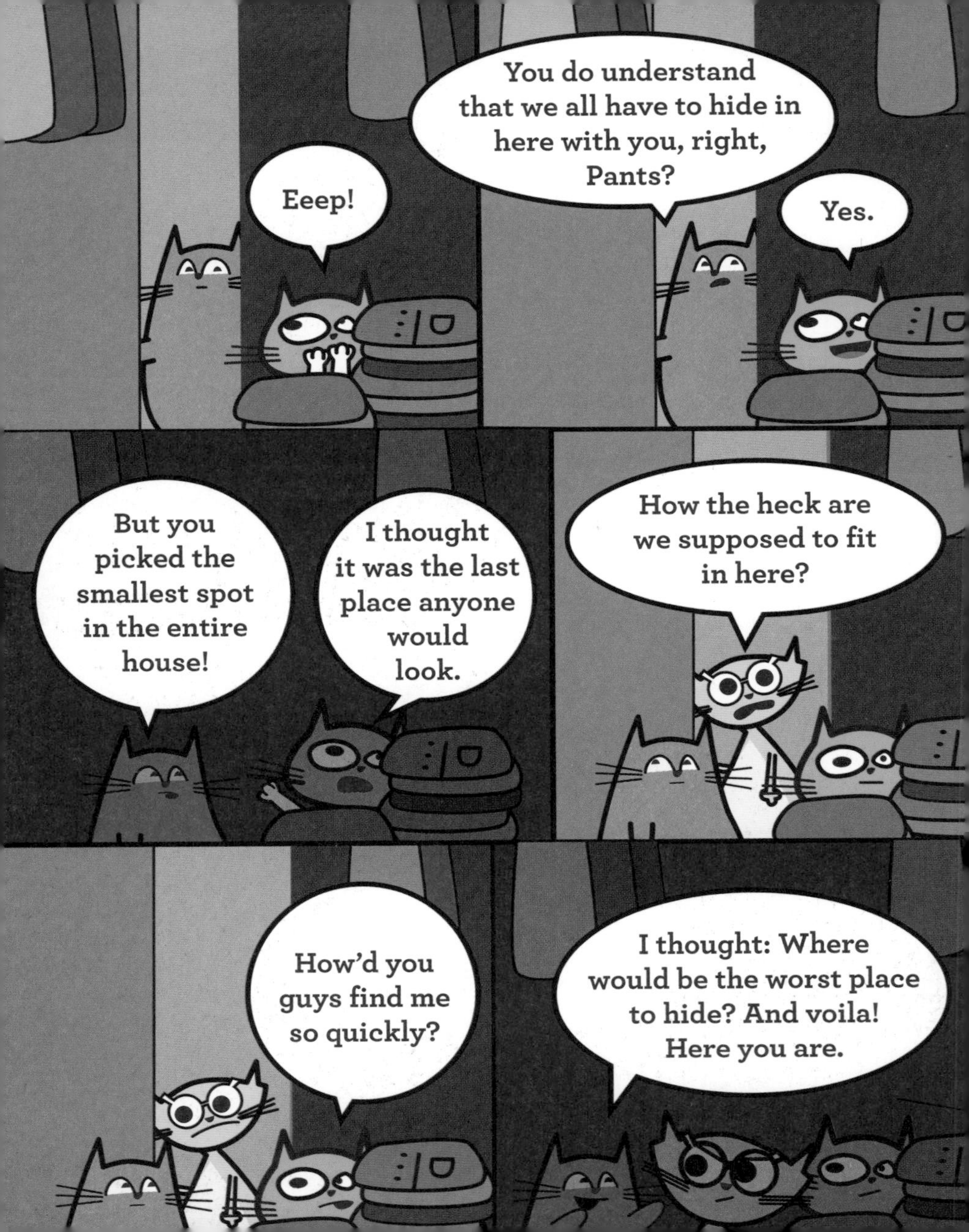
Eeep!
You do understand that we all have to hide in here with you, right, Pants?
Yes.
But you picked the smallest spot in the entire house!
I thought it was the last place anyone would look.
How the heck are we supposed to fit in here?
How'd you guys find me so quickly?
I thought: Where would be the worst place to hide? And voila! Here you are.

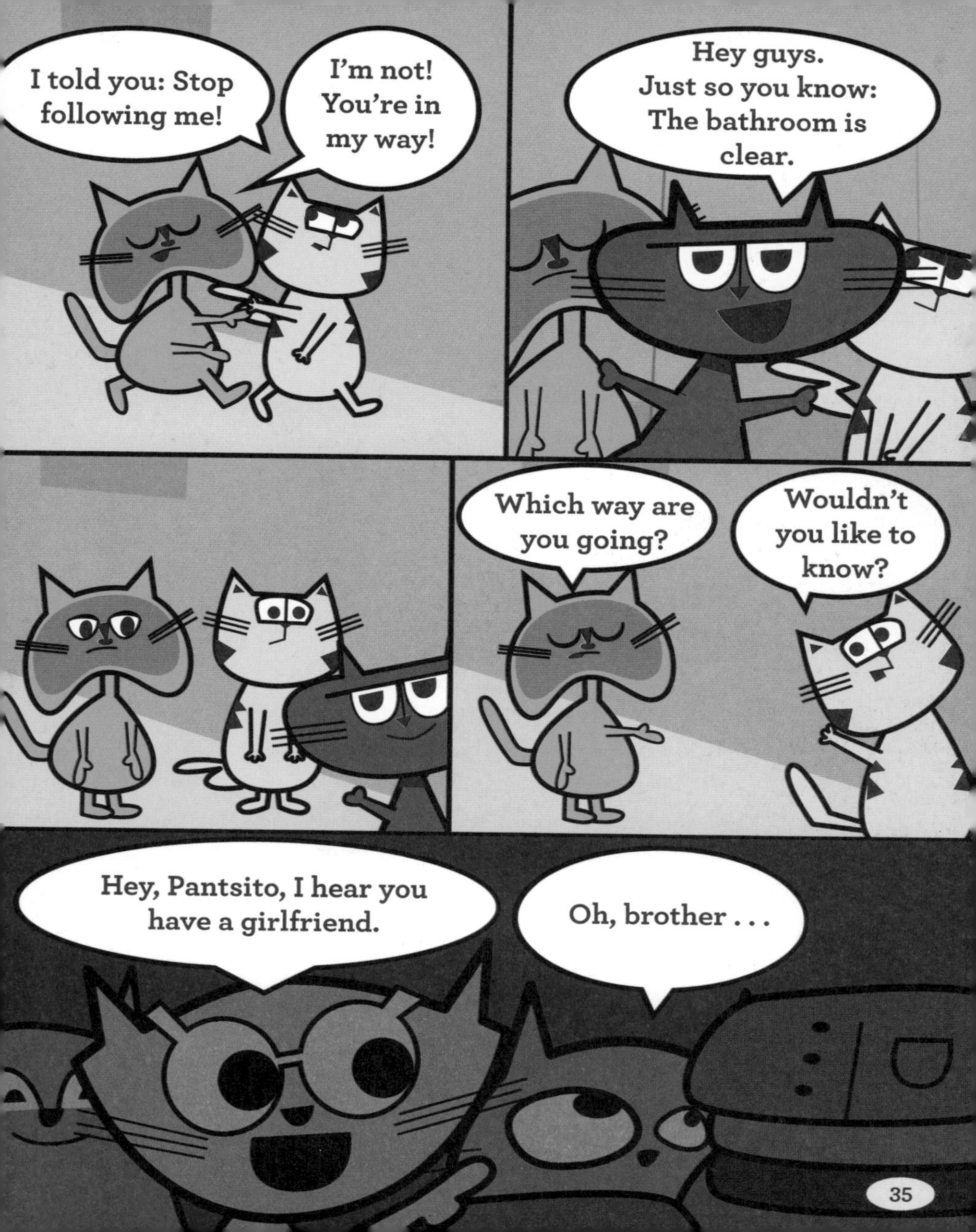
I told you: Stop following me!
I'm not! You're in my way!
Hey guys. Just so you know: The bathroom is clear.
Which way are you going?
Wouldn't you like to know?
Hey, Pantsito, I hear you have a girlfriend.
Oh, brother . . .

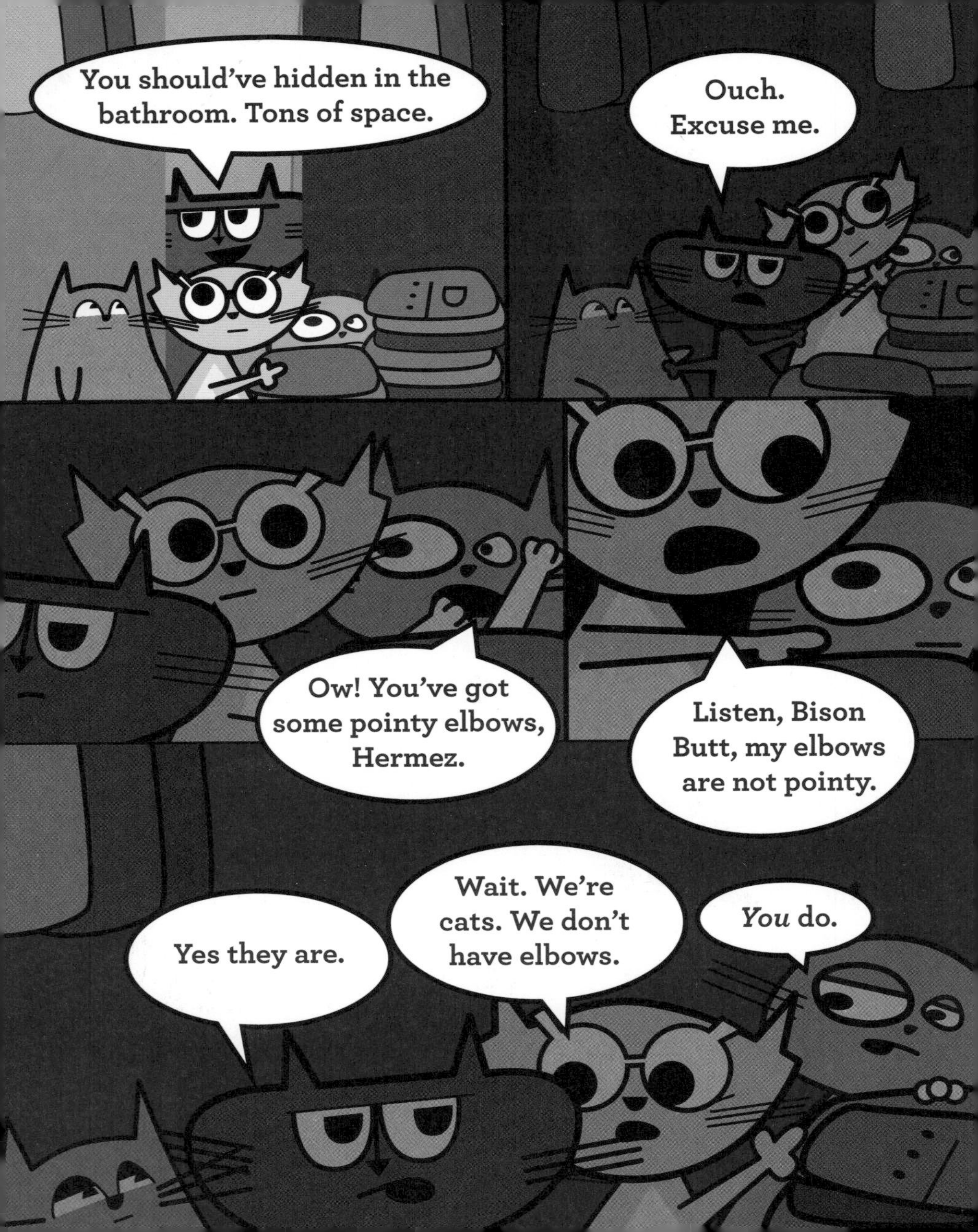
You should've hidden in the bathroom. Tons of space.
Ouch. Excuse me.
Ow! You've got some pointy elbows, Hermez.
Listen, Bison Butt, my elbows are not pointy.
Yes they are.
Wait. We're cats. We don't have elbows.
You do.

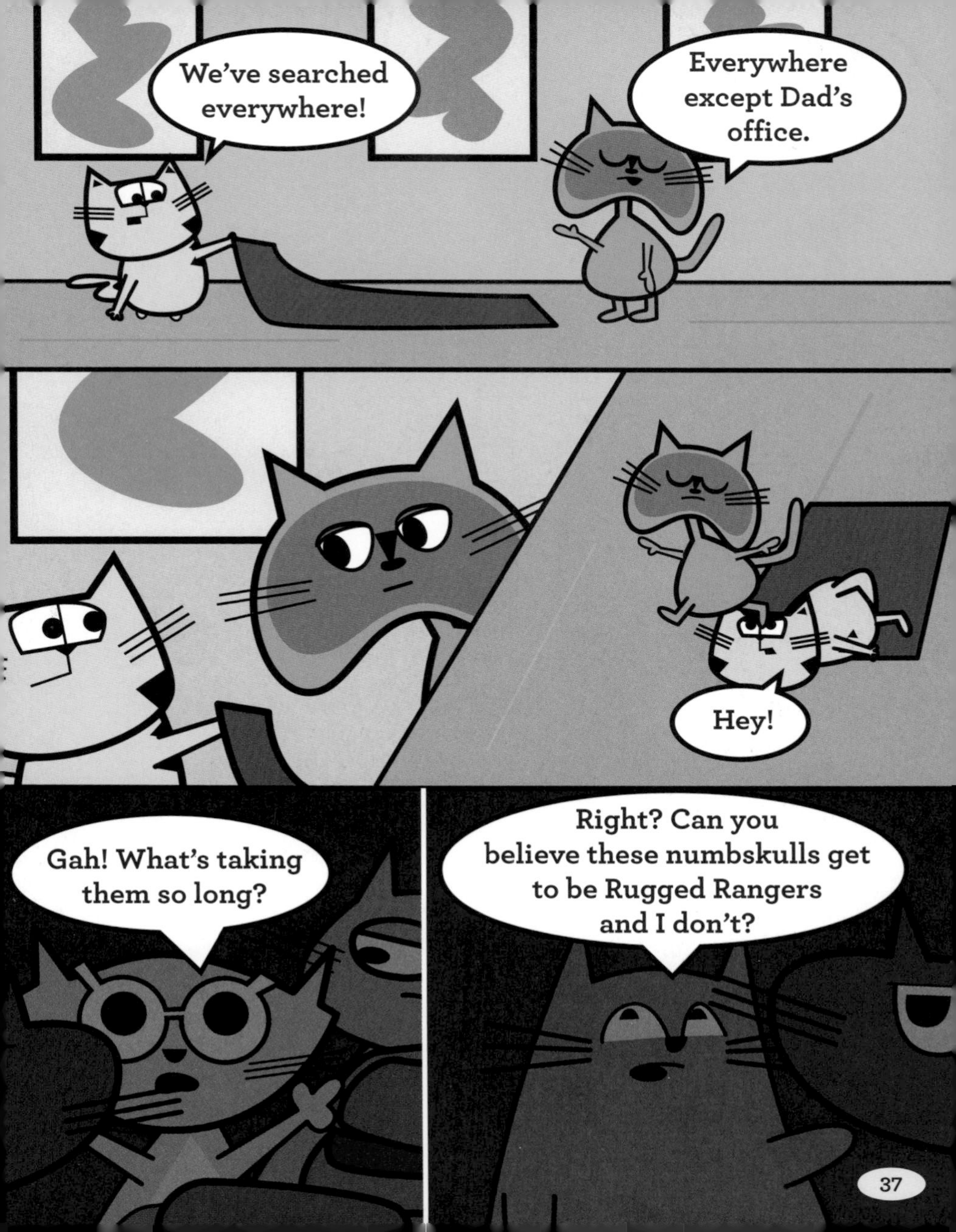
We've searched everywhere!
Everywhere except Dad's office.
Hey!
Gah! What's taking them so long?
Right? Can you believe these numbskulls get to be Rugged Rangers and I don't?

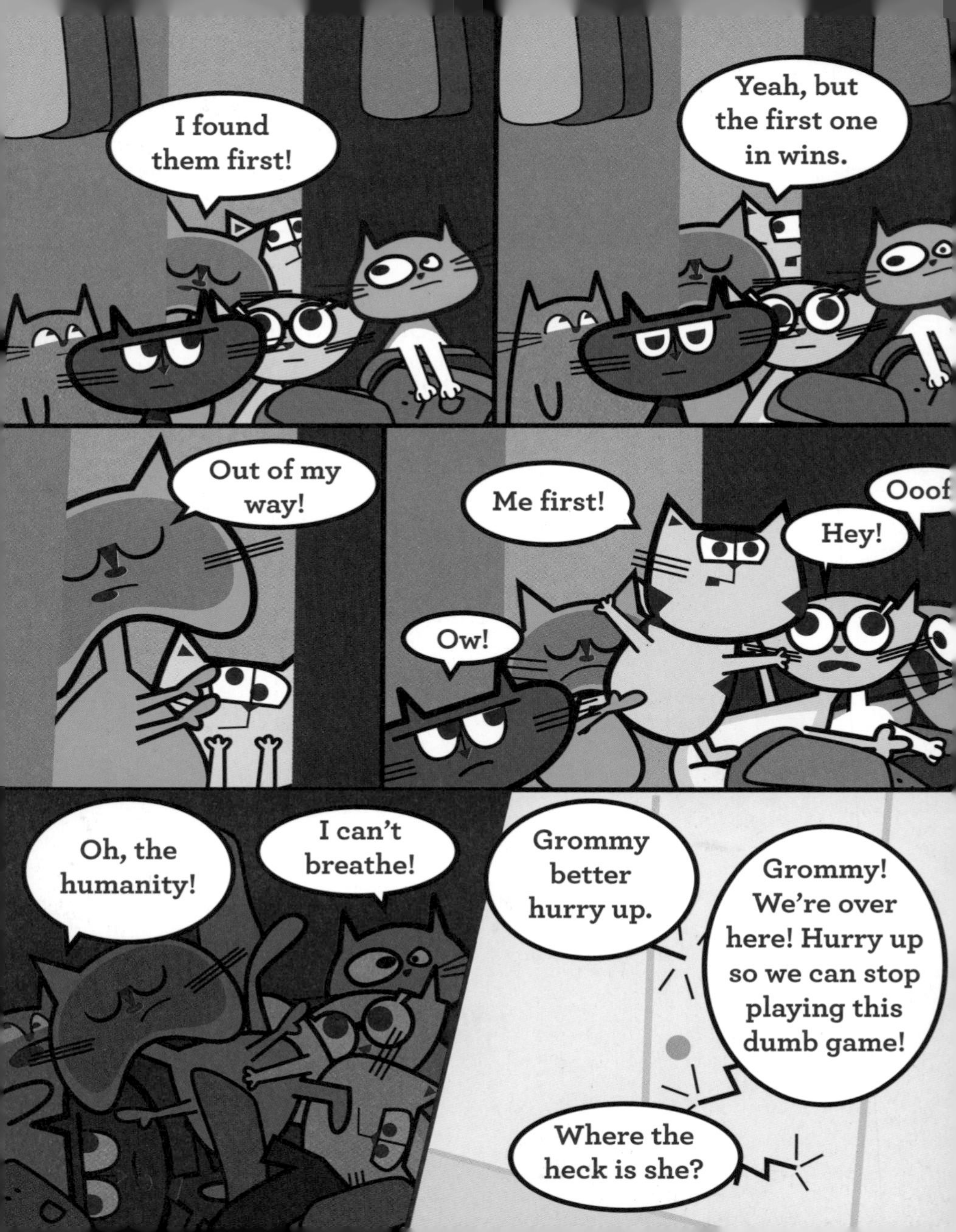
I found them first!
Yeah, but the first one in wins.
Out of my way!
Me first!
Ooof
Hey!
Ow!
Oh, the humanity!
I can't breathe!
Grommy better hurry up.
Grommy! We're over here! Hurry up so we can stop playing this dumb game!
Where the heck is she?

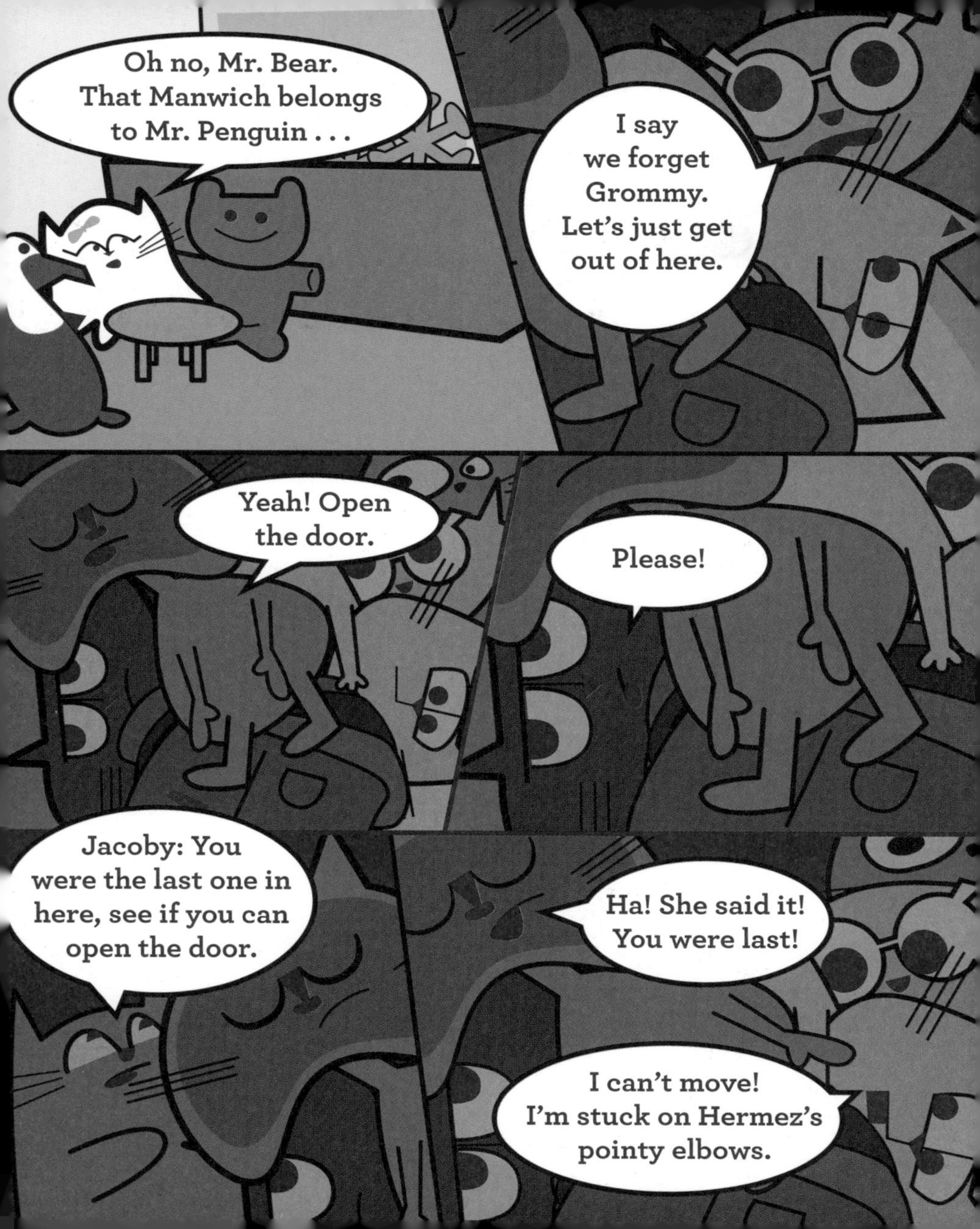

Oh no, Mr. Bear. That Manwich belongs to Mr. Penguin . . .
I say we forget Grommy. Let's just get out of here.
Yeah! Open the door.
Please!
Jacoby: You were the last one in here, see if you can open the door.
Ha! She said it! You were last!
I can't move! I'm stuck on Hermez's pointy elbows.

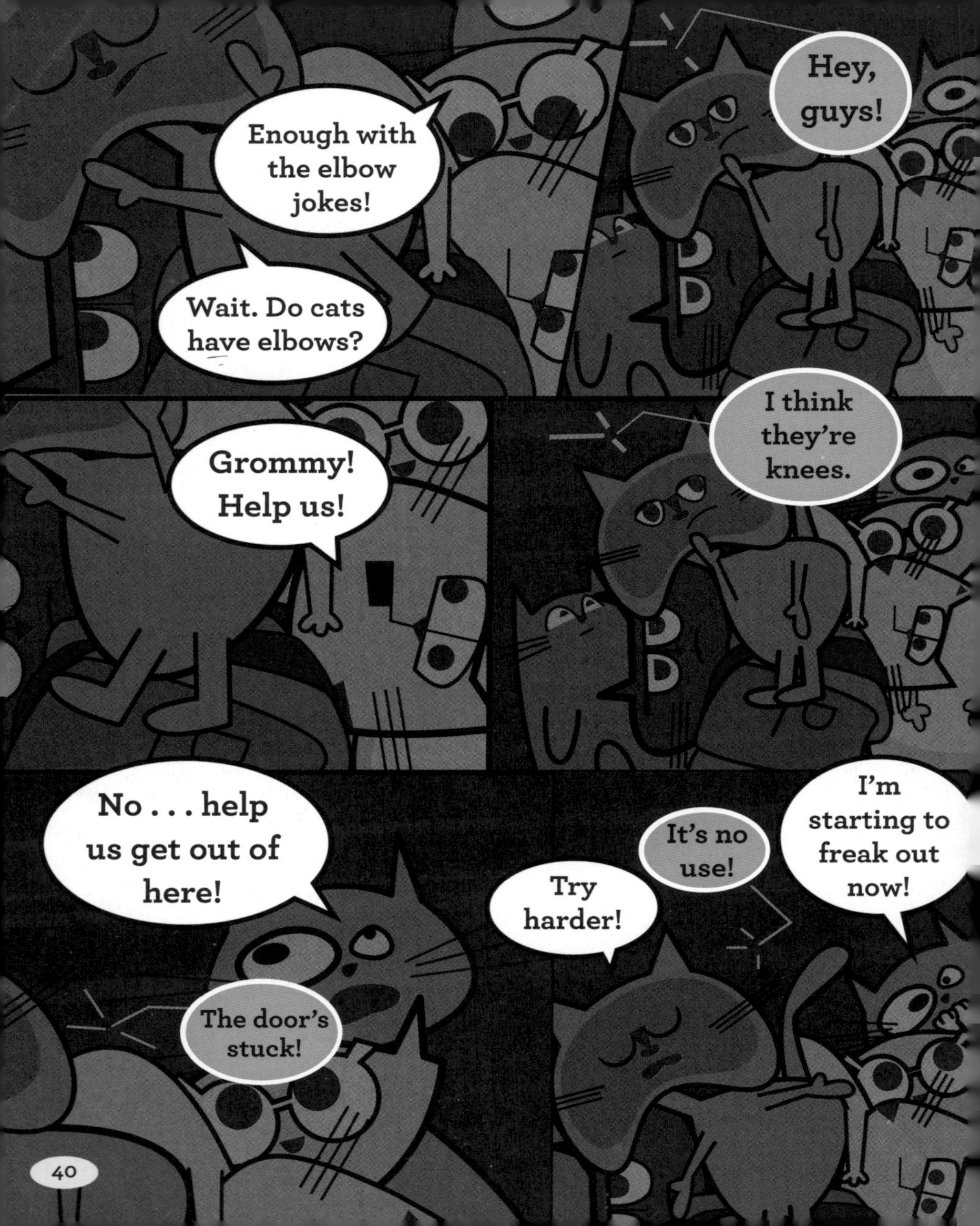
Enough with the elbow jokes!
Wait. Do cats have elbows?
Hey, guys!
Grommy! Help us!
I think they're knees.
No . . . help us get out of here!
The door's stuck!
Try harder!
It's no use!
I'm starting to freak out now!

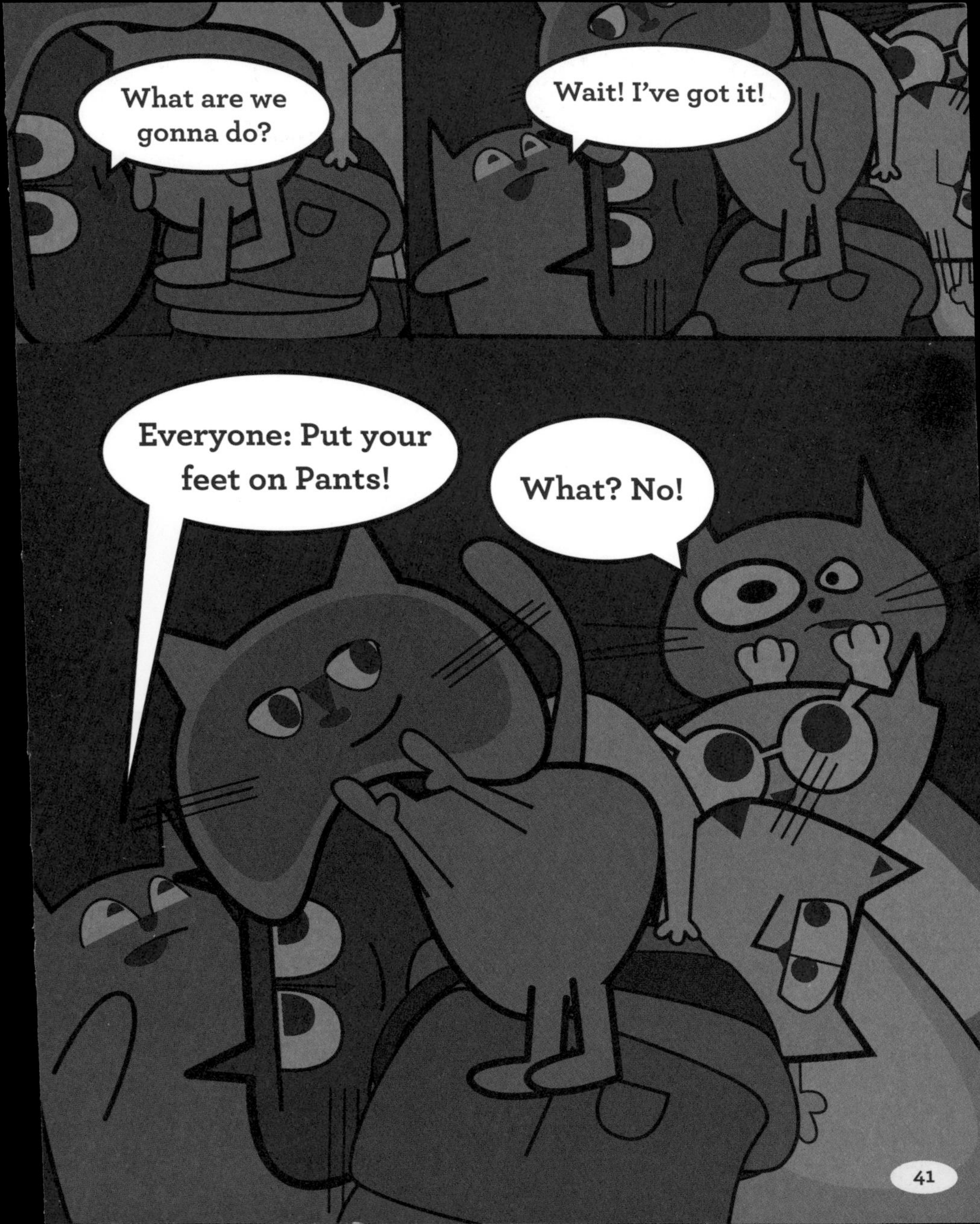
What are we gonna do?
Wait! I've got it!
Everyone: Put your feet on Pants!
What? No!

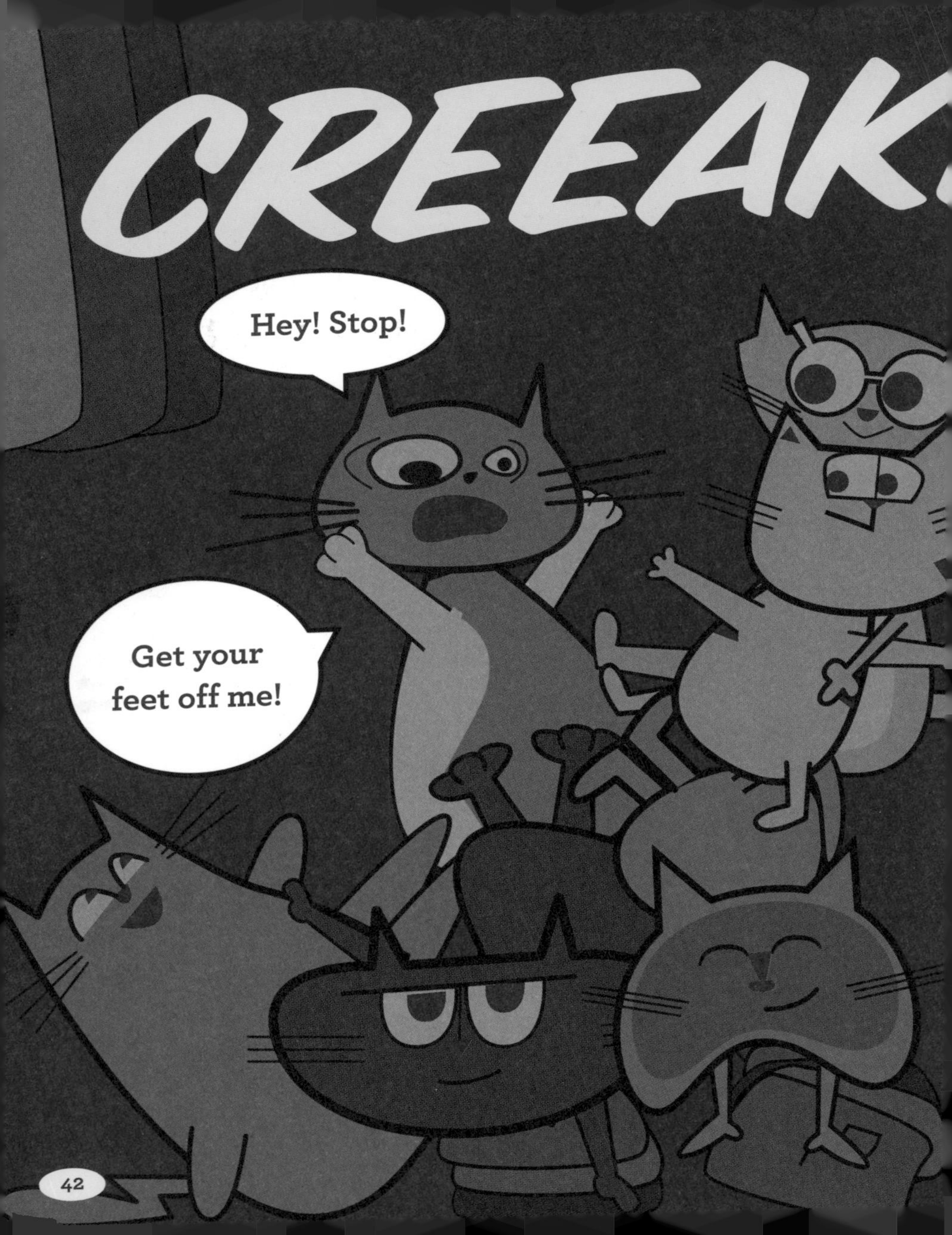
CREEAK!
Hey! Stop!
Get your feet off me!

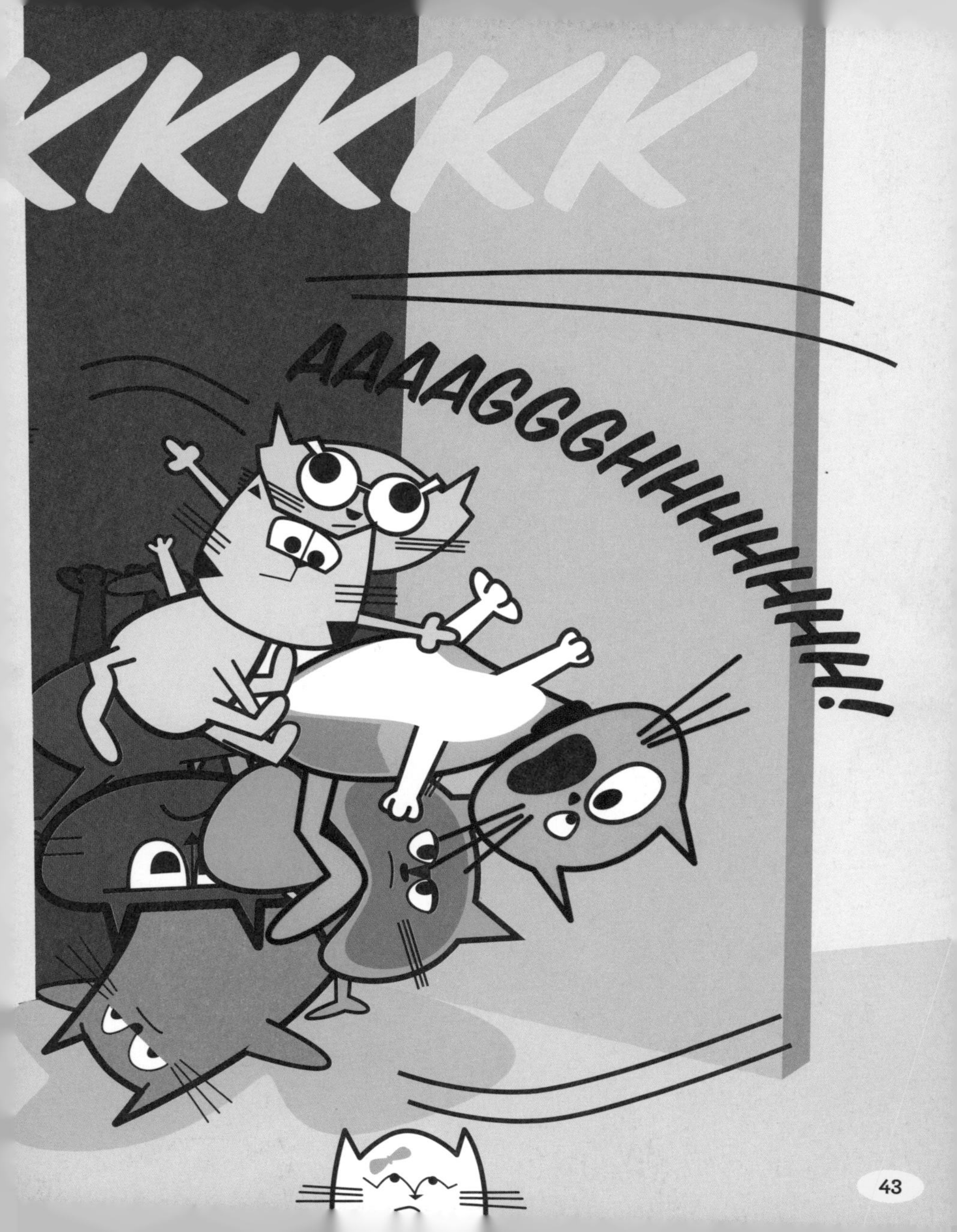
KKKKK
AAAAGGGHHHHHHHHH!

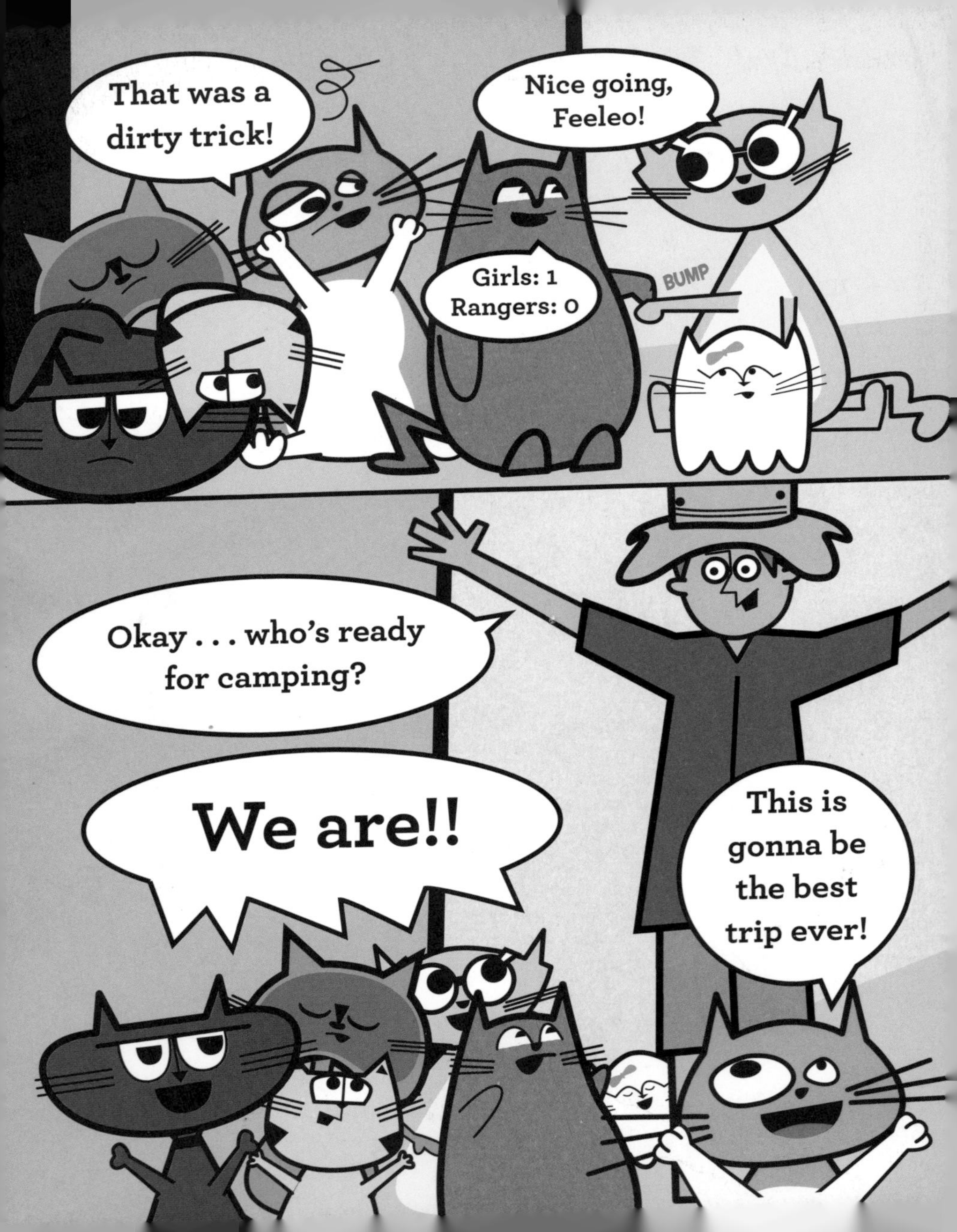
That was a dirty trick!
Nice going, Feeleo!
Girls: 1 Rangers: 0
BUMP
Okay . . . who's ready for camping?
We are!!
This is gonna be the best trip ever!

Chapter Four:
FEET'S FEATS

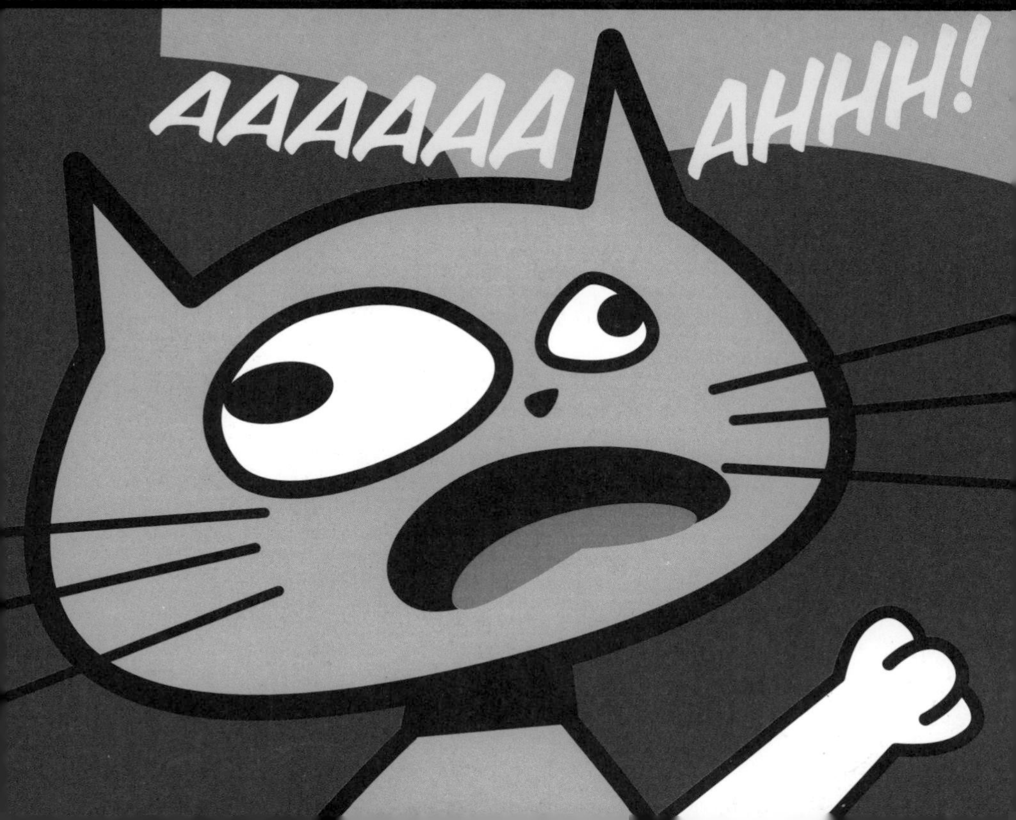
AAAAAAAHHH!

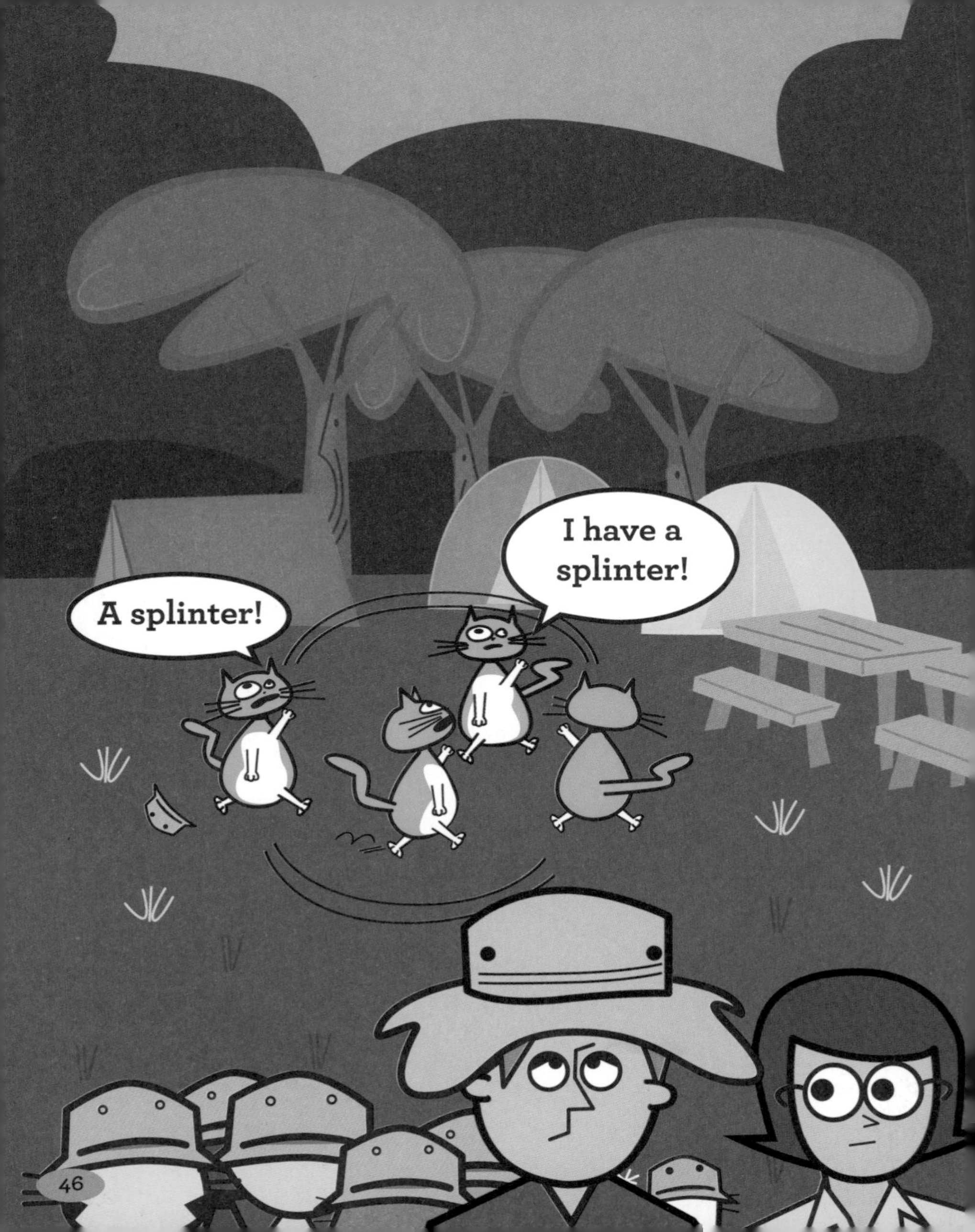
A splinter!
I have a splinter!

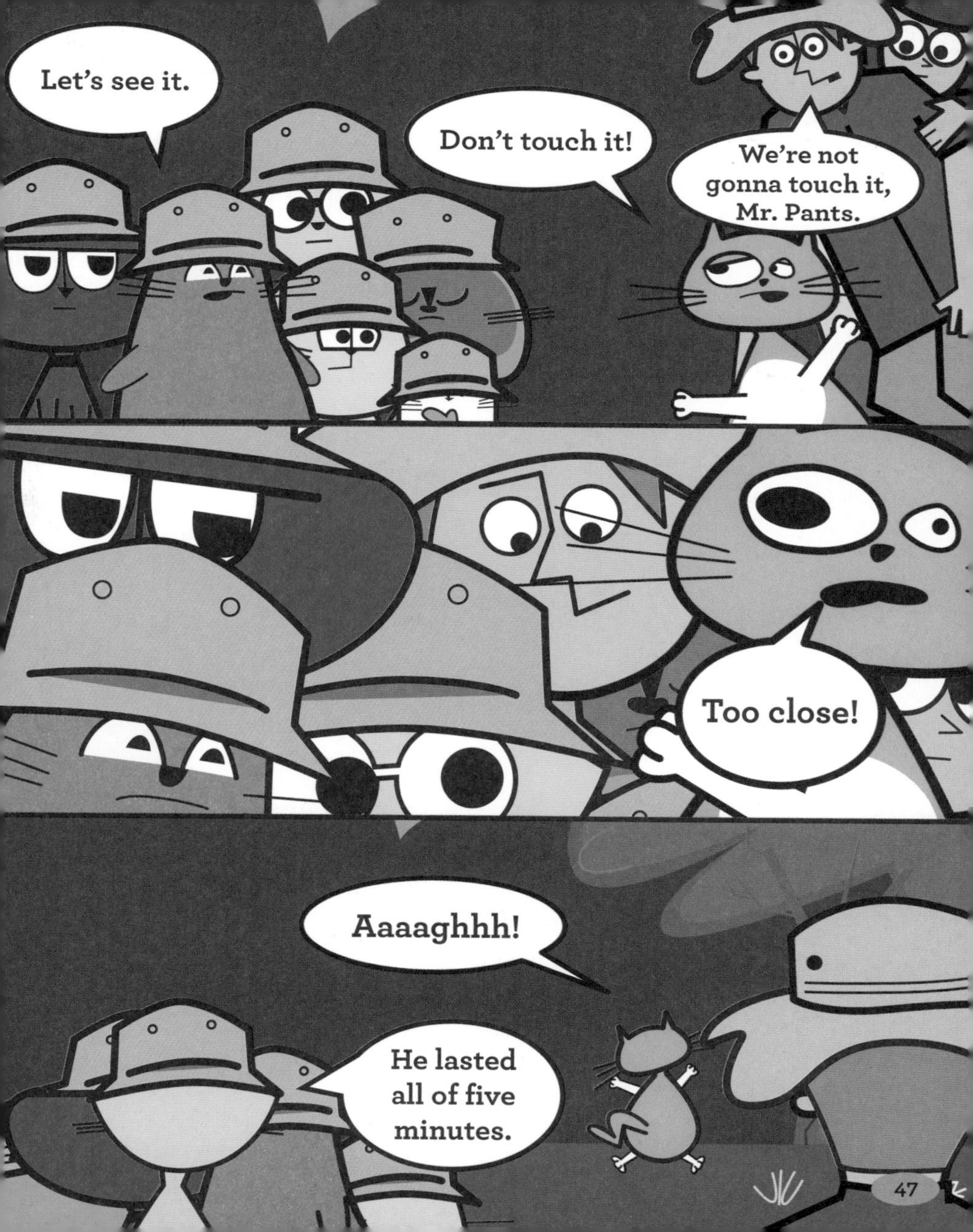

Let's see it.
Don't touch it!
We're not gonna touch it, Mr. Pants.
Too close!
Aaaaghhh!
He lasted all of five minutes.

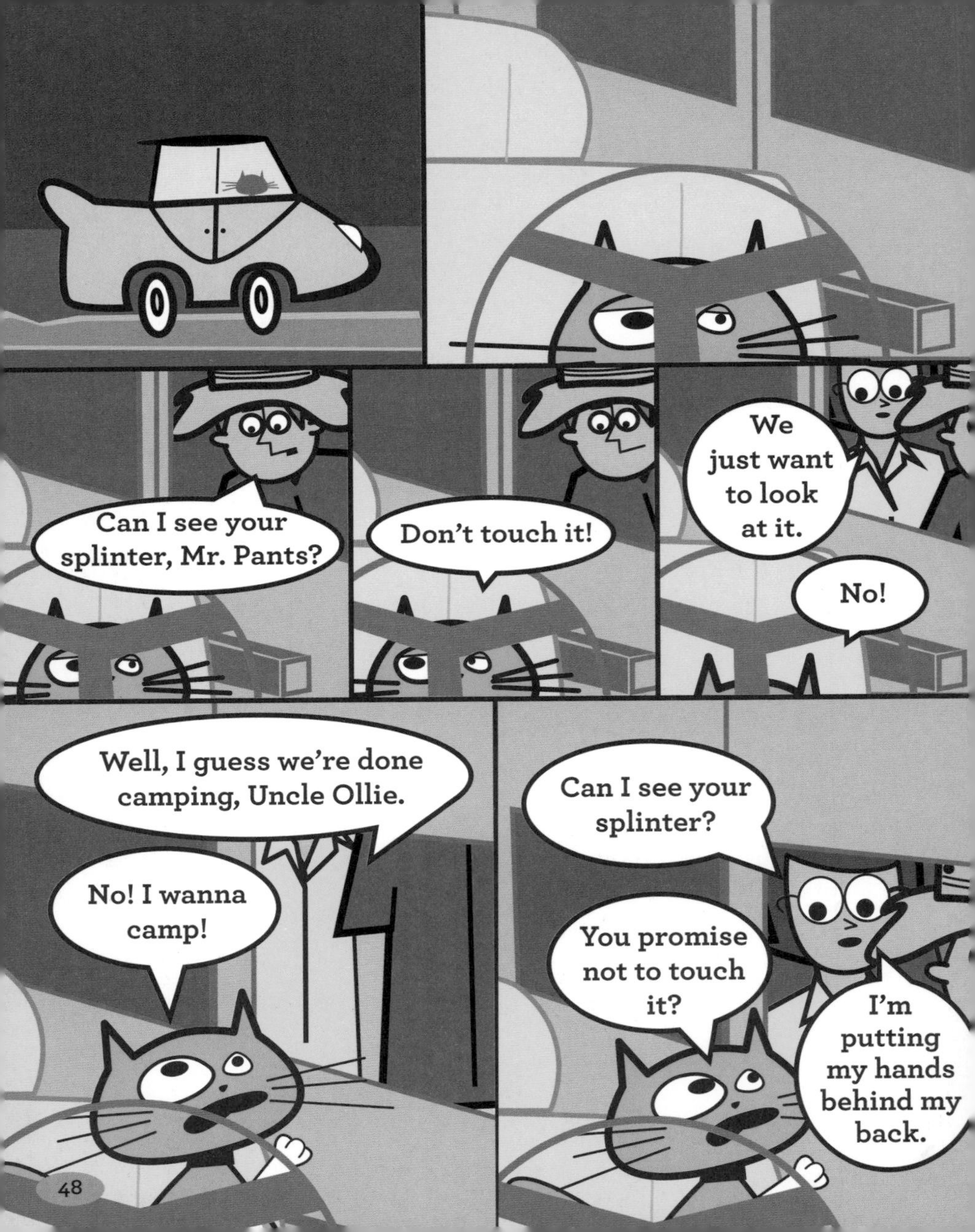
Can I see your splinter, Mr. Pants?
Don't touch it!
We just want to look at it.
No!
Well, I guess we're done camping, Uncle Ollie.
No! I wanna camp!
Can I see your splinter?
You promise not to touch it?
I'm putting my hands behind my back.

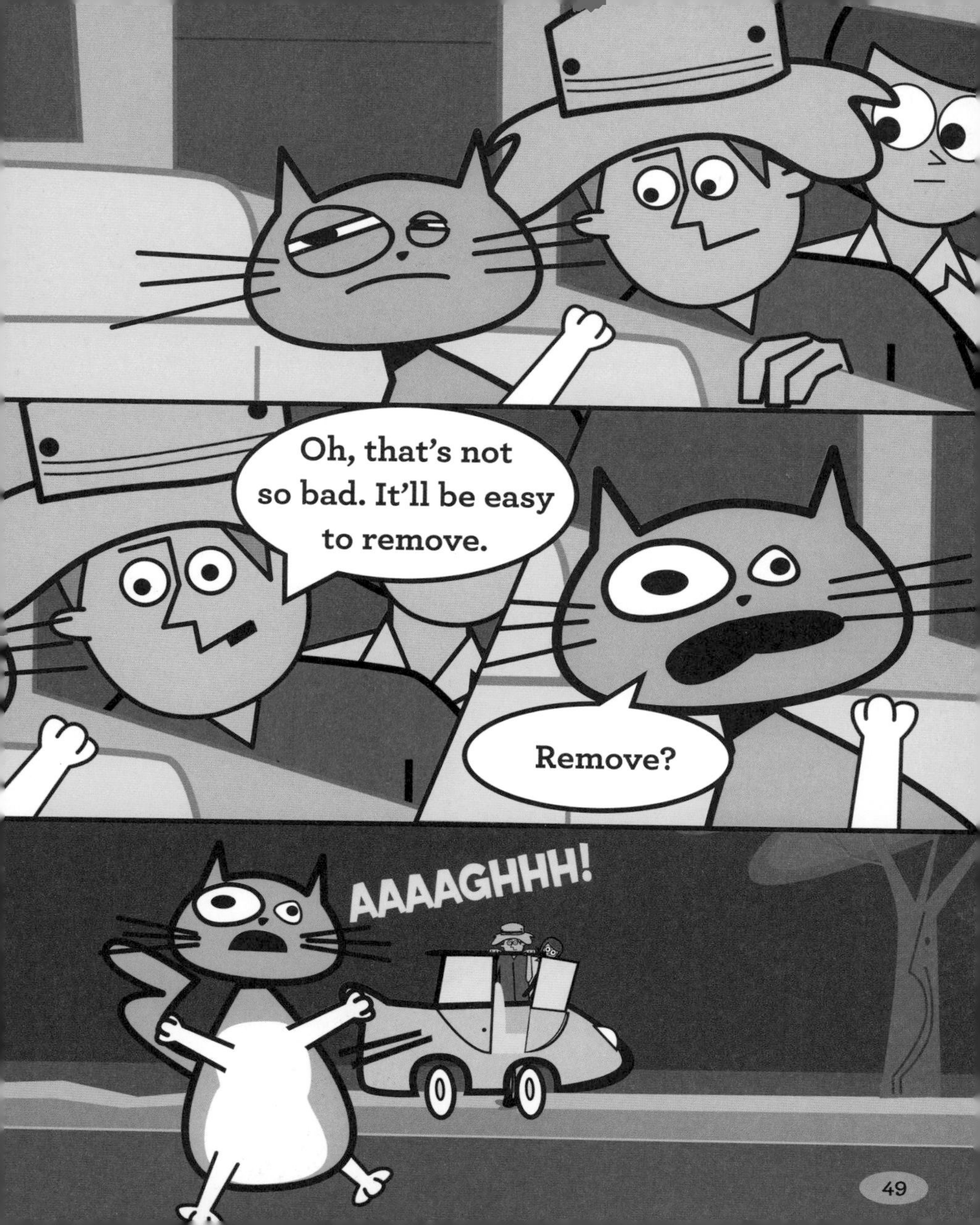
Oh, that's not so bad. It'll be easy to remove.
Remove?
AAAAGHHH!

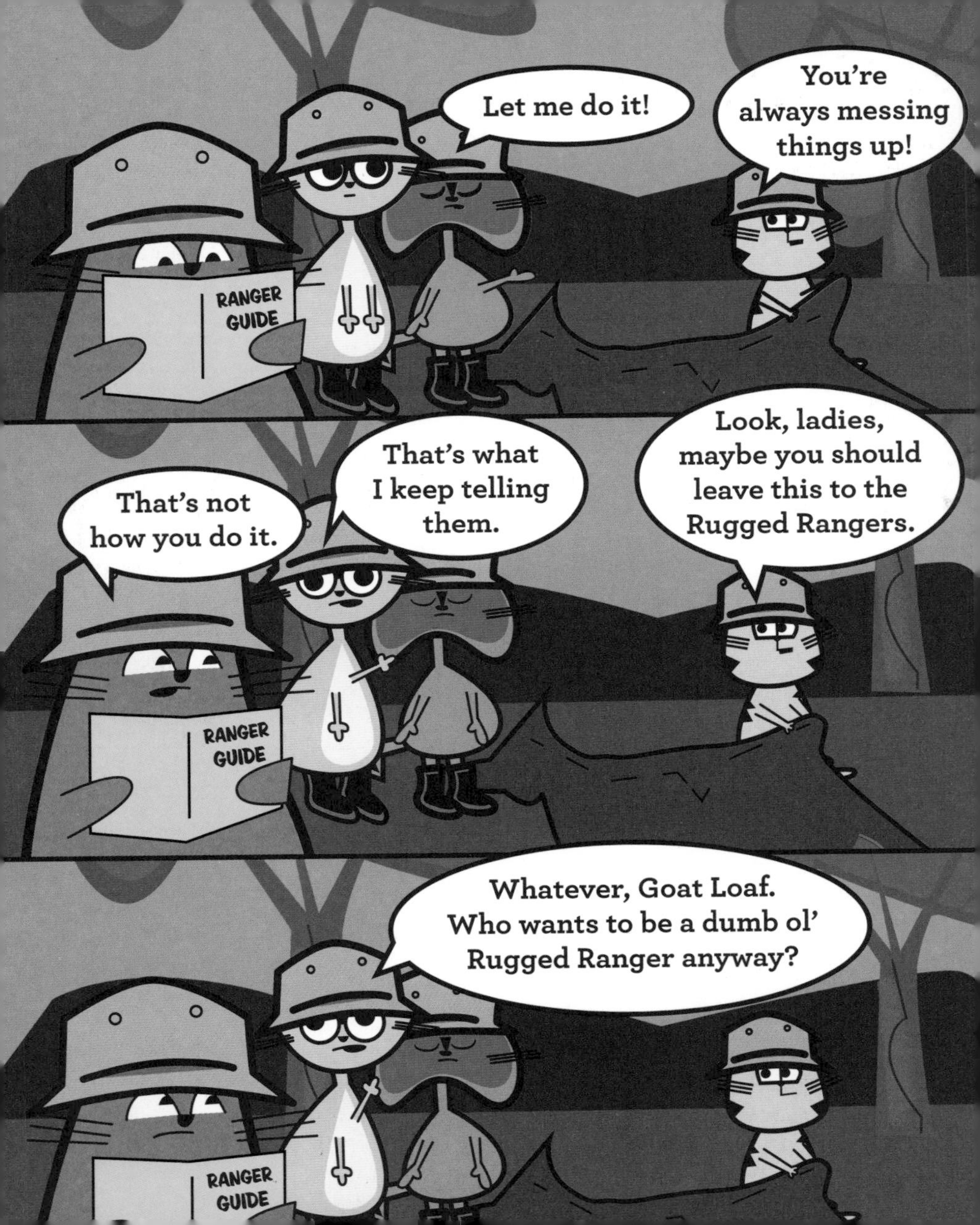
Let me do it!
You're always messing things up!
RANGER GUIDE
That's not how you do it.
That's what I keep telling them.
Look, ladies, maybe you should leave this to the Rugged Rangers.
RANGER GUIDE
Whatever, Goat Loaf. Who wants to be a dumb ol' Rugged Ranger anyway?
RANGER GUIDE

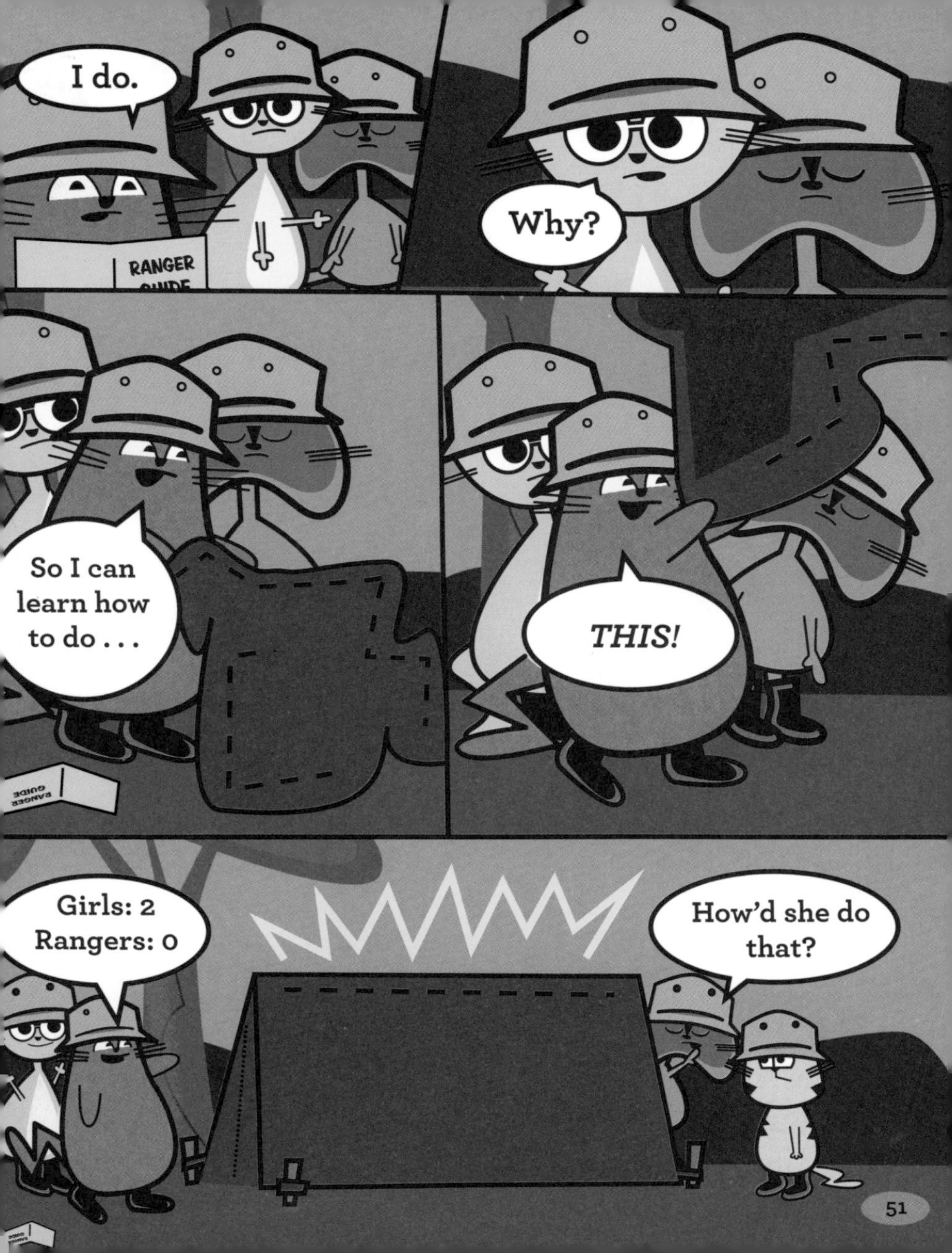
I do.
RANGER
Why?
So I can learn how to do . . .
THIS!
Girls: 2
Rangers: 0
How'd she do that?

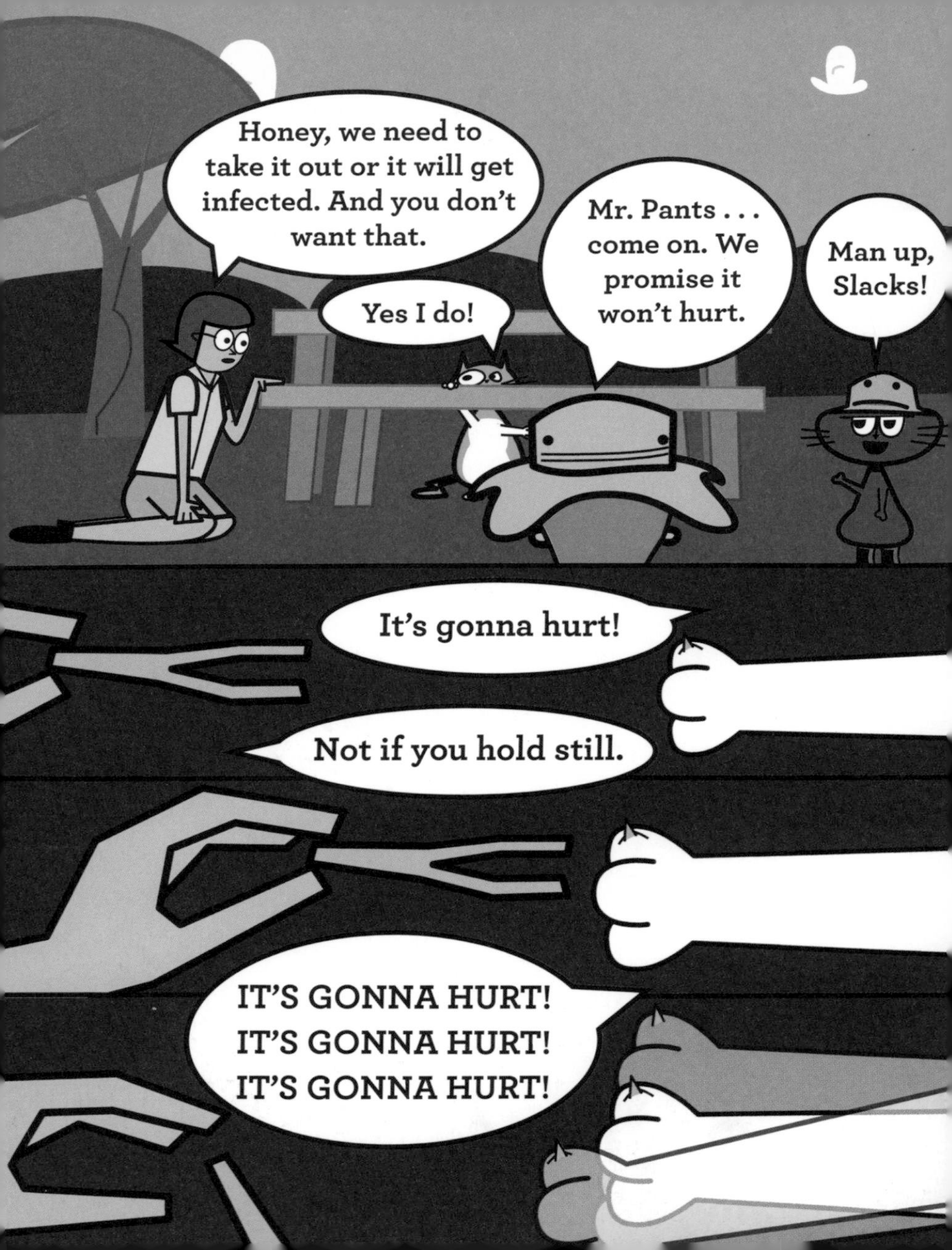
Honey, we need to take it out or it will get infected. And you don't want that.
Yes I do!
Mr. Pants . . . come on. We promise it won't hurt.
Man up, Slacks!
It's gonna hurt!
Not if you hold still.
IT'S GONNA HURT! IT'S GONNA HURT! IT'S GONNA HURT!

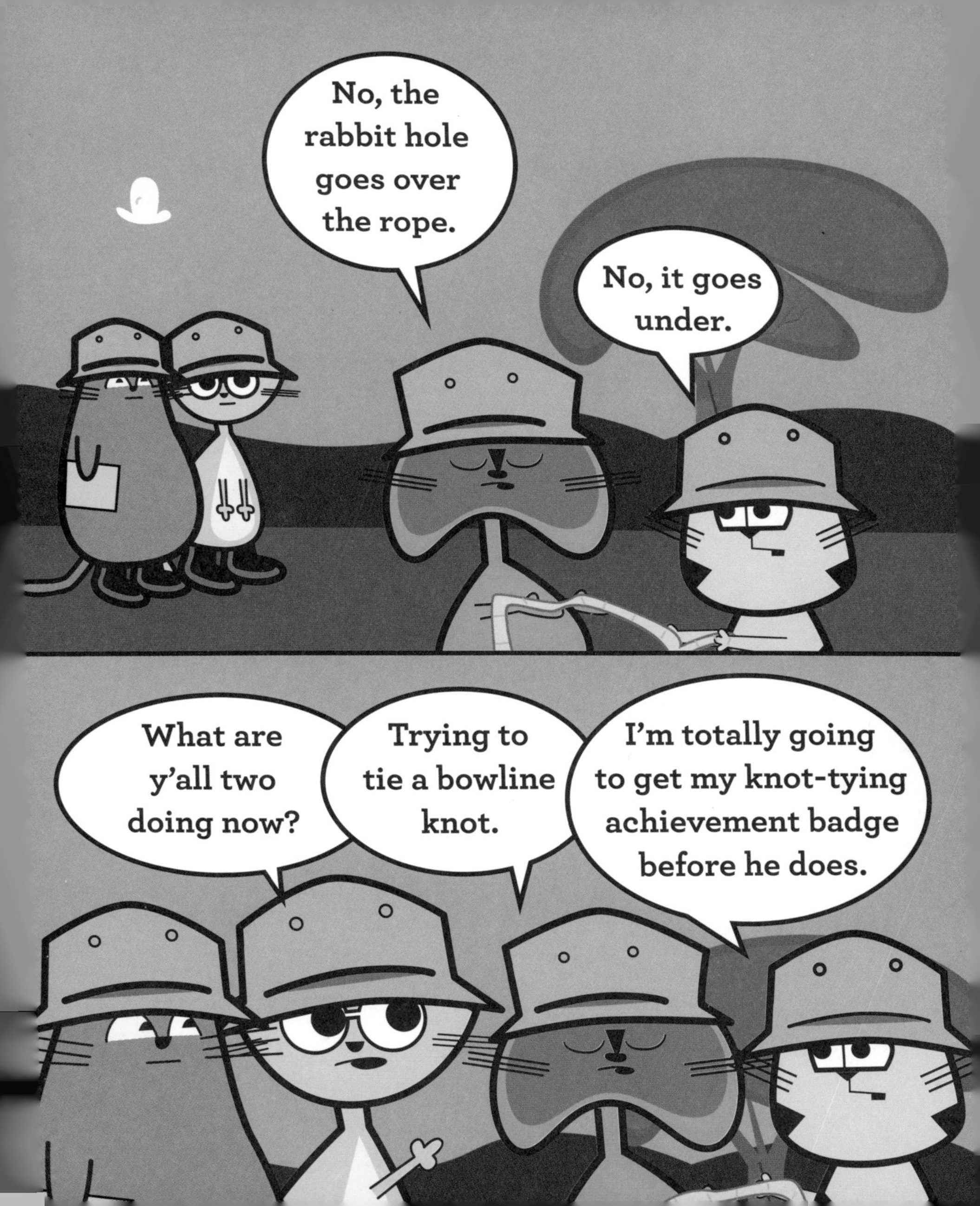
No, the rabbit hole goes over the rope.
No, it goes under.
What are y'all two doing now?
Trying to tie a bowline knot.
I'm totally going to get my knot-tying achievement badge before he does.

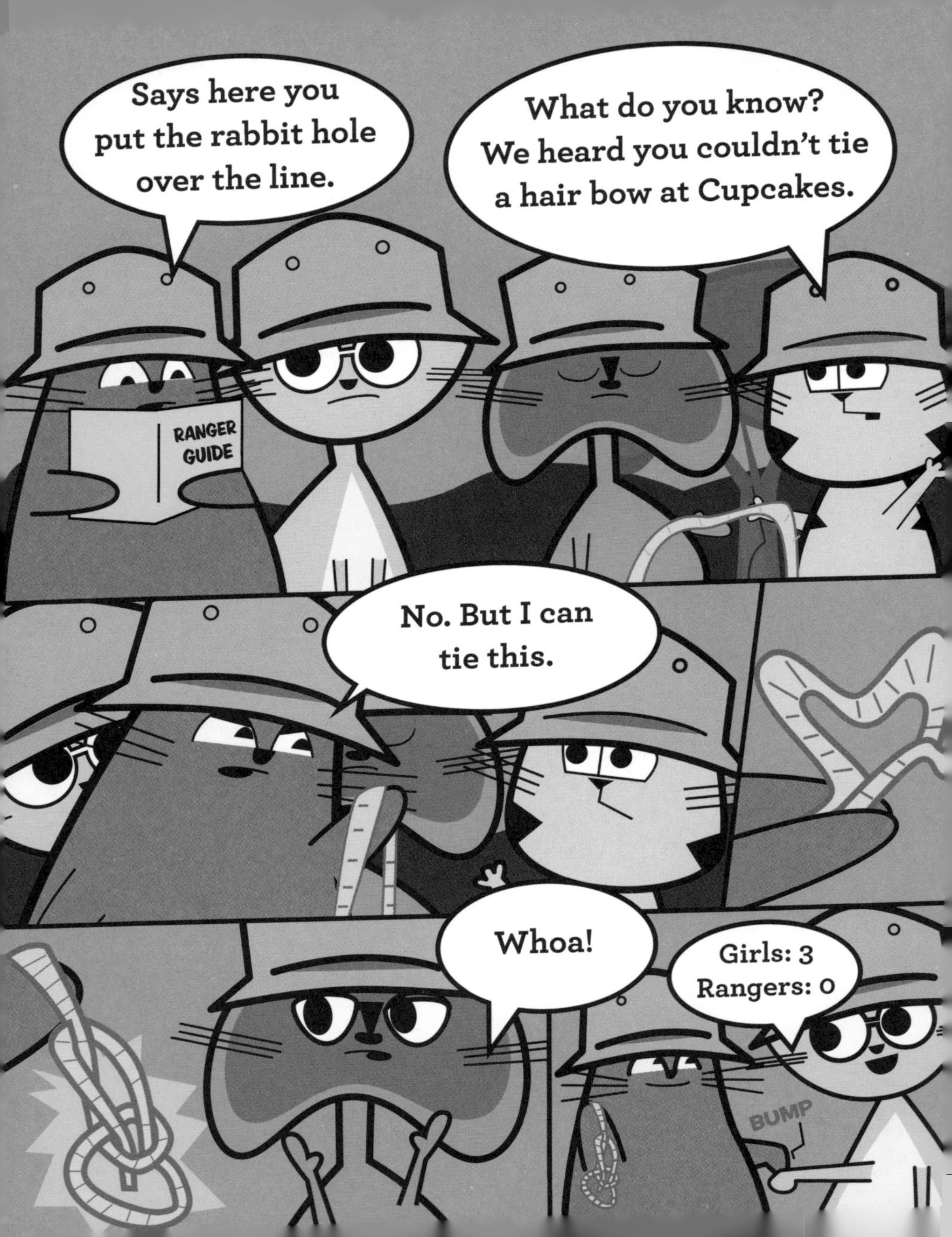
Says here you put the rabbit hole over the line.
What do you know? We heard you couldn't tie a hair bow at Cupcakes.
RANGER GUIDE
No. But I can tie this.
Whoa!
Girls: 3 Rangers: 0
BUMP

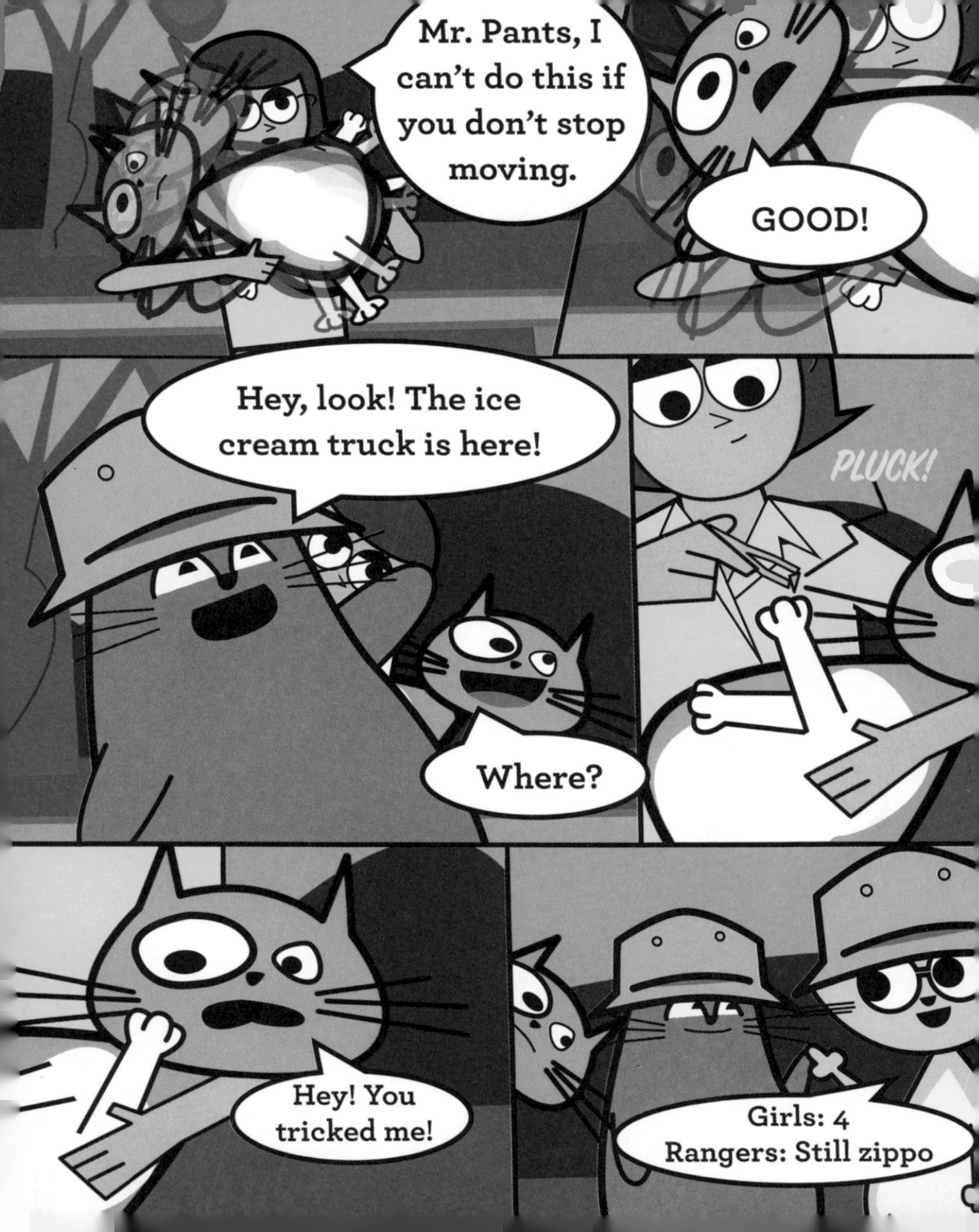

Mr. Pants, I can't do this if you don't stop moving.
GOOD!
Hey, look! The ice cream truck is here!
Where?
PLUCK!
Hey! You tricked me!
Girls: 4
Rangers: Still zippo

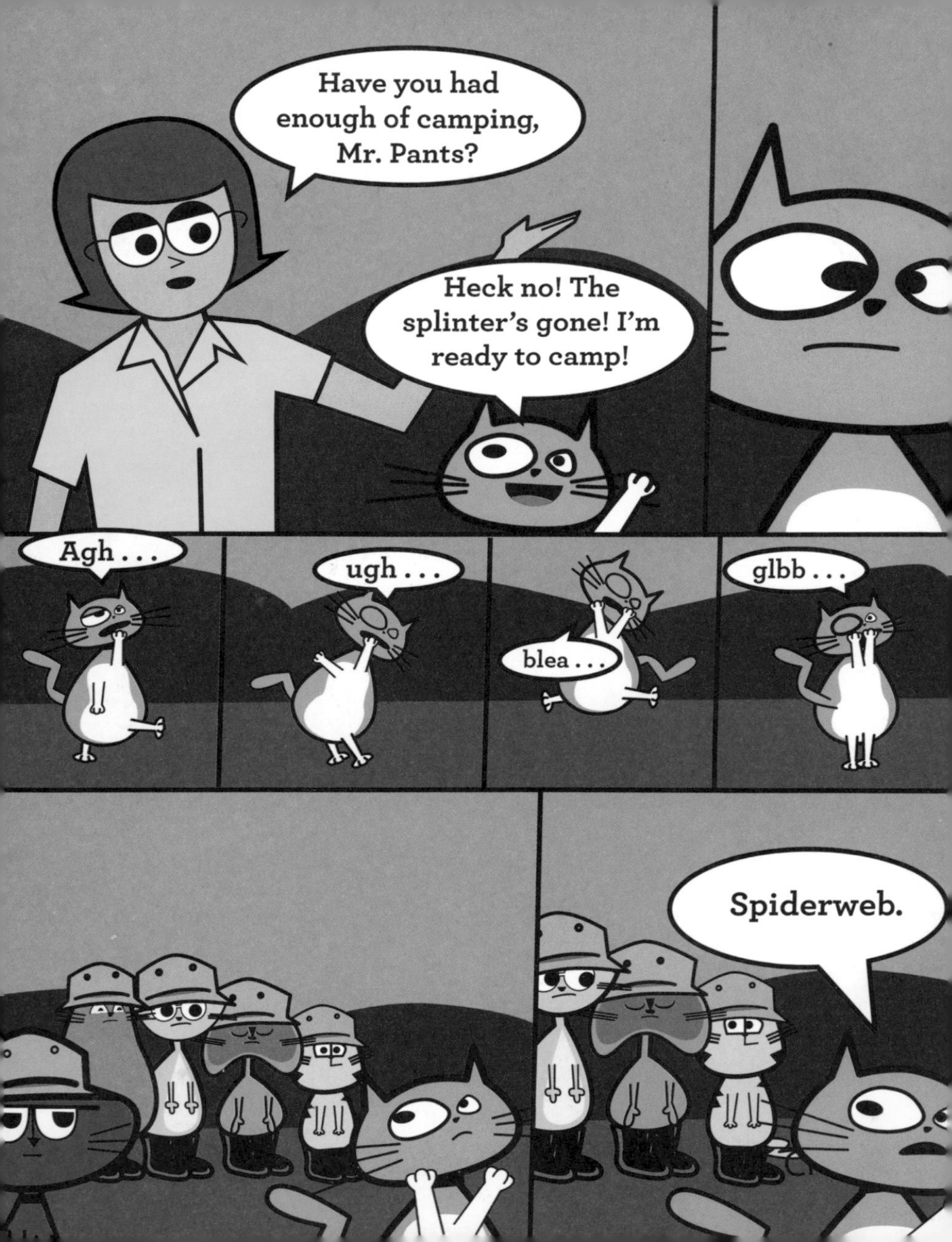
Have you had enough of camping, Mr. Pants?
Heck no! The splinter's gone! I'm ready to camp!
Agh . . .
ugh . . .
blea . . .
glbb . . .
Spiderweb.

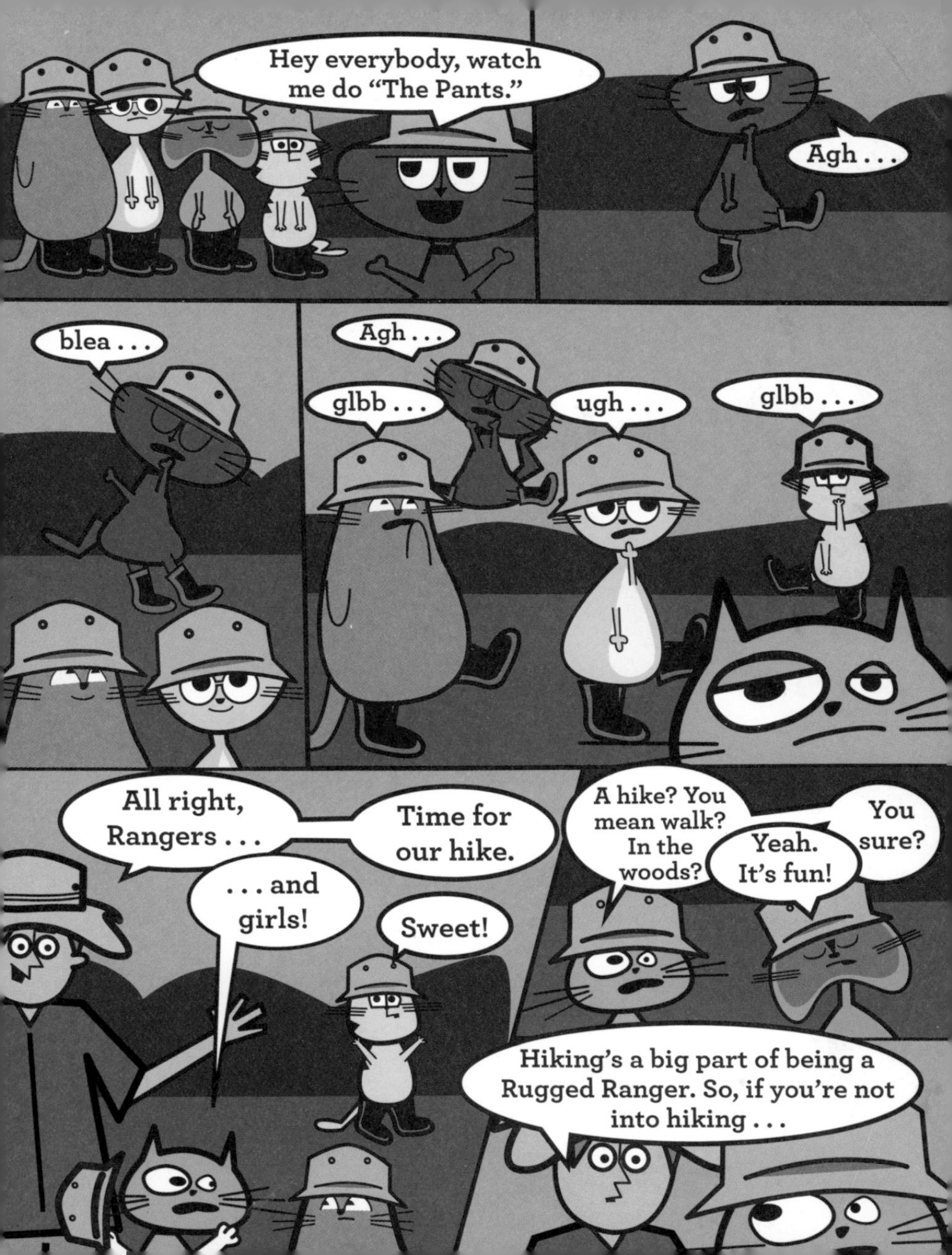
Hey everybody, watch me do "The Pants."
Agh . . .
blea . . .
Agh . . .
glbb . . .
ugh . . .
glbb . . .
All right, Rangers . . .
Time for our hike.
. . . and girls!
Sweet!
A hike? You mean walk? In the woods?
Yeah. It's fun!
You sure?
Hiking's a big part of being a Rugged Ranger. So, if you're not into hiking . . .

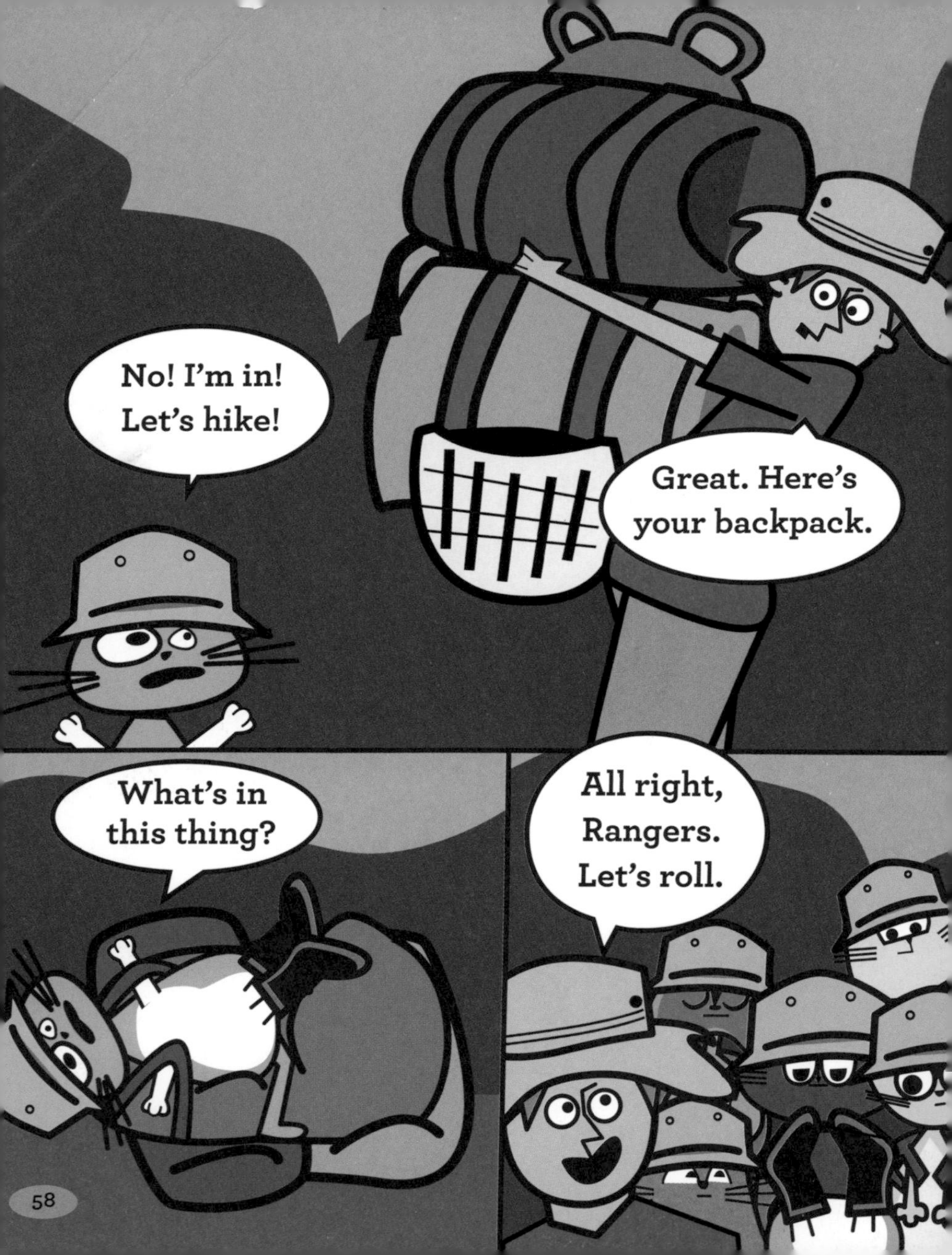
No! I'm in!
Let's hike!
Great. Here's
your backpack.
What's in
this thing?
All right,
Rangers.
Let's roll.

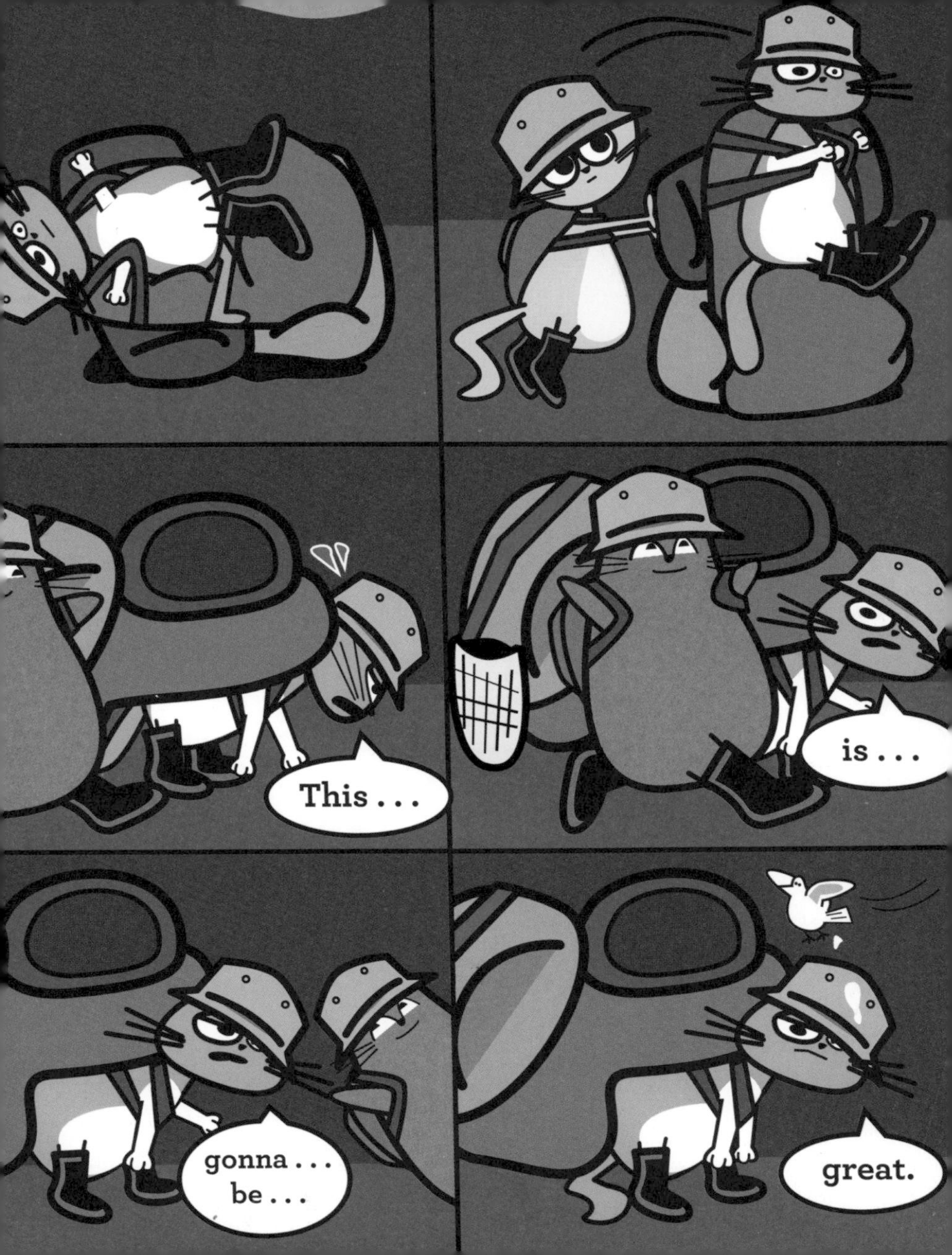
This . . .
is . . .
gonna . . .
be . . .
great.

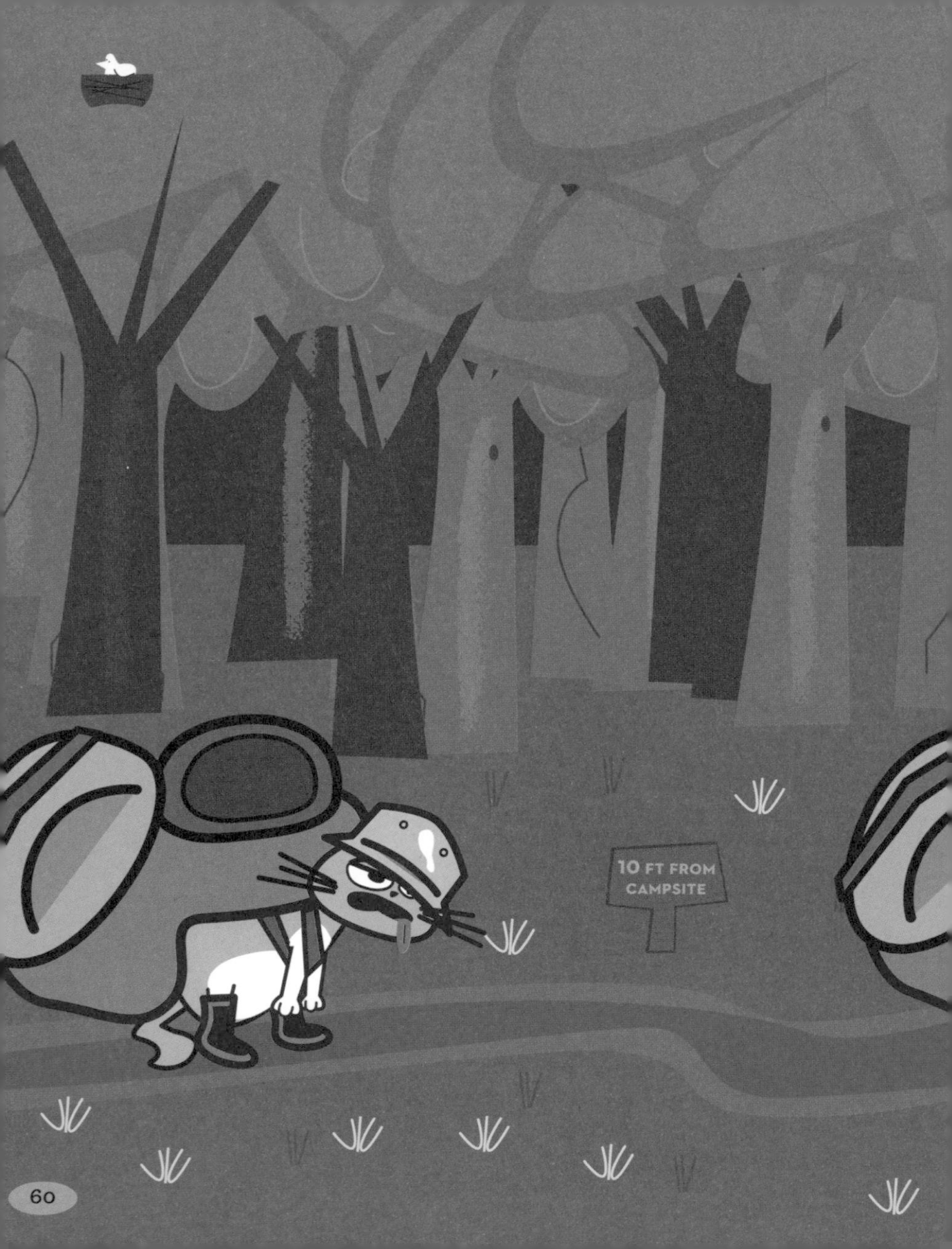
10 FT FROM
CAMPSITE

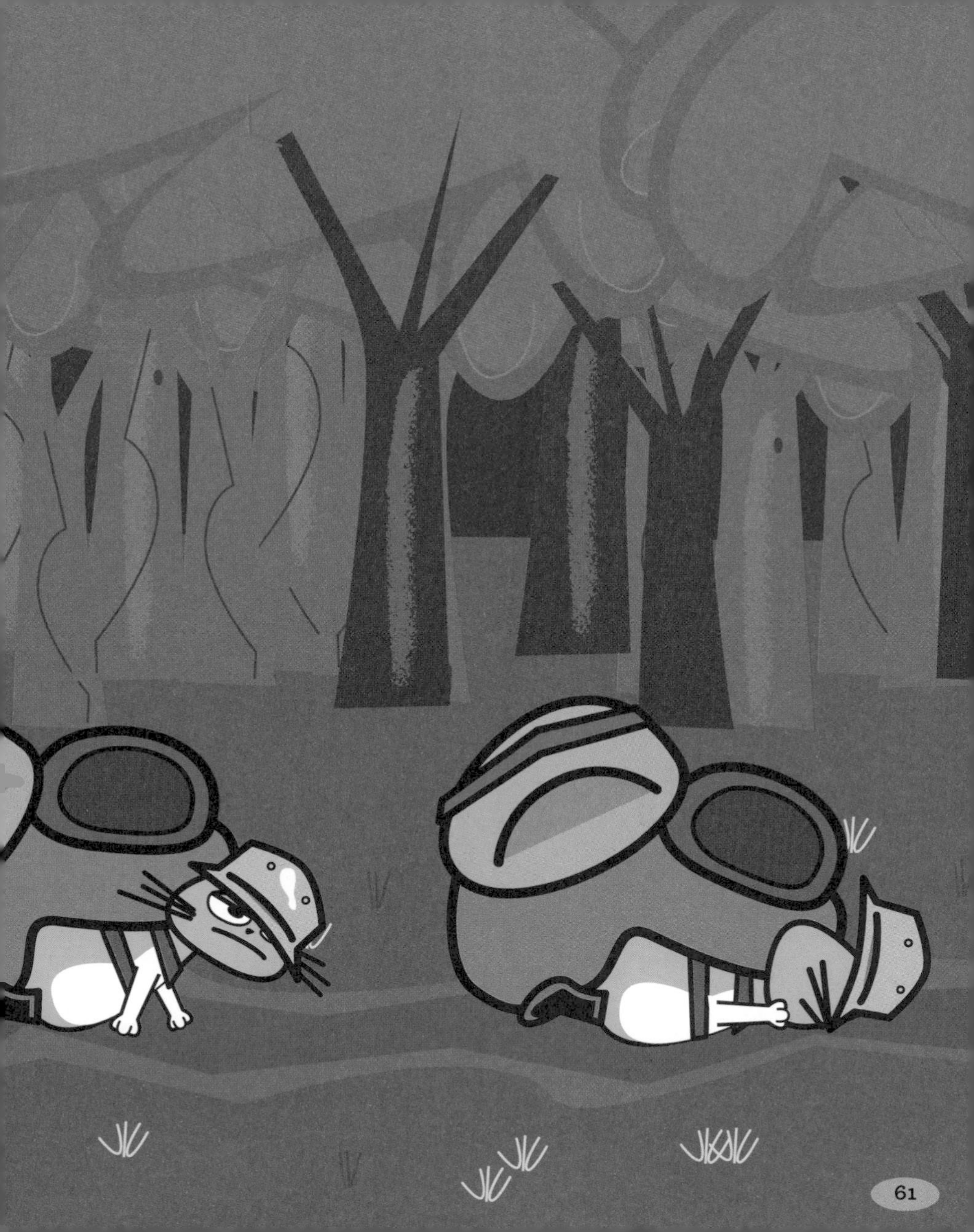

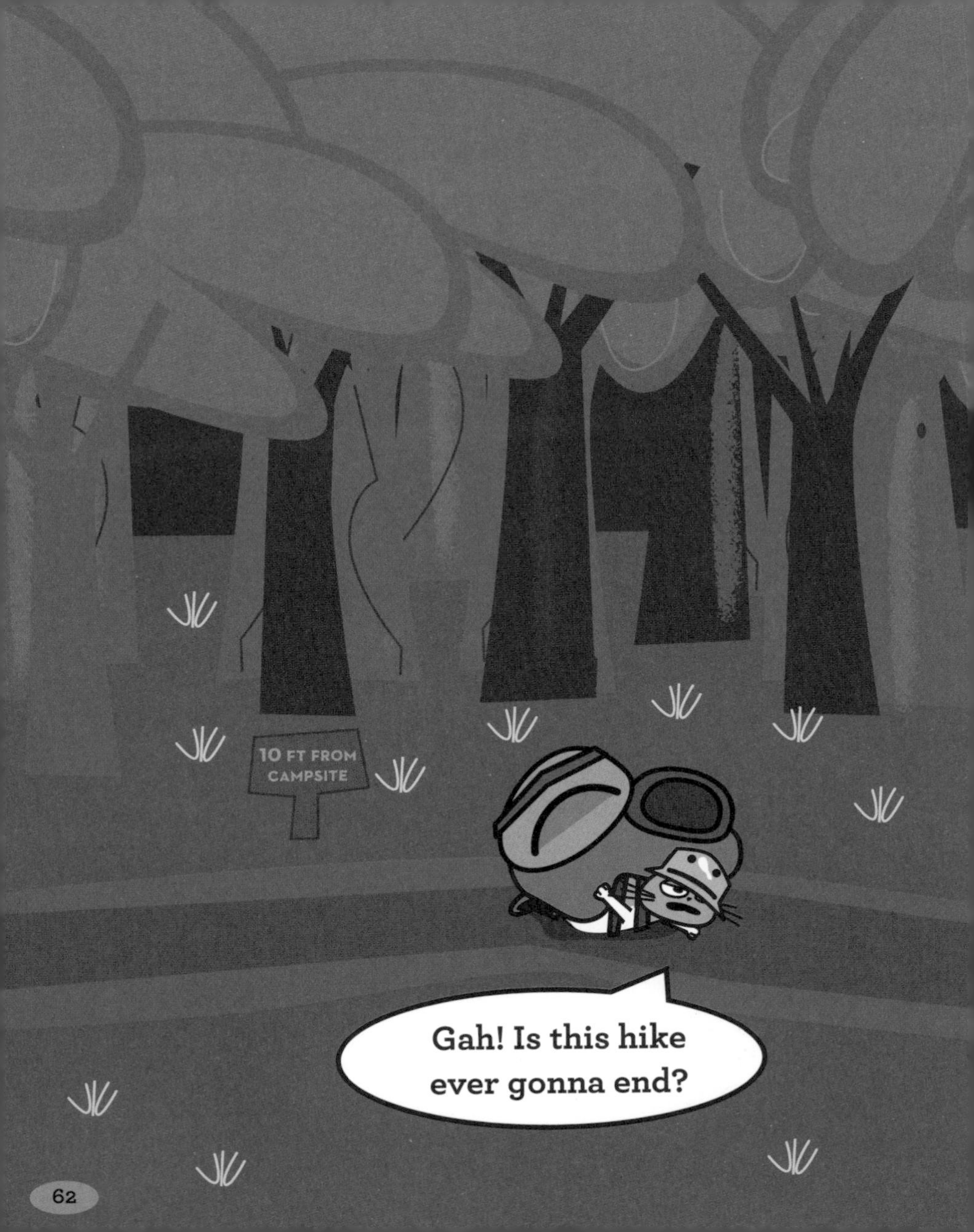
10 FT FROM CAMPSITE
Gah! Is this hike ever gonna end?

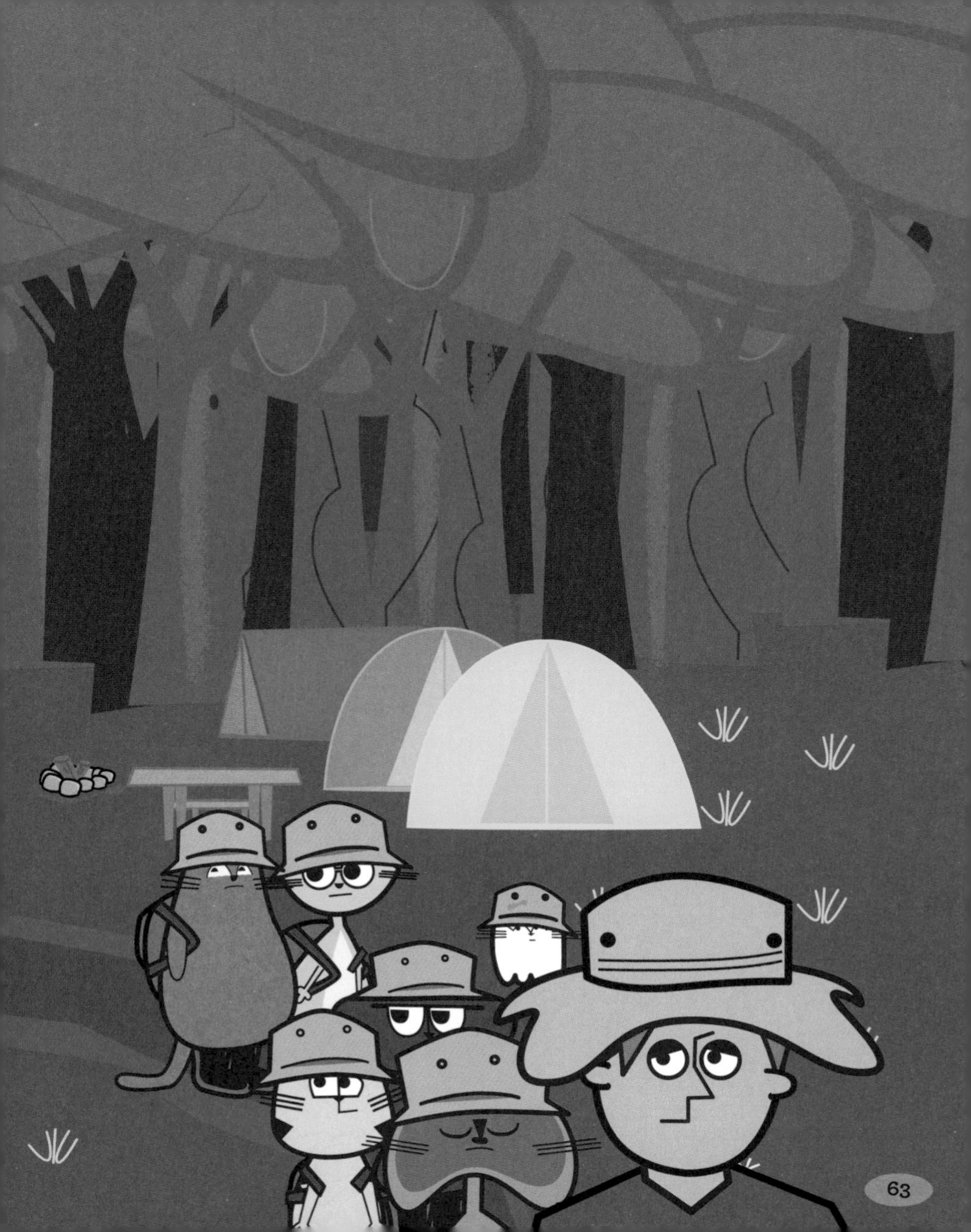

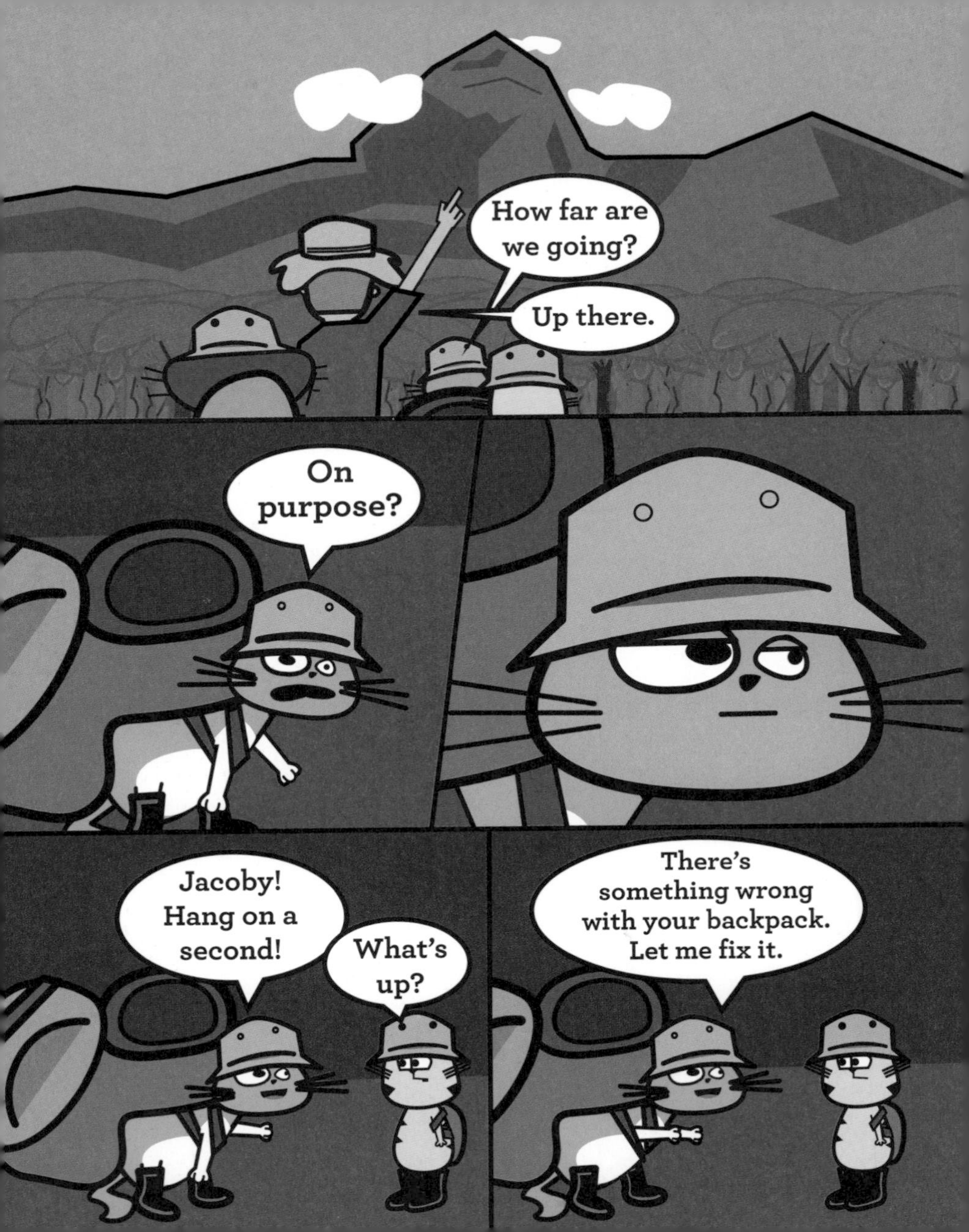
How far are we going?
Up there.
On purpose?
Jacoby! Hang on a second!
What's up?
There's something wrong with your backpack. Let me fix it.

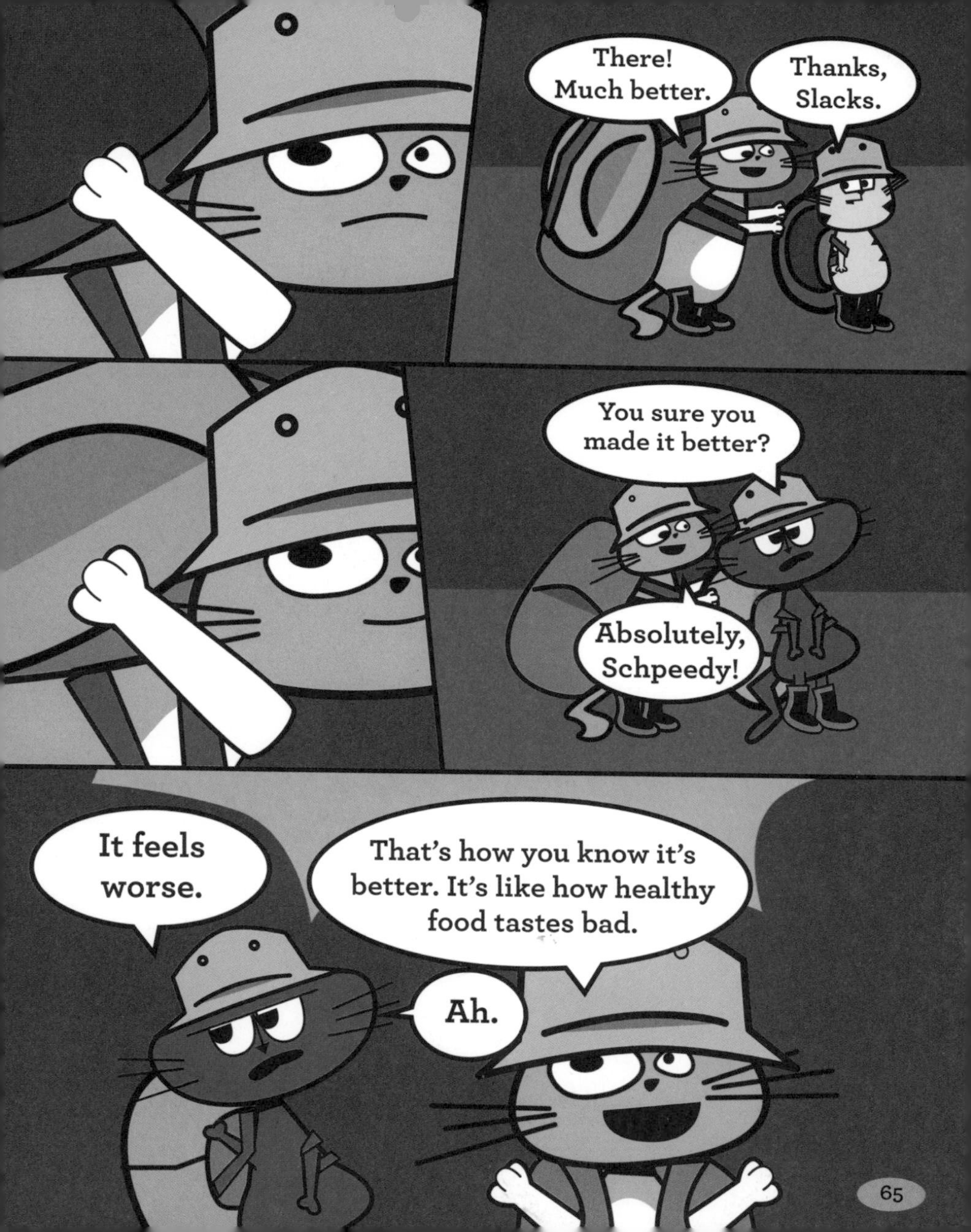
There! Much better.
Thanks, Slacks.
You sure you made it better?
Absolutely, Schpeedy!
It feels worse.
That's how you know it's better. It's like how healthy food tastes bad.
Ah.

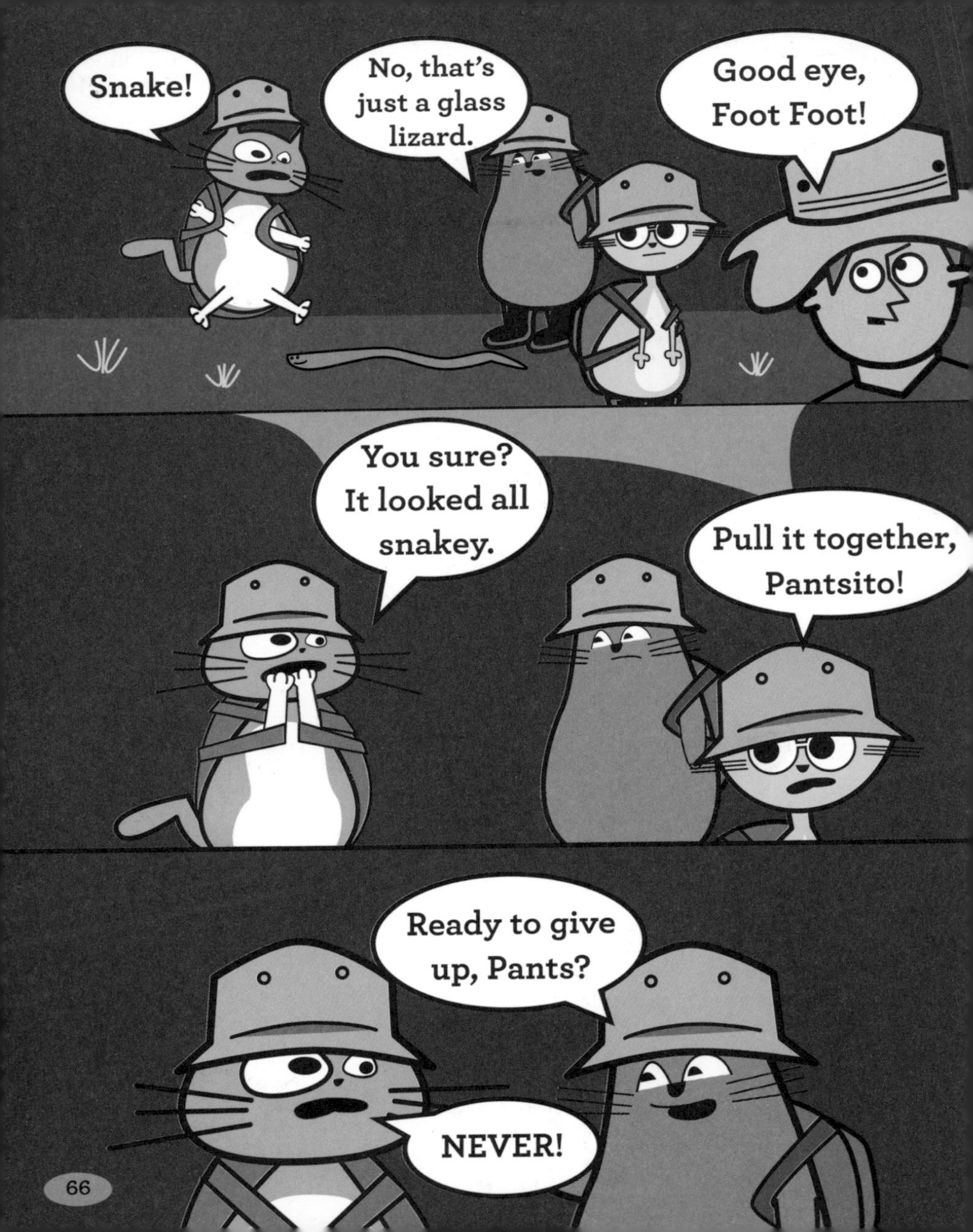

Snake!
No, that's just a glass lizard.
Good eye, Foot Foot!
You sure? It looked all snakey.
Pull it together, Pantsito!
Ready to give up, Pants?
NEVER!

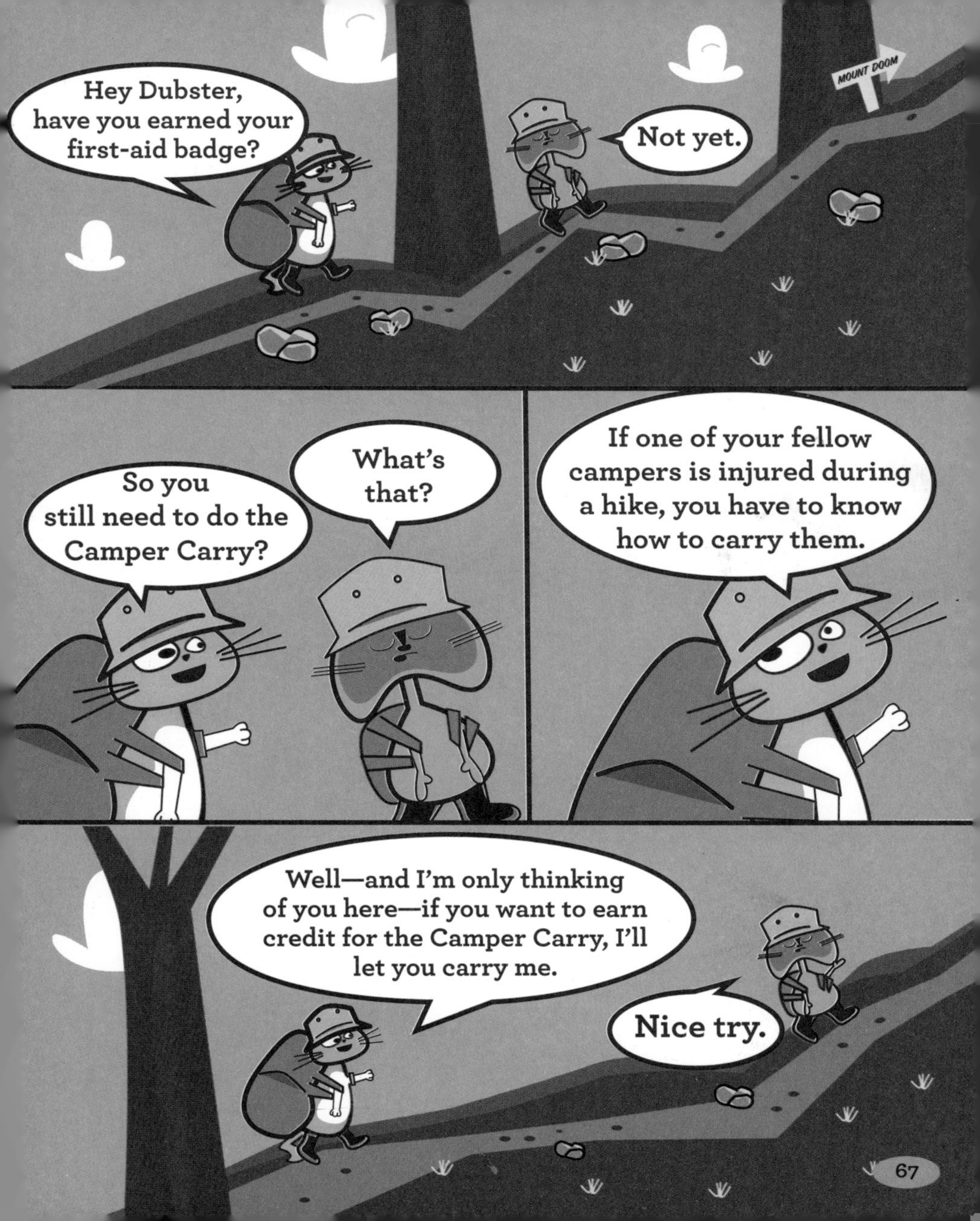
MOUNT DOOM
Hey Dubster, have you earned your first-aid badge?
Not yet.
So you still need to do the Camper Carry?
What's that?
If one of your fellow campers is injured during a hike, you have to know how to carry them.
Well—and I'm only thinking of you here—if you want to earn credit for the Camper Carry, I'll let you carry me.
Nice try.

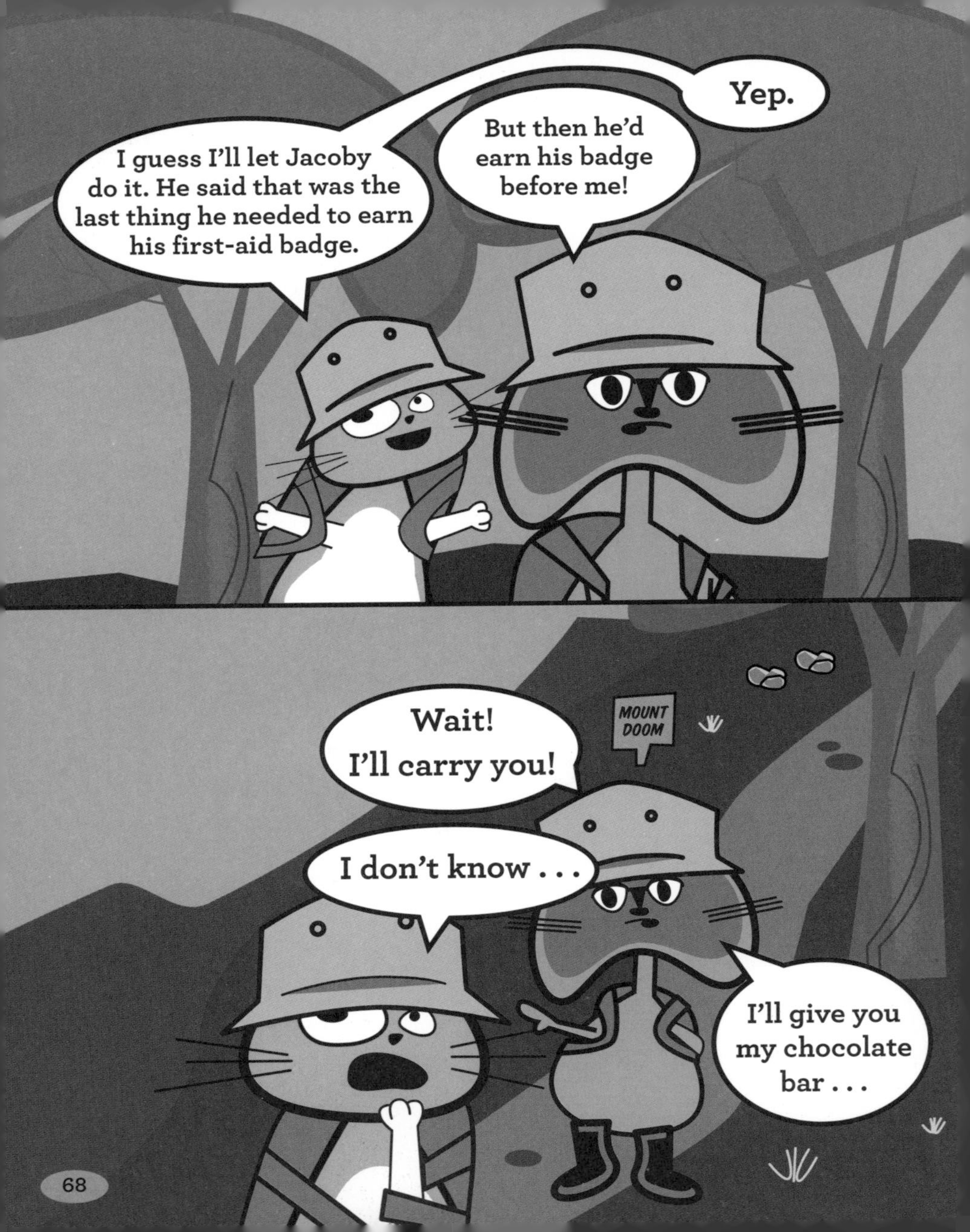
I guess I'll let Jacoby do it. He said that was the last thing he needed to earn his first-aid badge.
But then he'd earn his badge before me!
Yep.
MOUNT DOOM
Wait! I'll carry you!
I don't know . . .
I'll give you my chocolate bar . . .

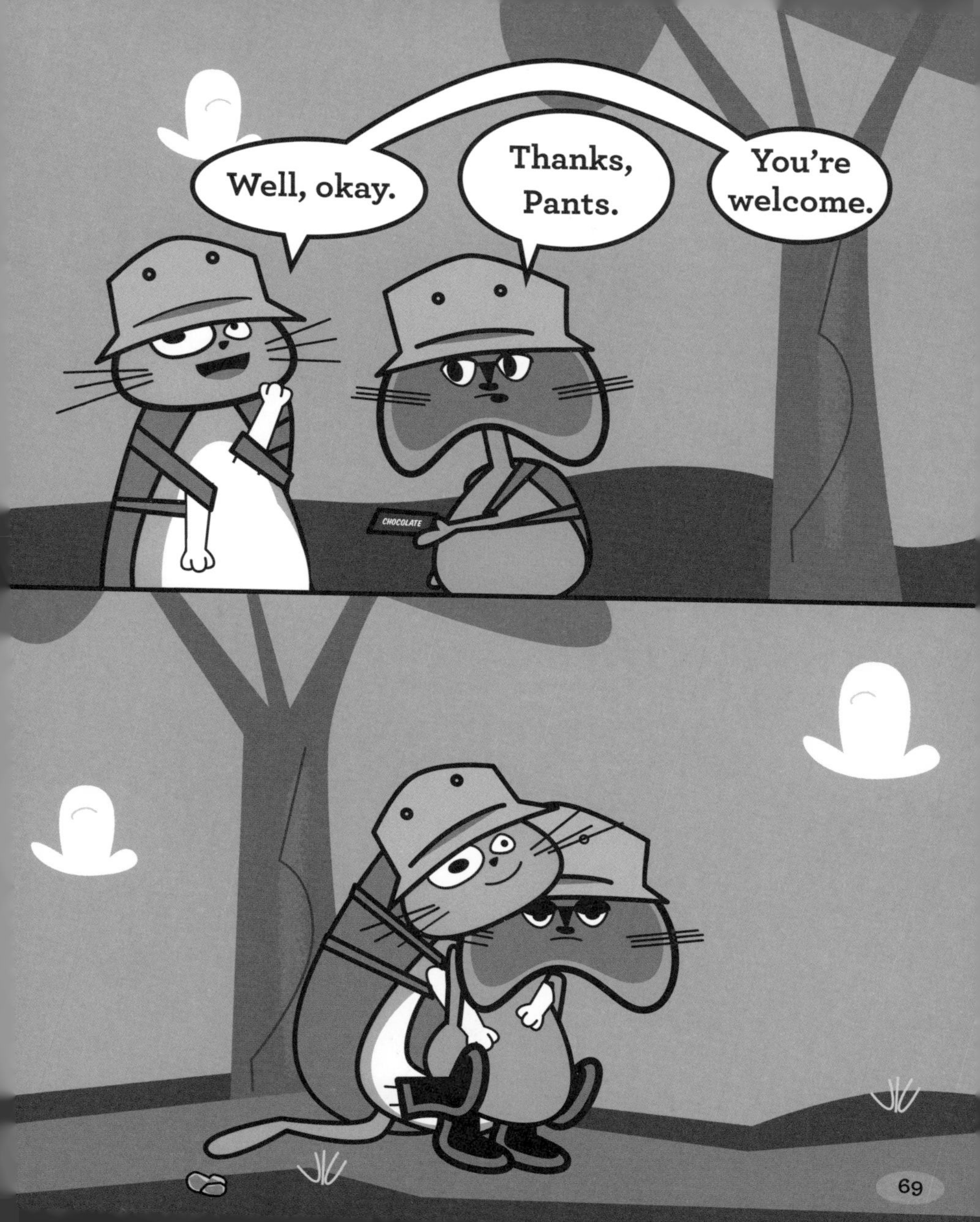
Well, okay.
Thanks, Pants.
You're welcome.
CHOCOLATE

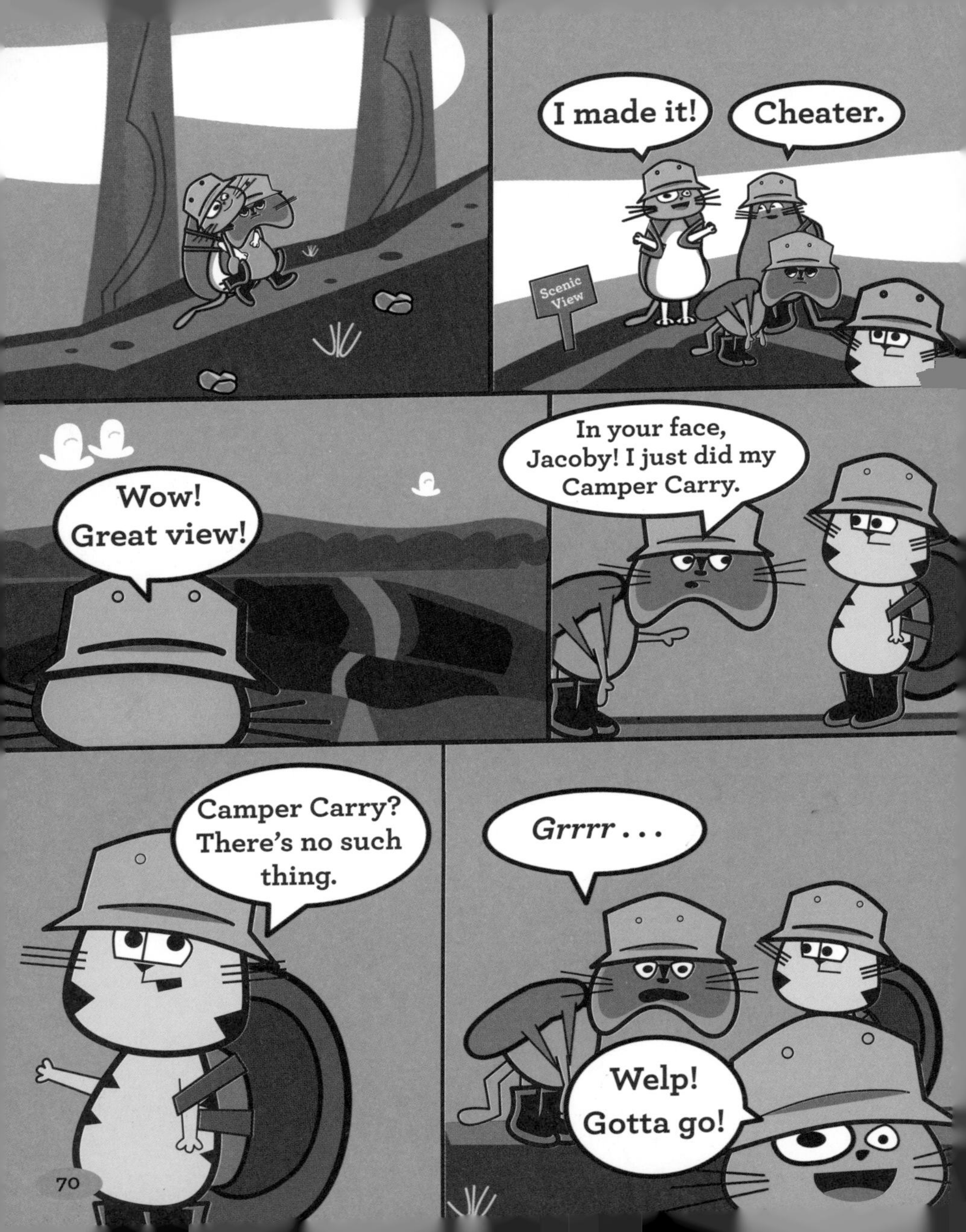
I made it!
Cheater.
Scenic View
Wow! Great view!
In your face, Jacoby! I just did my Camper Carry.
Camper Carry? There's no such thing.
Grrrr . . .
Welp! Gotta go!

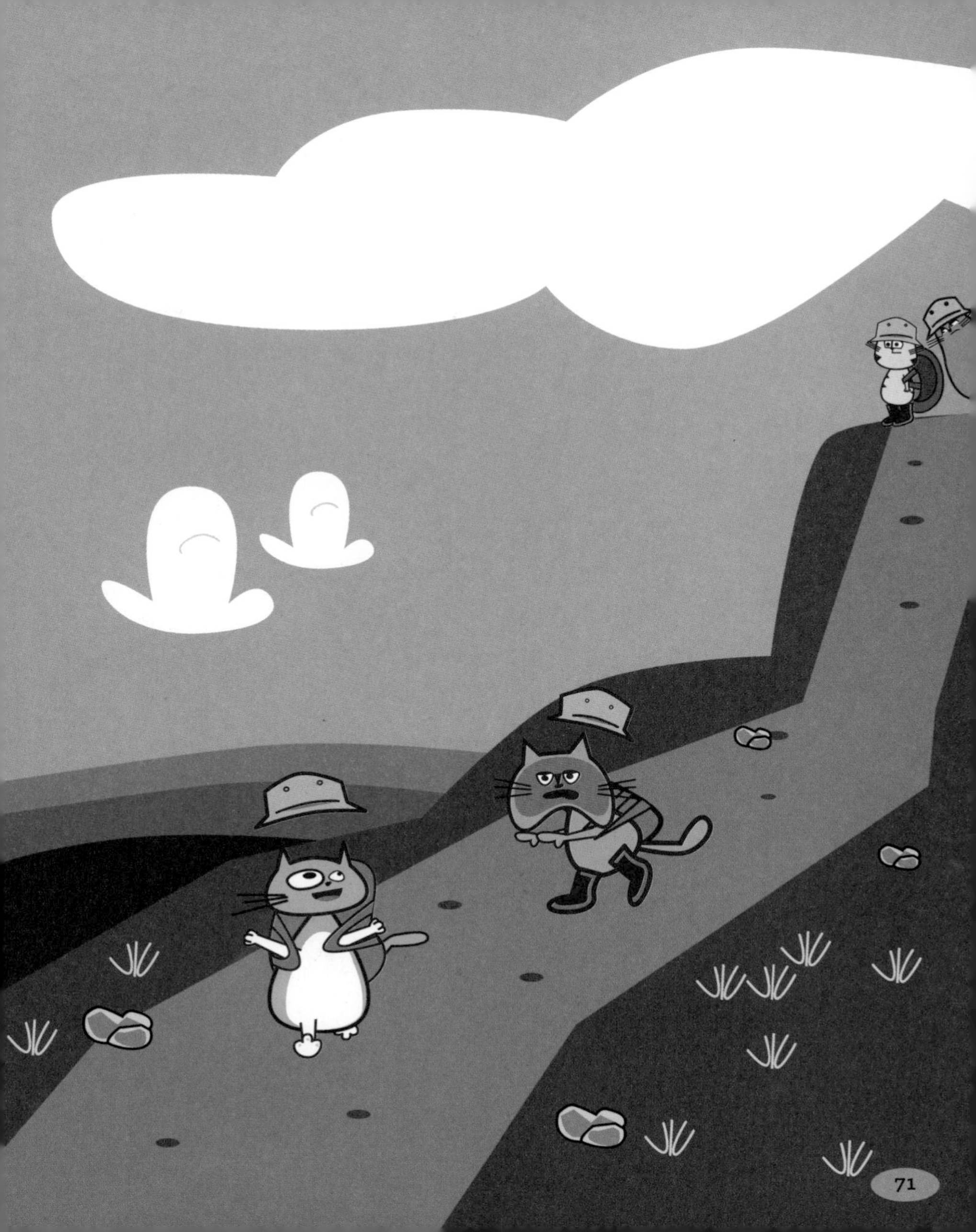

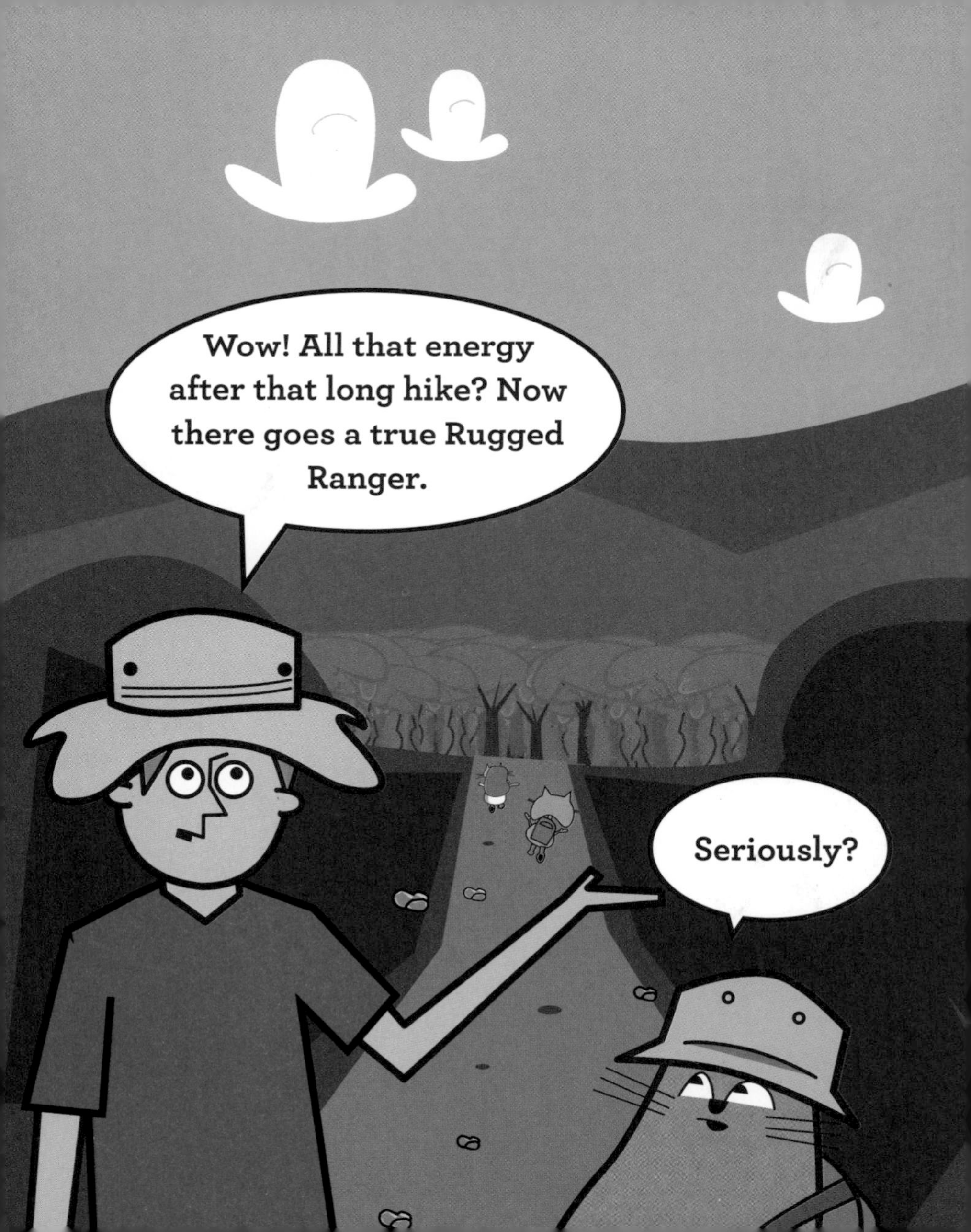
Wow! All that energy after that long hike? Now there goes a true Rugged Ranger.
Seriously?

Chapter Five: THE ITCH

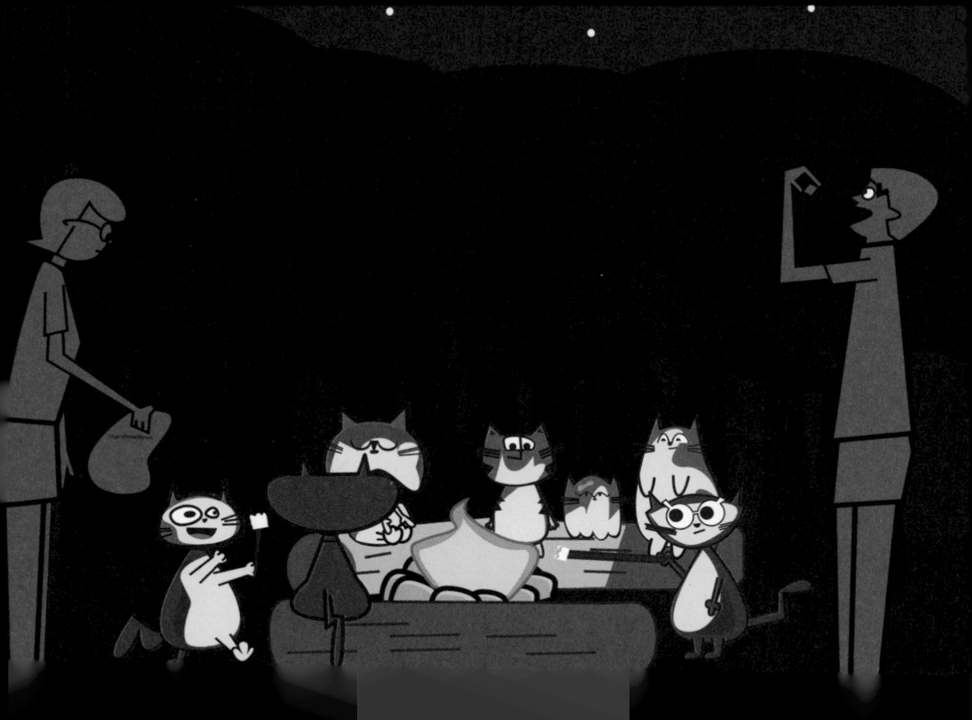

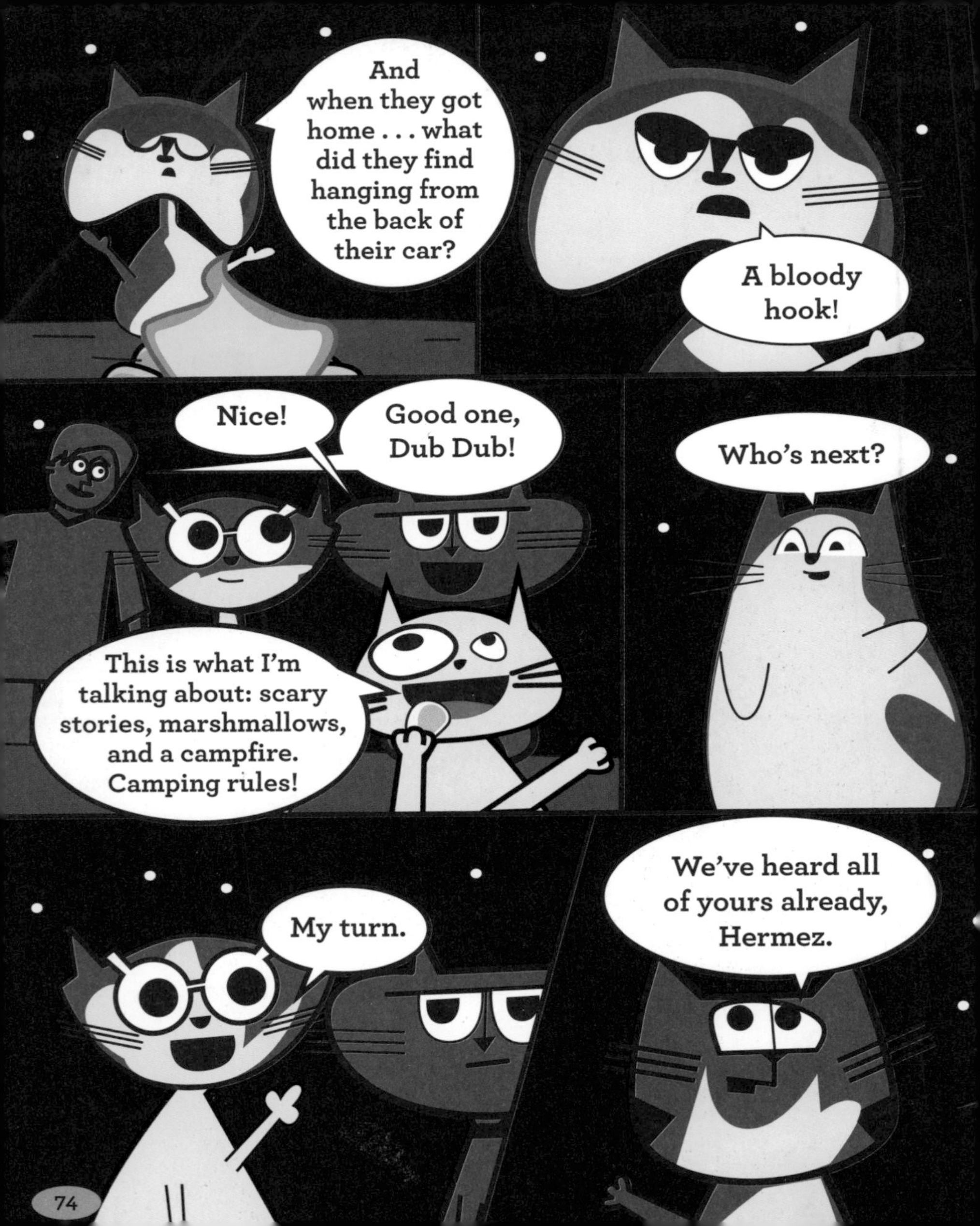
And when they got home . . . what did they find hanging from the back of their car?
A bloody hook!
Nice!
Good one, Dub Dub!
This is what I'm talking about: scary stories, marshmallows, and a campfire. Camping rules!
Who's next?
My turn.
We've heard all of yours already, Hermez.

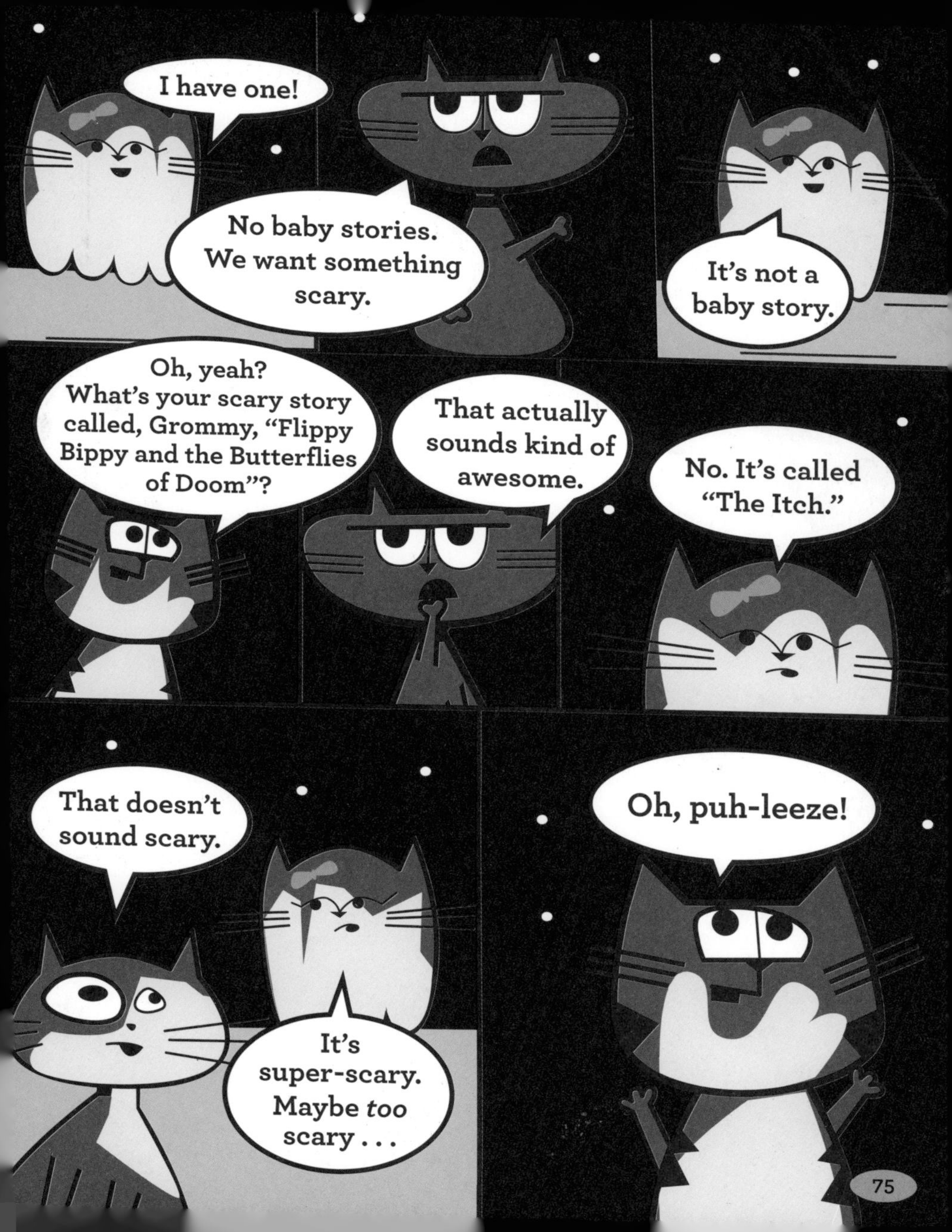
I have one!
No baby stories. We want something scary.
It's not a baby story.
Oh, yeah? What's your scary story called, Grommy, "Flippy Bippy and the Butterflies of Doom"?
That actually sounds kind of awesome.
No. It's called "The Itch."
That doesn't sound scary.
It's super-scary. Maybe *too* scary . . .
Oh, puh-leeze!

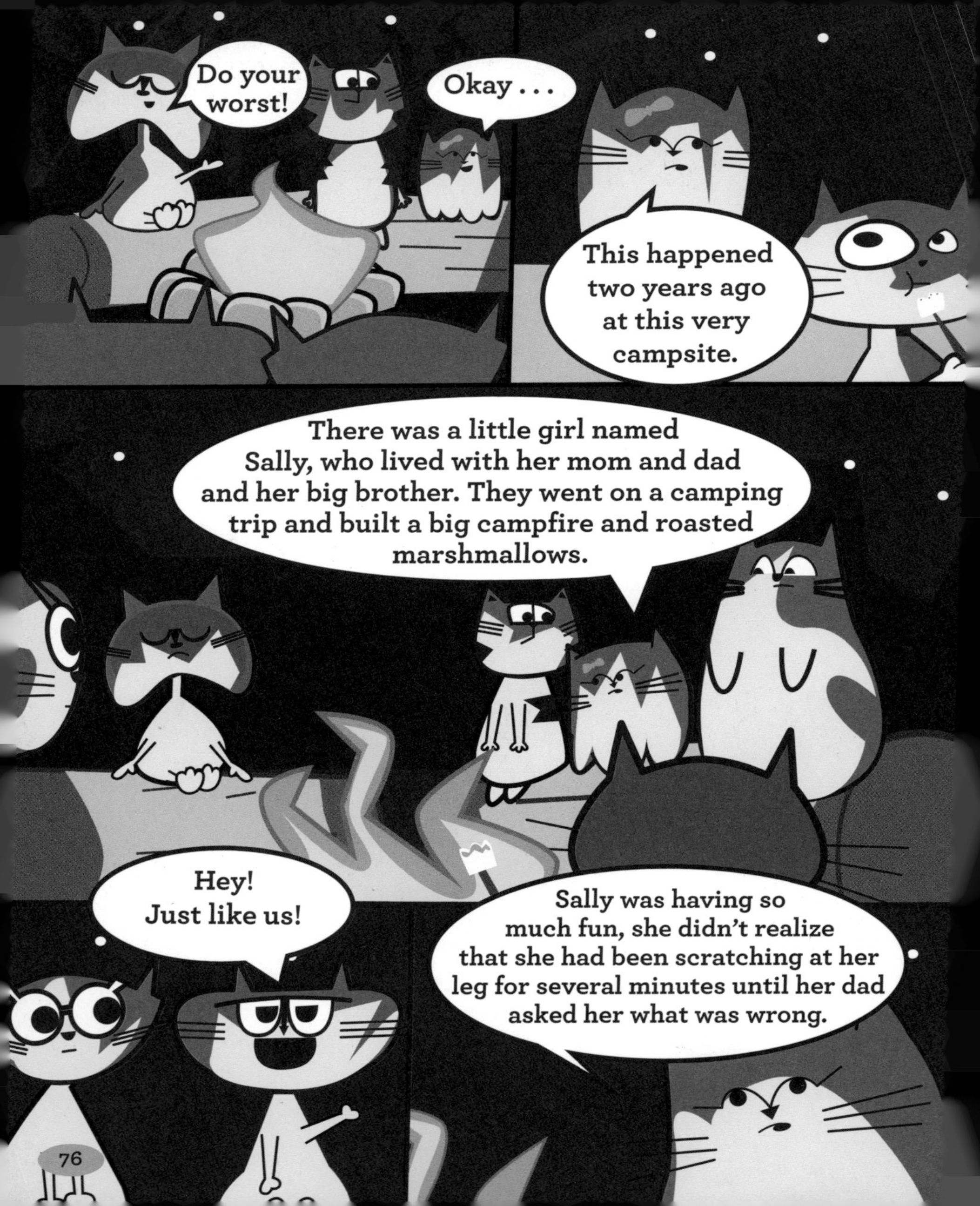
Do your worst!
Okay . . .
This happened two years ago at this very campsite.
There was a little girl named Sally, who lived with her mom and dad and her big brother. They went on a camping trip and built a big campfire and roasted marshmallows.
Hey! Just like us!
Sally was having so much fun, she didn't realize that she had been scratching at her leg for several minutes until her dad asked her what was wrong.

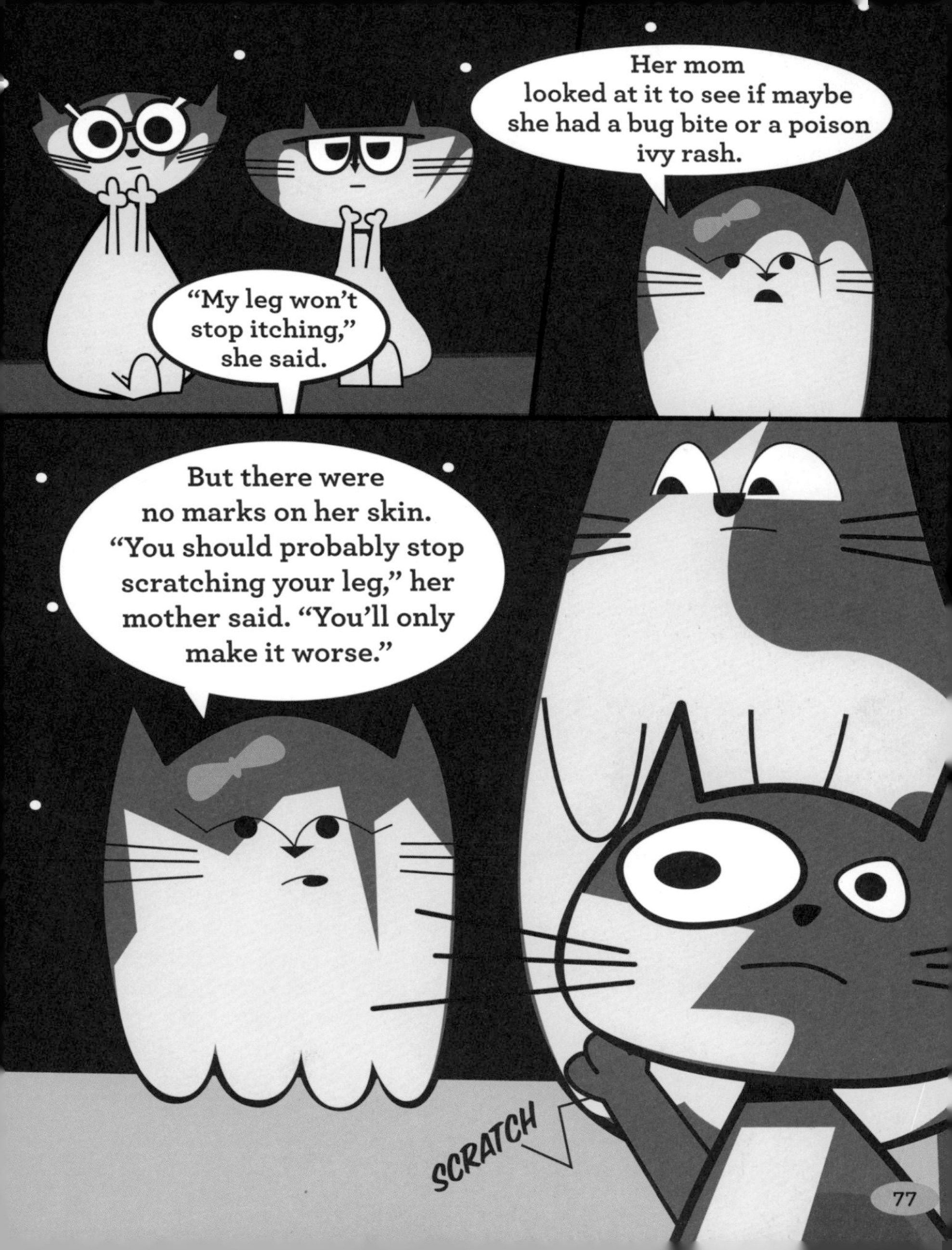
"My leg won't stop itching," she said.
Her mom looked at it to see if maybe she had a bug bite or a poison ivy rash.
But there were no marks on her skin. "You should probably stop scratching your leg," her mother said. "You'll only make it worse."
SCRATCH

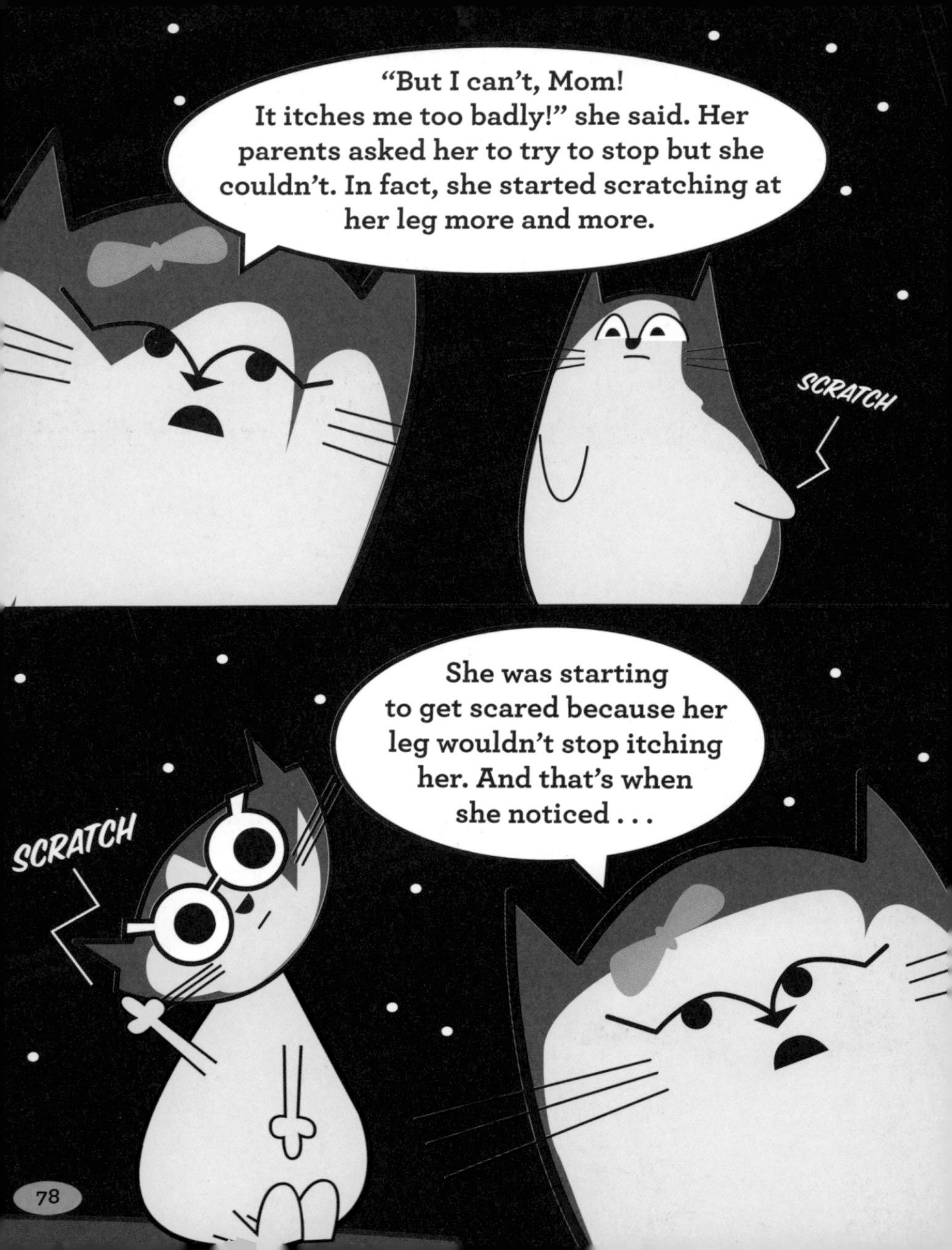
"But I can't, Mom! It itches me too badly!" she said. Her parents asked her to try to stop but she couldn't. In fact, she started scratching at her leg more and more.
SCRATCH
She was starting to get scared because her leg wouldn't stop itching her. And that's when she noticed . . .
SCRATCH

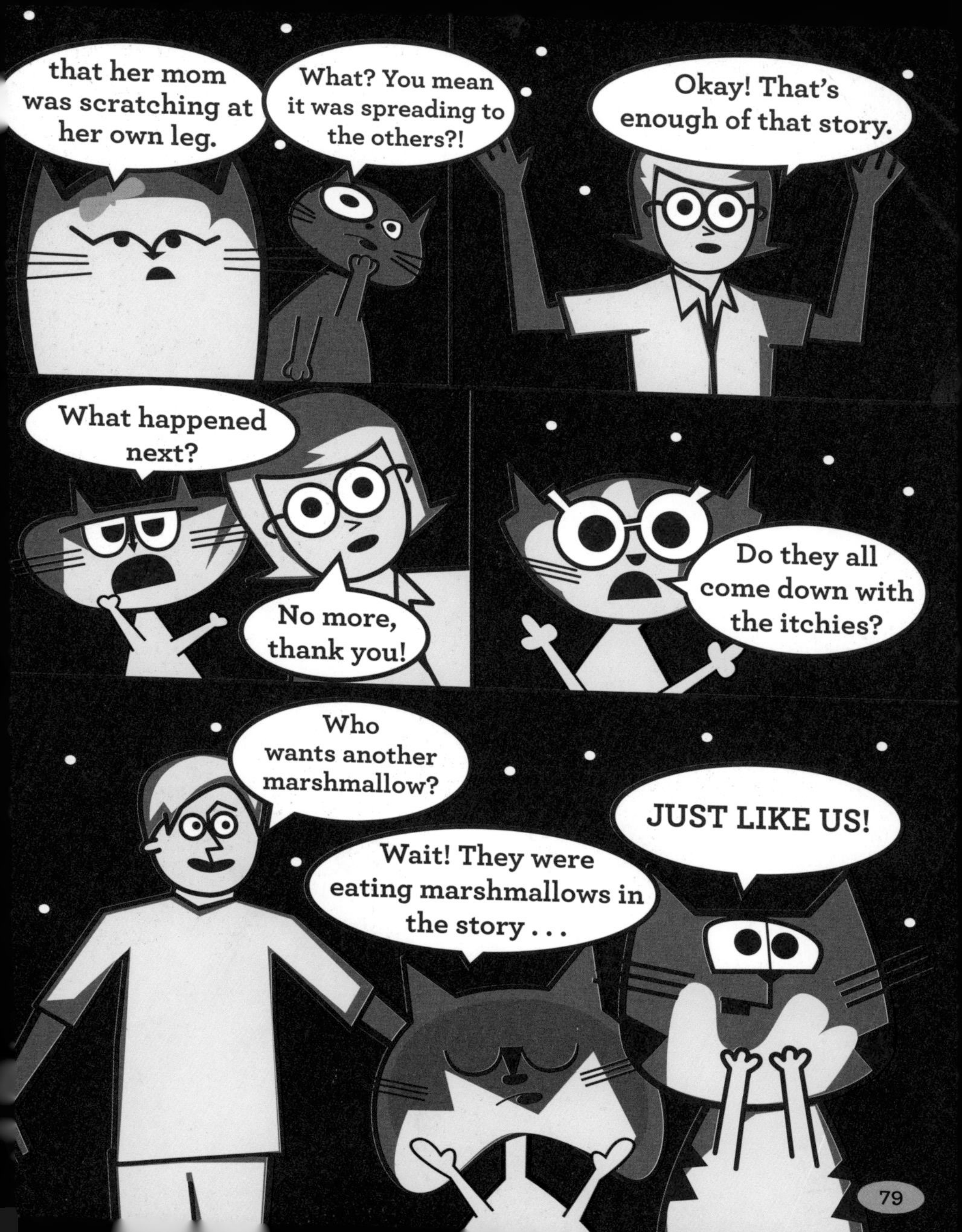

that her mom was scratching at her own leg.
What? You mean it was spreading to the others?!
Okay! That's enough of that story.
What happened next?
No more, thank you!
Do they all come down with the itchies?
Who wants another marshmallow?
Wait! They were eating marshmallows in the story . . .
JUST LIKE US!

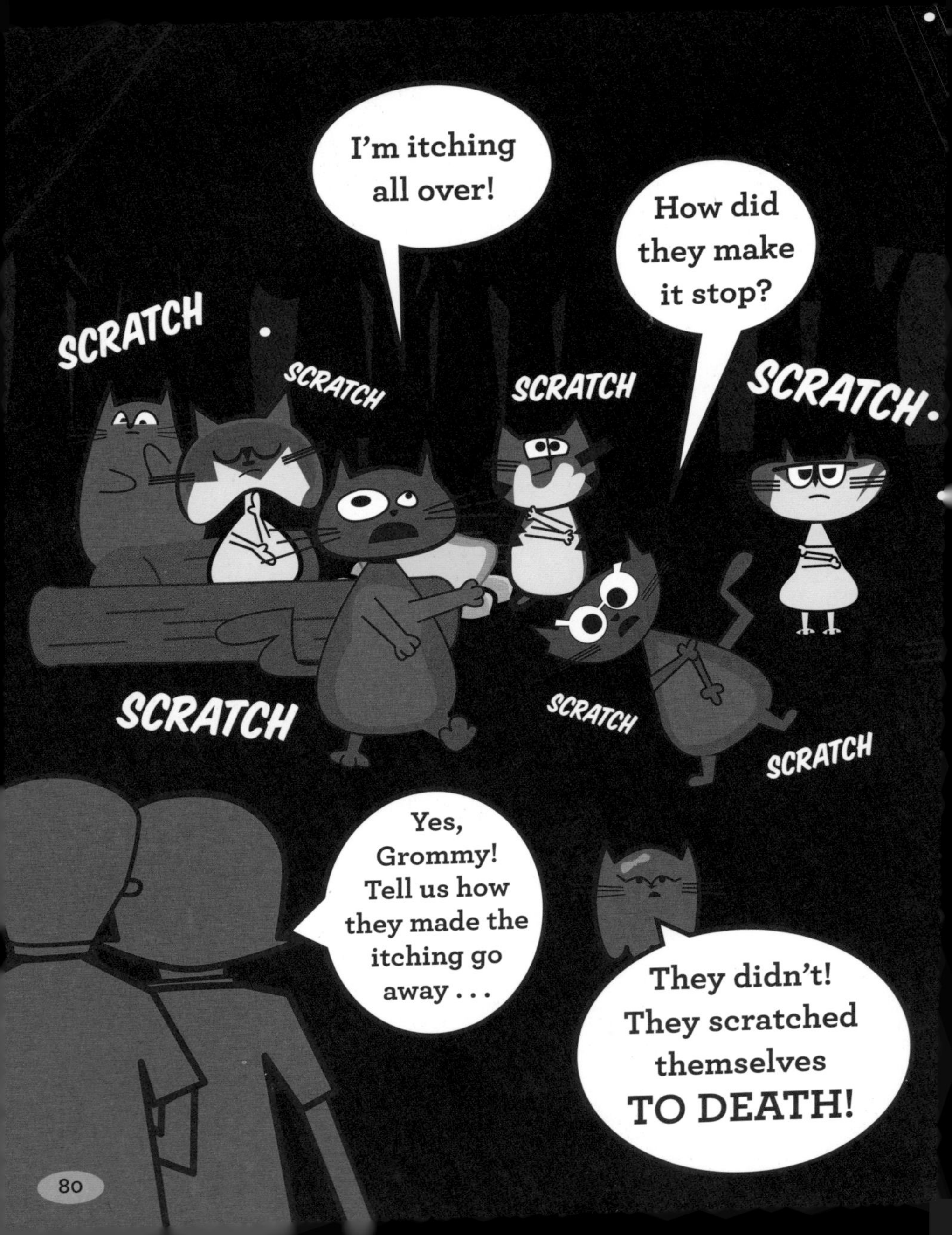
I'm itching all over!
How did they make it stop?
SCRATCH
SCRATCH
SCRATCH
SCRATCH
SCRATCH
SCRATCH
SCRATCH
Yes, Grommy! Tell us how they made the itching go away . . .
They didn't! They scratched themselves TO DEATH!

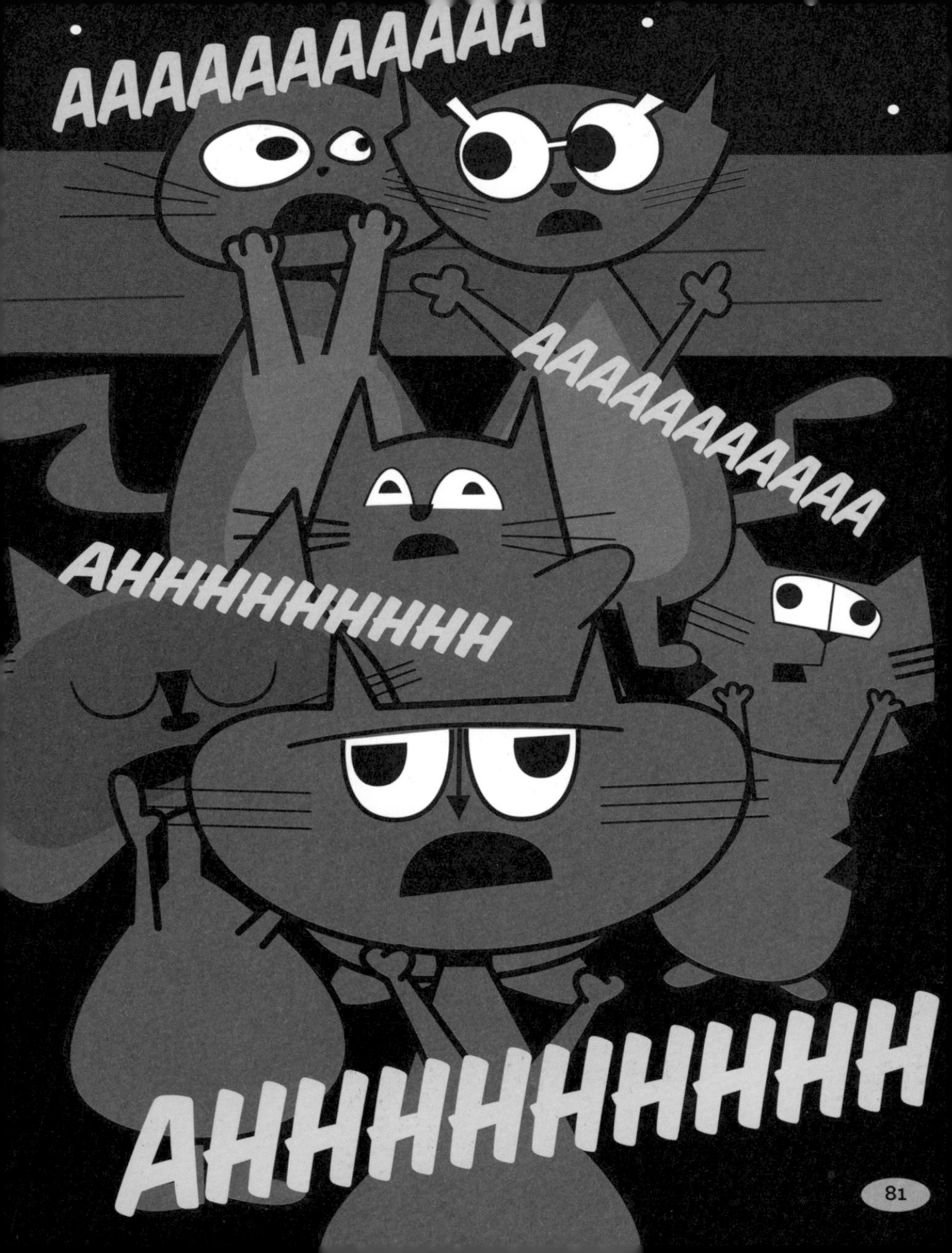
AAAAAAAAAAA
AAAAAAAAAAA
AHHHHHHHHH
AHHHHHHHHH

AAAAAAAAAAHHHHHHHHHHHH
AAAAAHHHHHH
AAAHHHH
SCRATCH
SCRATCH
Great. Thanks, Grommy.
That was a good one, right?
Sort of.

Chapter Six: The CAMPING CATASTROPHE

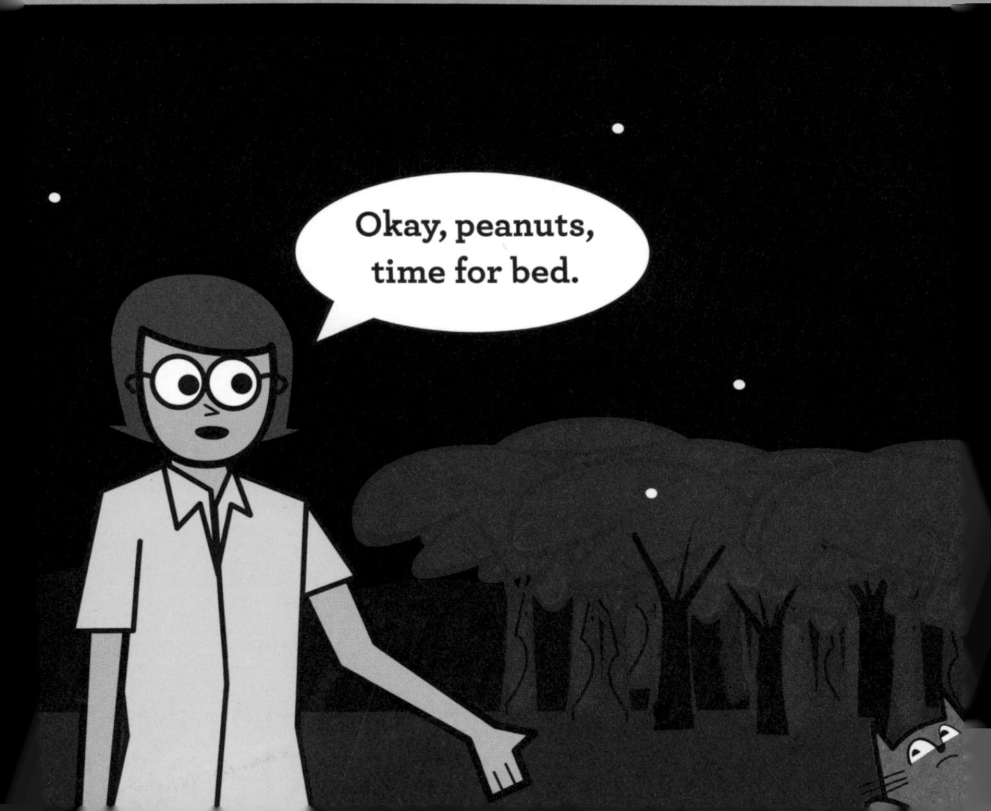

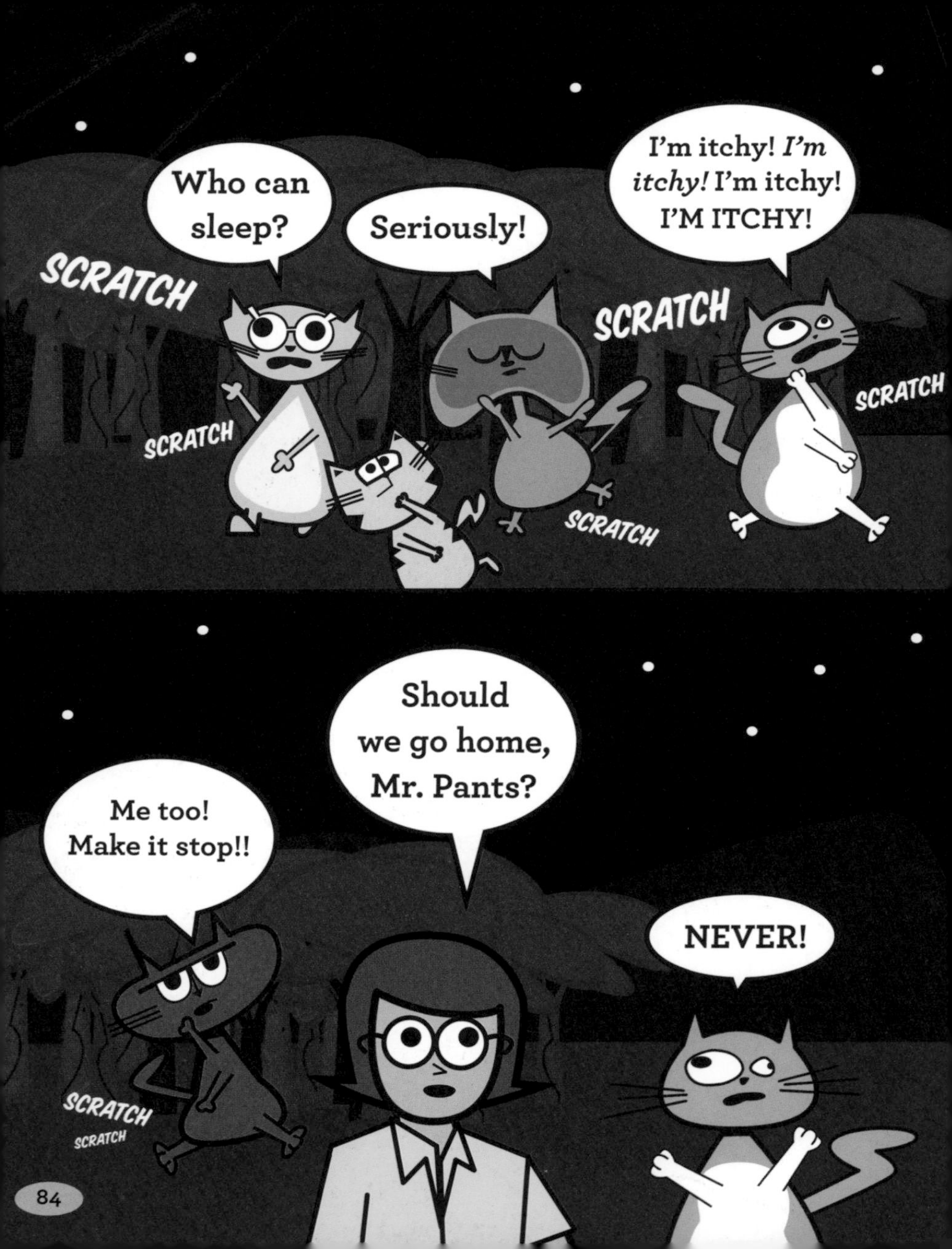

Who can sleep?
Seriously!
I'm itchy! *I'm itchy!* I'm itchy! I'M ITCHY!
SCRATCH
SCRATCH
SCRATCH
SCRATCH
SCRATCH
Should we go home, Mr. Pants?
Me too! Make it stop!!
NEVER!
SCRATCH
SCRATCH

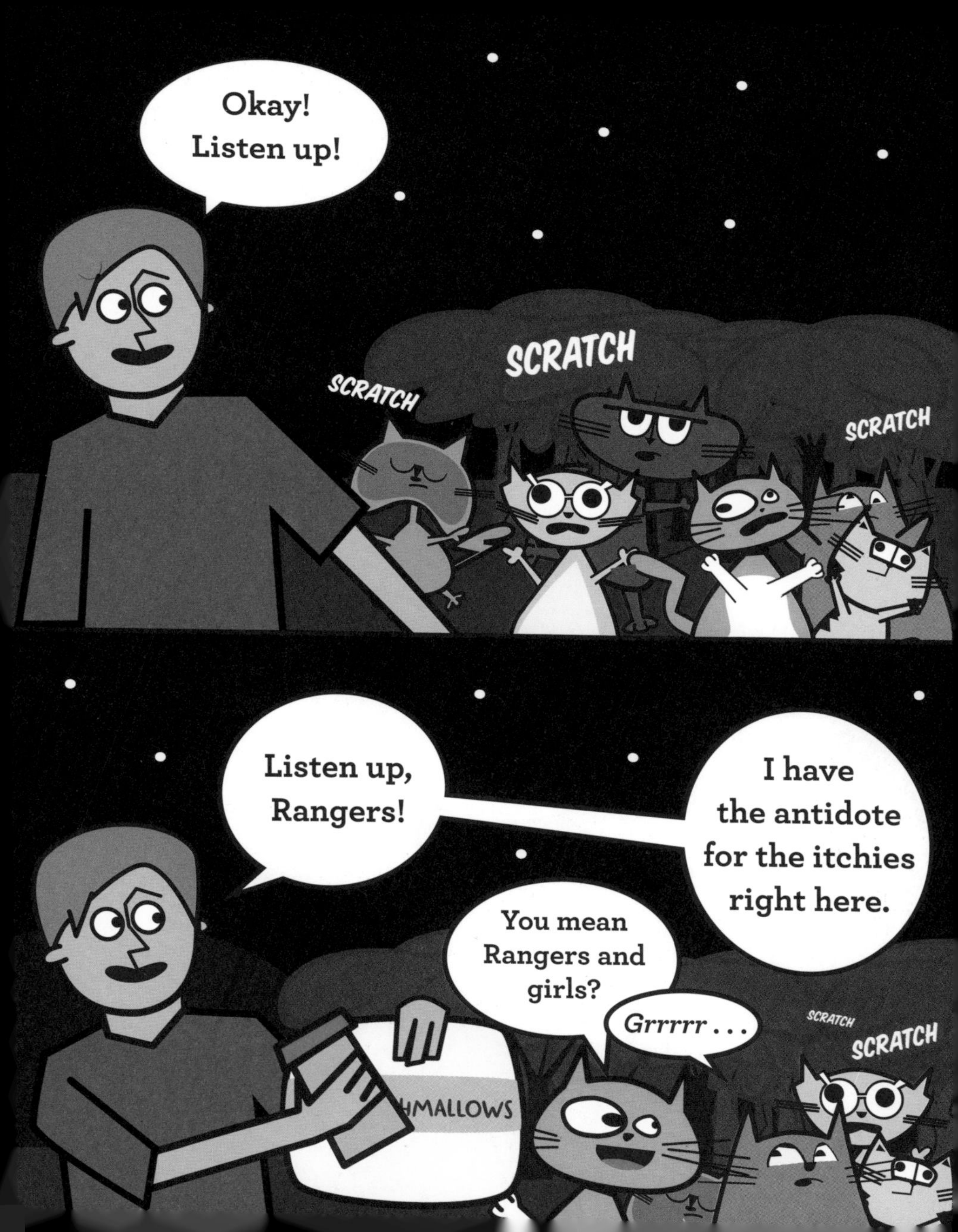
Okay! Listen up!
SCRATCH
SCRATCH
SCRATCH
Listen up, Rangers!
I have the antidote for the itchies right here.
You mean Rangers and girls?
Grrrrr . . .
SCRATCH
SCRATCH
HMALLOWS

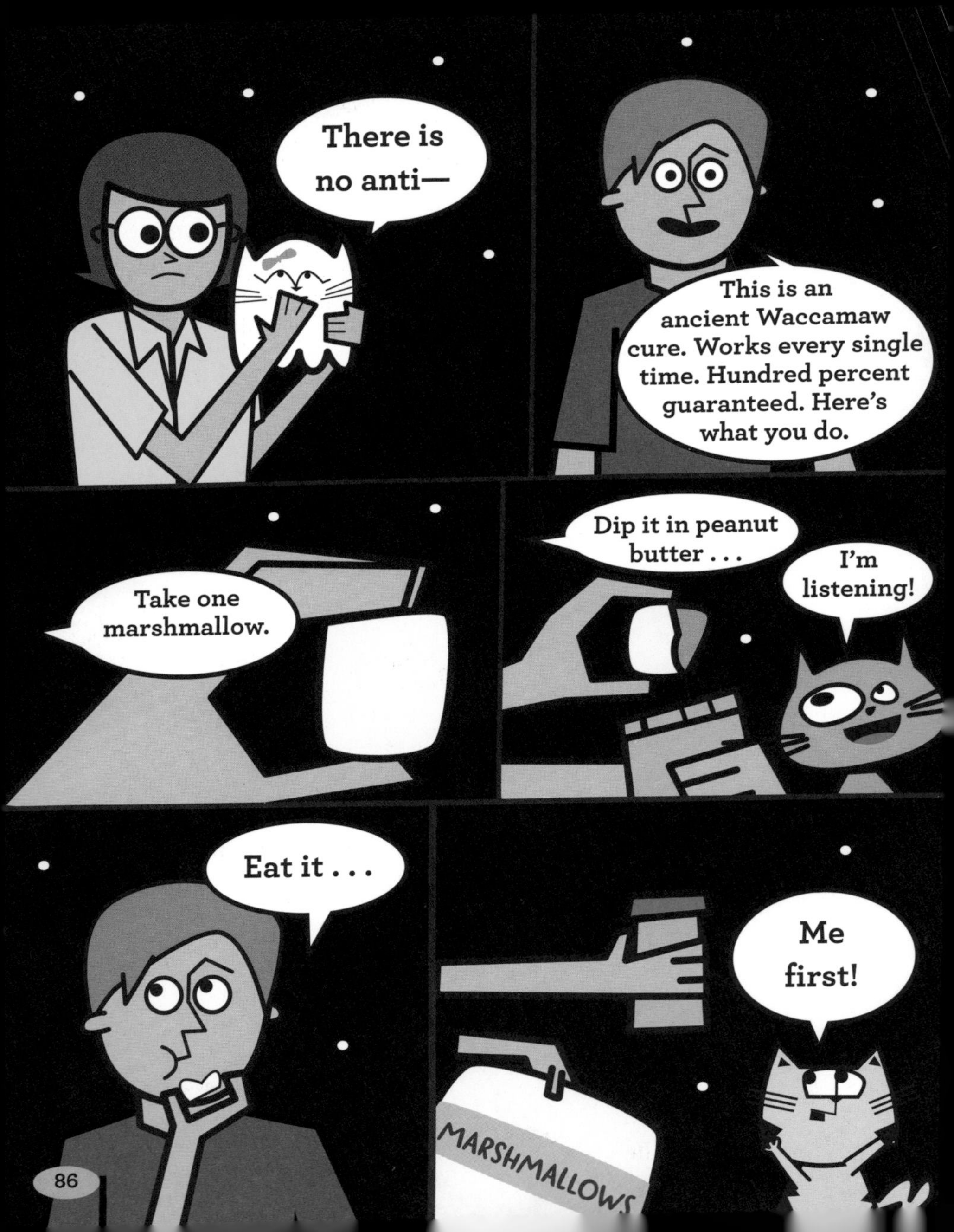

There is no anti—
This is an ancient Waccamaw cure. Works every single time. Hundred percent guaranteed. Here's what you do.
Take one marshmallow.
Dip it in peanut butter . . .
I'm listening!
Eat it . . .
Me first!
MARSHMALLOWS

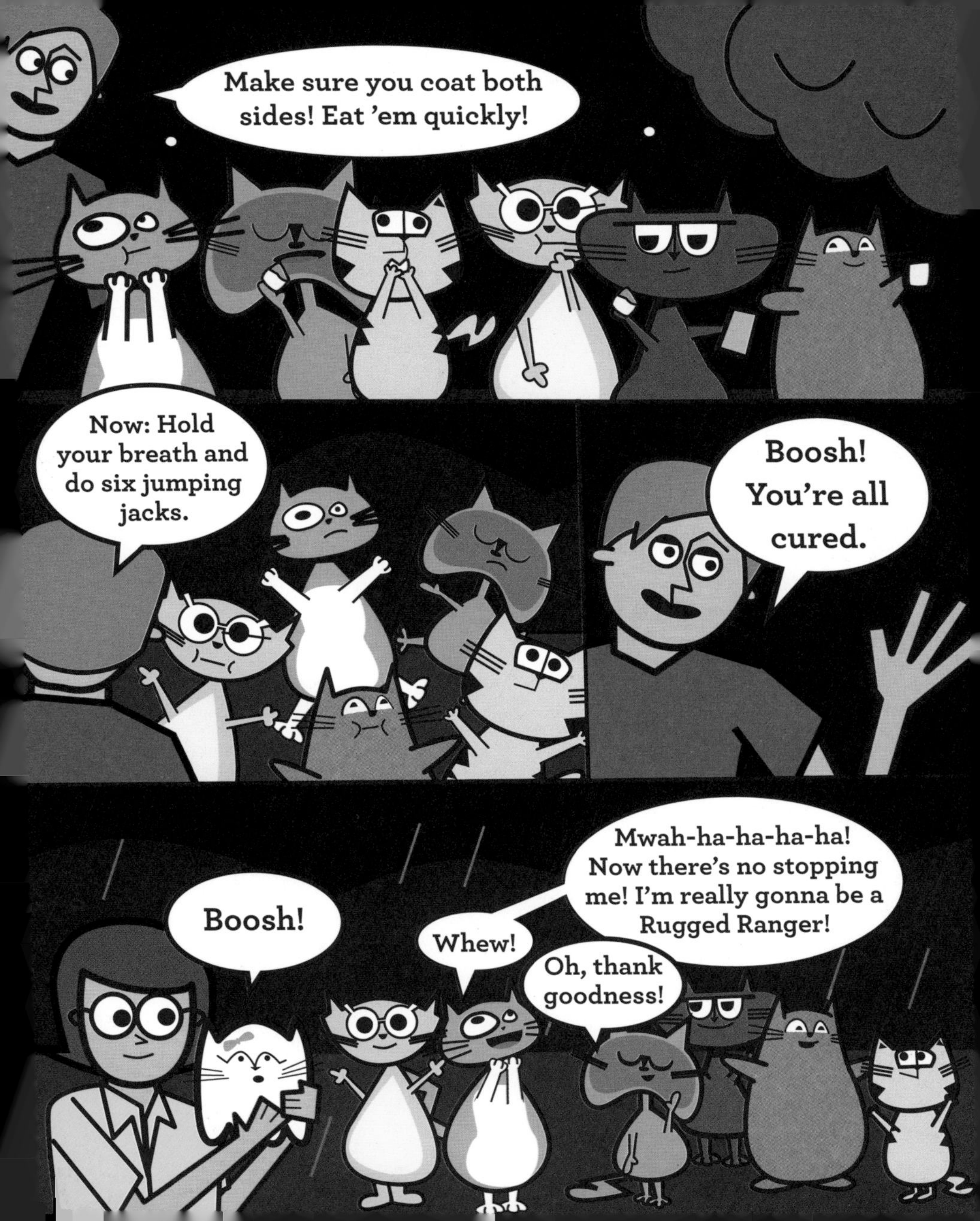
Make sure you coat both sides! Eat 'em quickly!
Now: Hold your breath and do six jumping jacks.
Boosh! You're all cured.
Boosh!
Whew!
Mwah-ha-ha-ha-ha! Now there's no stopping me! I'm really gonna be a Rugged Ranger!
Oh, thank goodness!

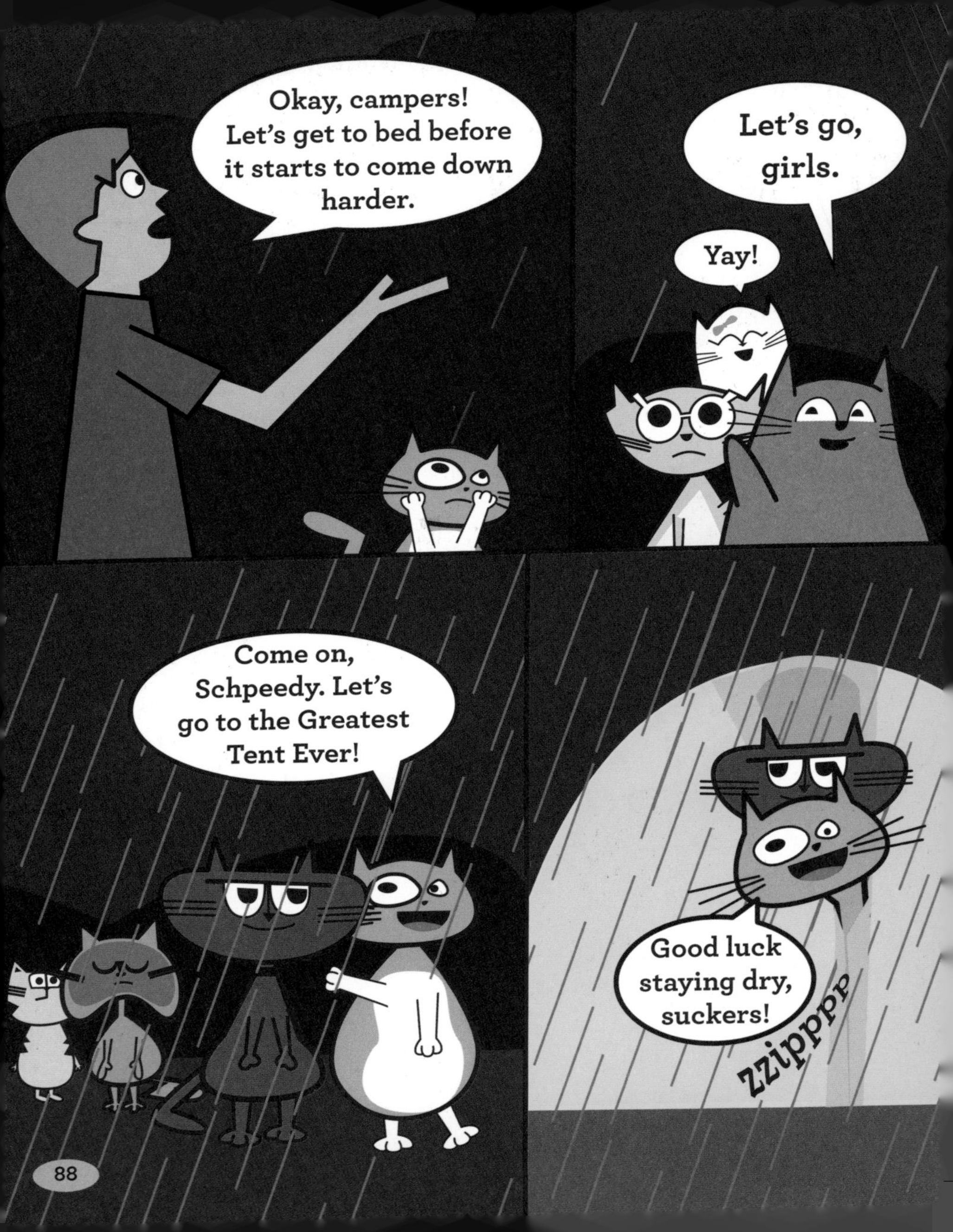
Okay, campers! Let's get to bed before it starts to come down harder.
Let's go, girls.
Yay!
Come on, Schpeedy. Let's go to the Greatest Tent Ever!
Good luck staying dry, suckers!
ZZIPPPP

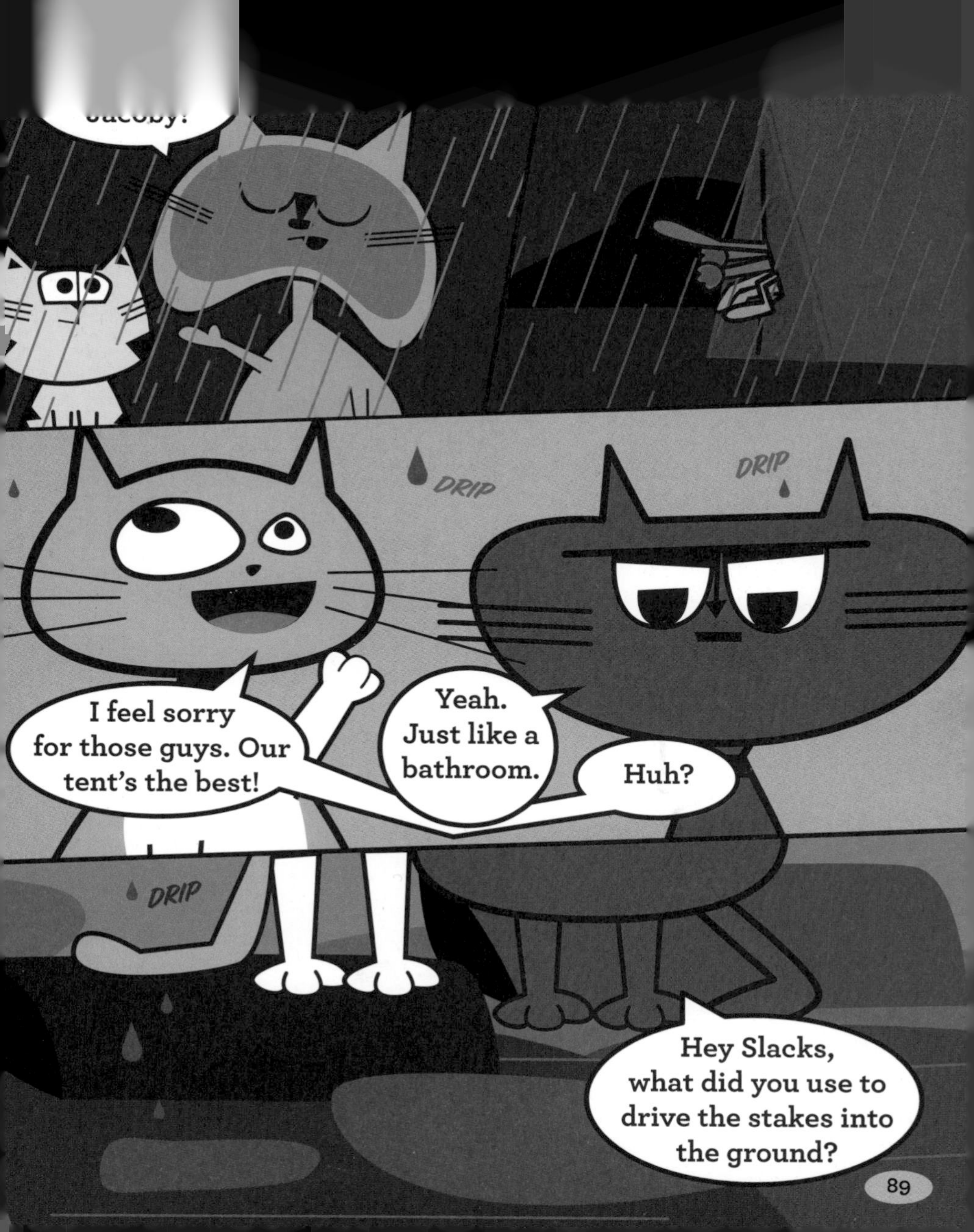
DRIP
DRIP
I feel sorry for those guys. Our tent's the best!
Yeah. Just like a bathroom.
Huh?
DRIP
Hey Slacks, what did you use to drive the stakes into the ground?

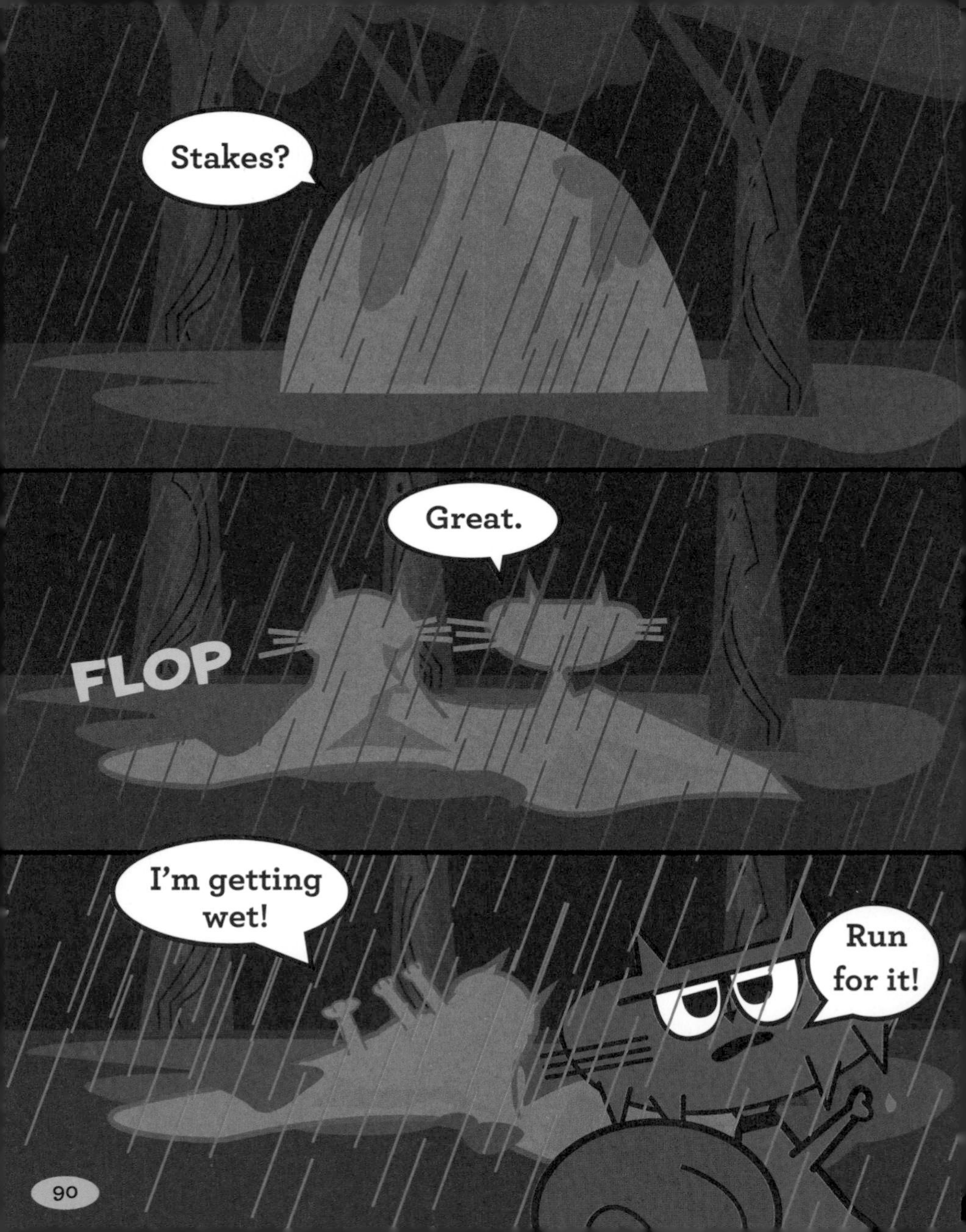
Stakes?
Great.
FLOP
I'm getting wet!
Run for it!

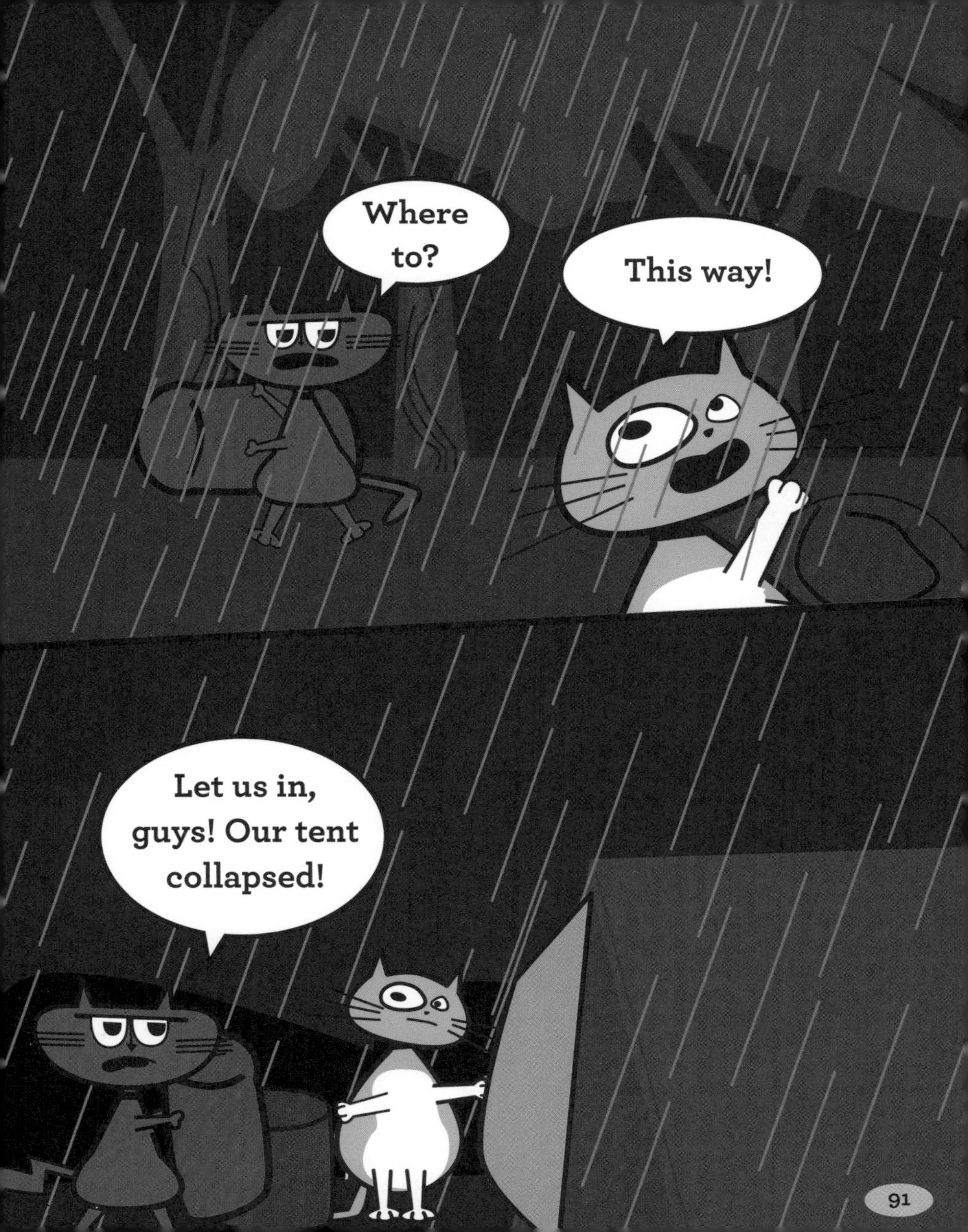
Where to?
This way!
Let us in, guys! Our tent collapsed!

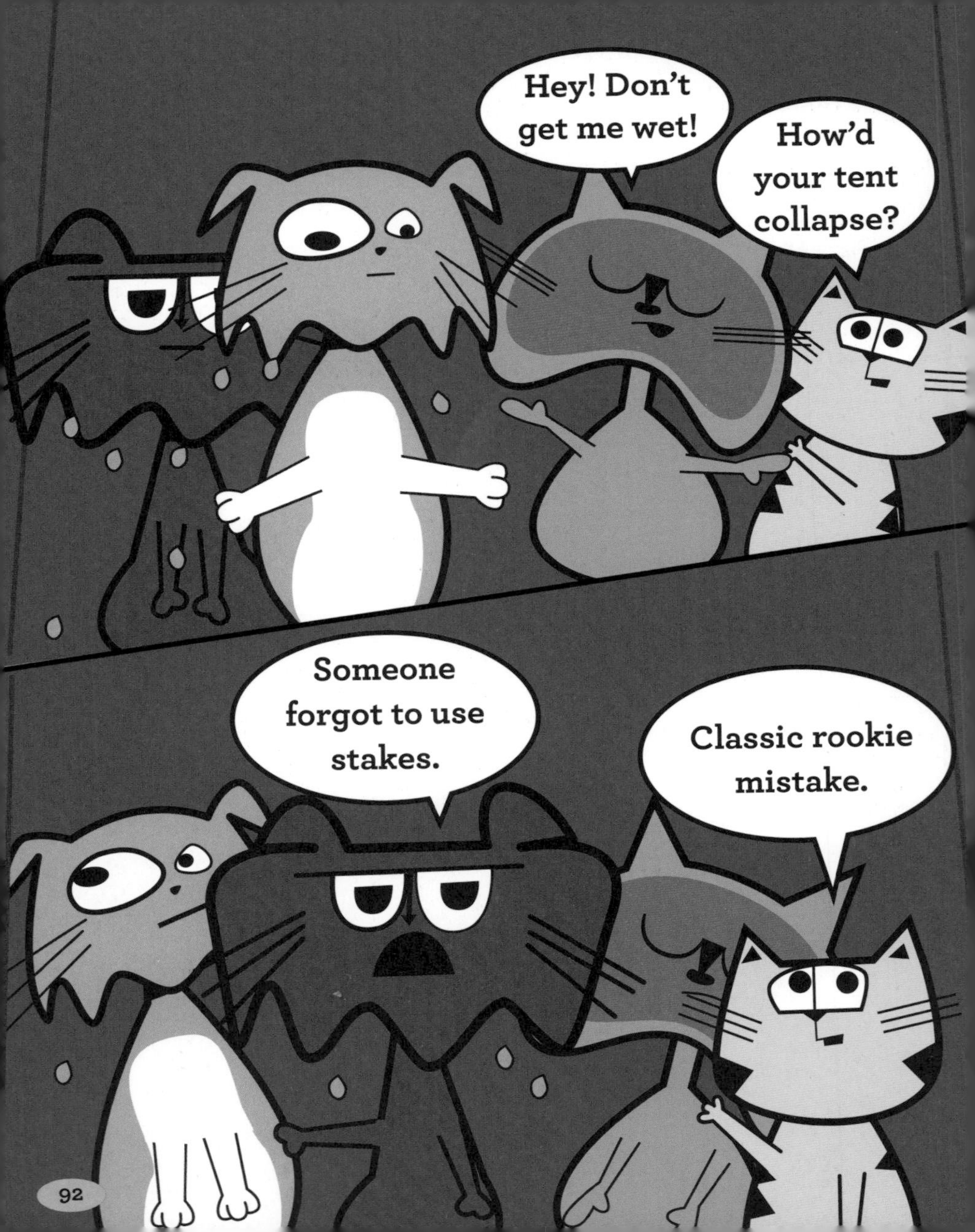
Hey! Don't get me wet!
How'd your tent collapse?
Someone forgot to use stakes.
Classic rookie mistake.

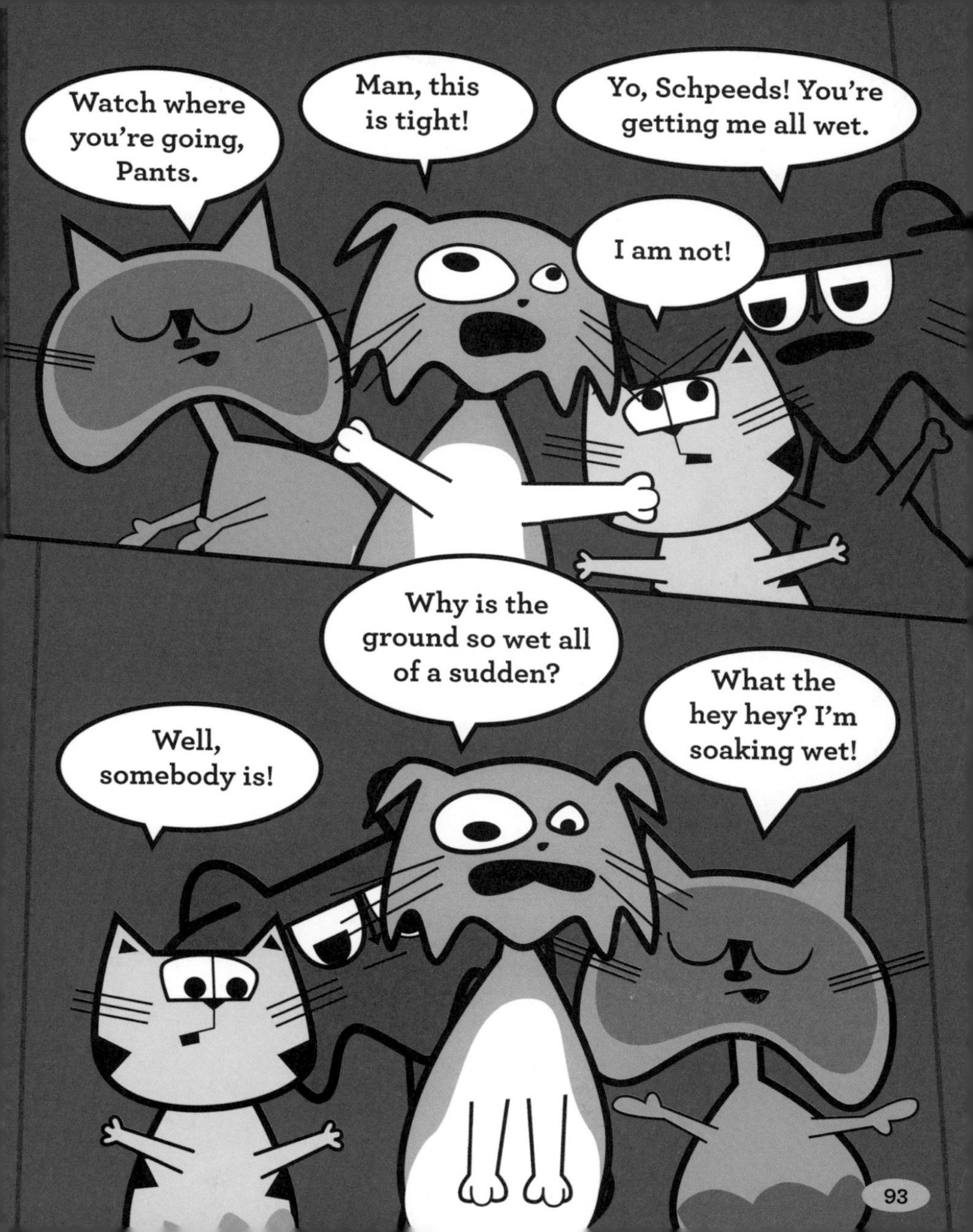
Watch where you're going, Pants.
Man, this is tight!
Yo, Schpeeds! You're getting me all wet.
I am not!
Why is the ground so wet all of a sudden?
Well, somebody is!
What the hey hey? I'm soaking wet!

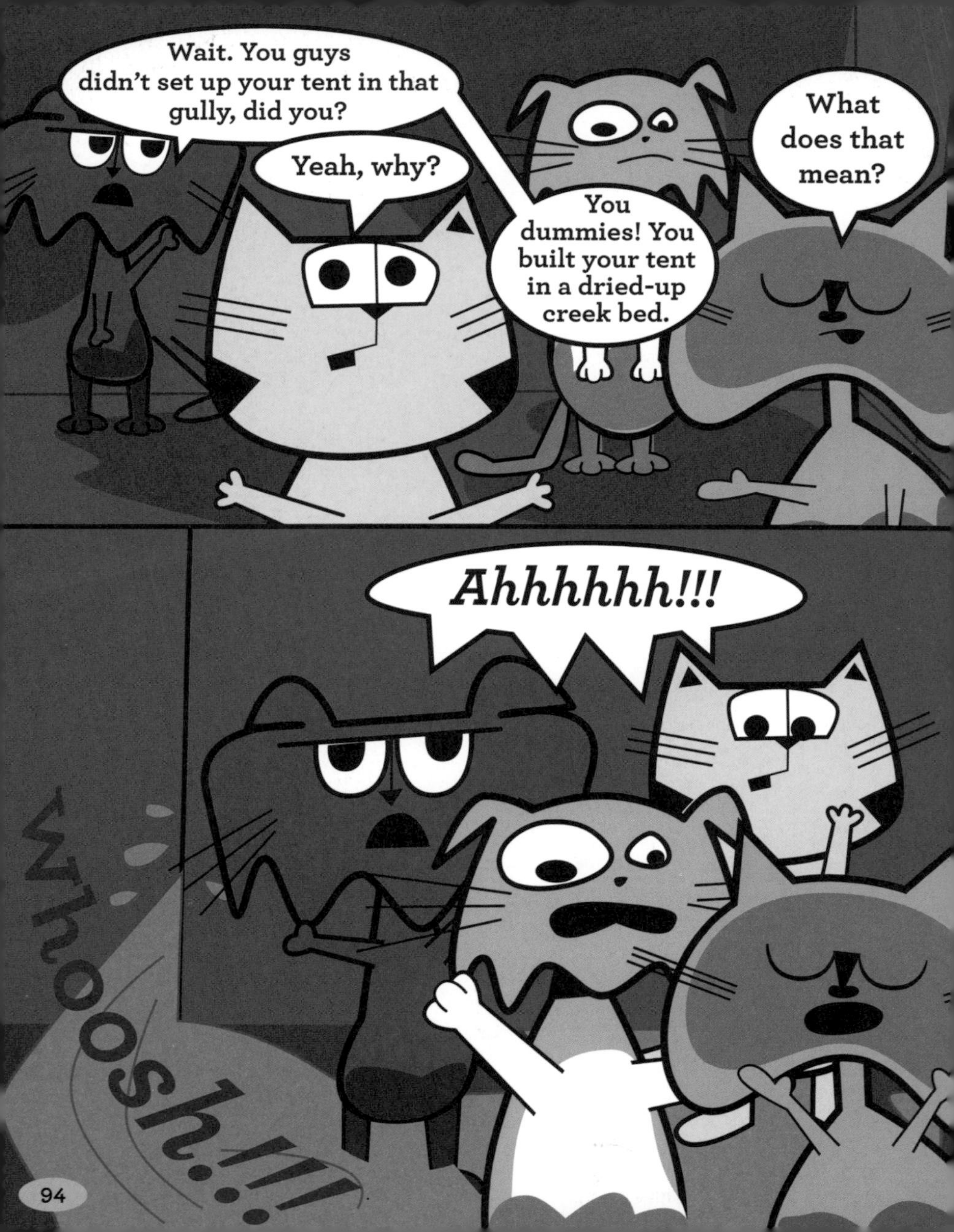
Wait. You guys didn't set up your tent in that gully, did you?
Yeah, why?
You dummies! You built your tent in a dried-up creek bed.
What does that mean?
Ahhhhhh!!!
Whoosh!!!

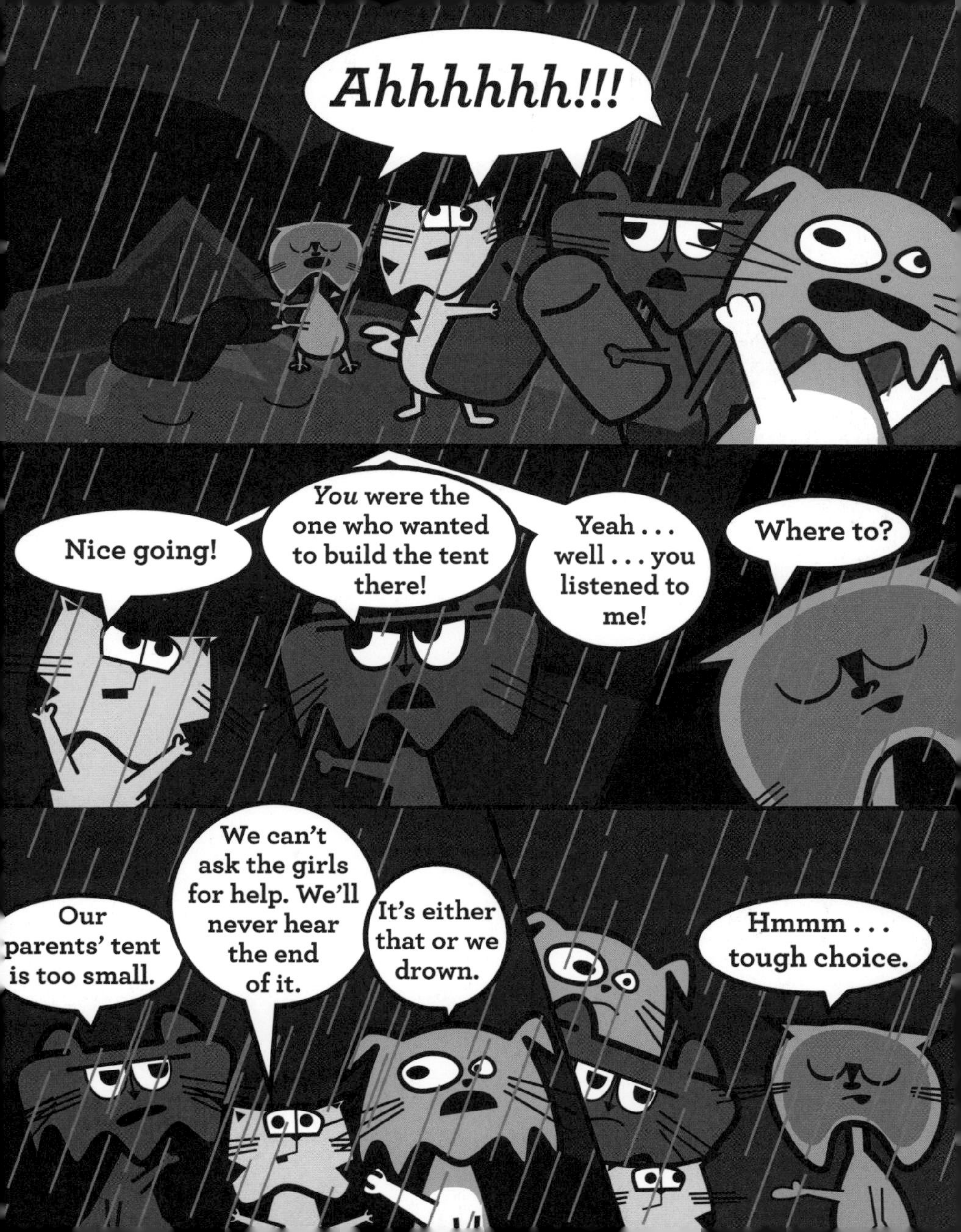
Ahhhhhh!!!
Nice going!
You were the one who wanted to build the tent there!
Yeah . . . well . . . you listened to me!
Where to?
Our parents' tent is too small.
We can't ask the girls for help. We'll never hear the end of it.
It's either that or we drown.
Hmmm . . . tough choice.

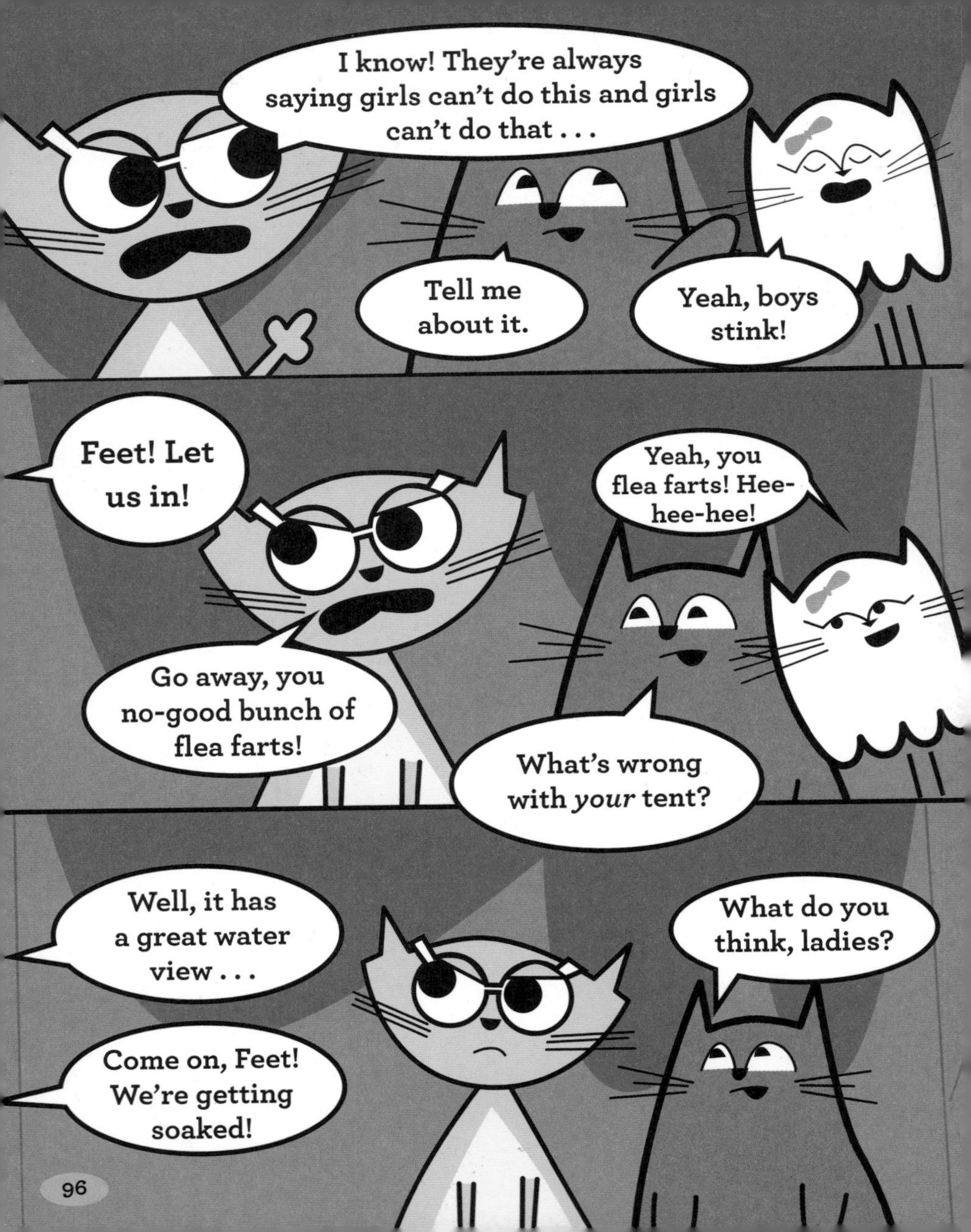
I know! They're always saying girls can't do this and girls can't do that . . .
Tell me about it.
Yeah, boys stink!
Feet! Let us in!
Go away, you no-good bunch of flea farts!
Yeah, you flea farts! Hee-hee-hee!
What's wrong with *your* tent?
Well, it has a great water view . . .
Come on, Feet! We're getting soaked!
What do you think, ladies?

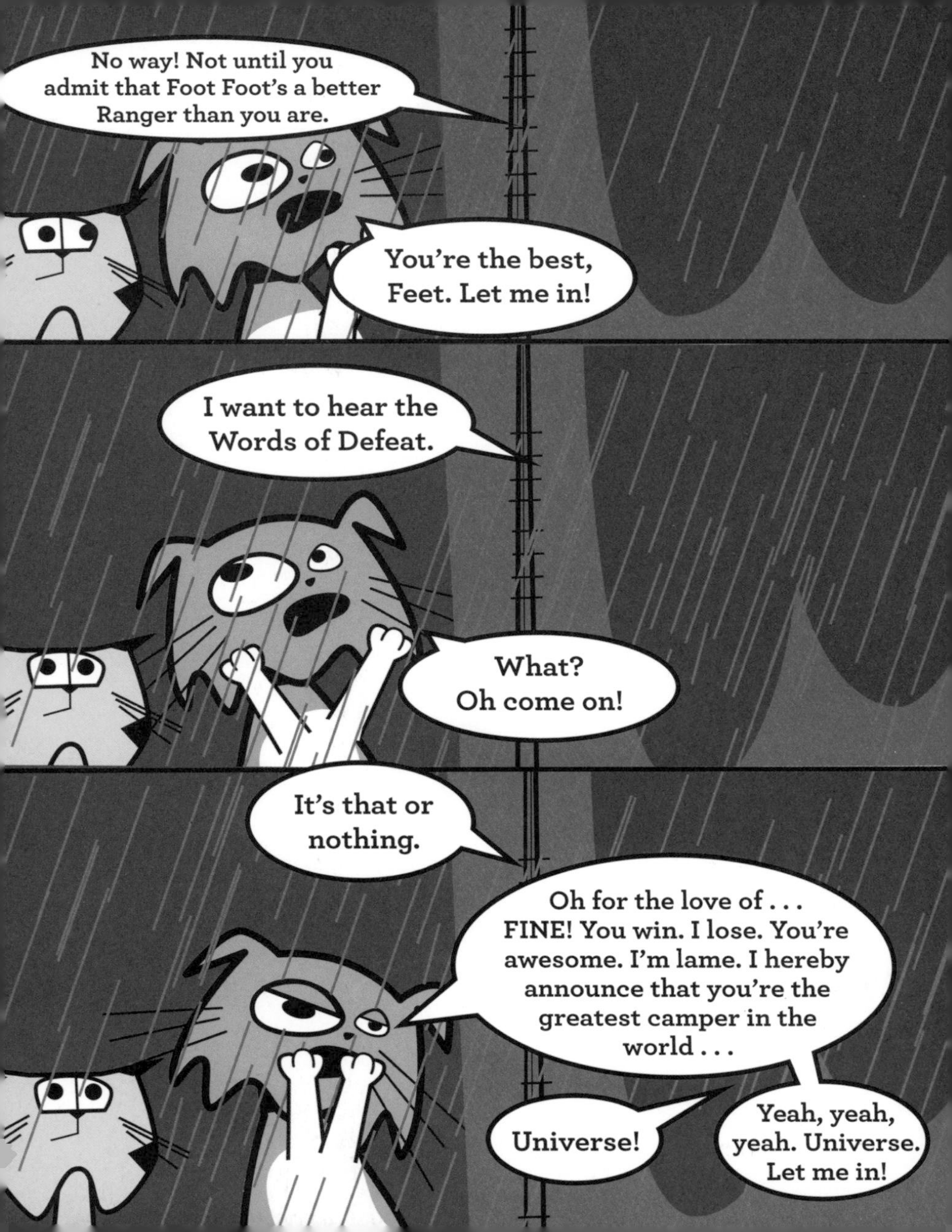
No way! Not until you admit that Foot Foot's a better Ranger than you are.
You're the best, Feet. Let me in!
I want to hear the Words of Defeat.
What? Oh come on!
It's that or nothing.
Oh for the love of . . . FINE! You win. I lose. You're awesome. I'm lame. I hereby announce that you're the greatest camper in the world . . .
Universe!
Yeah, yeah, yeah. Universe. Let me in!

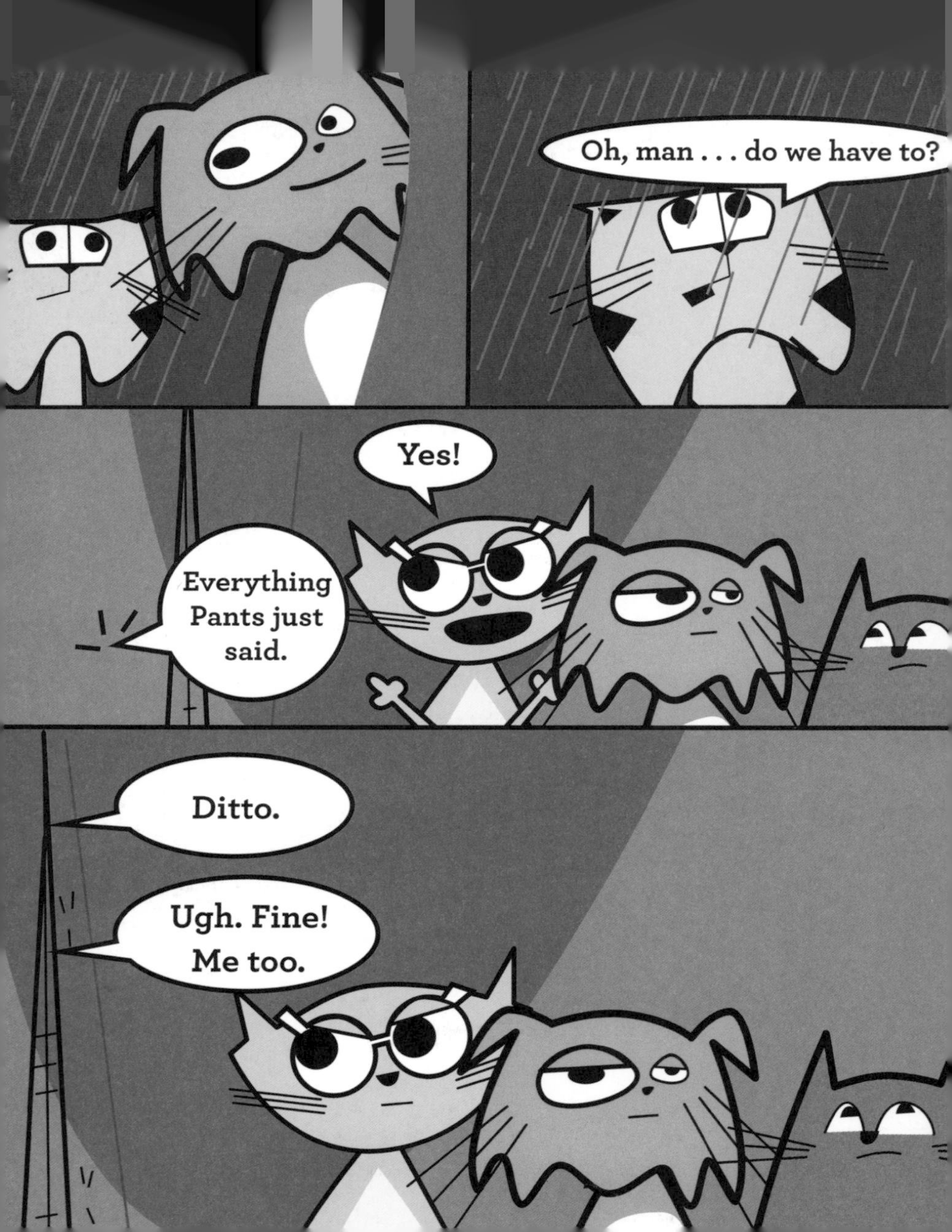
Oh, man . . . do we have to?
Yes!
Everything Pants just said.
Ditto.
Ugh. Fine! Me too.

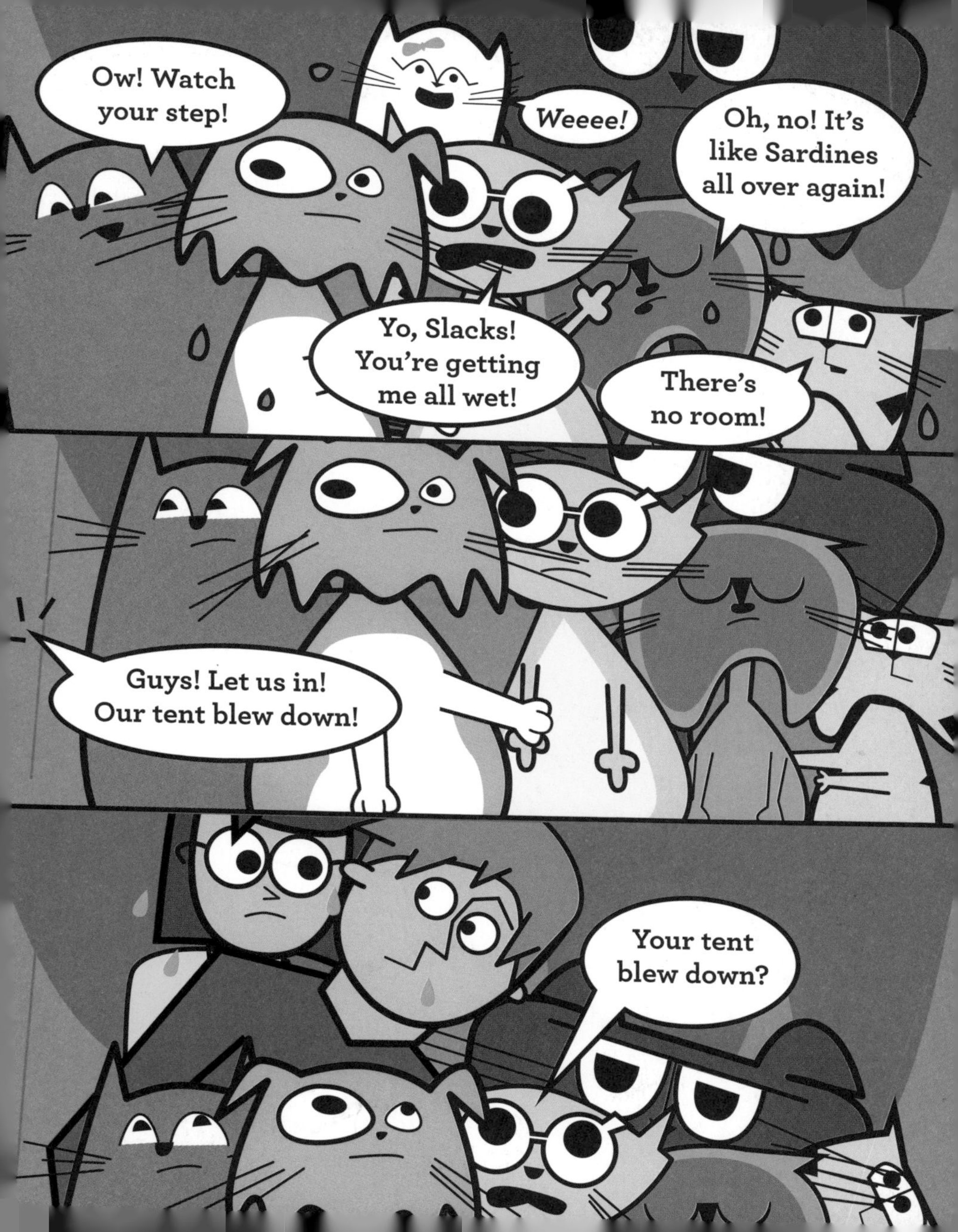
Ow! Watch your step!
Weeee!
Oh, no! It's like Sardines all over again!
Yo, Slacks! You're getting me all wet!
There's no room!
Guys! Let us in! Our tent blew down!
Your tent blew down?

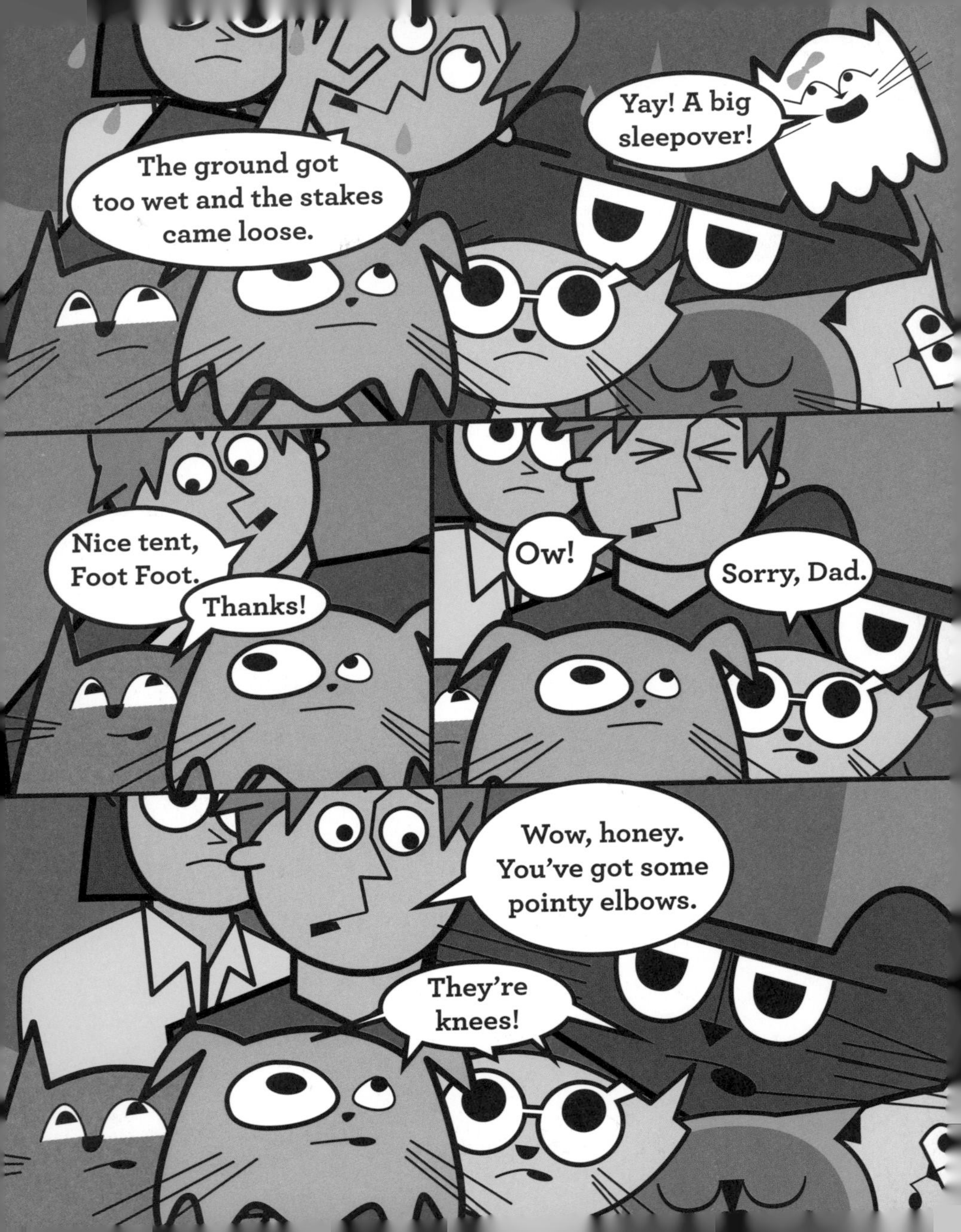
The ground got too wet and the stakes came loose.
Yay! A big sleepover!
Nice tent, Foot Foot.
Thanks!
Ow!
Sorry, Dad.
Wow, honey. You've got some pointy elbows.
They're knees!

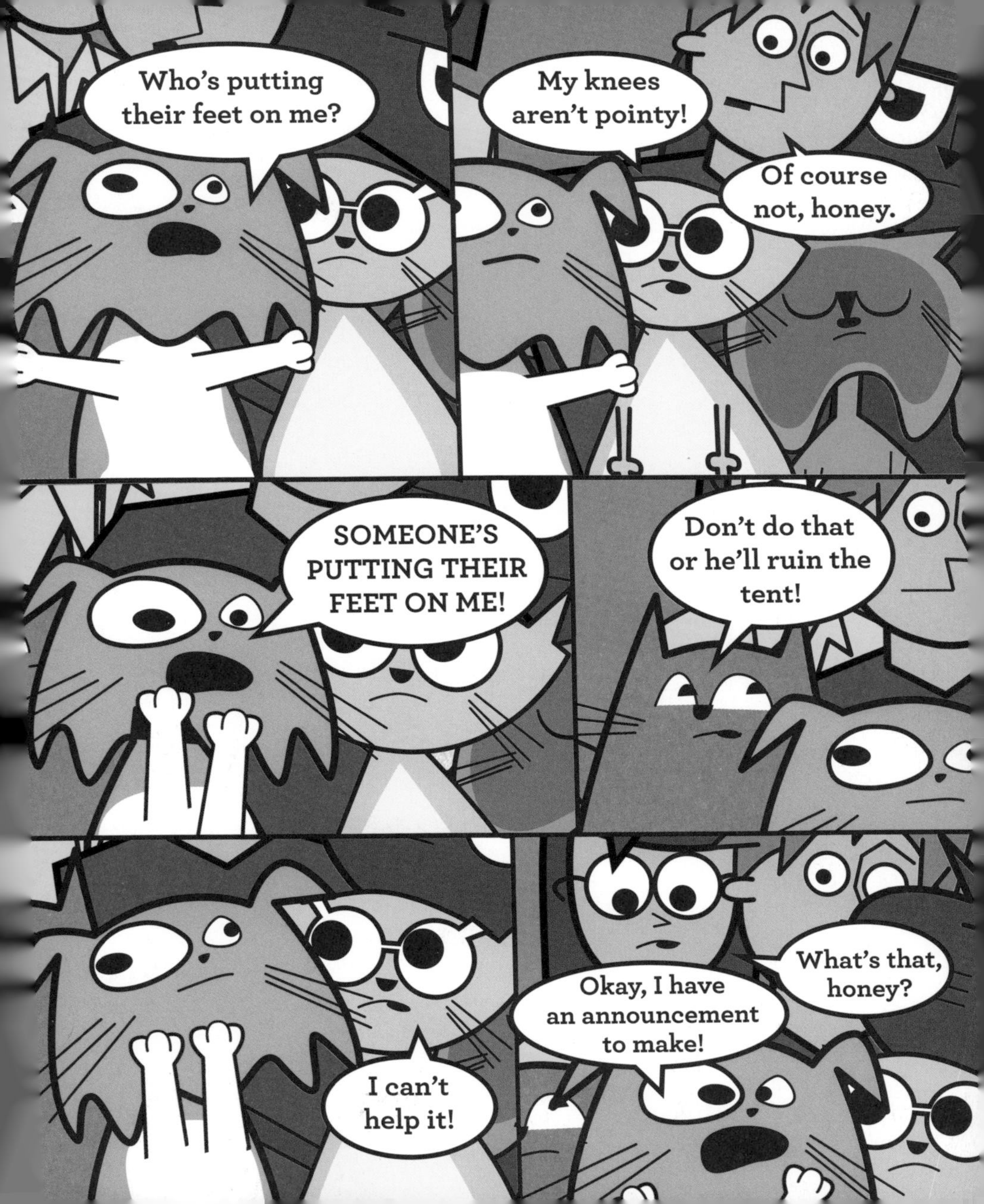
Who's putting their feet on me?
My knees aren't pointy!
Of course not, honey.
SOMEONE'S PUTTING THEIR FEET ON ME!
Don't do that or he'll ruin the tent!
I can't help it!
What's that, honey?
Okay, I have an announcement to make!

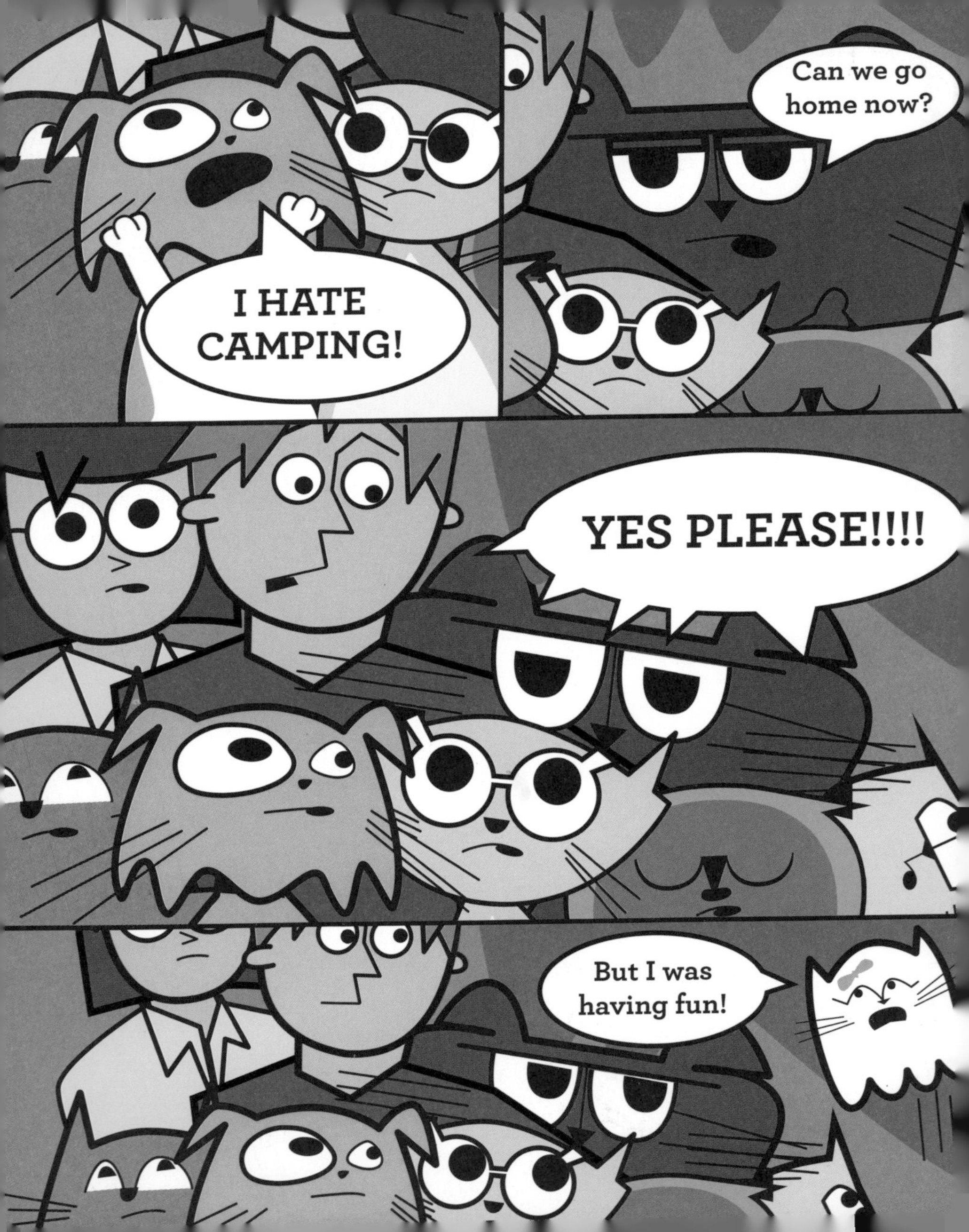
I HATE CAMPING!
Can we go home now?
YES PLEASE!!!!
But I was having fun!

Chapter Seven:

I HOPE YOU KNOW, THIS MEANS BAKE SALE

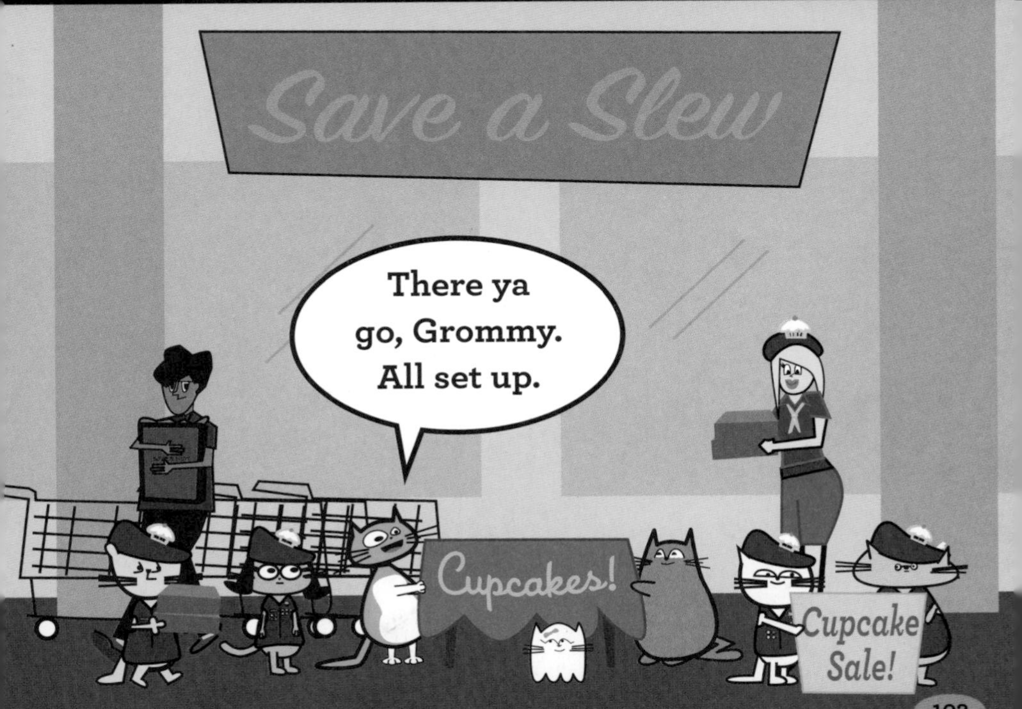

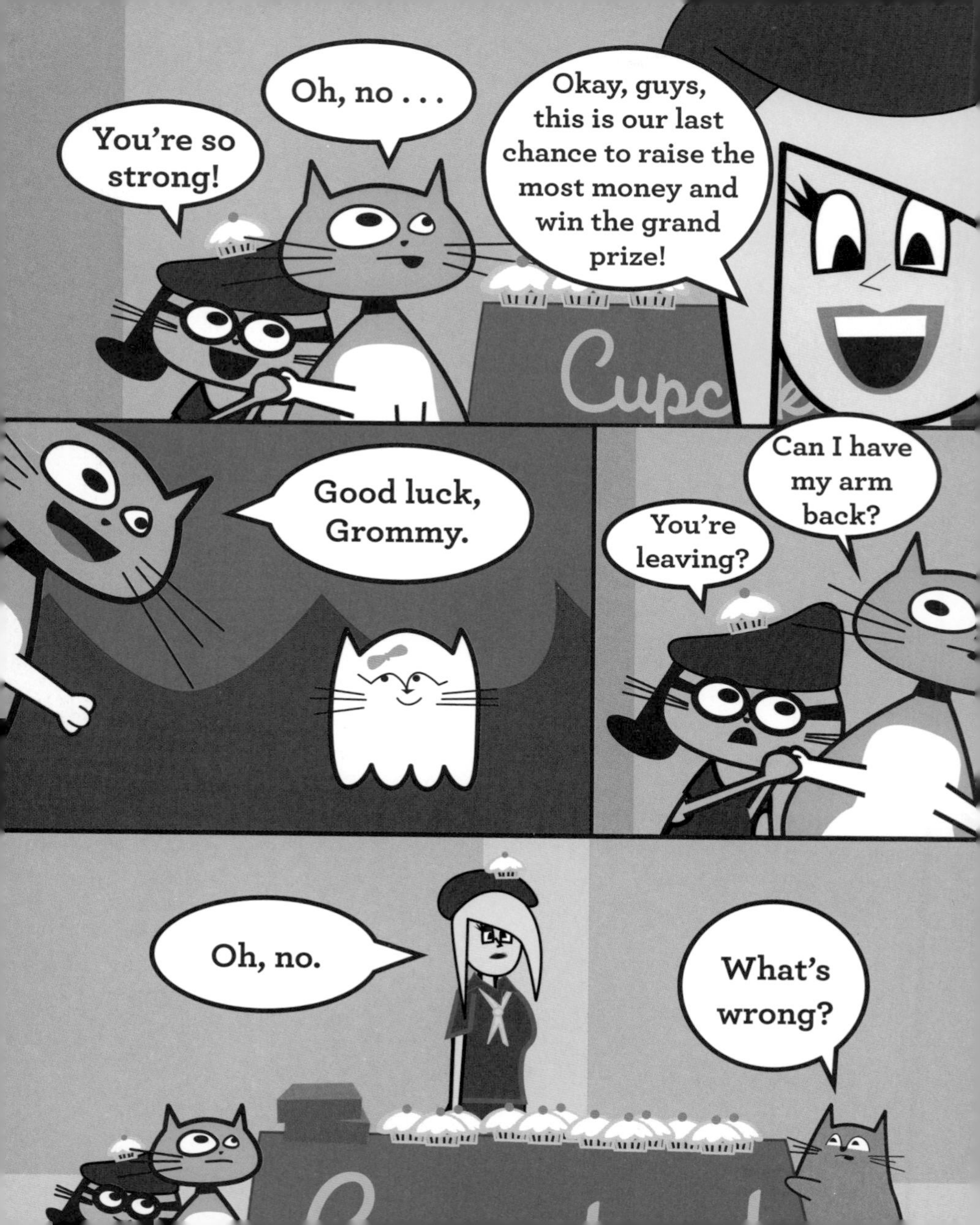
You're so strong!
Oh, no . . .
Okay, guys, this is our last chance to raise the most money and win the grand prize!
Good luck, Grommy.
Can I have my arm back?
You're leaving?
Oh, no.
What's wrong?

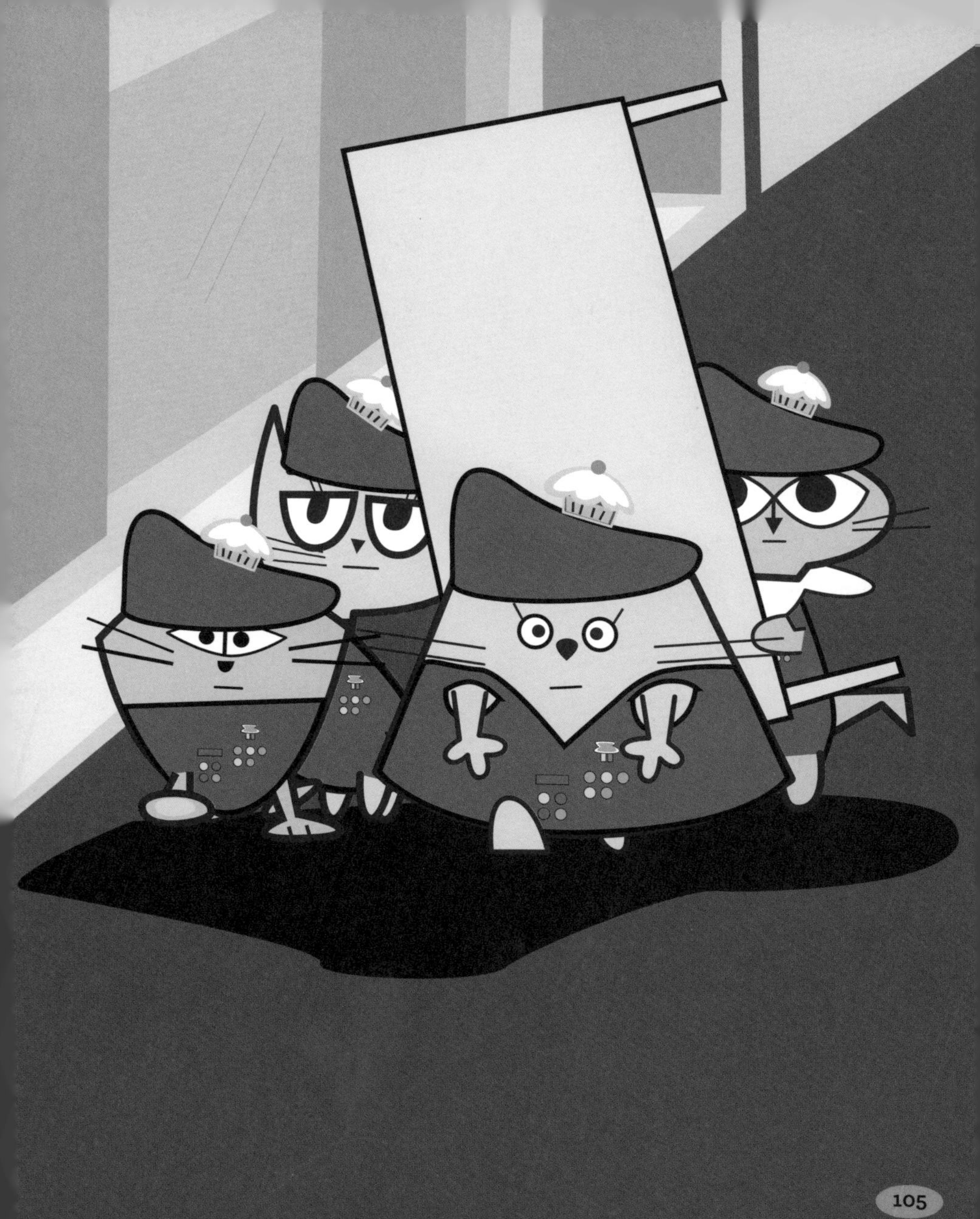

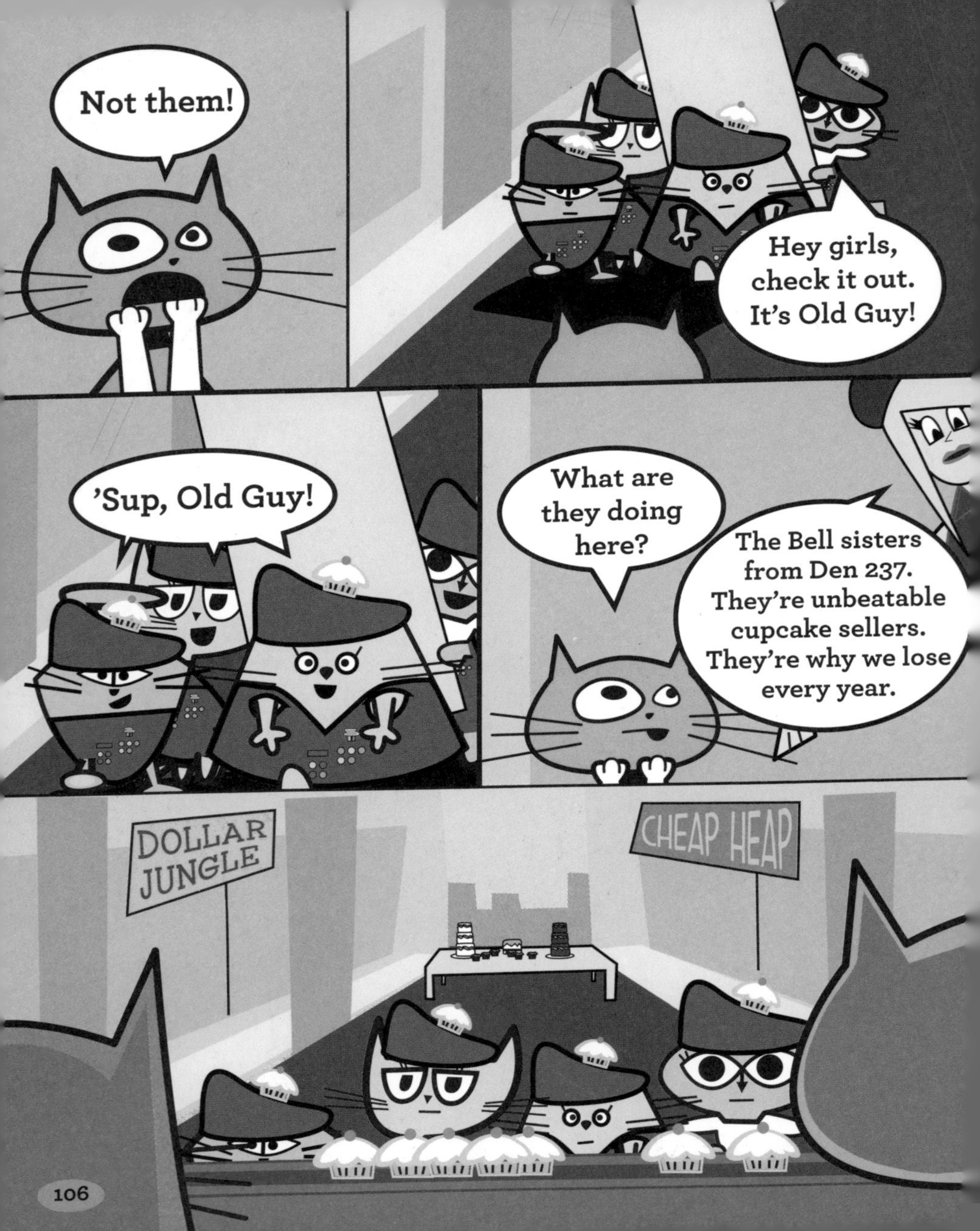
Not them!
Hey girls, check it out. It's Old Guy!
'Sup, Old Guy!
What are they doing here?
The Bell sisters from Den 237. They're unbeatable cupcake sellers. They're why we lose every year.
DOLLAR JUNGLE
CHEAP HEAP

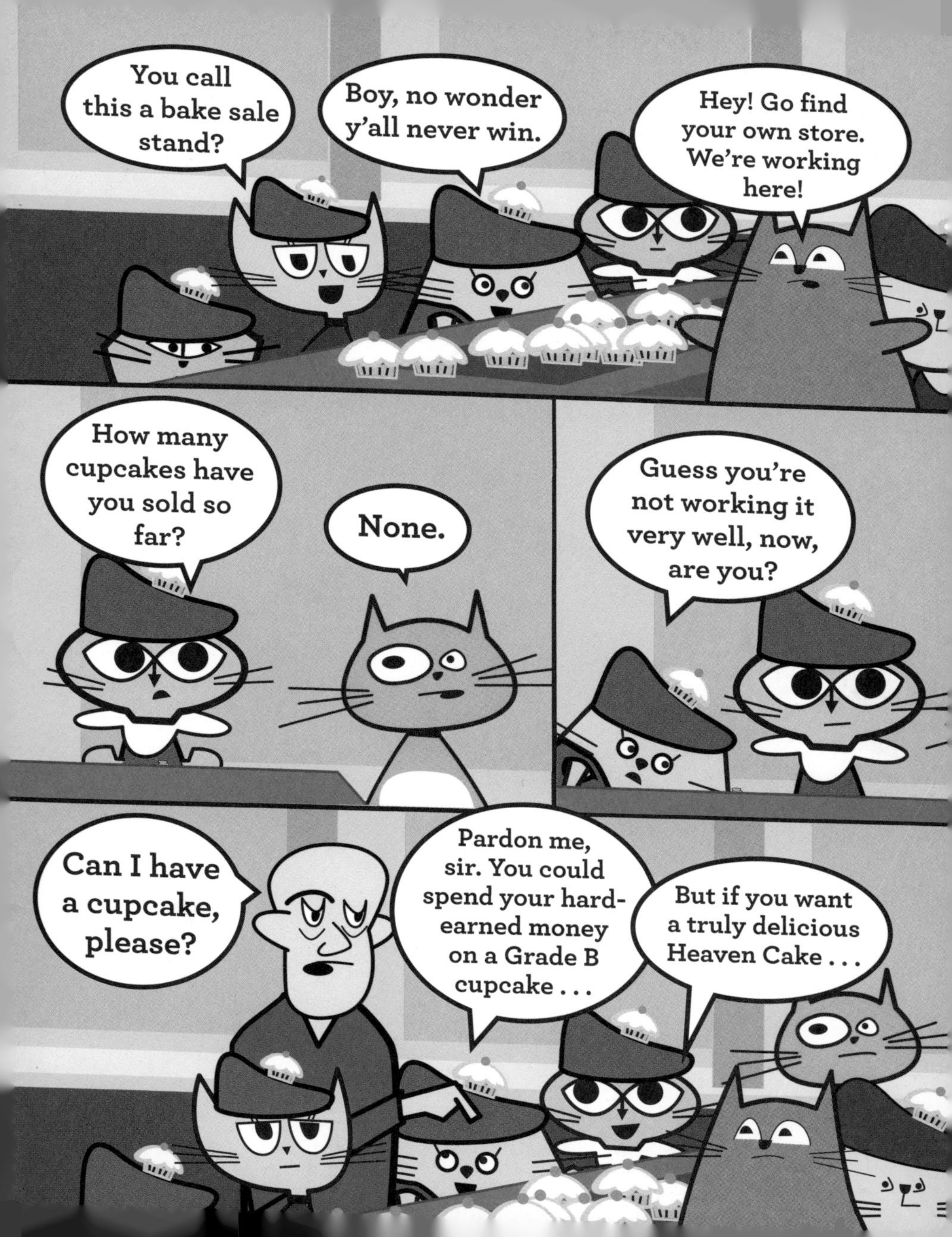

You call this a bake sale stand?
Boy, no wonder y'all never win.
Hey! Go find your own store. We're working here!
How many cupcakes have you sold so far?
None.
Guess you're not working it very well, now, are you?
Can I have a cupcake, please?
Pardon me, sir. You could spend your hard-earned money on a Grade B cupcake . . .
But if you want a truly delicious Heaven Cake . . .

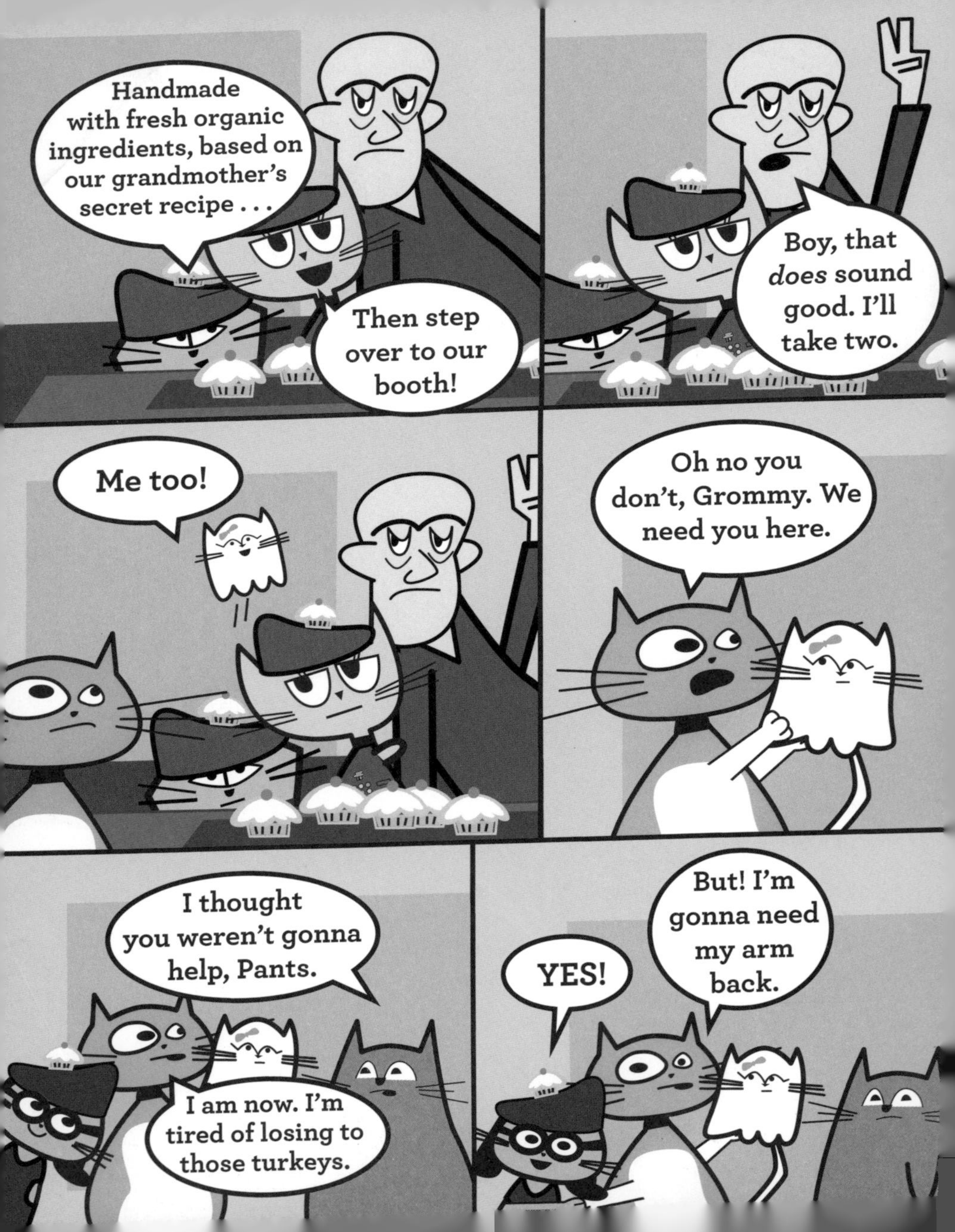
Handmade with fresh organic ingredients, based on our grandmother's secret recipe . . .
Then step over to our booth!
Boy, that *does* sound good. I'll take two.
Me too!
Oh no you don't, Grommy. We need you here.
I thought you weren't gonna help, Pants.
I am now. I'm tired of losing to those turkeys.
YES!
But! I'm gonna need my arm back.

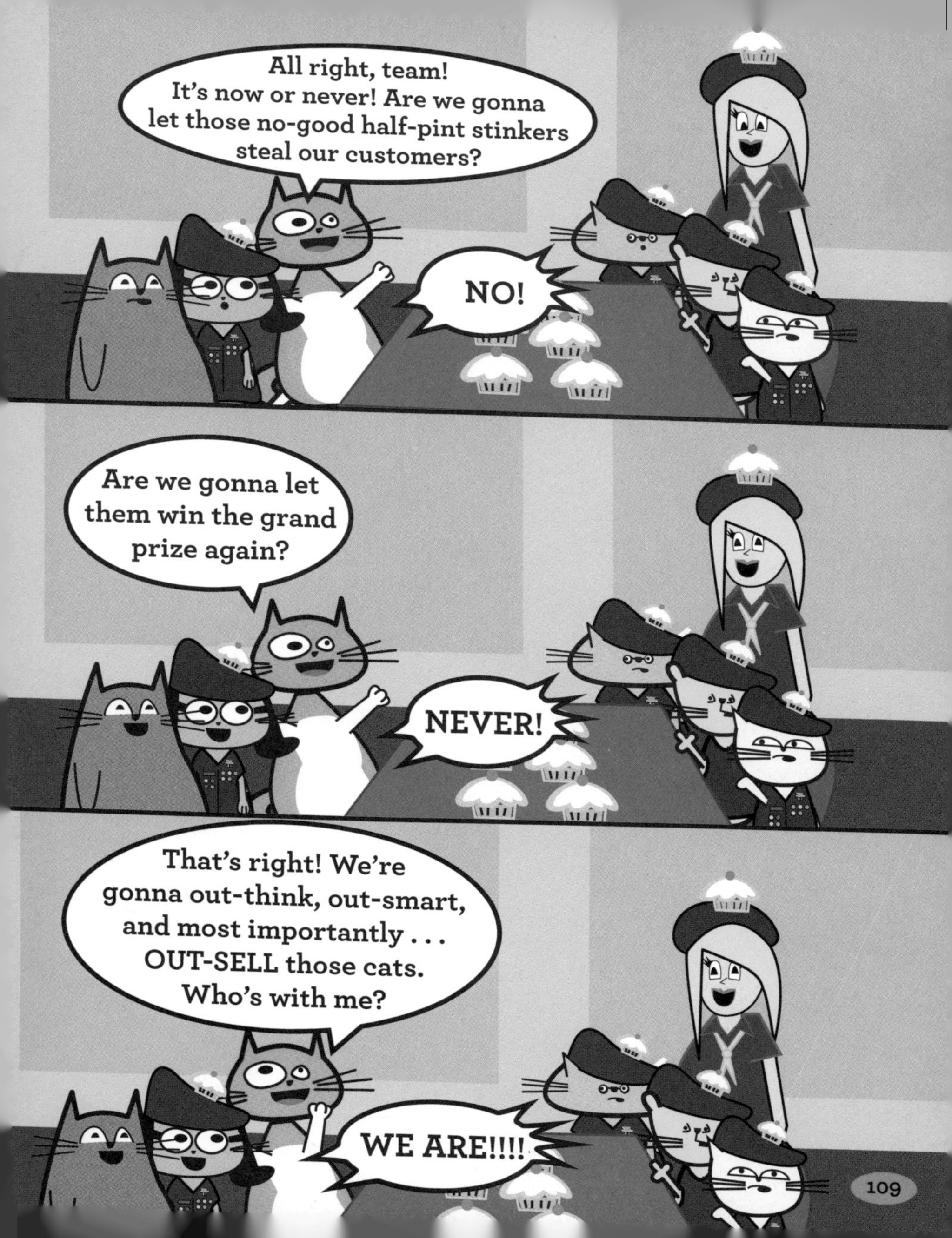
All right, team! It's now or never! Are we gonna let those no-good half-pint stinkers steal our customers?
NO!
Are we gonna let them win the grand prize again?
NEVER!
That's right! We're gonna out-think, out-smart, and most importantly . . . OUT-SELL those cats. Who's with me?
WE ARE!!!!

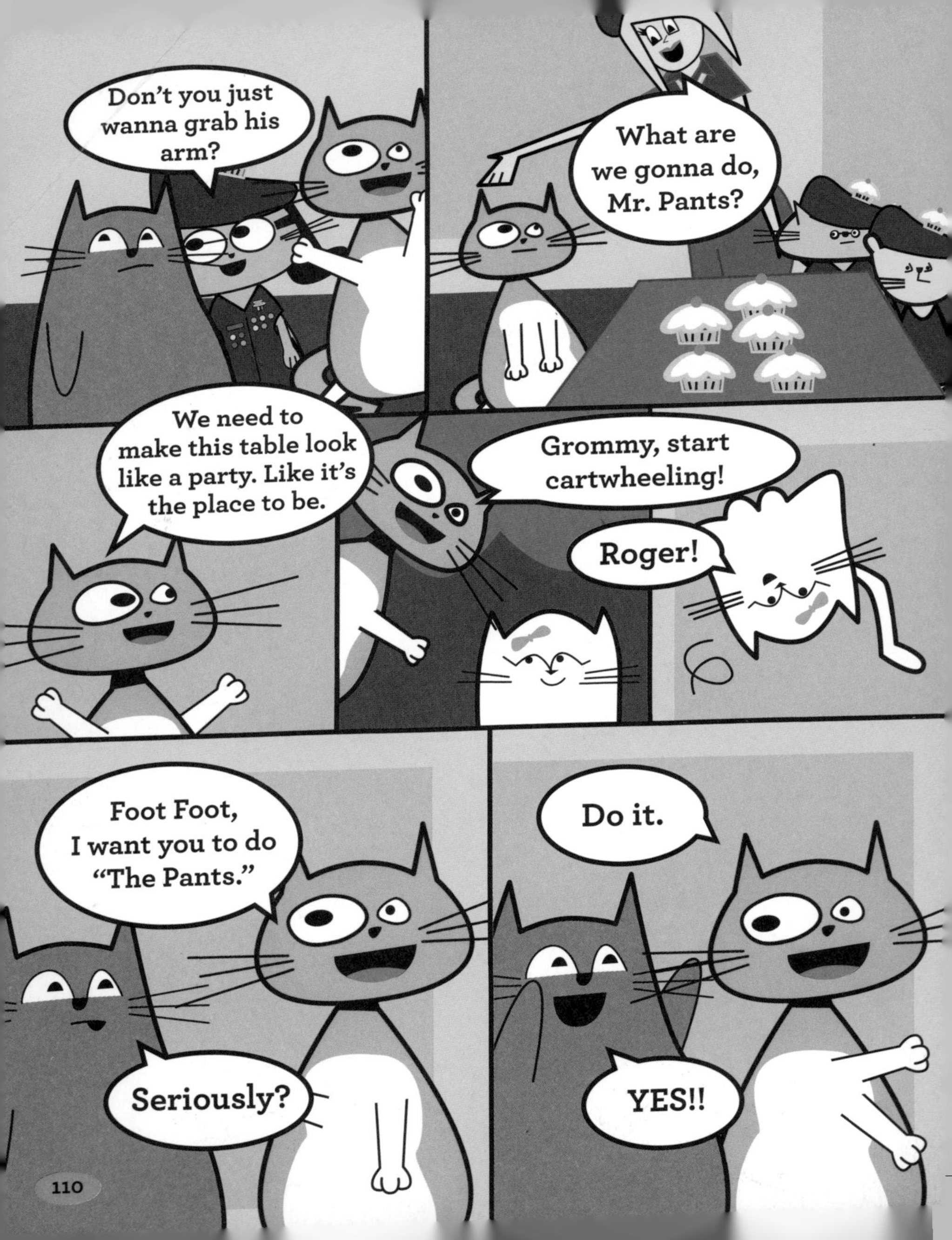

Don't you just wanna grab his arm?
What are we gonna do, Mr. Pants?
We need to make this table look like a party. Like it's the place to be.
Grommy, start cartwheeling!
Roger!
Foot Foot, I want you to do "The Pants."
Seriously?
Do it.
YES!!

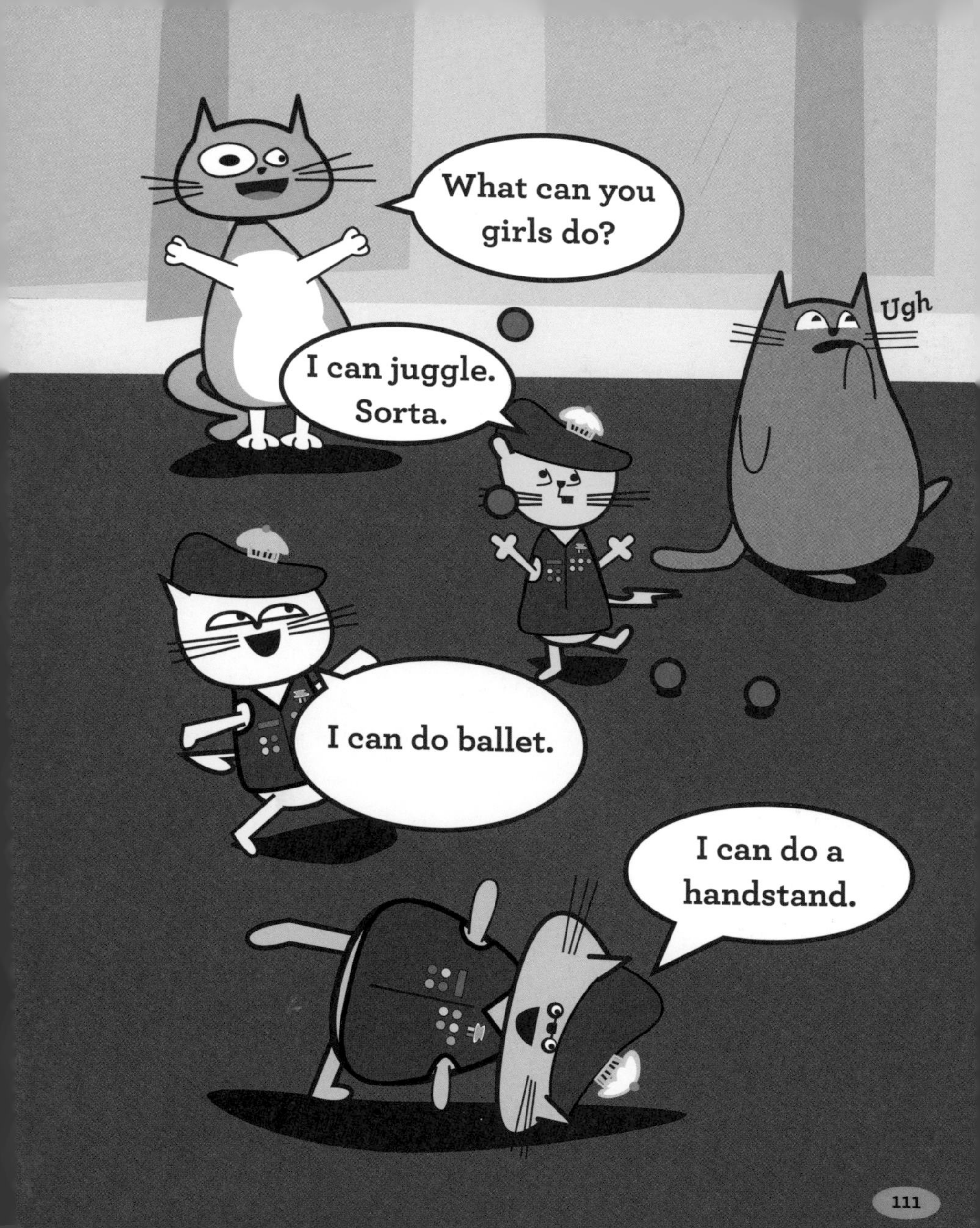
What can you girls do?
Ugh
I can juggle. Sorta.
I can do ballet.
I can do a handstand.

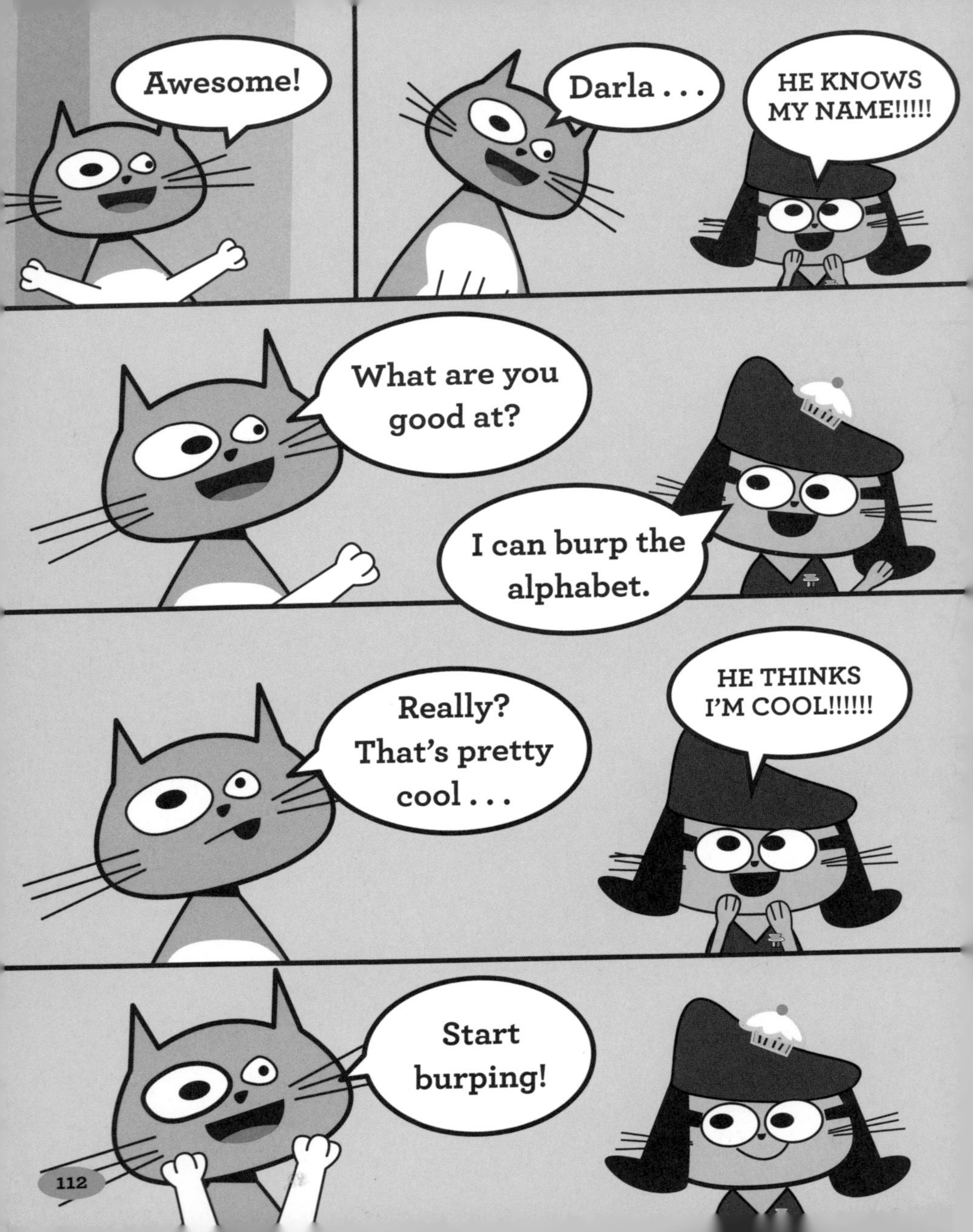
Awesome!
Darla . . .
HE KNOWS MY NAME!!!!!
What are you good at?
I can burp the alphabet.
Really? That's pretty cool . . .
HE THINKS I'M COOL!!!!!!
Start burping!

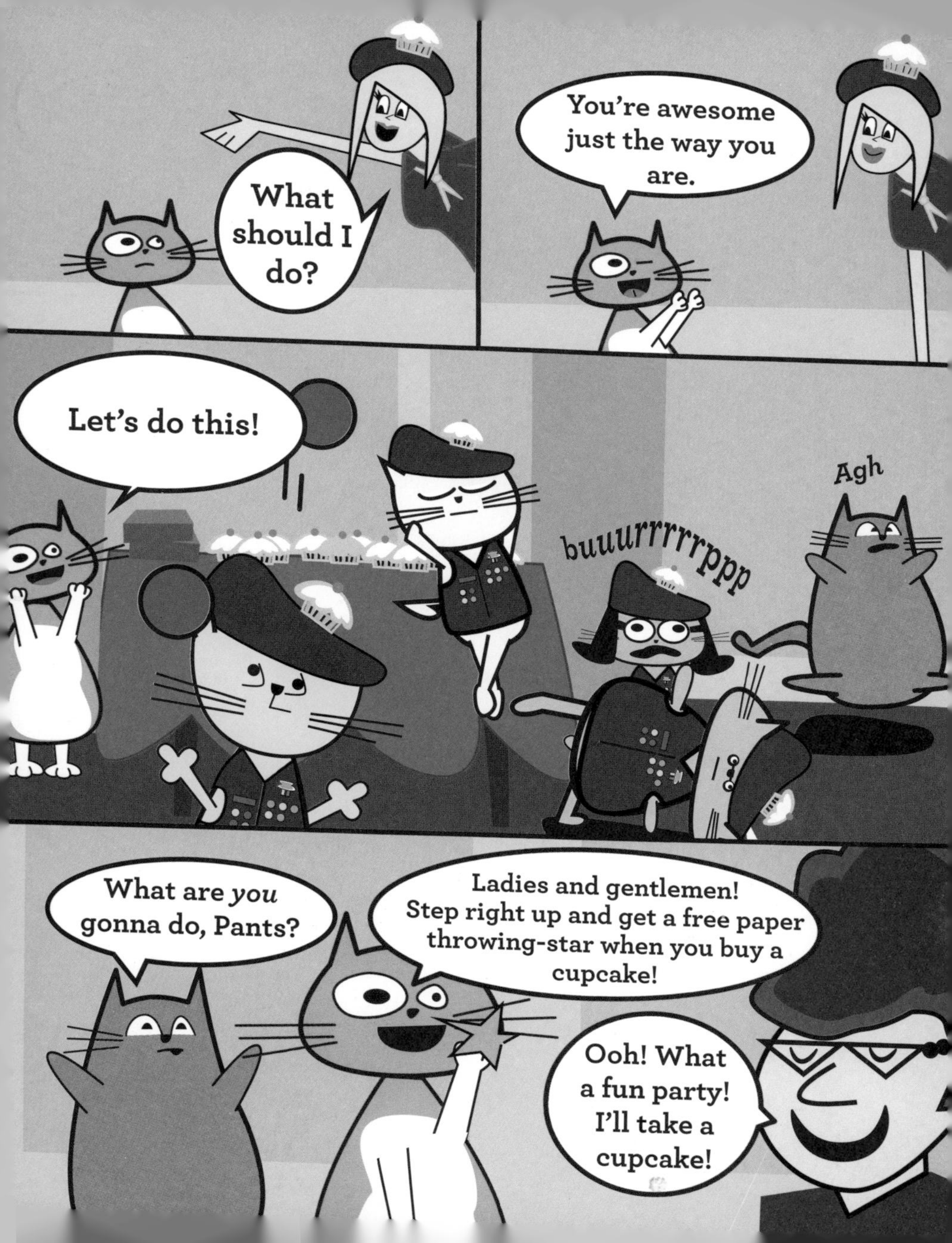

What should I do?
You're awesome just the way you are.
Let's do this!
Agh
buuurrrrrppp
What are *you* gonna do, Pants?
Ladies and gentlemen! Step right up and get a free paper throwing-star when you buy a cupcake!
Ooh! What a fun party! I'll take a cupcake!

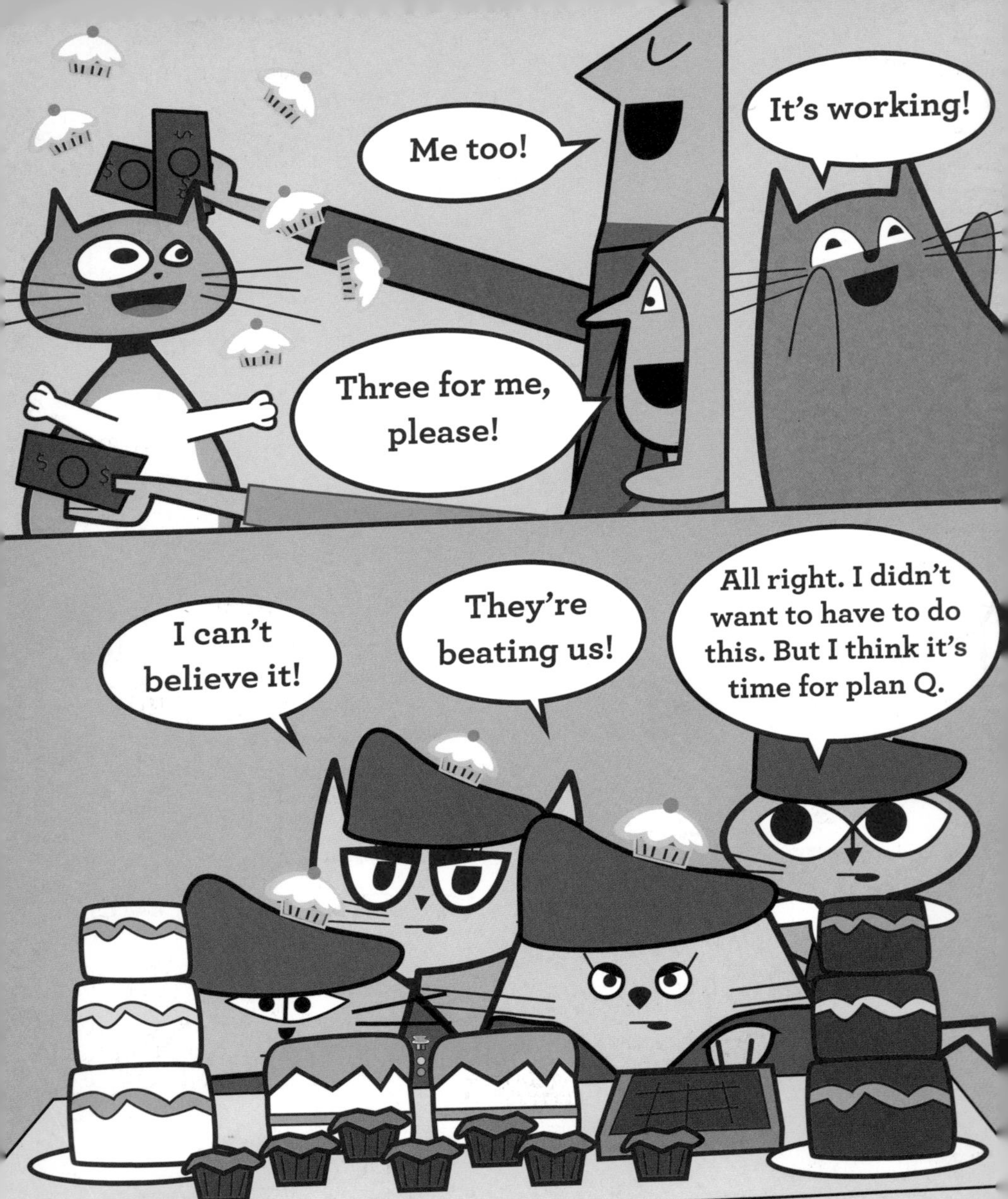
Me too!
It's working!
Three for me, please!
I can't believe it!
They're beating us!
All right. I didn't want to have to do this. But I think it's time for plan Q.

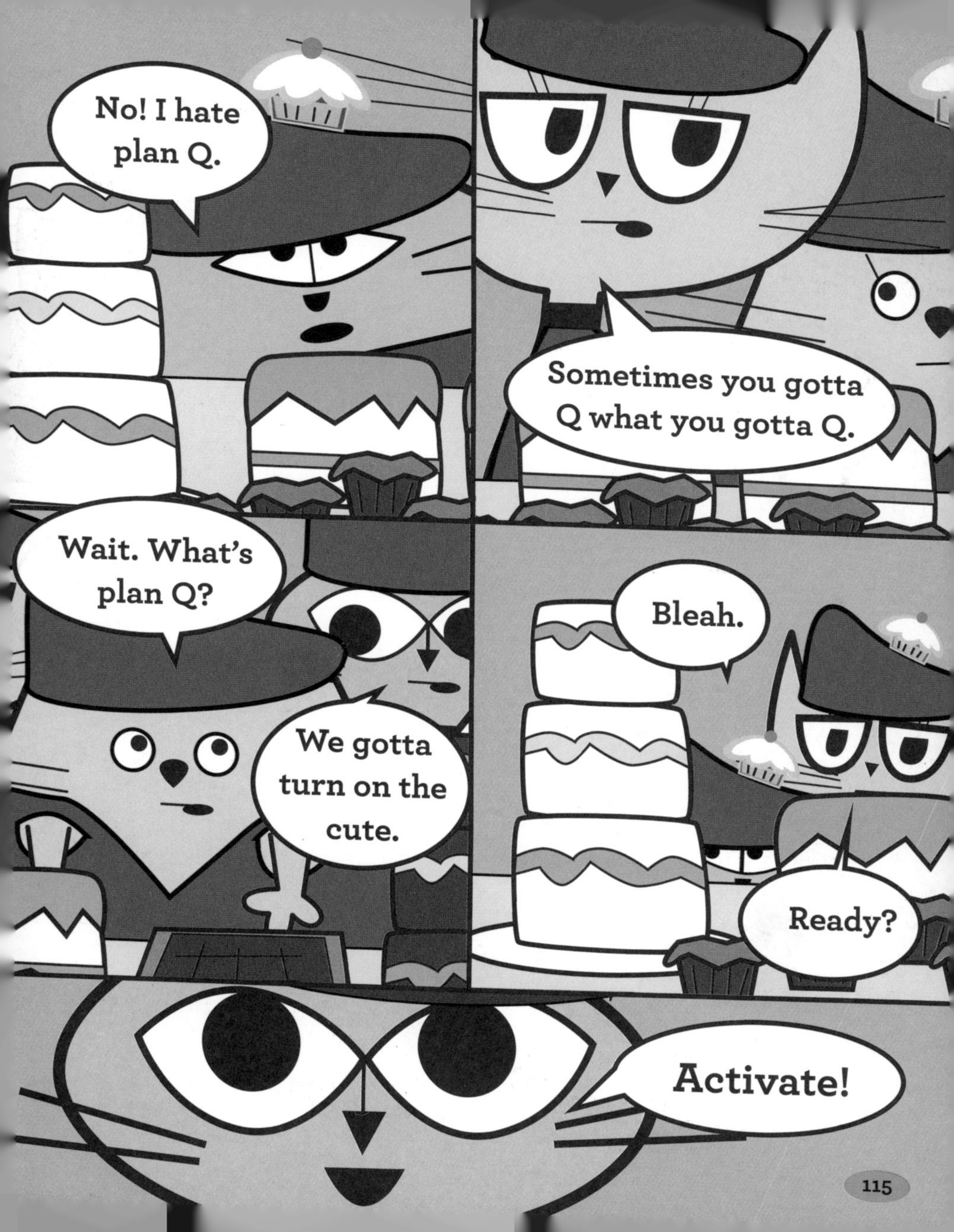
No! I hate plan Q.
Sometimes you gotta Q what you gotta Q.
Wait. What's plan Q?
We gotta turn on the cute.
Bleah.
Ready?
Activate!

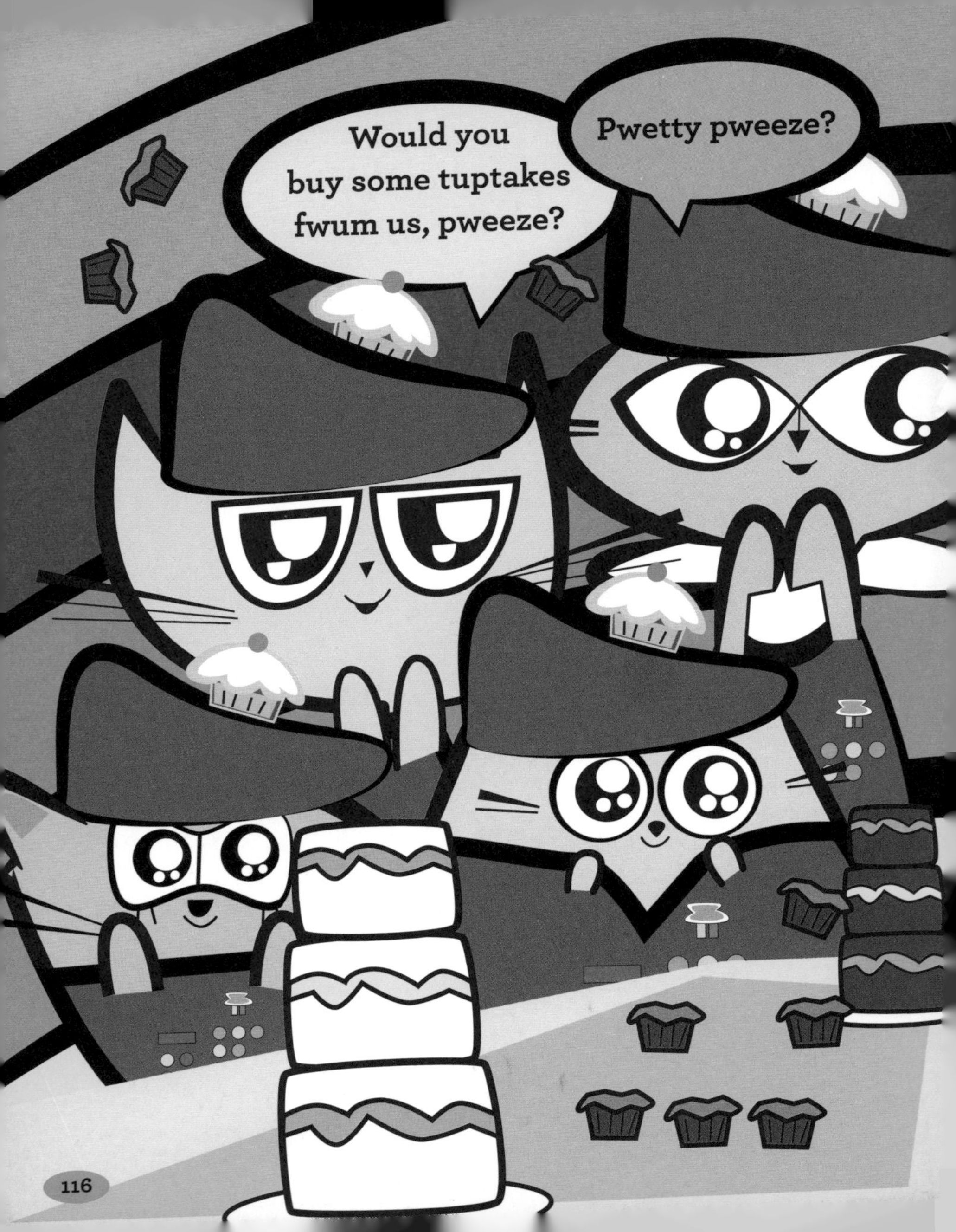
Would you buy some tuptakes fwum us, pweeze?
Pwetty pweeze?

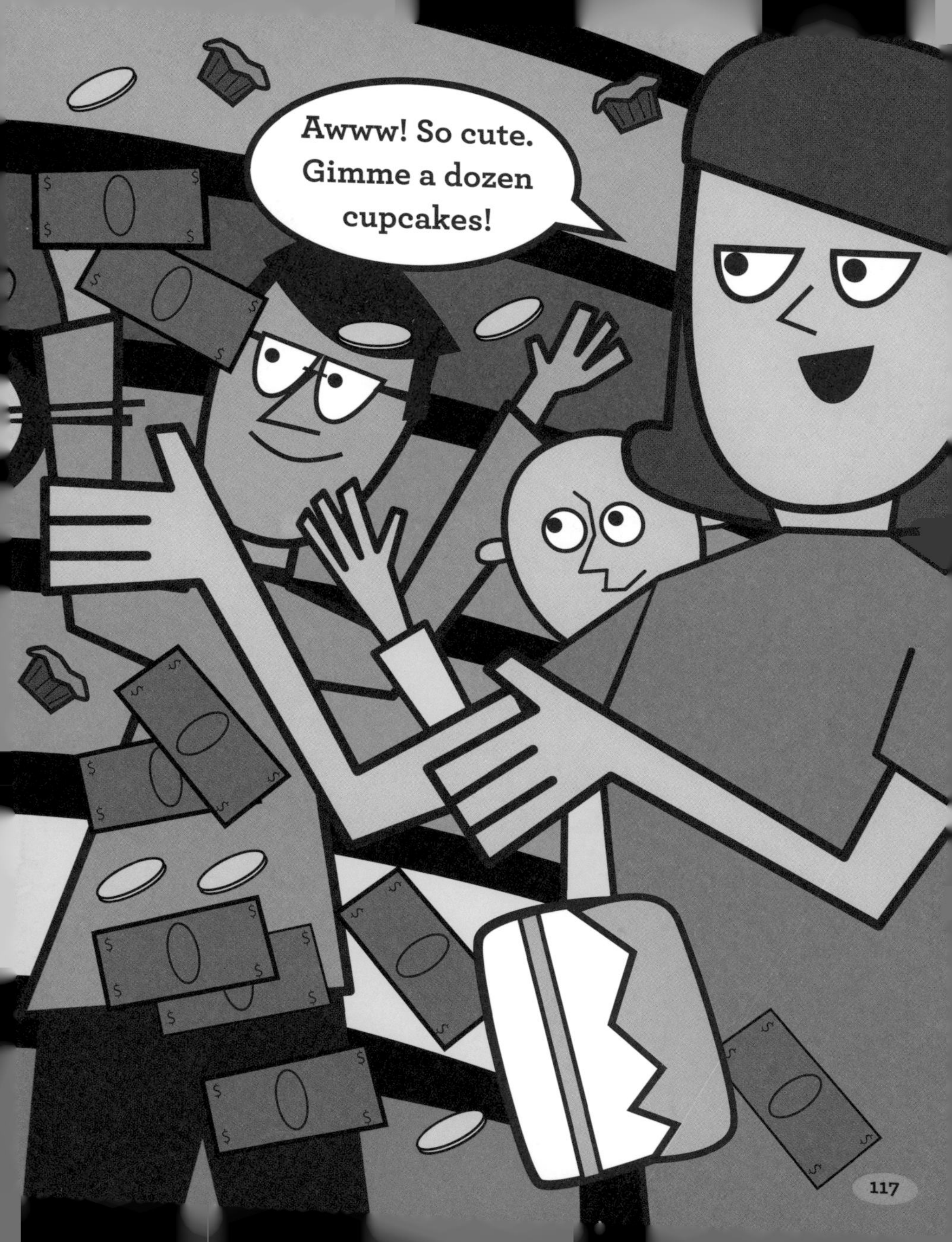
Awww! So cute. Gimme a dozen cupcakes!

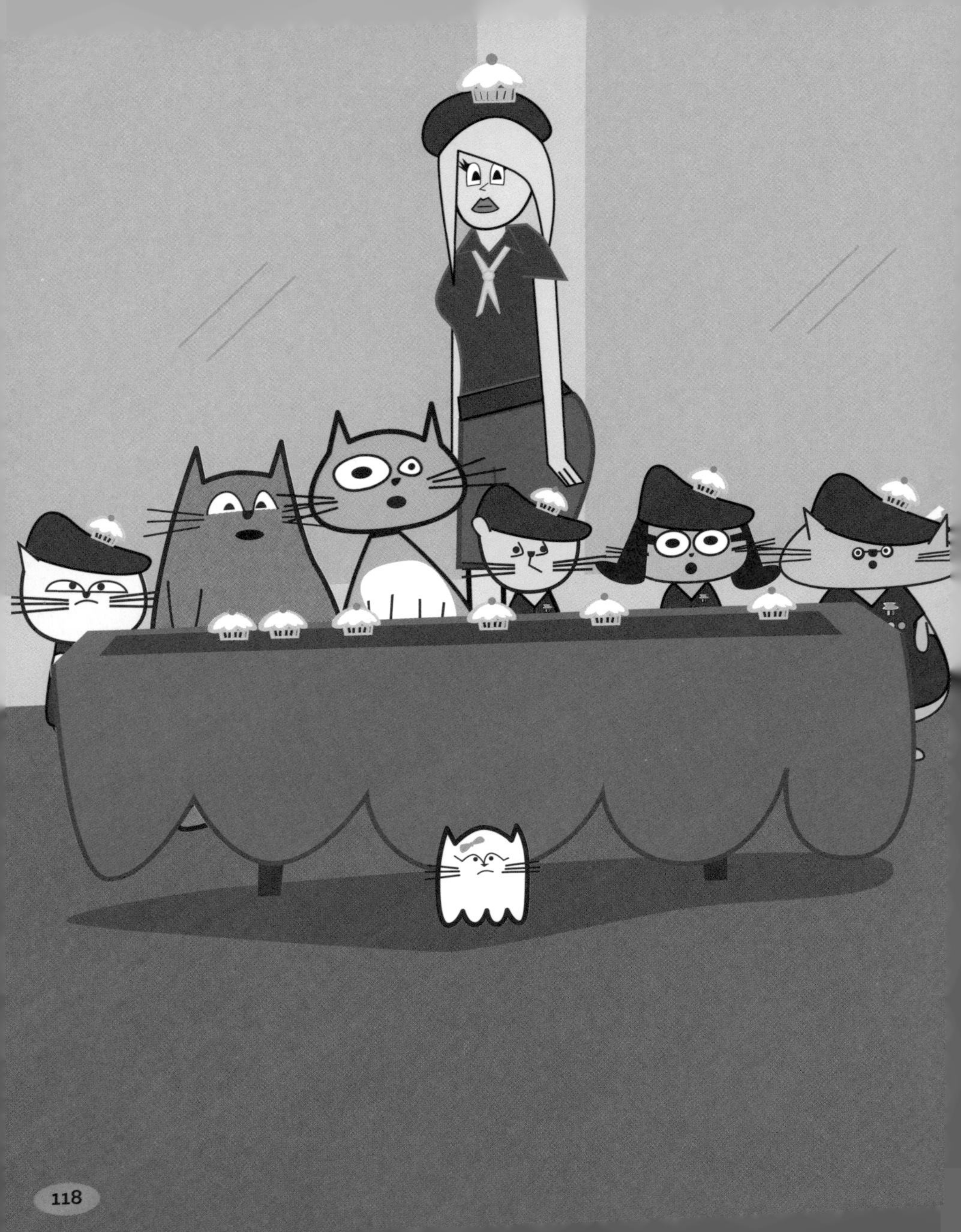

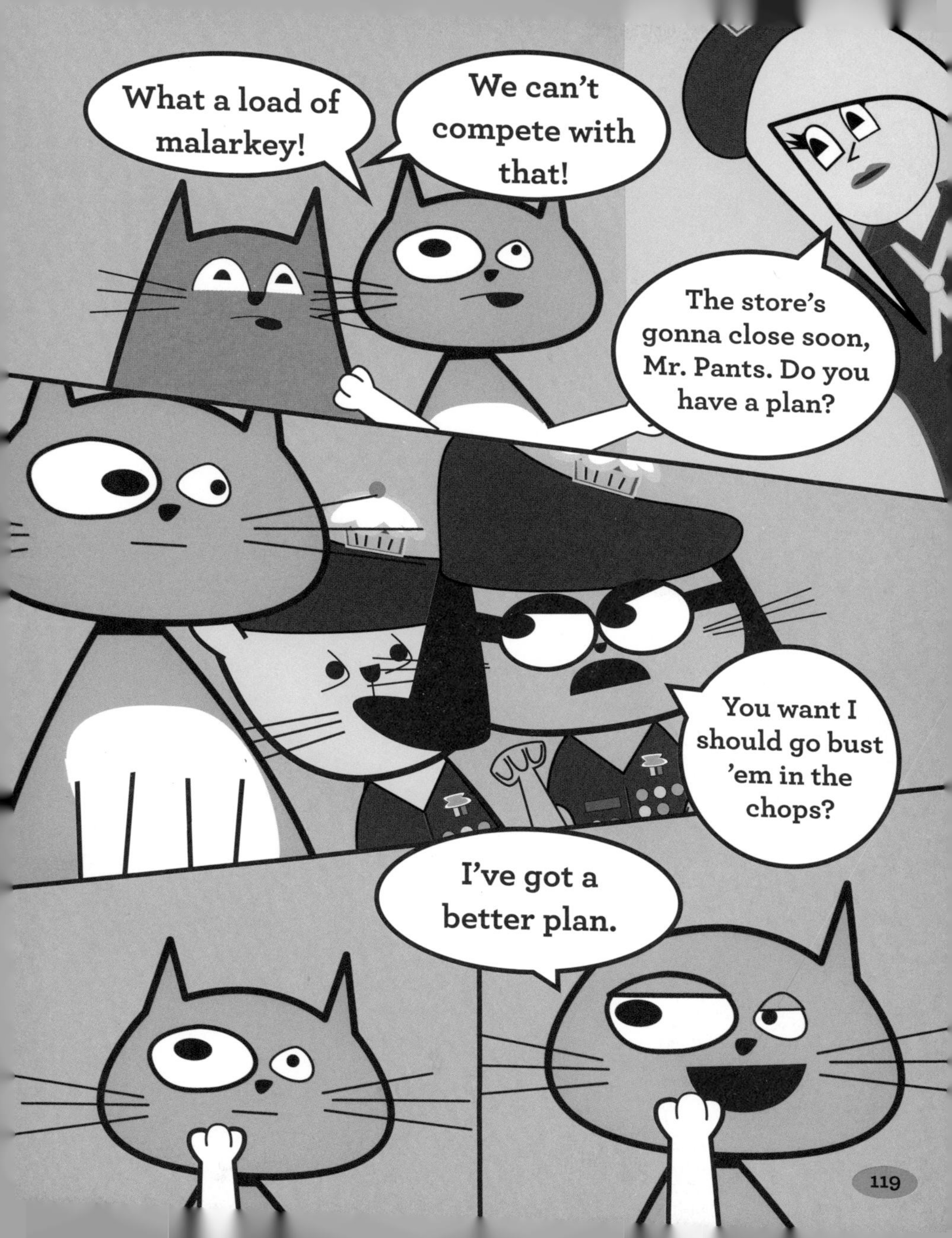
What a load of malarkey!
We can't compete with that!
The store's gonna close soon, Mr. Pants. Do you have a plan?
You want I should go bust 'em in the chops?
I've got a better plan.

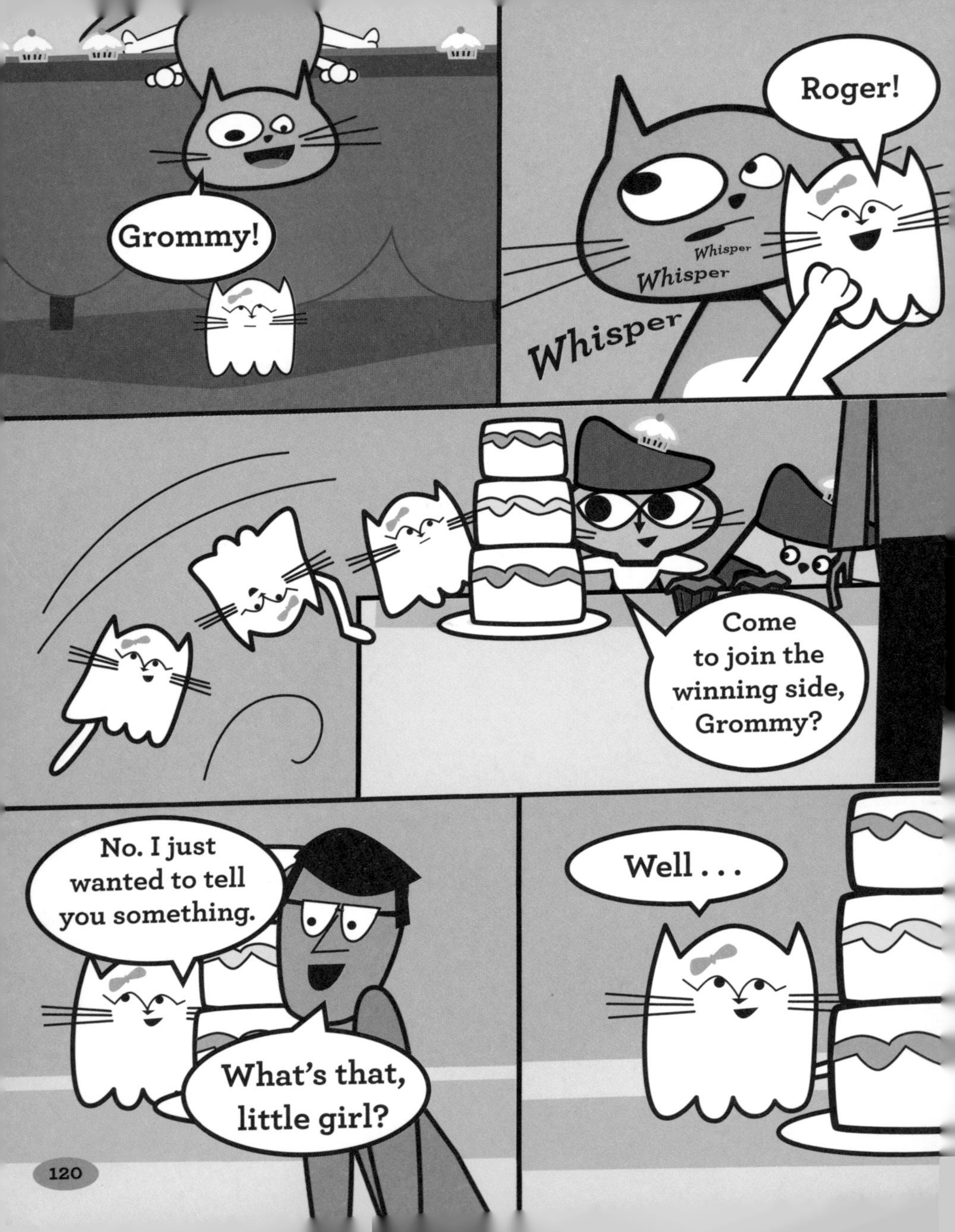

Grommy!
Roger!
Whisper
Whisper
Whisper
Come to join the winning side, Grommy?
No. I just wanted to tell you something.
What's that, little girl?
Well . . .

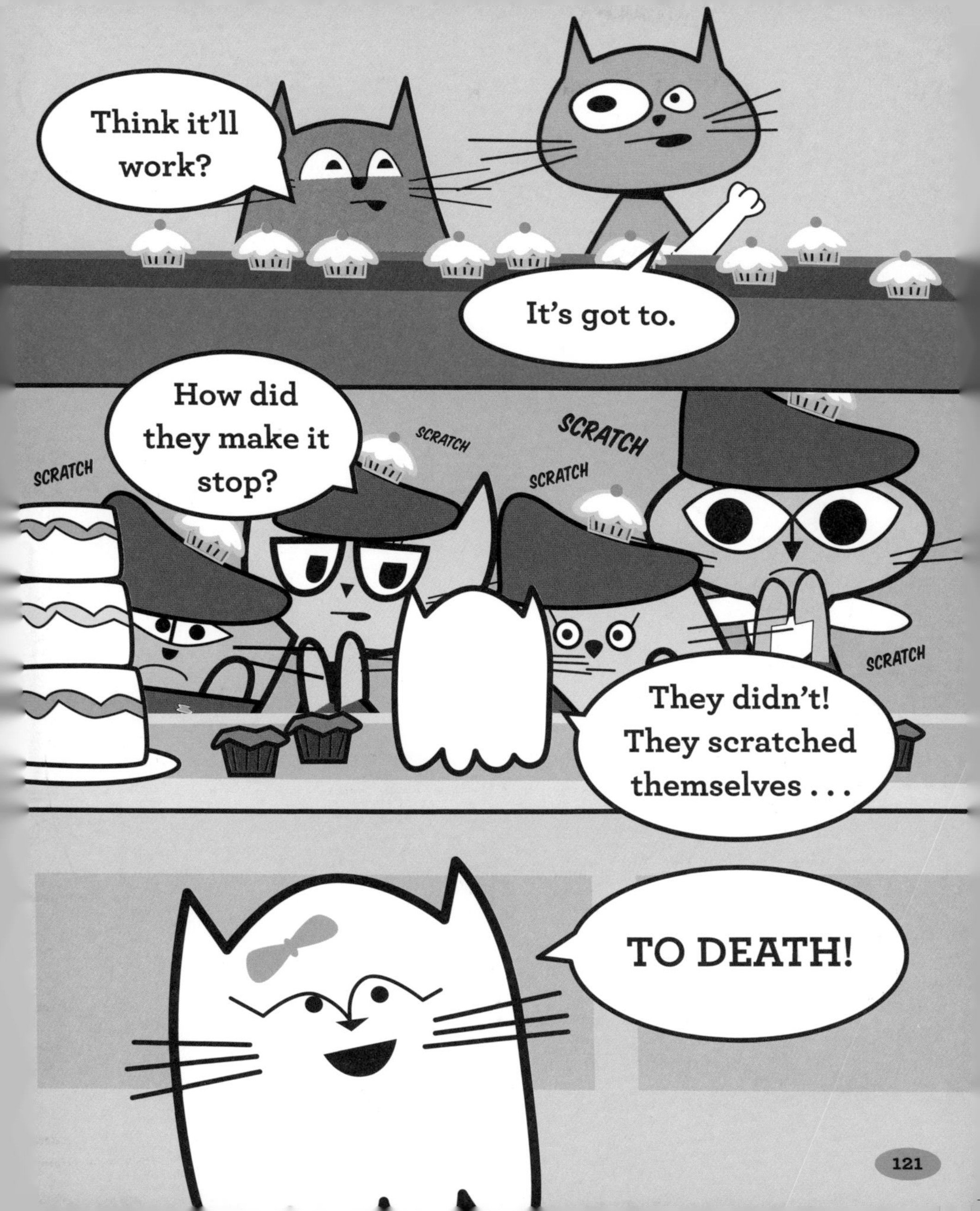

Think it'll work?
It's got to.
How did they make it stop?
SCRATCH
SCRATCH
SCRATCH
SCRATCH
SCRATCH
They didn't! They scratched themselves . . .
TO DEATH!

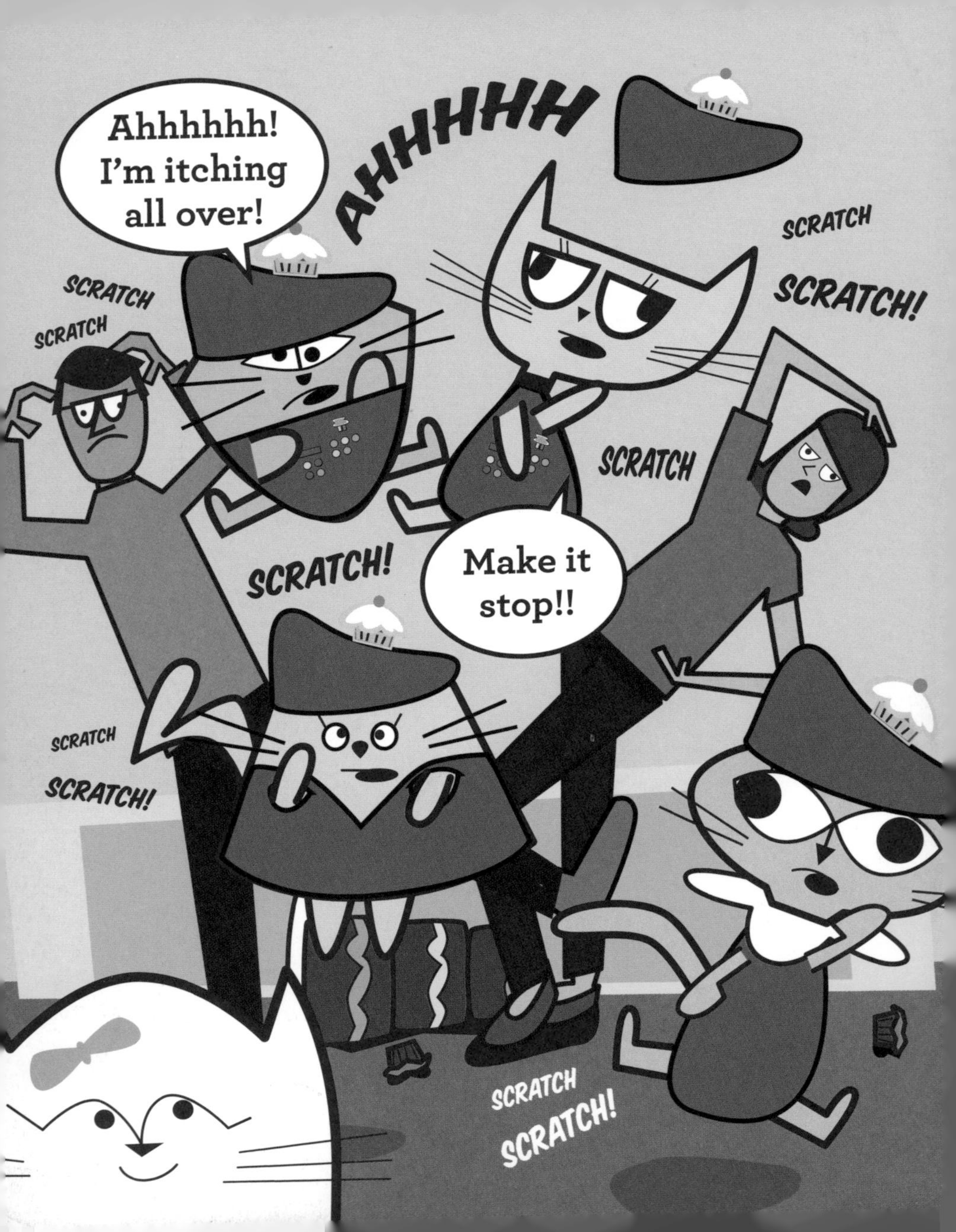
Ahhhhhh! I'm itching all over!
AHHHHHH
SCRATCH
SCRATCH!
SCRATCH
SCRATCH
SCRATCH
SCRATCH!
Make it stop!!
SCRATCH
SCRATCH!
SCRATCH
SCRATCH!

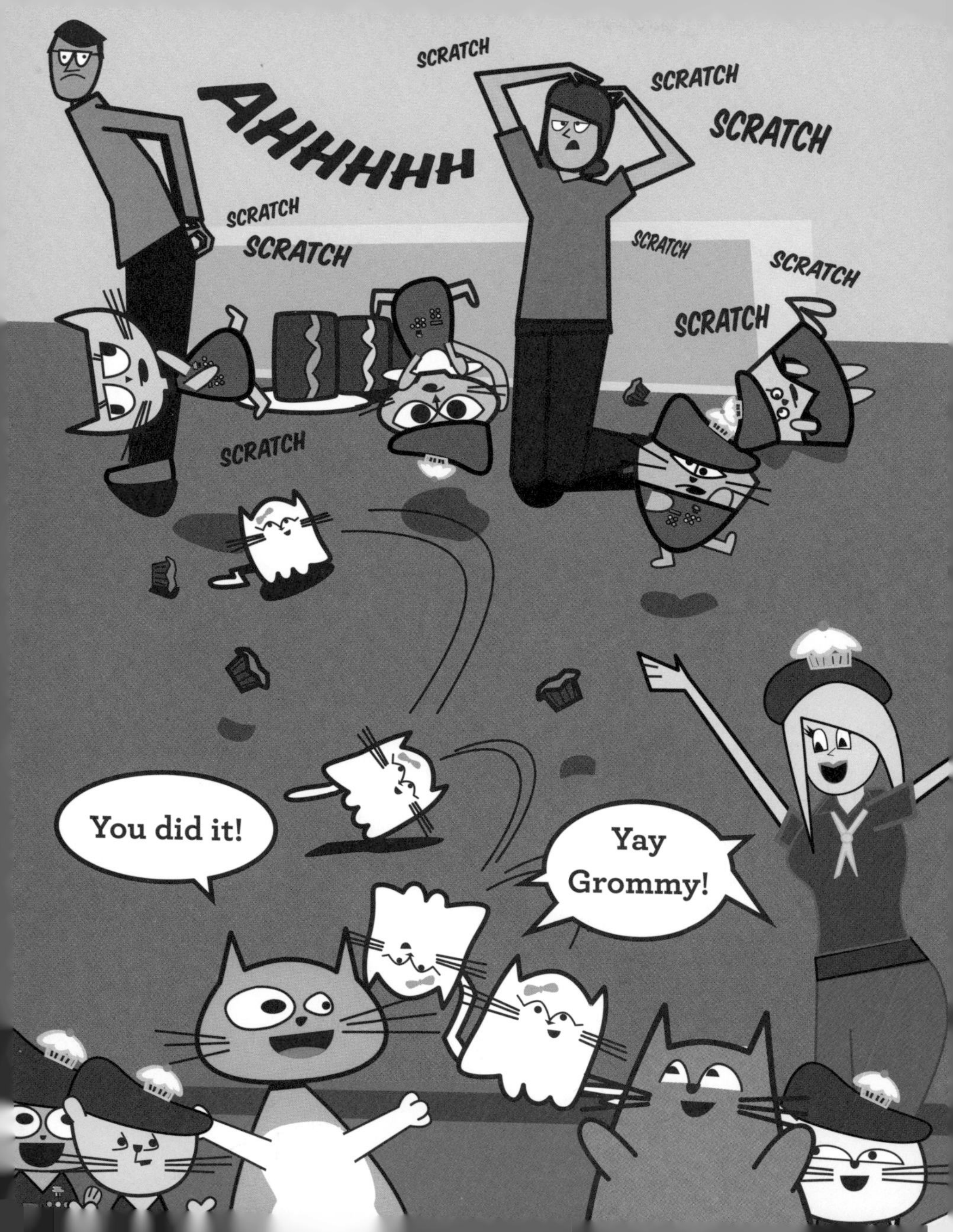
SCRATCH
AHHHHHH
SCRATCH
SCRATCH
SCRATCH
SCRATCH
SCRATCH
SCRATCH
SCRATCH
SCRATCH
You did it!
Yay Grommy!

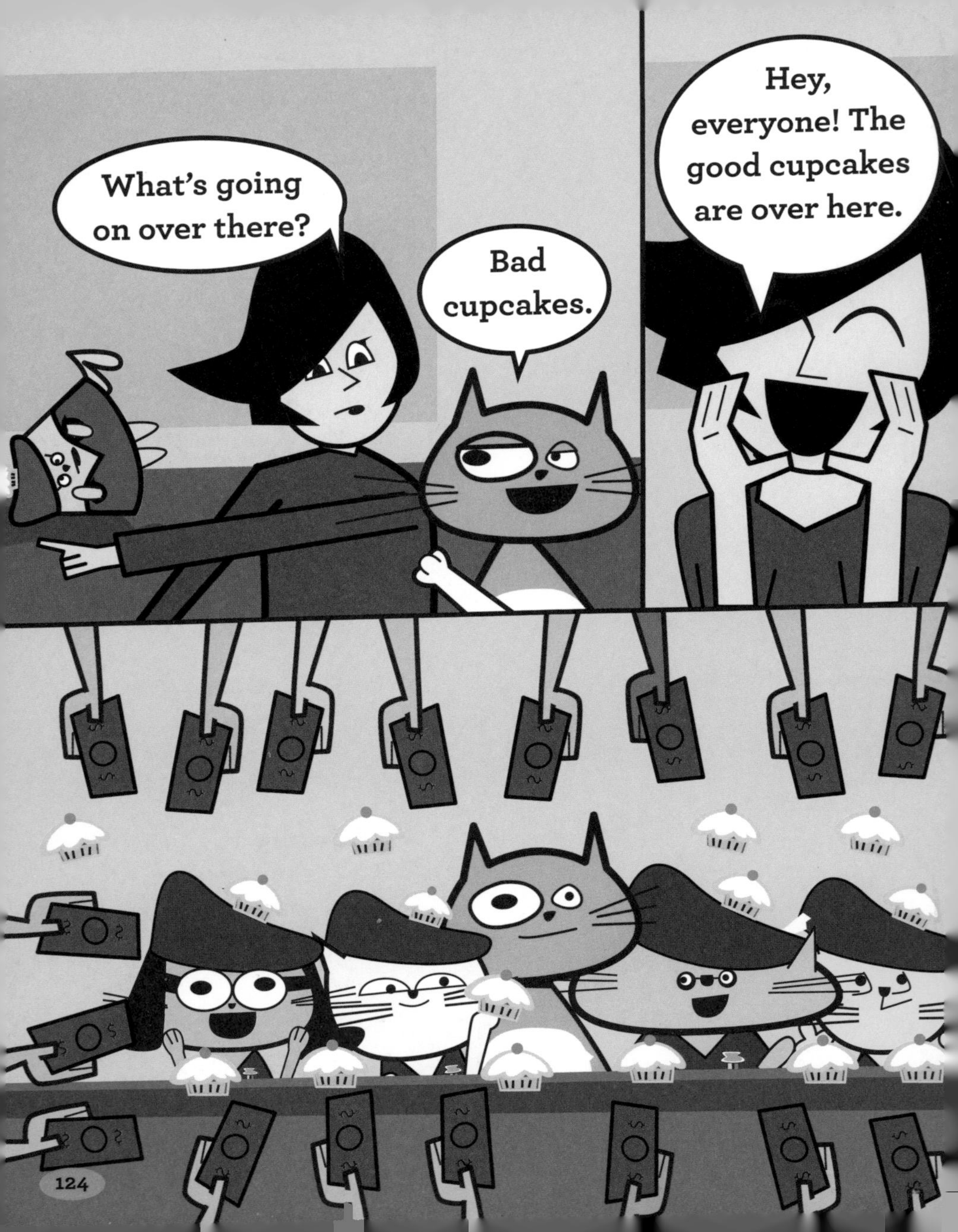
What's going on over there?
Bad cupcakes.
Hey, everyone! The good cupcakes are over here.

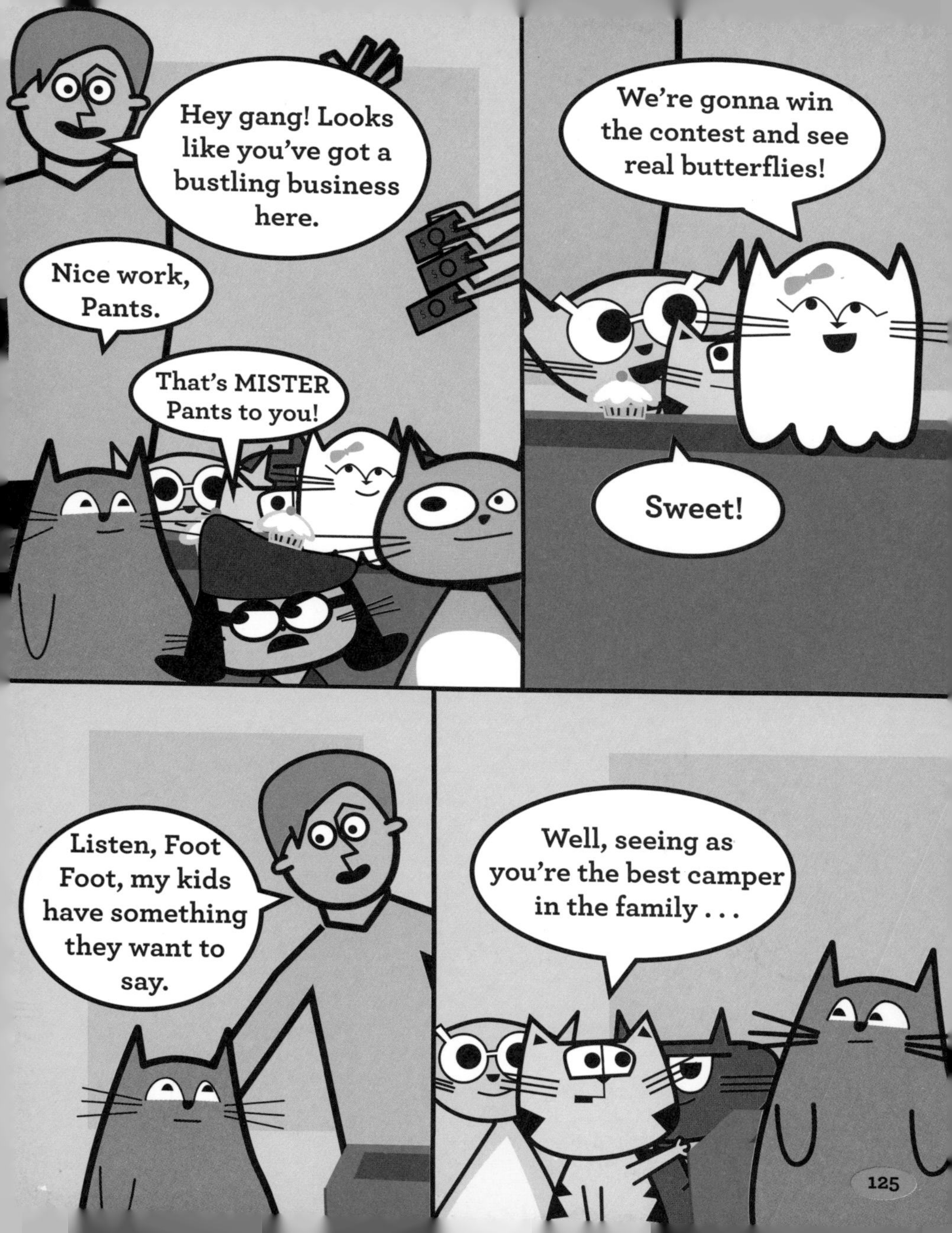
Hey gang! Looks like you've got a bustling business here.
Nice work, Pants.
That's MISTER Pants to you!
We're gonna win the contest and see real butterflies!
Sweet!
Listen, Foot Foot, my kids have something they want to say.
Well, seeing as you're the best camper in the family . . .

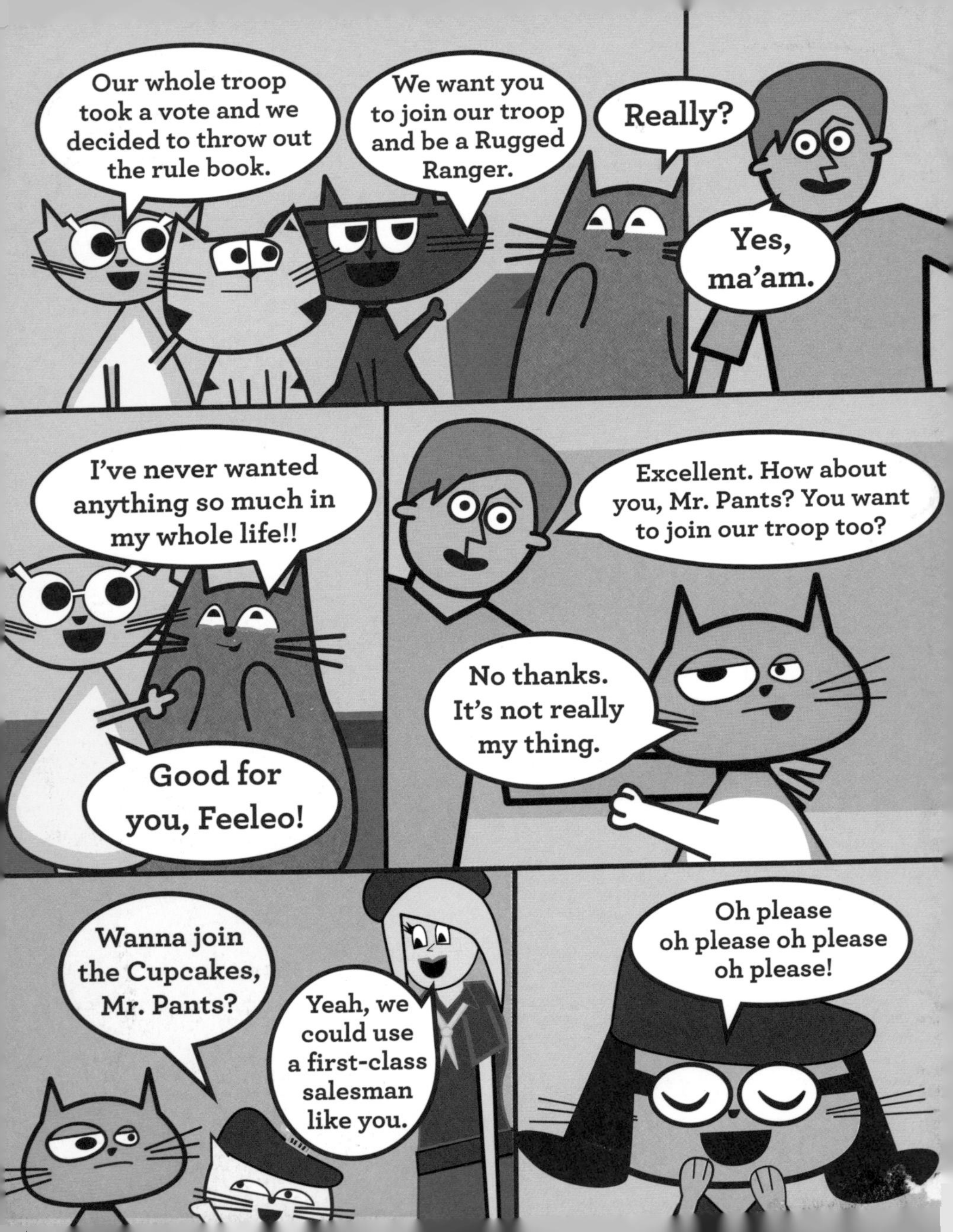
Our whole troop took a vote and we decided to throw out the rule book.
We want you to join our troop and be a Rugged Ranger.
Really?
Yes, ma'am.
I've never wanted anything so much in my whole life!!
Good for you, Feeleo!
Excellent. How about you, Mr. Pants? You want to join our troop too?
No thanks. It's not really my thing.
Wanna join the Cupcakes, Mr. Pants?
Yeah, we could use a first-class salesman like you.
Oh please oh please oh please oh please!